A WRESTLING SEASON

ALSO BY SHARON STARK

Stories

The Dealers' Yard
(*1985*)

A
WRESTLING
SEASON

SHARON SHEEHE STARK

WILLIAM MORROW AND COMPANY, INC.
New York

"Notes Toward a Supreme Fiction," copyright 1942 by Wallace
Stevens. Reprinted from *The Collected Poems of Wallace Stevens*, by permission of Alfred A. Knopf, Inc.

Library of Congress Cataloging-in-Publication Data

Stark, Sharon Sheehe.
  A wrestling season.

  I. Title.
PS3569.T33574W7   1987   813'.54   86-21681
ISBN 0-688-06755-7

Printed in the United States of America

First Edition

1 2 3 4 5 6 7 8 9 10

BOOK DESIGN BY RICHARD ORIOLO

To Howard, with love

The author wishes to express her
gratitude to the National Endowment for
the Arts and the Pennsylvania Council on the
arts for support while writing this book.
Special thanks to Richard Bond for
his help with the dialect.

Life's nonsense pierces us with strange relation.
—WALLACE STEVENS,
"Notes Toward a Supreme Fiction"

CHAPTER

1

Trover Kleeve had never gone to a wake in his life. As a lawyer he knew the value of precedent. You don't *go* to funerals, he reminded himself like a life-long friend. And to his wife, asleep beside him, he said, "It feels like snow."

And Louise Kleeve, who could manage wisdom only in emergencies, and then only when it became clear that nobody else would furnish it for her, opened her eyes. This time she did not hiss, "Snow? In November?" Did not turn her sleep-stuck face to his, trying to mold a groggy stare into stiff suspicion. Wisely said nothing.

Trover watched his wife lift weightlessly out of bed. The fact that her nightgown was really a yellowing nineteenth-century choir robe rankled obliquely, the ghost of annoyance only. He was mainly engaged in the satin cunning of her getaway. It reminded him of a movie he once saw in which an adulterous couple surprised in the act respond by calmly rising from beneath the sheets. They make the bed and slip out of the room, out of the house. The outraged husband is left in the hands of a finagled reality, the serene expanse of the smoothed-over crime. Trover had not yet decided what Louise's sin would be, and now that she was getting away, he had to think fast.

"You know how I am," he called in the direction of the bathroom and her fragile morning sounds. "I *worry* about bad roads." No reply. He waited. Countless ways to get to this woman. This time he rounded his tones. "Roses are red, violets are blue, flush the hopper when you are through." If the woman had any sense she'd ask for a divorce immediately, but except for the amenable answering rush of the flushing john, not a peep out of her.

The morning light thinned at the window, and sorrow broke through to him. Shivering, he drew the blankets to his chin. He tried not to breathe. If he could sleep all day, he could face things rested. If he could sleep all week, he'd wake with the worst of the trip behind him. Sleep would burn up grief like diesel.

He listened in panic to the perfunctory sputter of tap water. "Please don't ask me to jeopardize the lives of those two little kids," he said.

When she appeared in the doorway, he said, "Would a solid family man like my dad want blood? Now would he?"

"I'll wake the kids," she said. Her face was benignly stern, the way they portray prairie women or the wives of great but difficult men. Who was she trying to kid, her in that ratty seraphic robe, her morning-matted hair, head-to-toe monotone, that long drink of Louise? Why couldn't she just fire up a cigarette like she always did first thing and he could gag and cough and turn loden green if need be? Instead, she was throwing on a loose wrap and preparing to float away, trying to be a dream or a memory, and nothing about this morning was quite as solid as the thousands holding it up by threads spun thin as a breath.

He screwed his face tight. "I'm not going."

She whirled around, the fabric of her gown twisting prettily along the tapering length of her. "Get up," she said. "Up. Before you shame yourself forever."

"My throat is scratchy."

"You should be spanked. Think of your mother."

At first the remark threw him. What could his mother decently expect from a boy who'd just lost his father? When he finally hauled his legs over the side of the bed, it came as almost a surprise that the size ten shoes on the floor fit, that the boy in the bathroom mirror had a mature, rather splendid red beard and mournful, pouched eyes, the crumple-faced, slumped wariness of a tired middle-aged defender. Him all right.

Trover trailed his wife downstairs, where she began her meager kitchen ministrations. He took quick stock of the countertop. Some years back he had embarked on a rapid-fire series of best-seller diets. One of them required strict attention to weights and measures: sixty-two grams fish, eight grams parsley flakes. For breakfast, an unvarying quarter cup cereal, three ounces fresh fruit, a half cup milk. Although Trover's diet phase eventually collapsed under the sheer weight of its painstaking, he could still be counted on to come out, on a regular, if unpredictable, basis, against red meat or white bread or anything pretending to be anything, and when it came to breakfast, he continued to hold Louise to the original ritual of apportionment.

Recently she'd inquired of him, "If I submit to this nonsense, then will I look silly enough to suit you?"

"Louise," he'd said solemnly, *"you're* the one you have to please." He'd caught her looking with that one, and then, while she stood there speechless, asked if he couldn't maybe have his cereal in a wineglass from here on out.

It had not escaped him that she often cheated on his portions anymore, serving up mere guestimates, and nearly always she refused to dirty the stemware because it didn't ride well in the dishwasher. Today, though, much to his chagrin, the measuring cup and postage scale sat on the counter next to a sparkling Waterford goblet. He watched her shake Mini-Wheats to the second mark on the cup. Then she transferred the ponderously impecunious quantity to the pretty glass. With her usual awkward hacking whacks she sliced a banana onto the tiny scale. He was partial to thin and even. Ah! "Thin slices," he said, "are apparently too much to ask."

Whatever his methods, they continued to come up short. He moved away and stood against the refrigerator, one arm girding his middle, the other supporting his chin. He wanted her to think he was thinking. "I know what," he said, as if just now stumbling upon the subject. "The sensible thing is to go back next week. By then she'll *need* company."

Slipping a Mini-Wheat to the young beagle begging at her feet, Louise said very quietly, "This is purely outrageous." But Trover noted that the milk carton trembled in her pouring hand. Soon that lone tear would leap into the corner of her left eye. And wouldn't that be just the loose edge he required? It would be like pulling up the floor, boards cracking, chairs flying, everybody screaming *yeow-eee.* And then what? Beyond that he didn't have to see. For the moment, for his purposes, simple pandemonium would do.

He drummed a rat-a-tat rhythm with his pointer nail on the range hood and addressed his wife's back. "You're not planning to leave the kitchen looking like this?"

"Like what?"

Making his gestures large and righteous, he started humping around the room, cuffing at incongruities. "For starters, this wrestling jacket. And this jump rope."

"That's your jump rope."

"Gawwwwd—are these green stamps *stuck* to the Formica? How long's that turtle shell going to sit around?"

"The kids found it in the woods," she said protectively.

"Oh, I get it, a *stray* turtle shell. Well, by all means, let's give it a good home." He shook a paperback at her. "This greasy *Guinness Book of World Records*—kids find that in the woods, too?"

She drew in a breath. "Why don't you do your toilet paper number and get it out of the way?"

Pretending not to have heard her, grateful for the suggestion, with a grunt, he hurdled the glove-and-hat box and left the kitchen.

Pounding down the hall, he had a sudden flashing vision of himself looking small and pestilential in his clean white underduds: a well-kept, wholly indestructible brat. Homunculus Munchkin, Louise had called him once. Hunchkin. Muchless. Muncle Sam.

He found the toilet tissue in the powder room sitting defiantly on the lip of the sink. "And when," he boomed through cupped fingers, "was the last time you put the roll on the *holder,* Louise?"

The trick was to get her actually to *answer* questions like that. Defending one's self turned a person into a defendant, and defendants, even innocent ones, were necessarily rabbity, panicked, tongue-tied and, in general, made a bad impression on themselves. Normally it was easy to goad her into raging after him, foul-mouthed and murderous. "I'm calling them right this minute," she'd shriek (referring no doubt to her private corps of hit men). If he could bring her to that, he'd have what he needed, a dangerous broad—a cutthroat, crime broker, ball-bustin' amazon (she was also taller than he)—to be avoided at all costs.

Bounding back into the hall, he nearly collided with his son. Michael's real name was Banfer, after Trover, whose real name was also Banfer. He'd picked up Trover in law school, Trover, after a term he'd missed on a test. When his son was only several weeks old, Louise started calling him Michael Scott, in a kind of playful parody of the current vogue in naming babies. Trover's wife was a pathological namer. She could not stop naming things, again and again, especially what she loved. As if no one name could possibly suffice to honor all that a favored person was. Every part and every phase and every similitude had to be acknowledged, and each name, containing its own dynamics, went on then to ramify. The boy had lived through his own endless progressions—Parsnip to Parisfal to Parsippany, Scuff to Tuff to Mr. Puffin. Fergus and Flute and McNertney. Yet through it all Louise had not let Michael drop. A strong and providential name to break the baptismal grip of Banfer. Trover's mother had done him the same service, calling him Bud, seeing to it even the nuns complied. So no Banfer had actually to face the day as such except for Trover's dad, who'd lived in the musty breath of his name as effortlessly as he lived his last years in the damp of his basement den.

A man born to go nicknameless.

A collar of burning almost closed Trover's throat, and he had to breathe deeply. Michael, having taken a grip on his father's shoulder, pressed a quick, self-conscious hug. He let his hand slide lingeringly down the length of Trover's arm, in that slow, hesitant new way of his. At fifteen he was at that startling stage of diminshed roundness, just before a boy firms to his final architecture. He was awkward, saucer-eyed, and, despite his considerable strength, defenseless.

Trover stepped back into the white light flooding through the door at the end of the hall. "Don't you have homework?"

Michael nodded, guardedly.

"I guess it's against your religion to keep abreast of things."

"I won't be in school the rest of the week. No sweat. I got all next weekend to do it."

"How about wrestling practice?"

"Starts tomorrow."

"Good old Sparkle Plenty doesn't have to work out."

"Dad, it's OK. I mean, a death in the family . . ."

"Always got an answer, don't you?"

"Want me to stay home by myself?"

Trover huffed twice, as if the boy were just too dense to be endured. They filed around the corner into the kitchen. Trover whipped a balled black satin garment off the counter and held it open. "Yours?" Across the back it said BAUSCHER COUNTY ALL-STARS. 138. "Well, is it?"

Michael lowered his eyes. "Dad, you know it's mine."

Dropping the jacket onto the boy's sneakers, he said, "Put it somewhere."

"Da-add."

Trover looked away. The pleading in Michael's eyes was not on his own behalf, but for his father, to save himself.

Sighing, the child stooped to retrieve the coat. His bony white hands, smallish, in fact, for the gripping needs of a wrestler, bunched up the slick stuff of the jacket. The hands and the vulnerability of his bent neck caused Trover to wince. He swallowed and swallowed against whatever kept working in his throat. He blew into his fists. Nothing was panning out. Not a single belligerent to be had. The one thing he had not figured on was his family's sudden ironclad protocol. The unwritten law of the civilized world: You don't fight with invalids or lunatics or people in mourning.

After Michael had left to hang up his coat, Louise drew her husband close to her side, furtively, the way you might confide to someone his fly is open. "Remember," she whispered, "when Bagel was a pup, how she used to chew the leg of the piano bench?"

With arch forbearance Trover awaited the birth of a parable.

"Remember how, whenever we'd try to get her to confront the damage, she'd dig in her heels and have to be dragged to the spot. And even then she'd have her head twisted backwards. You could not get her to look at it."

The parable, thank God, was defective. "My father's passing on," he said, "is hardly a mess of my own making."

"Just the same," she said, "that's how *you* behave when you refuse to face something."

"Ribbet," he said.

"Don't you ribbet me," she said, adding, oddly, "Please."

"Ribbet," he repeated.

"Oh, brother." She was standing with the tinny November light slicing sideways at her. The light crazed her skin, and the turn of her cheek reminded him of her old white restaurant cup. Very slowly, with just a hint of malice, she said, "Should I go back without you—again?"

He gave her a hard look, but her face held, as enduringly fragile as the cold curve of that cracked cup.

"Was it my fault when your grandmother died I had to be in court all week?"

She sipped her tea and said nothing.

Candyass nonsense, he thought. But now that she was dragging him back to the chewed wood, like it or not, he had to look, had to see more even than she wanted him to see. He saw her in the heat of July, getting into her precious Hornet, getting first into the passenger side before remembering she was the only one old enough to drive, the kids already squabbling in the back seat. Trover had watched from the porch, keeping a conspicuous grip on his briefcase, the main prop to his cowardice. Louise came back around the front of the car, scuffing like a child, eyes dazed. And the part he never told anybody—not that he ever told anybody anything—but the part he tried not even to think about was this: As she went to step into the car, he saw the melted chocolate stuck to the seat of her pale summer dress, acquired no doubt during that short mistaken occupancy of the passenger's seat. It was his, Trover's half-eaten Hershey bar. And he'd let her go like that, brownly soiled to a spotless woman's wake. A mess of his own making. Why hadn't he stopped and advised her? In a flash of insight as pitless as the late-autumn light, he saw now that indeed, the time it would have taken her to change clothes could have broken him. He'd wanted the pack of them gone posthaste, out of his sight, with all the mourners of the world and all the dead and dying and guilt and sorrow. He wanted these and all related matters swept without delay from his green, green hill, his own heart discharged of obligation, the driveway made innocent again, a smooth country lane knowing nothing but the way to town and the way home.

A mess of his own making. How did she always manage to nose so close to the worst of him without half trying? It enraged him, and the rage rushed him past any temptation to relent. "I'm not going anywhere trapped in a car with people whose only purpose in life is to pick me to pieces," he announced.

"I knew it!" Mighty had come in. Mighty, née Mary Ann. She stood hands on hips, feet apart, eyes narrowed. She was watching her father with what might pass for clinical detachment were it not for the slight crimp of trembling in her lower lip. "I knew he'd pull something." She tossed her head and strode forward. "Do you two *mind?*" she said, forcing her parents apart to gain access to the cereal cupboard.

Mighty's long hair had been darkening at the crown since summer. Freshly washed and blown dry, it broadcast fragrance in bothered air. Trover's girl was beautiful.

Michael came in and went to the refrigerator.

"Know what doesn't seem right to me?" said Mighty, throwing peevish tones in with the full line of Krispies and flakes and Chex.

"What's that?" her mother said.

"Him running around in his BVDs on a day like today. Looks like he just escaped from someplace awful in the middle of the night."

Trover threw up his arms, and at the same time Michael turned away from the open refrigerator, holding a cut lemon. He gave his sister a sadly reproachful look. "Can't you just let him alone when he loses his only father?" The awkward phrasing lent his words a cast of archness and parody he could not have intended. He sank his teeth into the shriveled lemon flesh.

Mighty said, "You kidding? He look all broken up to you?"

But Louise had taken hold of the girl's arm, digging her nails in hard enough to impress fair warning. And Mighty said, "Look, Ma, it's your funeral. Well, you know what I mean. You have to spend your life with the little monkey . . ." She unhanded herself. "Mind if I invite Gideon along?"

"Yes," said Louise. "He still in bed?"

"I'll run up and tell him to watch the house while we're gone."

"But will we get it back, is my question."

Trover was poring over a letter left lying open on the Toast-R-Oven. "Who's this Sister *Innocent?*" He thrust out his hand. "Pleased to meet you, Sister. I'm Attorney Truthful."

"Hey," said Louise, "don't read my mail!"

"Then put stuff away," Trover said. "This nun coming *here?*"

"Might."

"Well, Louise, if you're expecting company, don't you think you'd better get the house in shape?"

"Certainly. Mighty, give your grandmother my regrets. Tell her I had to stay home to straighten up."

Trover's eyes bugged at her. "What about the dog?"

"Get Bagel's leash, Michael. We'll take her along."

"We won't all fit in one car," Trover argued.

"We'll take the Hornet."

"Hornet's a piece of junk."

"It'll make it to Lackawanna and back."

"I'm not going."

In the end, of course, they all went, as Trover knew they would from the start. He knew as much even as he addled and deviled and danced his dances. They put him in the back between Mighty and Michael. Bagel, who could be trusted, sat up front with Louise. What was he if not a hostage, as always, in the heart of his own family? As they peeled out between the two large fields, he noted dimly the plucked and stubbled landscape and that their man Sprecher was out in the cold, mowing yellow grass. Wasn't this November? Wasn't it going to snow? And how suddenly open the land was, haze in the distance, the horizon revoked and nothing, *nothing* mediating between him and the unopposable outwardness of things. He closed his eyes.

Well, they could drag him along, and they could wedge his butt between their bodies. They could strap him to the ski rack if they wanted. But he'd be damned if they could block his escape. Before the Hornet reached the highway, Trover Kleeve was fast asleep in his son's arms.

CHAPTER

2

"Well, look what turns up in the bushes," Maddy Kleeve said when she saw them. "Take a load off, folks. The place is filthy with eats." She led them straightaway to the table, where cakes and casseroles were arranged like wedding gifts, and circling slowly with sagging paper plates were the three family priests, Father Pat, Father Bill, and Father Ron. There was no choice but to eat immediately, and after palpating every belly for fullness, Maddy set about dispensing cushions, slippers, teabags, and toothbrushes. Brand-new Squibbs sealed in their tubes. Toothbrushes all around. Louise had little doubt that the first thing Maddy did after the hospital phoned was dash down to Rite-Aid for toothbrushes. In her ancient pedal pushers Maddy fussed embarrassingly over the priests, all sons of her sisters, all red-headed as she once was. Boys Trover had beaten at something. Boys he'd beaten up, for their pennies and bubble gum.

In this tiny house Louise always felt not big exactly, but bony and conspicuous. Around and around the room divider she walked, a cigarette in one hand, ashtray in the other. The ashtray bore two names. *"John F. Kennedy,"* in red letters across the bottom, and, written on a strip of adhesive stuck to the underside, "Louise." By now Maddy had got around to labeling nearly everything she owned. Every book and bud vase and salt cellar; every jug and jelly jar. Her entire sum and substance commended to someone's eventual possession. As Maddy put it, "so yins don't squabble over no turkey platters when I'm gone." The family's only surviving smoker, Louise would doubtlessly fall heir to all the ashtrays.

Next day Louise vowed to make herself useful, but trying to fall in with Maddy was tantamount to boarding the Hershey Park Looper moving at full tilt. "Brrrrrrrrr-up," the older woman trilled into Kerry the canary's cage as she scampered past. "Brrrrrrrrr-up." She scrambled up the high-risered attic steps and skittered down. She hopped onto chairs to reach high places. She skated around the kitchen, her feet wadded in lavender slipper socks, a T-shirt tied around her mop. Up and down the house she went, dustrag in one hand, Pledge in the other, chin tipped up in the air of someone who'd been hoodwinked and would never let on.

Trover ventured out from under the Lackawanna *Herald*. "Didn't I tell you Mum would be fine?" he said.

"She looks like someone just told her her kid won an ugly child contest."

"Ribbet," he said, diving back under.

Louise hoped to sneak off for a nap, but as she tiptoed down the back hall, Maddy shot out of the dead man's room and grabbed her upper arm. She yanked her daughter-in-law through the doorway, pointing everything at once, her eyes, her finger, her sharp little Irish nose. "As you say, Louise," she said ardently, "it was a heck of a thud. Whatever it was popped him right in the closet. Had a dickens of a time haulin' him out."

"I'm so sorry," Louise said, backing hard against the dresser and Maddy still coming on.

Maddy threw her a strangely blazing, hysterical look. "He kept trying to tell me something, you know. I put my ear up close to his mouth. 'Where's my glasses?' That's what he said, by golly. 'Where's my glasses?'" She angled her jaw at Louise and pursed her mouth. "Well, guess what."

"What?"

"Why, that man never wore no glasses in his life."

The priests left for the viewing in the big black boat Father Ron borrowed from his boss, the bishop. A slip of a woman, Maddy had no trouble squeezing in between Trover and Louise. She was roundly miffed with a sister-in-law who hadn't seen fit to show. "Looma chased our Paddy all over heck and back," she told them. "Them Repps was a brazen lot if ever they was one."

Michael leaned forward, attending dutifully. "What's a Repp, Gram?"

"What can I say? A Repp's a Repp. She was Looma June Repp. Her pap worked at the renderin' plant, and the whole outside of that there house was gussied up with lard-can lids. Now that should tell you what a Repp is. Anyhow, she figured if she could land herself a Moriarty, she'd come a ways up, if you git m' drift."

Michael smiled.

"Way-el, didn't little Miss Looma June have herself another think comin'. Sure she snagged our Paddy. Didn't do her a lick a good, though. *No*sir. Them Repps was already too far gone. As you say, Mikey, she still looked like a Repp, smelled like a Repp, and half them kids are Repps. Mean little stinkers, they are. Bad skin, beady eyes, them big yella choppers."

Bending gently toward his grandmother, Michael said, "Gram, we're here."

In the large perfumy room they nudged Maddy forward, bumping her discreetly up to the casket, where she waited stiffly for several seconds before scuttling back to where her family waited in a rigid phalanx. "Be my guest, Bud," she said, giving Trover a shove.

Trover and Louise stepped forward together, the children flanking them uneasily. Looking disconcertingly barrel-chested and oddly donnish, Banfer Kleeve rested in the same alcove of the same parlor as had Geggo two years before. The yielding inside Louise was not so much for him but a freshening of what she'd felt then, standing on the same spot, Mighty's jean jacket tied over a chocolate splotch, standing in the middle of a moment imagined so often over the years that even that reality seemed mere reenactment and the grief a revival. Geggo, who'd raised her after her mother left and then passed easily on to life after Louise, and she'd loved that life as she'd loved the granddaughter. She cried when Louise left home, and one lovely day of her last spring she wept for herself, quickness and clarity gone, some light escaping now with every breath. There was dismay in her eyes and brightness under the skin, and on her bedroom sill, a carnival glass jar burned with a fire like stoppered joy.

Now Trover went suddenly rigid, and a slow shuddering passed from his body to hers. He slipped into a tremor so severe that Louise had to respond in like measure, grabbing him into an ungainly sidewise embrace, cupping his elbow in one hand, pinning his left arm across his paunch. With her own parts, she was strapping him down, binding him in for turbulence. So reduced, overtaken, laid low, Trover was a pleasure to look after. Now he could be loved with impunity.

When the trembling stopped, he stood stock-still for a moment before turning agitated again. He motioned into the casket.

"Shhhhh," she said. "What is it?"

"That man is wearing glasses. *My* dad never wore glasses."

The glasses were droll little bent wire spectacles of the sort indigenous to old daguerreotypes, small enough to belong to a child. Maddy, the supplier. What bag of heirlooms, what forgotten cache had she raided to rustle up a dying wish?

"My father had twenty-twenty vision all his life," Trover was saying indignantly, as if the matter were something she had personally to account for. "Or didn't you know that?" It was one of his stock one-two combination. Those words, that look. "I have to work for a living," he might say. "Or didn't you know that?" "I was raised in an *orderly* household. Or didn't you know that?"

Two tiny sprigs of baby's breath from the family floral spray affixed to the casket lid lay on the dead man's shoulder. Gently Louise detached herself from Trover. She stepped forward and, when she bent to brush the debris into her palm, spotted a curious slip of white showing just beneath the edge of Banfer's lapel. Glancing furtively to her right and left, she flipped the lapel back. She peered closer, scarcely believing her eyes. Then she smoothed the fabric flat again, forcing a fist of something like laughter back down her throat.

The children shuffled and gawked like visitors in a strange church. Mighty occupied herself with twisting a crocheted scarf into a nervous noose around her neck. Michael looked wretched. He would feel very bad for not feeling bad enough, for being unable to cry over a long-distant grandparent.

Trover was the first to break away, and they followed him to a row of seats against the long wall in the center of which sat Maddy, looking canary-bright and perky. Brrrrrrrrr-up. They filled in around her. Warily Louise watched her husband fan the air around his face, rummaging among thoughts like somebody looking for a pen that works. He drummed his knees and bounced his heels and scrubbed his knuckles and then stood up. He bent to his wife. "I'm going out to buy an apple," he whispered.

When he was gone, Maddy chirped. "What's up? Bud have bees in his britches?"

"He's going out to buy an apple," Mighty said, inviting Maddy to share in their exasperation.

Maddy made little nibbling motions. "Shoot," she said then, "he shoulda said something. I could have brung him one out of the frigiator."

All around them the silence swelled, fruity and humid and overripe. Gladiolus heads seemed to thrive, but the heads of the sorrowful drooped. Along the contiguous wall Trover's sister, Rita, and her brood of five looked fixedly ahead. Rita's children, who lived but a block from the deceased, wore the unstable puckers of the truly afflicted. Loved more, they had deeper reserves of grief as well. The carrot-topped priests sat in a row. Maddy often expressed dismay that with "three stubs in the bucket" the family had not yet drawn a monsignor. They sat legs crossed at the knees, arms folded high, the glint of gold watches, more gold under that. Here lay the vein of family ore. Three celibate men and hair on the back of the hand to break your heart. Trover had inherited the same red-gold fuzz that turned to ground fire in full sun. Hair so fetching that Louise would never be entirely sure she hadn't married a man for his riches.

Maddy's arm sprang out of nowhere and gave Mighty's scarf a jerk. "Mercy, girl, some mouse chew a hole in your muffler?"

Mighty blinked.

"Way-el, don't lose no sleep, chickie. Tuck here, stitch there, we'll have you fixed up lickety-split."

The words "lickety-split" dispelled slowly as skywriting. Across the room Rita frowned. Her lips molded, "What's wrong with that woman?" and Zig, her husband, leaned back, shook his head, and yawned.

For the funeral Maddy selected not just any pink brocade dress but the one she'd bought for Trover's wedding nineteen years before and, despite the bone-soaking damp, in her new confusion, set out cloaked in no more than a white acrylic cardigan of the type sold from hangers in budget basements. The priests took turns leading the rosary. The joyful, the glorious, the sorrowful: a set of mysteries for each. Then Doheny rose to close the casket for the long drive to Holy Redeemer. When he gave Maddy the signal to step forward, she shot out of her seat and, with her pale little face angled proudly into the lights, tocked across the room and was about to vanish into the foyer when Rita flew after her and, whispering instructions, coaxed her sternly back to her duties. Maddy stood at the casket for an obligatory second or two, then, without as much as a backward glance, whisked her spring-weight presence out of their sight. The outside door settled heavily against its jamb.

When the others had completed their farewells, they, too, went out. Maddy was waiting under the sidewalk canopy. Just as Michael reached the bottom step, she hopped up next to him. "How's the wrasslin' man?" she asked.

In a kind of processional hesitation step, Doheny approached. Seeing him, Maddy saluted, trundled out of the crowd and into the lead car.

The strange thing was that just as the smallest grandchild laid the last white rose on the coffin lid and just as the mourners began to disperse, it started to snow. Nothing really wintry or calming or cathartic. Just the grudging flecks the local people called "trying to snow." Louise looked out over the rolling cemetery. One of those serpentines of well-kept roadway led to Geggo. Louise knew she could never find her without a guide. The cemetery was laid out like a maze, endless oxbows and circles and switchbacks, planned, it seemed, to confound, to keep the living looking. The air drew tight around the niggle of winter.

Louise climbed into the second car with her children and watched the mourners come off the hillside. Moriarty upon Moriarty. It seemed that all the attendees derived from Maddy's side. She was the oldest girl in a brood of fifteen. By contrast, the dead man seemed not to have derived at all, but to have sprung pastless and full-grown from the shoe department of Pincus Brothers Department Store. If there were Kleeve kin extant, Louise had never encountered any. Lucky for Banfer, he began a line when he did. Abbreviated and unspectacular as it was, this immediate family made certain guarantees, an album page, a standard grave—frames and corners and context, now and for always. They'd laid law upon his head, often set their whims and purposes against his own. In a limitless universe, bestowed limits. Without Maddy and Rita and Trover and this anchoring entourage of kids, he would already be vapor rising. Not dust to dust, but air to air. Even living men could lose themselves that way, as heat on a clear winter day goes out into endless space.

Maddy started down off the hillock. She seemed to be picking her way with an invisible walking stick. Behind her, several yards to her right, came Trover with his sights lining out over the horizon. The unmistakable identical set of shoulder and spine, the small similar smiles of bravado tugging at Irish skin suddenly looking too thin to withstand the strain. Trover, with the fuller stride, moved quickly parallel to Maddy, and just before reaching the roadway, in precise synchronization, they turned face-to-face. Hesitating briefly, Trover took a step toward her, another. Almost as if expecting a jab to the jaw, Maddy drew back, and Louise saw that she was shivering. A slip of a thing in a plucky pink dress and single-ply sweater.

Then Louise caught it, a lapse not lasting a moment, but old, so old, the look that passed between them, a look of perfect longing, son to mother, mother to son. A look that was almost a prayer. For what seemed an eternity then, long after their eyes had fluttered and fled, Trover equivocated, adjusting his stance, testing and rejecting gestures, a raised arm, an upturned palm, awkward now as a father with his firstborn. From behind rolled windows, barely daring to breathe, his family looked on. "I can't take the suspense," said Mighty.

"Come on, Dad," said Michael. "Go for it."

Mighty shrugged. "Two bits he chickens out."

Indeed, already Trover was turning from his shaky purposes, recomposing his face to the old strained geniality. He struggled out of his jacket and tried to toss it over Maddy's shoulders even as his lower body crabbed backward. Cross-purposes came close to pitching him on his ear. And Maddy, always at the ready, had grabbed him by the shirtsleeve. With her free hand she shoved the jacket back. She enacted this not with indignation, in a gesture of wounded refusal against an insufficient gift, but fussingly, the same way she offered bridge mix and toothbrushes and cushions. "I ain't cold, Bud," she said. "Here, feel," and she forced his fingers into an appreciative pinch around the sweater's heft. She spun forward then, walking in a girlish, swinging way, down to where Doheny waited by his dove gray Caddy. Trover stood alone for several moments. Then he, too, came along, his jacket dragging forlornly on the yellow grass.

The table around which they gathered was in Rita's house, a massive trestle type that Zig Messina had made himself out of pine and polyurethane. Louise guessed the polyurethane part was the gelatinous tier on top in which were embedded seashells and pebbles. Father Ron did vanishing tricks with quarters while the old aunts picked at abstemious portions of baked limas, tuna noodles, and sunshine salad. Zig sat at the head of the table, but it was Rita who held court. Her approach was always headlong, her style unblinking, and she was possessed of a very effective managerial mix of wholesomeness, competence, and rectitude that Louise attributed to her nursing degree and a wide rictus of perfect teeth.

Conversation followed a lumpy course of plodding monologues, none of which seemed to require comment and to none of which was such offered until Maddy struck up a lively disquisition in support of chunky key ring ornaments. She clattered away from the table and returned seconds later with her purse, plunging a fist in and out, to demonstrate how untroublesome a task it was to locate her house keys when they were linked up as they were with a chrome-plated *M* the size of a lug wrench.

One of the ancient aunts squinted hard at her. "But don't it make your pocketbook awful heavy?"

"I keep m' burdens to myself," Maddy said cheerily, and Trover rose without excusing himself and left the room.

Then all the lost-key and lock-out stories came out, and keys led to cars, and then Zig allowed how quick Rita was to let the kids take the car anymore. "You're a patsy, hon," he said. "Admit it."

"Well," she said, the corners of her mouth tucked primly, "I guess I'm just a born giver."

Michael and Mighty exchanged wide-eyed looks that clinked in the air like fine glassware. "Here's to us," their eyes said. "Thank God we're not like *them*. Born givers, indeed." Silently they enticed their mother as well into this tight circle of superiority, within which, for the moment at least, Louise felt closed off from the surely more certifiable superiority of the sister-in-law. Sheltered, too, from the letters that came from Rita with hammering regularity. Letters thick as catalogs. Letters that were catalogs. Lists of Louise's flaws and failings and insufficiencies. And hadn't Rita once called her a "taker"? She'd longed to write back, demanding to know what it was she had taken and how much was owing, but Trover had said, "Let it go, Louise. You want to drive a wedge between me and my family?"

Said with the same stunning illogic and twisted causality that could so discombobulate a jury that they'd fall like battered apples into his lap. His hold on a point, true or false, could be so tenacious that you would begin to doubt your own perceptions, and while you stood puzzling, he'd send you crashing out of common sense. His eyes would blaze their certitude and burn you to the ground. That will—primitive, relentless, impenitent—that will would, in the end, seem indistinguishable from the man it ruled, another heart, though a heart unhoused, thus always vulnerable. Whatever her heights of rage, however vituperative and wild and spiteful, Louise always stopped short of a direct drive against that openly pulsing, vital-organ will of his, and thus, she believed, it was by her sheer good graces that Trover was permitted to live.

So to Rita's continuing critical declensions Louise turned one or another of her broad Slavic cheekbones; to absorb the shock to her Irish spleen, she wrote lacingly literate, annihilating replies which she would sign flamboyantly, then scrap. But how she and the children would go on about the matter, burlesquing the more ovine, compliant, tacky ways of the other household, hardly neglecting a single phase of the aunt's complacency, not sparing her unshaved legs or pronated feet or passion for macramé? And Trover would put up with it as long as he could, and as long as they could make him take it, they dealt it out. It was the price he had to pay for shirking his share of their defense.

With his dark, sensuous looks and jocular ways, Zig always seemed, at these assemblies of the pale and absolute, like something left from a heartier party. Pushing the cold-cut platter at Mighty, he said "Provolone's domestic, but try the proszoooooot." He kissed his fingertips. She helped herself to a slice of hard salami. "Take two," he urged. "They're small."

Mighty took a second slice. "Guess I'm just a born taker," she said, sighing.

In a way Louise hoped nobody would tell Trover. In a way she wanted him privy to every amazing shading and detail of what followed. The initial clotted silence broken only by the steady crunch of Bagel chewing on the leg of Zig's table. Then how Rita's youngest set to stuffing her face with globs of solid butter. How two of the priests, already flushed with dago red, turned even pinker. Father Ron, like Trover, always paled. After several moments of tapping her jowls, Maddy leaped up, crying, "Who wants catsup for their baloney?" And then the remarkable finesse with which the home crowd took this alien chord and nudged it from their midst and, when the air was neutral again, allowed their own breathing into the cleared space; then, one by one, their words and throat and chewing sounds, until the room was ringing again with familiar strains, with essence of them.

Mighty's retort would have thrown Trover into aphasia, for he did not bear up well under embarrassment. But a part of him, she knew, would have been spoken for. Among these people he felt no more condoned than did his wife. They were all four of them outsiders here, and now Louise understood what it was she had "taken." In her youth and ignorance she'd run off with him to the opposite end of the state. With hardly a second thought, they'd settled elsewhere. They'd forgotten the name of the local bakery, the hometown beer, the way to the stadium. They'd come to say "soda" instead of "pop," "nosy" for "nebby," "wash" for "warsh." The stress fell closer now to the end of the sentence. Louise couldn't even keep the toilet paper roll on a standard holder, let alone enshrine it, as did her in-laws, in the crocheted skirt of a southern belle, in a shade to match the tank cover.

Unpoliced, they'd grown less vigilant against the many enemies of democratic and Christian life; they let their table manners slide, stayed home from church. Anyhow, *their* churches were bursting with Germans, Protestants at that. Softer women and rounder mountains, a landscape as precise and vibrant as fine writing. The clop of horse-drawn buggies. Home.

What Louise had taken could not be absolved. She—they—had taken away themselves.

Cheeks burning, she slid out of her seat and dropped to her knees and crawled under the table and detached Bagel from the table leg. "I could use some air," she said.

Mighty and Michael jumped up saying, "Me, too," and Trover fell in with them on the way out.

In the brotherly light of late afternoon they walked down to the shopping mall, then up past the church where Trover and Louise had been married, down past the fire hall, where the reception had taken place in a blur of baked ziti and spilt beer and ceaseless banging on glasses. Trover shambled a half step ahead with his hands in his pockets, his lips set for whistling, though no sound came out. Mighty said, "These guys know Dad's a porn lawyer?"

Trover turned a puckish, sweetly regretful smile. "A First Amendment man," he corrected.

"Well, check out this scenario," Mighty pressed. "We're all gathered around the snottop table, and Uncle Zig says, 'Heyyyyy, Bud, how's tricks?' And Dad says, 'Got my hands full just keeping the smut palaces open.' "

"Come on, Mighty, give the guy a break," said Michael.

"Then old Papadopolis looks Aunt Rita right in the eye and says, 'You oughta see the jury trying to act casual when they hold up the dirty pics.' "

Trover shook his head, making a token effort to look harassed, and Louise took Bagel in her arms and buried a giggle in the animal's fur. Someday she would look back on this moment as one of the good ones, a time they felt ostracized and sleazy to the core and very close. "That's not funny," she said.

"Yes, it is," said Mighty.

"You win." She easily agreed. "It is."

That night, as soon as they returned to Maddy's house, the old woman set about giving away her husband's worldly goods—his retirement watch, velour bathrobe, the Swiss army knife. The priests filled black satchels with booty and foil-wrapped leftovers. After they left for their rectories, Maddy decided to clean the refrigerator. Even though it was soon obvious that what they were doing was cleaning the clean, Louise pitched in. Trover sat at the kitchen table reading a Spiegel catalog. Under the amber dome lamp, every time he moved, his crowning bald spot filled with winged light, like small dancing hands or canaries. Maddy thrust out a cabbage. "Isn't this a nice solid head, Bud? Eight cents a pound at the Shop 'n Save."

Trover stared as his mother turned the head slowly for his perusal, and when she took it away, he laid his reading matter aside and pushed away from the table and walked to the basement door and started downstairs.

"Leave the crisper for me," Louise said, handing her mother-in-law the sponge. "I'll be right back." It did not seem wise for Trover to go down alone. Who knew what might turn up in a dead man's cellar?

Banfer Kleeve had been proud to own a heated basement. In the larger section the usual appurtenances—furnace, freezer, scrub sink, boxes filling with Good Will. But if you turned left at the foot of the steps, you entered the old man's world. On the cement floor, a threadbare braided rug, and the mauve-tinted air overhead was webbed with a network of crisscrossing strings, each dangling a washer-weighted pull chord over a makeshift plyboard desk. From this jerry-rigged console Banfer Kleeve had activated his world without leaving his seat. A bookcase Trover had made in woodshop was packed with Boy Scout handbooks and how-tos and souring classics. A rock polisher, the tumbler full of pretty stones stopped in their slurry partway to becoming gems. Stained-glass angels and triangles and bells. A planter cut from a rubber tire. A world organized around an appetite for simple machines and petty inventions.

Trover moved to the other wall, where his father had installed his punctilious filing system. Shoebox upon shoebox painstakingly labeled. "Toggle screws," "door hinges," "rubber bands," "binder rings," "pencil stubs," six "What Have You" in a row. When the larger world got beyond him, he'd organized his bits and pieces. "Campaign buttons," "color chips," "standing granby."

"Standing granby?" said Louise. The only standing granby she knew was a hotshot wrestling maneuver. Trover slid that box out of the grid. Inside, tightly rolled, was an ancient *Playboy*. The loose centerfold slipped out. A sunny six-foot strawberry blonde with one bare foot on a milking stool, a tiny calico apron around her waist. Her name was Allison Granby. Next to her face a margin note said, "What a doll!"

Trover shrugged and carried the magazine over to the desk. Louise moved behind him, sidestepping, her arms out like a basketball guard or a guardian angel casing for danger.

Behind another stack of boxes set ingeniously lengthwise Trover uncovered a small secret grotto concealing a jug of elderberry wine, a fluted cup over its neck. Trover brought out the jug as his father might have, often did for special occasions, when Maddy would permit it. He set it on the plyboard desk and resumed his inspections. Paper clips. Lighter flints. A gadget to fuse soap scraps into marbled multicolored cakes. He moved slowly, pottering, poking, as if his father had slipped inside his skin and was steering him along his accustomed routes, according to his worn rhythms. The hunched back, and that endless melancholy burning low behind the eyes.

Louise remembered the old man's sporadic attempts to make a life for himself upstairs. Trying to help Maddy with the dishes, he'd kiss the back of her hair and call her sweetie. She'd snap a playful tea towel at his legs and order him out from underfoot. Or maybe he'd try to draw his boy into man talk, a worldly exchange of automotive wisdom, high or minor finance, hockey, always deferring in a slow unraveling of pride to his son on matters litigious or political. Trover suddenly taking fright as the old man drew closer, waxing, with every word, happier. Invariably, in due course, Trover would vanish before his very eyes, slipping between almanac facts or the maps of an atlas, or maybe he'd run out to the kitchen for an apple.

His father would wait awhile longer and then, sighing, go back through the sliding doors to his room, come back dressed for bed and head downstairs to do whatever a retired shoe salesman does among his old and clever boxes.

Trover meandered back to the wine. He unscrewed the cap and filled the cup. He took a sip and cautiously tasted his lips.

"What's wrong?"

He poured another. And another. "Bitter," he said.

"You mean sour?"

"I mean bitter."

"Well, don't drink it."

"Have to." He refilled the glass and handed it to Louise. "Here," he said, "help me out, Bibs."

Louise bore no particular love for homemade wine, and Trover was starting to sway from the shoulders. She looked long and hard at him. He drove her crazy. The year was 1982. The man was unacceptable by present-day standards. And so was she, for consorting. The tide was against him and on the rise. She looked at him now as if he were drowning. Alarmed, she accepted the cup. The wine was like silt, thickly sweet with an after-print of bitterness.

Overhead, Maddy's springy footsteps tapped across the vinyl tiles. Down below, they drank, their lips turning purple, their teeth black. Footsteps tracing the worn triangle from refrigerator to table to sink, and Louise could envision the blurred figure held in the gleaming floor brushing by under the clacking feet. Clack, tap, thump, squeak. The polished chrome and scrubbed cupboards. A woman busy with kitchen business, above-the-earth business. How lovely, thought Louise, how purely good the sounds from above. But by now she'd had too much to drink. How beautiful, she was still thinking when Maddy came looking for them. They were sitting splay-legged on the musty rug, playing with a plastic yo-yo they'd found in one of the boxes.

Maddy Kleeve clapped her hands like someone shooing pigeons. "Git up, Bud!" she said. "Git to bed, go on."

Trover patted the rug. "C'mere, Mum. Wanna tell you something nice."

"I can hear you good where I'm at."

His eyes were large and raw, skinned-looking things. His lips moved noisily, smacking like a three-day thirst. Smacking came, but no sense.

Maddy clapped again. "Everybody out of the pool," she said, her voice high and cracked. Insouciance was a balloon drifting just beyond her reach.

"Mum," said Trover, lopsidedly solemn, "I loved that sad old man."

As from a social indecency, or the one demon that could undo her,

Maddy spun away. For a moment she stood in the harsh light, looking confused and old. Then she swooped down on the dirty glasses and the jug of wine and the dilapidated *Playboy*. Gathering them into a jumble, she dashed back up the stairs.

The wine and Trover's sorrow acted like ballast on Louise. She could float forever like this, and long after they'd turned in, she continued to drift in the soupy gray that was not quite sleep, not quite wakefulness, her big yellow night eye turning in its black socket. She saw again the mother and son on the brown hillside. She saw the parsimonious snow. She made a dutiful effort to see the dead man one more time before his big day folded into forever.

Two weeks earlier they had driven down, Banfer and Maddy, in the only car they'd ever owned. Banfer had set right out to the orchard to gather the last fruit into a paper bag. He returned to the house before Maddy and helped himself to a fast glass of wine. "Don't tell your mother," he cautioned Trover, as if he wouldn't give himself away with that pulpy Kleeve look and too much loose talk. Later Louise caught him pointing out to Maddy the fingerprints on her walls, the graying sheers. She pretended not to notice his notice. Nobody had guessed how close he was that day to all he would ever be. What he was, it seemed, was a slow-witted nipper with a critical eye on his daughter-in-law's incompetence.

He'd worn his denmaster's belt that day. He was a clock stopped in his Scouting years, those years the spawn for all his stories. Twenty-six Eagle Scouts; he was proudest, of course, of Trover, who'd earned four more badges than required. A flannel shirt and voluminous gabardines hiked with plaid suspenders. Eyes soft with surreptitious wine and the memory of singing boys. He called his grandchildren names like Sugar Peach and Handsome Man, and he was as gentle as he was tedious. The final product? Singing boys and standing granby. How much of a person tapped along the floor; how much glided tenuously in reflected light; how much of him moved in hunger and solitude under the kitchen? What did a person make of himself down there?

And then she lost sight of the living man entirely.

Her eyes swept and stopped at the moment she'd straightened the dead man's lapel. What she'd uncovered on its underside was a printed name tape. The kind you'd order in slim, silky rolls for summer camp. Maddy had neatly hemstitched around all four sides. Maddy, the labeler, commending everything she owned to responsible hands. Maddy, the expediter. *Remember who we have here, Lord. Lest he be misplaced in the breadth of forever, remember. Lest thou forget, I have marked him. Banfer Kleeve. He is ours.*

Many minutes later Louise nudged her husband. "Are you sleeping?" she asked.

"Maybe I am."

"I love you."

"Who?"

"Are you sleeping?"

"Yes, I am, Louise."

CHAPTER

3

Perma would know, he told himself. In the saddle of the old John Deere, mowing the dogleg that lay between the driveway and the woods from the cement bridge to the first bend in the macadam, Sprecher tried to tally up his years. A man had to be soft in the head *yuchsing* around in the damp at his age. He figured himself between eighty and eighty-five. But Perma would have been able to say for sure. She could even tell you how old so-and-so's stillbirth would be today. If he'd been the hands and back of his marriage, Perma had been the head. She'd known ciphering and Scriptures and how to spell and keep ledgers and write checks. In addition to the Pennsylvania German names, she knew the English words for things, for marsh plants and trees and birds and body ills. That the wildfire was also called erysipelas, though it scorched the cheeks just the same.

And Perma understood about him and the cold. As a schoolboy Earl Sprecher shrank from winter; even as a young farmer sufficiently robust to hoist two bales at once, brave enough to drive off a pack of gypsies with nothing more deadly than a wire fruit picker and a spunky wife at his side. Cold weather clogged his bones and slowed his blood, and now that he was old, how the chill dug in, turned to lead in his spleen, gas in his gut. Made him bawl like a *bubbel* for no good reason. It had gotten so he wore his union suit year-round, and only when the mercury was nudging ninety and the skies hovered white and toxic as a cough did he begin to get comfortable. When Perma was alive, she'd bundle him in her own warm body dough and fix him up with lemon whiskey. Dire times she'd call in the powwow man, but not with all his potions and rhymes could he thaw the ice in Sprecher's plumbing.

And if cold cursed him, then he was doubly cursed, for habit had at him, too. He lived as prisoner in the rhythm of seasons and tides and cycles. He used liniment not by dose or direction but according to the half or quarter moon; unfailingly he rose at five, retired at nine. And much as he would have it otherwise, he drove himself mercilessly to perform his offices in *all* weather, heat or cold, his gray face taking rain like granite, snow welting his cap.

Today he wore two sets of long johns under three flannel shirts and a pair of bib overalls, a dungaree jacket, all of it unwashed since Perma died. At the crest of the rise he crossed the road and swung around the edge of the field and headed back downhill. He always cut this section in diminishing concentric circles, and he pursued this pattern the same in spring, when the grass was lush and deliciously cuttable, as now, when mud-colored straw matted beneath his blades and no festive ridge of clippings bannered behind. He traveled eyes to the ground, especially on the downswings, to avoid seeing the chicken house and what was left of the red barn.

He used to think of these structures as great weights holding down if not the whole of his property, then its troublesome southern edge. In recent years, however, it looked more like someone in a hurry had herded them there, the way they huddled and hunched, the barn's forebay all but collapsed, borning stalls sagging, dragging down the lower end of the henhouse he'd annexed the very week of his wedding. His great-grandfather had built the barn, using hewn crossbeams and wooden pegs and hand-cut nails, and Sprecher had left seven peahen feathers in the root cellar to discourage the elements, set them there himself the day he signed over the deed. Remembering now, he let his head hang low.

There were four hills running up and down behind the barn, easy up and down all the way to the state gamelands. Those low hills had been his. Once he had dressed them in barley and rye and wheat and alfalfa. That land had been the world to him and all the world-to-come he wanted. He'd loved it maybe too much not to fly into untimely and ruinous rage when it betrayed him. Two dry years in a row, two years of cornstocks rattling in hot winds, the dirt sucked white as the river of rocks down in Hiester's Valley, the rocks themselves white as knucklebones, his own fist pistoning heavenward. Well, spite didn't so much as dent the will of God, but it did make Sprecher sell out to the first one who asked: a man from Ohio with yellow boots and eyes looking east and west.

A declaration of intent had not been required of the buyer, but as Sprecher told Perma a year later, "I thought he'd at least behafe hisself." As it turned out, the Ohio rogue was no farmer. By then that seamless piece of God's work and Sprecher's lay packaged in chunks like a butchered steer. Six acres to this one; ten to that; the wooded western slope of the third hill shaved flat by the lumber company. His farmhouse to progressive thinkers, who promptly leveled the place and swept up the pieces. His best top lands were turned into Tumbling Run, a camp for smart-mouthed city coloreds who routinely overran their bounds onto the soggy half acre Sprecher'd kept for himself and Perma. On this small plot he'd built a bungalow out of aluminum and plastic and a gas-powered sawmill from ancient parts with which he turned trees into boards for a price and which (at his bitterest and most bilious) he hoped would learn to catch and eat Tumbling Run rowdies. His barn and chicken coop the Kleeves bought from the walleyed man a couple of years after they took over the Knoll. For that he'd been grateful. He expected educated folks to know enough to keep after things.

Well, that was how much he knew. The *dummkupps* went to work on the Knoll house instead, a place that was plenty good to start with. They knocked out windows and put in windows and took out walls and walled up porches and made the attic higher and the dining room lower. In the meantime, when the wind blew, sheets of tin slashed off the barn roof and the timbers creaked and moaned and glass shattered just to hear itself talk. The boards of the henhouse were warped so bad the whole swollen structure put him in mind of his own belly, blown out with gas.

No, he daren't look on this as he worked. The sight was such to bring on stroke. But it didn't matter; the heat from the vision burned behind his eyes anyway. He saw without looking, and even from a hundred yards he caught the smell of dry rot and the rich, hot stink of the henhouse floor burning to black earth. In his sleep he saw Perma's bones and his own bones and the damp boards settling together in a sweetish heap.

The section finished, he moved on. All that remained now was the upper third of the orchard and the small grass island around the swimming pool. He hated this part, the work winding down, the only job on earth worth doing anymore. He'd spent fifty years of his life on tractors; his youth had moved out from under him at that puttering pace, the days unfurled in swaths and furrows. Without the vibration under his bum and the hum in his ears, how would he know himself? Who would he be unseated but a hot-headed coot who'd sold the best of himself to a man from Ohio with eyes like tunnels running east and west.

Now, in mid-November, the distress that always accompanied these final rows turned to dread as long and hard as the coming freeze. The Knoll people would put up a devil of a squawk if he tried to mow again this year. Last week, when he'd come up to shut down the outside water, the Kleeve woman said, "Don't bother with the grass anymore till spring." Of course, he'd gone ahead and done as he pleased. If they called him on it, he'd act like the deaf-and-dumb Dutchman they figured him for.

Anyhow, hadn't he cut every single week over the long summer, even through the August drought, when they'd begged him to skip a week or two? In the end they gave up and let him go. He's old, they were thinking. He's nutsed. Don't argue with him. *Da orm aldernarr*, let him have his tractor ride if it makes him happy. It had been years, too, since they pestered him about edging or raking or planting flowers. Well, he was too damn stiff to bend so low, too impatient anymore for the precise or fragile or fancy.

He rumbled up over the top of the sour grass meadow and down to the upper orchard. This he mowed the way a house painter paints, in nice wide strokes right to left, left to right, back and forth, to and fro. *Remember me when far, far off where grundsows die of whooping cough.* He rubbed his eyes. Now who the heck put that in his head? *Remember me.* Where had he picked up such a rhyme? Ground-hogs dying of whooping cough. He almost laughed for the foolishness of it and for the rush of sudden pleasure under that.

Crossing the tarmac, he bounced up onto the last section, the large egg-shaped swimming pool island. The mower was beginning to skip some. He didn't like the John Deere, never did. Belts forever ripping, power dropping off on him, cylinders misfiring. And it was way too puny for the job. Three years now he'd been angling for a replacement, a new forty-four-inch to-mato red Massey-Ferguson, with disk harrow, corn picker, and front-end loader attachments. "See if you can make the old one last one more sea-son," they'd say, season after season. So he'd taken matters into his own hands. A hammered valve, a scored ring, Aspergum under the locknuts. "Fix it, just one more time," they'd say time after time, and they'd go out and buy new parts, and what choice did a handyman have but be handy? Next May he'd think of something else. He could see himself sitting high and wide on the Massey-Ferguson, spring everywhere and all around him the friendly scent of new. He had to consider, though, that the larger ma-chine would cut a broader swath, and that meant he'd get done all the sooner. Well, he'd just have to go over the front lawn and the orchard twice. Not for the extra pay. Earl Sprecher was no chiseler! No, it would be twice around to stretch out the pleasure.

The lower, narrower end of the egg he cut by zippering back and forth, making wide turns onto the driveway, swerving to clear the willow roots. He shook his head. It was a sure bet the mower wasn't a hundred percent. But Sprecher knew the knocks and pings and clinks that signaled real trouble. This engine would last the job. He gave the tractor's nose a conspiratorial pat. "Easy big fella," he said. "Take your time. Conk out good come spring."

For the wider half he reverted to his nested circles, always moving to the center. So true to his patterns was he that he always began at a flat engraved memorial stone. It said, "Boots Dutt. 1926–1937. Boots was a fine German shepherd." Sprecher remembered the dog kindly, even as he reviled the memory of his master. Harvey Dutt had owned the Knoll through the Depression, and by the sweat of the locals, he'd improved it. People willing to work for pennies and Neisstown beer built the pool, the gazebo, the high stone walls.

During the same black era he swindled Sprecher's pop out of eight choice acres, a transfer that moved the common boundary to the dirt road and the barn. On a township map the dividing line looked tidy and harmonious, if anything, more natural than the original, but the same line lived under Sprecher's ribs like a rattlesnake, and every time the serpent was poked, there was that bad taste and a sharp pain and chaos. Sprecher turned a flashing glance over that selfsame ground: the orchard, the meadow, and then some to the road. In the orchard chinkapin burs dangled spiny and open from black branches, the nuts dulling below, muddy with worms. Men like Dutt left the land encumbered, debts for those who followed to work off. That was the law, thought Sprecher: Sprecher's law.

Across and over and around the juniper bank (Sprecher hadn't pruned in years, so the shrubbery planted by Dutt's corps of underpaid neighbors now groped unruly limbs or tufted weirdly from areas Mrs. Kleeve had yet to figure how to reach). Sprecher stared directly front as he rode. "Mind your own cabbage rows," his grammy always told him. And wasn't Sprecher good at making it look that way? He could put on like he hadn't a mind at all, just a plodding instinct for completion. But now, as he swung a second time past the pool, he found it near impossible to keep ignoring the bobbing glob of bright yellow. On the third pass he cried aloud. *"Dunnerwetter! Gott fadommt!"* He set the mower on idle and lumbered down.

It was a six-man rubber raft, and he'd met this raft many times before. It had drifted into the usual corner, where it rocked gently in a flotilla of pine needles and pin oak leaves. The water was the color of wintergreen, the air pressing and achy. It hurt Sprecher to suck such air into his system, and by his tingling gums and marrow he knew it would soon snow.

At the water's edge he stopped and squinted north to the ridge. The white cliffs of Pulpit Rock embedded in solid gloom. It stood to the left of the lone perfect peak the *ausländers* had renamed the Pinnacle when they shaved it for ski runs but that had always been known to Sprecher's people as Himmel's Hahn. Horn of heaven. Well, now, all creation was that, wasn't it? And today the mountain stood stiff and judgmental as the Maker himself. But the Hahn, he knew, wore many moods and took its cue from the hour and the weather and the mood of the man on the plow. Sprecher went suddenly weak with remembrance. His eyes swept over the junipers and across the road to the terraced ground rising on the other side. It was no task at all to see himself, square-built and strong, a glad-hearted young farmer turning stubble under, spading through deep purple shadows laid by the foothills. The April morning mellow as milk and Himmel's Hahn standing clean against sky, green and yellow meadows patching its fore-flanks, goshawks circling. And how he would fill with the goodness of the world, and yearnings turned his blood sweet. He could hardly wait for eleven, when he'd go home to Perma's lunch. When he'd lay the knife-edge of his hand in the valley between her bosoms, she'd cuff him playfully and push him off. They both knew better than disrupt a day's labors for hanky-pank. He'd return to the fields, the give of her flesh alive on his skin and the mountain still breathing as before, and then soon enough, as the shadows crept eastward, the light would begin to lean on him and a hush lay on the land and his loins would turn toward evening. Lord!

Remembering so overpowered and possessed him that the gray November reality met him like a swung shovel. He stood dazed in the present, desolate and disbelieving. Could it really be he was old, old, rheumy eyes, gut full of sewer gas? And those priceless acres—had he really cast them off? *Remember me when far, far off where grundsows die of whooping cough.* In the same flush of grief it came to him. Ten-year-old Perma Warmkessel had written those words in his sixth-grade autograph book. The pink of smokehouse apples was on her cheeks, and she had that yellow hair and those dark smudges under her eyes. On her feet the big brown cloppers come down from her brothers. Always noisy and too big. *Remember me.* Well, *wass fer dumm.* Who's far off now? And what kind of fool business was it to sit peeling rhubarb like life and rhubarb tarts were yours forever and the next second hit the floor with the helpless thump of stunned meat?

He could smell his own helplessness in the air. Coughing up panic, anger, a terrible taste rising out of his cold maw, he dropped to his haunches and took hold of one of the boat's three strap seats. Hiking the boat out of the water, he tried at the same time to compress its buoyancy and whip it sideways over his shoulder. So vehement were these strokes that the highly resilient thing was forced to react equal and opposite. With a bladdery whack it slapped apart and sprang away. Sprecher hung on, dragging it again toward him, trying to gather it up like a wiggling pig. It flung apart again and fought savagely back. It punched the old man backward and wrenched him off-balance, and as he reeled and let go, with a triumphant galumphing, chuckling sound, it leaped back into the water.

Sprecher came up against a wave of swaying gray, and when his head cleared, he stumbled forward and stood breathless above the boat as it settled dreamily into its pine needle nest just inches beyond his reach. He fired an arc of tobacco juice and missed. Then he clomped off for the broom in the back of his pickup. When he returned, he easily drew the boat close and, giving it one grunting heave, hauled it up over the side onto the walkway.

He continued to squat while he hammered the tubular walls with both fists. Then he stood and high-stepped into the center, where he proceeded to stomp and dance, and when he stopped, his curses went on ringing off the limestone croppings of Pulpit Rock.

How often had he told them to keep the boat out of the pool? Every time he went to skim or vacuum, there it was, fat and sassy, a big yellow belly laugh having fun at his expense. Here I am. Try and catch me, *aldernarr*. Old plug.

Any day now he'd have to bring the logs from the shed, lash them together, and float them along the pool sides. Solid objects to absorb the expansion of ice. And there it would be, the banana yellow, boot yellow boat, in his way again. Always something underfoot. The boy leaving books and baseball gloves and soda cans on the lawn, and he'd have to interrupt the music, the consoling flow of mowing, to pick up after him. And when he'd dismantle the outside shower to prevent the kids from wasting water, they'd sniff out the spigots and screw them back, so he sliced through the copper tubing and blamed it on the houligans from up at Tumbling Run. The Kleeve kids invited playmates up, children who weren't happy unless they could monkey with his equipment and break off branches and leave underwear to dry on the bushes. Didn't mean heck to chase them off the property. Mrs. Kleeve would only scold him, in that tricky-nice way she had. "But, Mr. Sprecher," she'd say, "what is land for, if not for little ones to run and play and be happy?" Well, he had lots of good answers to dumb questions. Oi-dee, but wouldn't he like to give her what is land for? Never said a word, though, not him, just hacked off the tulip heads so they wouldn't bloom again for at least two years.

Well, it would snow slugs before Roscoe Hummer would've bided any wise-guy neighborhood smarties. Hummer bought the Knoll from Harvey

Dutt in '47, and not long after Sprecher'd given up the farm, Hummer hired him on to look after the Knoll. Estate manager, that's what he called Sprecher. The Hummers were well-to-do quality folk with local roots, and they didn't live like pigs either. No boxes of crab apples left to rot in the garage, no boards or bicycles to break your neck on. They'd kept the Knoll as a summer place, and they'd kept it like the jewel it was. They gave Sprecher a schedule and written instructions, and they liked everything just so when they came up from the city Friday nights. By late Sunday they were packed and gone.

Through the week Sprecher and the wife had the run of the property. Summer evenings they'd come up and sit on the front porch, facing out across the lawn he'd been the better part of the week tending. There was always a breeze on the Knoll, and the cut grass smell would mingle with the rich currents coming off the rose bed, wash over them as they rocked without talking. Perma would peel apples for *schnitz* or darn socks, and Sprecher was more than content to sit a stone's throw away, in the warm, sweet drift coming down from his old holdings. The fields were tucked out of sight just behind the black pines, but he could feel their breath on him, the orchard grasses ripening in his nostrils and pollen drift leaving a waxy yellow dust on the floorboards around their feet. He watched carpenter bees bore their perfect holes in the banister or a black snake drag across the macadam, and once in that honeyed light just before sunset, as the cicadas sang in full chorus, he had a sudden, startling vision of his mother, plump and young, standing above her babe, shaking an amber fruit jar full of pretty glass buttons.

He remembered the year the Kleeves came, the racket of seventeen-year locusts, such a crunching and singing and carrying-on. The air was a basket, an in-and-out of sound, cross weave of all that was quick and hungry and writhing. The wind rushing through the reeds in the low marsh corner where he could never get anything to grow. Pheasants thrashing out of the grass, drumming grouse; as long as they were this close to his heart and imagination, his fields were safe. The land sighing and his woman beside him breathing in and out. His life in a basket. His world, his wife. He loved Perma as he loved the fields, and his love was always a fearsome, livid thing, knowing what he knew about how things came and how they could go. That love often made him ugly to her. So sometimes when she spoke, he didn't answer, just rocked and watched and rocked and listened and rocked and thought and closed his eyes over the good green visions flickering there.

The Kleeves moved in just as the locusts were winding down their time and digging their eggs deep. Seventeen years were a long time for life to wait. He led the Kleeves to believe the plague was perennial. Summer after summer life on the Knoll would be one long thunderation of bugs. Scared hell out of them. They moved in anyway, and after they took over, living there full-time, Sprecher and Perma could hardly have come up and plunked themselves down on their porch while the bunch of them were inside eating garlic or tearing out the kitchen or drinking whiskey or taking drugs or whatever the fools did to kill time.

It was a fact they ripped out the good birch kitchen Roscoe Hummer had installed the year Truman got in. They replaced it with some fancy *new* cupboards Mrs. Kleeve called *antiqued.* They closed up all the porches but the very spot where he and Perma used to sit on the green and white rockers. They did ask him to dinner—he'd give them that—but he wasn't so nutsed as to sit down before *ausländer* food like mushrooms and garlic. Mrs. Kleeve offered him a glass of buttermilk once. Buttermilk was what you fed chickens after the butter was made. No, he never put tongue to crumb in that house, never did and never would.

He climbed back on the John Deere and jammed the stick back; the machine lurched to its task, picking up the circles where he'd left off. His thoughts, too, looped in and out, always skeining back to the center, where the Kleeves stood as a single slipshod strangeness, united against him and his, indifferent to the plight of their surroundings, undeserving, finally, of a single nugget of Bauscher County mud.

Louise Kleeve had come to the funeral parlor alone. She wore a hat with tiny flyaway hairs like milkweed, and the hem of her coat was hanging out. Perma called her *franzel* because she always had something—a label, a string, a belt—hanging off her body. In plain view of Perma she'd sat with him in the first row, her hand lightly in his. Her hand was very small and sheathed in the softest skintight leather. It made his flesh feel funny. Funny but not bad. To this day he could smell that leather and her soapy scent. He near to fainted. She said, "Oh, Mr. Sprecher, can't you feel it? The room is permeated with her. She's right here with you, Mr. Sprecher." What a peculiar thing to say. He'd thought she was playing word games with Perma's name. *Permeated.* And still he took her in, breathed her deep, hardly resenting her at all. All he could think to say was: "You're too old to go around calling people mister."

Lawyer Kleeve was a different story altogether. He didn't come to the viewing, and he didn't show for the funeral. He never stopped on his way to work to draw Sprecher away from his chores to say, "I'm sorry." He waved and smiled, the same as he always did. Sprecher looked up toward the hills and down to where the orchard dropped to the edge of the woods. Sweet corn and field corn and barley. How had he come to divide his substance among strangers? He'd signed a deed, and now he was doomed to his tangled thoughts and endless circles. There was bile in his heart and cold in the crypt that was his stomach, and he rode a tractor inadequate to its task.

He came off the mower again, and while it idled, vibrating at his side, he rummaged deep in denim pockets until he found what he was after. He'd been presented the pocketknife at ten. His name was scratched into the yellowed bone handle. It had been his reward for perfect Sunday school attendance.

He used a dime in the thumb groove to work the blade out. The cast of his rage, until now diffuse and fragmentary, a painful rain of figments, suddenly formed a ball like the clot of water when the skillet is hot. A red-hot BB alive in his brain, and life was simple: this for that. He moved quickly up the slight grade to where the slackening raft lay like a small beached whale on the cold pavement.

CHAPTER

4

Louise woke to the soft jackhammer pulse of the Water Pik.

"What are you doing up so early?" she asked her husband from the bathroom doorway.

"Client wants to sue the airport," he said.

"So?"

"She'd like me to see for myself just how close she is to getting clipped by the eight-ten to Chicago."

"Airplanes playing chicken with people's houses? Surely not!"

"Sometimes you can be a very naïve person, Louise. Unfeeling, to boot. You've never lived under the gun. You've never been to war."

Louise blinked. "Neither have you, doughboy."

"Let me ask you this, oh, sheltered one. You ever heard of the nuclear age?" He bit back a smile.

"Who's the woman suing? Tri-City Airport or the modern world?"

"Louise, my license to practice is limited to Bauscher County."

Shortly after Trover left, Michael came downstairs, rubbing his eyes. "I couldn't sleep," he said. "My heart stopped again."

"Oh, honey, not that awful dream."

"I keep telling you. It's no dream. I was wide-awake the whole time. I wiggled my fingers. I made shapes on the wall. I could almost read the words on my regionals trophy. There were thirty-two seconds left on the clock. I felt my chest, and Mama, *Mama,* it was still as stone."

Even with the whole blessed spectrum of human reason at her disposal, Louise could do little more than gaze back with the same, almost radiant dismay. It was a recurrent thing, this experience. This dream. It had to be a dream, hadn't it?

"Don't you think I should see a doctor?" he asked.

"For prolonged cardiac arrest? I think not, Sweetness. No, there's just no right way to say it, if you know what I mean."

"But *you* believe me?"

"The clock," she ventured hopefully. "The clock in your room isn't calibrated to tell seconds left in the period. Doesn't that say something about what's real and what's not?"

He smiled sheepishly, but doubt still rumpled his brow.

"How is it now?" she asked.

He felt his chest. "Right now it's working like a charm."

"Good, get your shoes on and empty the boxes up at the pool."

The redwood planters held the frost-blasted remains of petunias dead since September. Soon the earth would freeze and split the seams at all four corners. She watched his all-star, black and white, slightly dejected back as he walked. His footsteps left dark prints in the frozen grass. He moved well enough, she thought, for a kid with a disabled heart in his chest. That dream of his always made her day precarious. She stayed at the window for some time after he had disappeared behind the twin larches filling the middle distance high and right. Then she put the teakettle on, and the water came to boil in the time she waited. She smoked two cigarettes. The boy would be up there watching a squirrel bear fuzz to its nest, watching intrigued, fond, amused, as if the squirrel were his smallest, funniest son. He would stop working to warble or cheep or trill to whatever sang to him from the top of the white pines. He was numb to the pressure of time or obligation. When the boxes were empty, he would turn them over and drum their bottoms with sticks or stones, or bongo with his palms, belting out Santana hits. When at last he emerged from behind the larches, he was dragging the stiffened carcass of the yellow boat.

The vaguely troubled timbre of Louise's waiting took on keener edge. She peeked out and pulled back, peeked out again, prickling with suspicion. She wiped the white of her breath from the glass and peered out again. Her eyes met Michael's, and she caught the look of someone burdened with bad news. She stepped sideways to the door, opened it a skull width, and poked her head out.

"It's cut," he said in a furtive voice, as if this were information he didn't want to get out. He stood just off the porch, the patient western sky wide behind him. Hurt always bleached the blue from his eyes. Louise watched them dull to a kind of gunboat gray.

"Maybe it was an animal," she said. "A wild dog. Groundhogs have nasty little teeth. Maybe it lost air from lying."

He showed her the slit. A foot long, hardly a jog of conscience in the clean length of the stroke.

She stepped out and let the storm door slam. They exchanged drooping looks, and their eyes turned in concert to the damage. Someone with a knife had stabbed their boat to death, and the basic components of their response were a kind of torpid curiosity, disorientation, and general stumpishness—all overshot with filaments of pity, for they could be moved as readily by the predicaments of things as persons. They felt for vacated homes and abandoned cars, discarded boots; for condemned buildings, gouged hillsides, supermarkets stinking of spoilage; for the thinness of old dimes. Maybe they were *too* sensitive, Louise had often thought. Empathy was a commendable trait, surely, but was it healthy to know exactly what it was like to be a dime?

"Well, don't worry," she said uncertainly. "These things happen."

"They do?" he said, his eyes still fading, the underrims gone oyster pale, as if the wound were inside, deep, draining him unseen.

The problem was not the loss of an object. Louise's children had always made short work of their possessions, though rarely with malice. It was the habit of casual handling generated mainly by their father's unlimited willingness to resupply. Come next summer, there would be another raft, so big perhaps it would simply tremble in the water as it lay helplessly wedged between the sides of the pool.

Michael said, "Who would . . . I mean, you have any idea . . . why would anyone—" He stopped and lowered his gaze, as if just thinking the old man's name shamed him.

"Who else?" said Louise, and she took the boy's cold hand between her palms and rubbed. Winter always coarsened his skin. Sometimes his knuckles bled.

"Maybe it wasn't . . . maybe . . . yeah, it was *him*," he said quietly.

He screwed up his face. "Remember the time Sprecher stuffed all our towels in the trash just because we left them up at the pool. And the time he threw my beer can collection over the hill. Even my good cone-top Neisstown. Hardly any rust on it."

Well, what more could be said? Michael dropped the raft where he stood. He followed his mother inside and directly to the refrigerator. She handed him an orange for breakfast. He had to get down to wrestling weight by the second of December. Mighty strode in, her face so perfectly composed, so purely bold it shocked Louise. "Get your tush in gear, mister," the girl told her brother. "I'm leaving in exactly two seconds."

"Here, have another orange," said Louise. "Mighty, you take one, too."

"Eat it yourself," Mighty said. "You probably got rickets from eating nothing but soda crackers all day."

"You mean scurvy?"

"You name it, lady." She pinched her mother's cheek.

"Aren't you going to be hot in that big sweater?"

"You have Tabasco for blood or what? It's *cold* out."

Louise smiled. Geggo was like that, too. Always yanking layers *off* Louise as she ran out the door.

Louise watched the squat red convertible bounce her children over the bump by the gazebo, around the bend and out. The VW hum lingered a long time, and then she picked up the strand again as they passed below on the township road. She heard Mighty gear down rather than stop at the intersection, upshift onto Hassler Road, and then the notched treble from first to fourth as she roared up the highway, the hum now like a thinning ribbon spinning out of her mother's ear. Then nothing.

A featherstorm of absences gusted and settled; the house took on quiet like another transparency of air, tinted aqua-gray, wavy. When the quality of quiet achieved a certain texture, a kind of clarified resiliency, Louise set the sack of oranges on the counter next to her teacup, and with something of the same mixed intrigue and dread with which she had watched Michael drag the boat through the yard, she went back to her room.

The room had been a porch, the back porch if you judged by its orientation, facing the woods; the front porch if you went by architecture, for the prettiest lintels and cornices, the fanciest windows gave on this porch, and it boasted a set of wide stone steps with great square stanchions holding two cracked concrete urns. It was a building trying to favor two milieus at once, a face for each world, a house by its own definition divided. That was fine with Louise. She would never be comfortable in a place with fixed ideas about itself.

Once she had nearly bloodied Trover over this room. By then they had enclosed both side porches, turning cubic yards of country wind into kitchen and sun room respectively. "You will not build a workshop off my dining room," she said, as if she were some sort of elegant person. "I'll do the work myself," he said.

She stood with her arms out, guarding the bow window. "Over my dead body," she said.

But in the end she was not willing to die for her views, and the next day Trover got started. The first thing he did was go out and buy the power tools that he needed to build the room that he needed to house them. In quick succession he acquired the drill press, arm saw, router, bench grinder, joiner-planer, jigsaw, band saw. The rage spent itself in the buying, so he hired somebody else to do the work. When the room was done, the equipment was retired. Only the drill press saw further action, and that was when Mighty made a hole in the roof of a birdhouse so it could be strung with wire and hung from a tree. Now these machines were the strong-arm boys to which all other rivals for space subjugated their claims.

Adjustable shelves were piled with small woodworking tools still in their boxes; wonderful arcane objects hung from pegboard, instruments to calibrate and perforate and bifurcate and true. Professional plumber snakes in three sizes when they always called the plumber anyhow. Glue gun. Linoleum knife, ratchets and hatchets and hammers for everything from upholstery to peening. Tiny watchmaker's tools and a jeweler's loupe.

The ski year stood in a staggering state of semicollapse behind the drill press. Trover's six sets, all with matching poles and boots and goggles. Her own skis were gone, having got away from her at the top of the Mount Mansfield chair in a blowing storm. She'd never found them; perhaps at that very moment they rested under a three-year leaf mold and tender early snow.

Trover came prematurely to mid-life; in this, as in everything, he'd jumped the gun. By his thirty-fifth year the artifacts of disaffection (both symptom and cure) had moved in and made themselves at home in the middle of the workshop. The barbells and lifting bench, little sandbags you tied around your legs. Punching bag bolted to the wall, an exercycle and chest expander. An unopened box marked "Atlas Gravity Boots." On the pegboard, stopwatches and metronome, plus monitoring devices for the less dependable rhythms of the self: electronic pulse readers, stethoscope, and blood pressure equipment. He stocked duplicates of these items in his office.

Jump ropes looped on hooks. Next to them, climbing tethers, pitons, crampons, and wondrously cunning harnesses and backpack accessories. Louise remembered the day he'd come slinking home with a suddenly squared chest and the telltale bag rattle under his overcoat. She'd knocked thrice on the hidden box, and Trover, found out, unzipped his cover and made public his purchases. A set of cleat plates for his hiking boots and the amazingly weightless aluminum pickax. "What's that for?" she asked.

"Ice climbing," he said, his voice scaling high on the word "ice," the contemptuous whine of the cognoscenti for the hopelessly benighted.

"Ice climbing?" she said stupidly.

"You got any better ideas?"

For a long time Louise didn't know what to call this annex. In that way the room was like her mother-in-law, on whom Louise had never been able to settle a simple designation for direct address. She tried Madeline, Maddy, Mum, Ma'am, even Miz Kleeve. Somehow every name managed to sound either false, presumptuous, mocking, or stodgy. She did not know how to say "Mother." She ended up calling her a mumble of mushed-up *M* sounds or nothing at all.

In like manner, she tried front room, back room, mud room, sun room, junk room, store room, studio, atelier. The only word that seemed to survive the convulsions of perspective was "room." The Room. "I'm back in the Room. . . . This belongs in the Room." Although one day, when Trover came home with a new ski wax barometer as big as a steeple clock, she closed her eyes and pointed. "Put it back in Purgatory," she said.

For how this husband and this room tormented her traditions, that long history of abstemiousness and denial. Her sense of proportion, of thrift, the law of use by which Geggo had reared her. And Louise with no gift for classification. Even when she managed to muscle the rest of the house into shape, this room lived on to shame her, the one unshriven sin, the mess that never left. With every passing year the stockpiles mounted, tangles tightened, early acquisitions sank into deep unavailability. Trover kept trundling home with his bags, and he plowed her under mountains of things she could not even name, and one day she crawled out and discovered the wheel.

The potter's wheel arrived at the height of his mail-order phase. It was the same year he ordered lime-colored underwear in ice-cream-cone packaging, the belt buckle made of sterling letters spelling "ME." He let his hair curl below the nape and banded his ringlets with a rolled red bandanna, and he bought a shoemaker's apron to hold his shaping tools. He assembled the wheel over one weekend, and then he bought the clay, in quantities large enough to qualify for an institutional discount. Then, wearing welder's goggles and a ferocious expression, he set himself to it. After an hour alone with the obdurate mud, he snapped the machine off, flicked the light switch, and slammed shut the Purgatory door. "You try it," he told Louise, and he sounded not defeated but insulted to the quick.

Louise was intrigued immediately. Unlike ice climbing picks, threaded snargs and chock tockers, the wheel was something she could pluck from the glut and put to good service. If there was a single advantage to the cumulative sums of her household, it was this: You rarely had to leave home to find what you needed. And Louise had if not a talent, then a hard knack for making, if not a living, at least a life out of whatever lay around getting dusty. Her grandmother had made fine soup out of hardly more than a dirty skillet. Tomatoes plumped on dishwasher; music came out of a comb. Double duty, the second law of use.

And sometimes for better and sometimes for bane, the other knack she had was perseverance. She gave the wheel more than a go, kept at it long after it aggrieved her for the "last time." She brazened out the mishaps, matter spattering, spinning into ribbons, flinging itself against the wall, the implosions and expulsions, the stupidly squat results, the sclerotic look and the woefully lopsided. And one day, to her amazement, behold, a bowl. In time, pots and pitchers and bowls enough to provision a small Hopi village.

Then one morning she awoke sick to death of symmetry. She could no longer bring herself to work along the same unchanging axis. But she went on courting the clay just the same. She especially loved its smug, dumb faith in the possibility of itself. More than medium, it was flesh of the earth's flesh, partner to her own in the active life of the cosmic imagination. An overblown notion if ever there was one, but Louise was sick, too—and maybe afraid—of the minimalizers and the grimly trivial. Sometimes she worked as burningly as if she were holding the flesh of God Himself in her hand. Other times she fancied herself "chosen" in the same way she once saw herself singled out to be His bride. Was she God's potter? Or God, the potter? It didn't matter; she was done with pots anyway.

She shoved the wheel back with all the other idled power doers and began to fashion free-form. She hand-built not the object itself but facsimiles thereof, things that were bug*like,* froglike, cowlike. Her people were abominations, unthinkable. Then, one day, from out the obdurate mud crept a man like unto a man and then a woman that looked like his wife. Then children and dogs, and in time confidence made her slapdash and playful. Laughing, Louise pushed the figures together into families.

She bought a book and taught herself how to make molds, that she might move quickly on to other mediums. She liked the calcimine, soakable whiteness of plaster. She aspired to bronze. In her rush to outstrip herself, perhaps she stopped practicing her craft too early. She should have studied anatomy, composition, consulted a theorist. She never did eliminate a certain mannered primness in her people, a stiffness in their carriage, and in the mode of the local populace, their waist and limbs were a shim too thick. One day she looked at the proliferating results and saw that what she had wrought was a pantheon of families, camera-shy, fetchingly stiff. The product of her flawed technology was oddly Victorian, but not bad at all.

And she came to see that the powers that governed art required all that she was, even the paranoia and impatience, the multiform confusions. The hand that acted too soon, too inexactly. They wanted her weaknesses as well as her strengths, the blind spot at the outer reach of a clean perspective, the pockets of darkness, the mote in her eye, the mild scoliosis that made for a certain lean. And wasn't a major component of "style" compensatory, how a person went about skirting the scary areas of flawed expertise? Once she read of a writer whose sweetest truth had surfaced from the slough of poor penmanship: how the line read, not what he'd written. And arrogance? They wanted that, too. The artist was a weed, every root and runner of which was edible. Arrogance, puh! With all of it, the willful stances, the fits of pride and ambition, Louise knew what she was doing. And what she was doing was exactly what she had to.

A small admiring public began to gather around her work. People were curious to see their own families rendered along the same quaint lines, the sweetly stern, tenderly baffled faces, and that other aspect, more elusive, as if they were waiting for something to happen, waiting for rebirth or second breath.

Years ago, when Trover was just getting started, she'd worked awhile for him without wages. Everybody looked askance at her in those days, and some of them asked, "Who's watching the babies?" Now the same acquaintances said, "Where do you work?" And Louise always said, "I don't." Well, she, too, was a product of her age and ethic, and even she didn't quite hold with sculpting as gainful employ. But whatever the world chose to call it, it kept her hands occupied and fragrant, her life pliable. What was extant could be reimagined, remade again and again. In the middle of Trover's expansionism, indeed, out of his overflow, she'd fashioned this small grotto for herself, in which she slapped at mud and hummed and cursed and learned the curve and heft and line that came from the pressure of her finger on things.

She took up a ball of new clay and threw it on the wedging table. The mass lay cold under her hand, unfriable, a slab of dead matter. Sometimes, at this stage, she was afraid of clay and slow to approach. She laid the side of her head on the mound and listened. It was silent, so still, and she remembered Michael's dream. She sat up and began working fast, pounding with the heel of her hand, turning it quickly, kneading in a rocking, spiral motion, pressing hard and twisting until the clay began to warm to her and soften, and then she worked even more furiously, as if she could restore that lost pulse, all the tiny stilled heartbeats, legion as grains of sand, that had gathered in the tectonic dark to make clay binding.

CHAPTER
5

The first time Michael ever saw a wrestling room, he thought of "soft-hearted." Imagine a room that said, "Come and play with me. I won't hurt you. No, sir, not me." Wall-to-wall mattress; even the walls padded half-way up. The room sighed and wheezed when pressed, reminded him of Rodney Reimert's mother, years ago, in the old neighborhood. He'd come upon her napping in a bedroom with drawn scarlet drapes. A great damp noodle-white asthmatic overflowing a rose bikini. The air in the wrestling room seemed to steam from the brick red mat, sweat-slubbed, shimmering pink.

The room was a repository of reek. No smell given over to it ever got out. What amazed Michael most was that the composite of all the body odors, each individual and distinct, made a single indivisible body. Every wrestling room he'd ever been in smelled exactly the same. Michael suspected that if he tracked this scent down, he would learn something elemental about the brotherhood of men.

He was always the last to get to practice, the last to leave. As far as he could see, he didn't do anything special after school. Toss his books in the locker, riff with some of the guys. He'd exchange a few strained pleasantries with his girl, Emma Jean, promise to phone later. In his hands, though, these trivial acts took on amazing tensile properties, tended to expand and branch. He seemed to lack a natural containment, that streamlining feature that kept others on course through an hour or two and allowed them to arrive somewhere intact and more or less on schedule. For Michael time did not seem to elapse so much as leach away, evaporate as through his own pores.

When he entered the wrestling room, his friend Spot Grayrain lifted his chin in greeting. "Scratch in the locker room?" he asked.

"On the phone—hey, you better cool it. He ever hears that Scratch jazz, he's gonna ask why."

Spot grinned. "I'll say, 'Kleeve here's our resident spokesman. Take it away, Kleevo.' "

"The heck you will." Michael went in fast on his friend's legs, dumped him with an immaculate ankle-pick. One, two, ka-boom!

"Whoop-de-do, the kid is hot!" Spot pressed his face into the mat and giggled. Then he rolled over and kipped to a sitting position, his face avid. "Two bits he's sweet-talking that chick from Alsace."

"Who is?"

"Who we talking about, denso? Scratch—pardon me—Coach Yoder. Chick's name is—get this—Erica Underdonk. Didn't you ever pass them coming in in the morning?" Spot crumpled his face. "Shit, how could you? You're always late. Anyway, point is, you *can't* pass them since they're usually blocking the road."

"I don't get it."

Spot hitched closer, chewing on his smile in the cagey, knowing way of the amateur informant. "Look," he said, "I'll draw you a diagram. Yoder"—he stabbed the mat—"lives in Alsace and teaches"—tap-tap—"in Lorraine. Underdonk lives in Lorraine and teaches in Alsace." Spot connected the dots. "Now this is the old mountain road, right? Suppose they happen to rendezvous, uh, X marks the spot. Skeeeeeeeek! Slam on the old brakes, roll down the old window, and start shooting the old bull, like they just rented the road or something. Sometimes Yoder gets out and stands there with his head in her window and his butt poking out. . . ."

"I never saw that," Michael said.

"Underdonk's not bad. Thin and kinda pretty . . . I see them all the time." He said this last proudly, as if he owned stock in their affair.

"Yoder's married, isn't he?"

"Big whoop. So's Underdonk." Gossip was rubbing color into Spot's cheeks.

"Maybe they're just friends."

Spot drew up his knees and knocked his head against them. "You for real, Kleeve?"

But Michael was off somewhere putting the finishing touches on his version of a girl who would be named Underdonk. Underdonk would be her husband's name. Ox Underdonk. Not her fault he was some hairy ape football player. Not her fault he had a foul mouth and hung out at the Legion Hall when he got through at the plow works. He'd eat Limburger for breakfast and then go out to the garage and gun a cold engine. Ox Underdonk. No wonder she was messing around.

She'd been born, of course, to a gentler name. Fairfield or Lavender. Erica Lavender, skin like talcum to the touch. Eyes dark, like his sister's, with a little of Mighty's friendly fire and none of the scorn. She wouldn't be blond—not yellow-haired like Emma Jean—but that pale brown that made a radiance around a woman's head when the light came from behind. He imagined her fingers resting lightly against the roof of the car as she talked, her hand blazing white in the sun, a green ring flashing like the steely glint in her husband's eye.

Snapping his fingers twice, Spot said, "Come out, come out, wherever you are."

Michael blinked the Underdonks away.

"Hey, Teach, what's the lesson plan for today?"

"Huh? Oh, that. Come on, cool it." Michael turned away, embarrassed.

All around them bodies flounced and rolled in a kittenish preliminary to serious working out. The younger ones, armed mainly with their freshly awakened, amazingly legal aggressions and their prodigal ways with precious strength, danced around the bigger guys. They threw feints, alit on backs, attached themselves to torso-thick necks. Like gentlemen giants, the upperclassmen would suffer their roistering awhile longer before whacking them flat.

Michael found himself suddenly having to field Kib Itterly, the 106-pounder. He dumped him forward over his shoulders, bracing the fragile neck as his head hit the mat. He hoisted the boy to his feet and patted his behind. Itterly skipped off. "I mean, hey, Coach is coming along great."

Yoder had been thrust on them last year when the regular coach quit. Coming from track and general math, he knew next to nothing of their sport. When they said "Peterson," he thought they were talking about one of the guys. He called the periods rounds. Without a tradition of excellence to fall from, the team had to brace itself for the more ignominious drop from mediocrity.

At Yoder's request, the few decent technicians on the team—Michael among them—started staying late to coach the coach. Starting from square one, they moved quickly through the fundamentals; the man turned out to be a quick study. By season's close Yoder knew even the esoteric stuff, bonus show-off moves, even some advanced razzle-dazzle. His was the wide-eyed buoyant zest of the beginner, and fueled by the clear pride of his tutors, he attacked his job with far greater passion than the real coach, the one who'd abandoned them. For his teachers, he brought apples, cucumbers and carrot sticks. Yoder was hooked. They were expected to have their best season in years. Michael gave Spot a look of mild reprimand. "Yoder's doing great," he repeated.

"Yeah," Spot said. "All things considered."

"Have the Leper today?"

"Yep."

"Gimme a lift home?"

"Sure."

Michael peered close at the whorl of white just below Spot's crown, the genesis of his nickname. Was it growing or just changing form? It appeared to be lengthening, less of a spot now and more like a chicken feather.

"Hey, here comes Scratch."

"Shhhhhhhh." Both boys looked down at the mat, swallowing grins. The coach had entered, fumbling at himself, scratching with such casual industry as to appear a happy confederate in his own labeling. Jock itch, they figured.

"Kleeve!" Yoder barked, tentativeness still undercutting his tone, eroding his command. Not until his teachers were graduated would he feel truly free to take charge. "Kleeve, get over there with Hunsberger. You suck on your feet, and he's even worse."

Michael was far more at home on the mat than chumming for the takedown. The main trouble was air. Air was the soup he had to get through before he could find his man, the ankle or arm, that human projection he could use as anchor or ground. He needed the conductor bone to connect him unmistakably to the mat. In a way, this reminded him of his nocturnal heart problem. He wondered if all vaporous people suffered such eccentric, nonspecific, and indescribable ills. Not a single reference to this trouble with air in the wrestling handbooks.

Still, it was hardly true anymore that he "sucked" on his feet. He'd spent all last summer learning freestyle, working the tournaments. And Yoder knew it. Much quicker now, he'd expanded his range with a good half dozen smart-looking throws, a hip toss, a suplay, a brilliant Japanese whizzer. Hunsberger was a piece of cake.

After ten minutes Yoder pulled Michael off Hunsberger and tossed him in with the Pack boys, Rob and Tom. Great blue-necked bulls. Headlock specialists, ten-second pinners. The home crowd worshiped these boys. Maddy had once watched the Pack brothers wrestle. Now she always asked after them. But they could be had. Anybody of similar heft, with half a brain and some staying power, enough savvy to avoid the early crunch, had a solid chance. Unaccustomed to going the distance, the Packs quickly ran out of both steam and character. Ten seconds into the third period they'd be supine, stalling like crazy or crying hurt to cop a few seconds' R and R.

Even at well over fighting weight, Michael was still skinny. Gut-sucked, he could be divided thrice: head and abdomen and thorax. The Ant King, his sister called him. Mesomorphs to his ectomorph, the Packs solidly out-scaled him. They were the only ones he ever actually attacked, and he would go at them like a bull, in a frenzy of brute, stupid desire. Michael was smarter, but what were brains against men who held their ground solid as plugs, smug as cudgels? Hell would not be fire but the endless back-to-back abutments of impossibility. After two minutes alternating Tom and Rob, Michael collapsed. He sat watching his sweat spackle cracks in the plastic. His face burned; it would be peony pink by now.

Yoder bent to Michael's ear. "Killer instinct," he whispered as if making a subliminal implant. Michael's style troubled him. Instead of initiating a series, he practiced something called countering—reacting in clever, unex-pected ways to the other man's aggressions. "Sometimes *you* gotta shoot," the coach said. Then he stood, letting his shoulders slump, smiling resign-edly.

In the corner Hunsberger was manhandling Paulie Bortz, the team cream puff. A heavyweight was a rare acquisition for a small double-A team. Yoder had managed to sweet-talk this butterball into joining up, wooing him with pizza and Häagen Dazs bought out of his own pocket. The only advice Paulie ever got was: "Just please don't get decked." His not so hidden, deceptively effective weapon was flesh. Flipping Paulie Bortz was like trying to turn a three-hundred-pound tub of noodle dough. When he waddled out in the full-face protector his mother made him wear, the crowd cheered. If he managed not to get pinned, his reward would be nothing short of general delirium. Such overapplause implied a derision that embarrassed Michael, but Paulie was hard put to keep from collapsing into the jelly-filled center of his own bliss.

"LaWall, *think!*" Yoder tapped his own skull. "You're in on a guy that deep and he's still got your ever-lovin' leg, how the hell you expect to roll him without falling under?"

Fuzzy LaWall was mammoth of muscle and minuscule of mind. He was unable to grasp fully the standard stratagems, so his moves were mainly custom jobs, invented for the occasion. Unorthodox, unwieldly, generally untenable, sometimes—by sheer dint of his awesome strength or the grace time gained through his opponent's dismay, sometimes by simple luck— they actually worked. When they missed, he usually managed to hang himself. The boys would see the fall coming the instant he locked into one of those ungodly configurations, and a gathering moan would rumble down the length of the bench.

Michael enjoyed watching Itterly and Kern, the shrimps. They hardly made any sound at all, their limbs conflicting dryly as sticks. In the hands of the lightweights, stripped to bone, so to speak, the sport seemed purest. They gave each sequence sharper play and delineation. Because the little guys couldn't stir a crowd with the theatrics of fat meeting fat, the meaty thrill of a resounding two-man slam, they had to rely instead on skill, speed, and a certain quirkiness of approach. You could count on the ninety-eights to be the ones to charge the mat like Apaches, devise eye-catching, often pretentious mannerisms. He watched Itterly pop around in a pixilated prance, while Kern stalked in counterpoint, slinky as a manx.

As for himself, Michael had never quite got used to the idea that he was a first-rate contender. He'd always been a C squad, bench-buffing member of any team that would have him. He spent one entire summer making triumphant leaps onto the back of the kid who'd already, quite decisively, made the tackle. Another year he went 0 for forty-six at bat. The first time he tried skiing he broke the T-bar operator's femur. He'd been glad his father wasn't the type who needed an athlete, though it was now clear that if Trover Kleeve had one, he'd best be a winner.

Michael's first wrestling encounter had been in eighth-grade gym class against a kid named Gilbert Krumrine. His teacher had been amazed— and so had he—with his ease in handling the larger, more experienced boy. Michael's reactions had been quick, instinctive, the first knee jerk in a long career of countering. In time he began to see what it was that set wrestling apart. In football, baseball, skiing—he could barely stand to think about tennis—he stood alone mostly, against little more than his old elusive opponent, air. It was as if he could not quite get a fix on himself in the physical dimension. He did not feel his own weight, had no sense of himself as muscle, as matter, as force. He seemed built of some infinitely expansive gaseous drift, and regardless of what he might try or with what ferocity, he would not make solid contact. Not with man or ball or mountain. He envisioned himself coming off these things harmlessly as light or flowing with ectoplasmic formlessness over whatever it was he wanted to challenge. And nothing—*nothing*—seemed particularly intrigued with the idea of challenging him.

"I want to beat you up," he'd once said to a kid on the school bus.

The kid flicked his thumbnail and said, "Bug off, yo-yo."

"When I grow up, I'm going to knock your block off," he'd told his dad.

"Fine," he had said. "So grow."

Ignored, unopposed, Michael ceased to exist, at least as true son of this embattled planet.

But encoiling the squirmy girth of Gilbert Krumrine, feeling the blood pump in the latter's throat, the jut of bone, the bump of skull—by the reference points of another—Michael was able to locate his own framework. He felt his soul shrink to a pinprick of incandescence, a pilot light, steady but recessive. With the clash of muscle and will, the animal in him awakened to the craft of physical resistance. For those few moments in tender time the animal prevailed. This made him real. It was only a bonus that he also turned out to be very good.

"Dagnabit, Kleeve!" Sometimes Yoder's voice cracked into a womanish whine. "Now do something, will ya? Try some escape combinations with Rascucci over there. *Do something.* So help me, you choke at states again . . . judas priest, what the judas priest's the use? Practice making a mean face if you want, but *do* something."

"Sure thing, Coach." Michael made a face, the one Mighty always made him perform for her friends, his Father Goose face: lips shoved up and out, nose sloped like a downspout, neck thrust into another plane.

"Christ, you look like a mallard." Yoder was laughing despite himself.

Michael shrugged, faking chagrin.

"OK, you guys," Yoder said, rapping his teeth with his pen. He tapped his clipboard. "Eliminations tomorrow. Bring your best stuff."

"Crack ass, Kleeve," Spot said. He landed a playful jab to Michael's chin. "The Wild Blue Leper don't wait on nobody."

CHAPTER

6

Trover thought the eight-ten to Chicago quite splendid in its husk of hammered light, even if it did rattle Mrs. Reeser's chimney some as it lumbered skyward. He took several snapshots and scribbled diligently on his legal pad. Mrs. Reeser could have no idea that what he wrote was a list of the cities he secretly lusted after: Rangoon, Katmandu, Dar es Salaam, Vladivostok, Machu Picchu. He reminded himself to renew his subscription to *National Geographic*.

He declined Mrs. Reeser's offer of eggs and scrapple. She was a plump, chignoned widow with emerald satin house slippers and the sort of guarded eyes he could imagine glittering to life in the steam of coffee and conversation. She would pretend he was husband or lover and forget, for the nonce, the menace overhead. Should he allow himself to be lured into somebody's fantasy life, he would have to live like the figment he felt this morning: "Thank you, no, ma'm." He had french fries and gravy at the Tiptop Diner.

He dawdled over hot chocolate until nine, when the stores opened. He drove up the road to Wilderness Travel, where he bought a glorious silver dome tent that revived the surge he'd experienced watching the radiant plane climb toward the sun. "Will you want the vestibule, sir?" asked the clerk.

"I'll take the nave, if you have one. The belfry. The works."

In the adjoining ski shop he bought a fat banana yellow down-filled jacket and a pair of 215-centimeter skis. The scrubbed and ruddy young man who waited on him raised an eyebrow, presumably because Trover, at five-six, would appear not only awkward but mortally imperiled, on boards that length. "Sure they won't be a bit too much ski for you?" the clerk said carefully. "Suckers really cruise."

"Speed's where I'm at right now," said Trover, and immediately felt foolishness drag like excess flesh on his face.

At Life Cycles he picked up a pair of racing pants, the kind with the chamois crotch. Then he bought all the Thomas Hardy Waldenbooks had in stock and everything they had on bicycling. He was due for a new bike.

Interstate east toward Lum Motors. Trover told himself he had official business there, even as he recognized Lum's as the last stop in his normal morning course, a follow-the-dots circuit through the wards of his chief suppliers.

Out on the pike he passed the Stud Shop. Unquestionably it would be tempting fate to take more underwear in. He owned drawerfuls, briefs of every cut and hue and stripe, candy-colored stretchies packed similarly to gourmet jelly beans, in hard plastic cases. Undershirts with round and scoop and V necks. Louise had had to resort to under-the-bed storage boxes. She pushed cardboard cartonfuls into corners, her face waxing stark with alarm and panic. Once she'd come bursting into the bathroom as he was toweling off. "What is it?" she demanded. She was dangling at an appalled arm's length a contraption that was hardly more than a wide elastic waistband with an attached electric blue jersey pouch to swaddle his parts.

"I bought it by mistake," he lied.

"What did you mistake it for, an oriole nest?"

He switched on the electric toothbrush.

"The truth!" she said. "*Who* did you buy it for?"

"Obviously I bought it for me," he said dryly, unplugging the appliance.

"From Frederick's of Hollywood?"

"That's right."

"Trover, you are a married man."

He opened the towel, and she peered at him first with hostility, next with uncertainty, then with the sullen interest of a child about to succumb to the bright enticements of a bad man. She sighed and stepped in close. He closed the towel around her, and they took tiny toy-soldier steps out to the hall, where the floor was more forgiving.

Trover professed no interest in knowing the limits, only in testing them. Certainly there was little room left in his marriage for stress, even less for underwear. Yet he could not resist bringing home an occasional three-pack, and he consciously looked forward to that look of almost comic incredulousness when Louise found them. In those seconds, caught in the narrowing vise of her vexed regard, he felt better and sounder and more complete than in all the moments of mutually self-conscious special handling that pretended to safeguard their union. Besides, didn't she always find room for more stuff? Soon he would start buying socks. Off-white and neutral tones, the fluffiest he could find.

It was a comfort to walk into places where people knew him by name. Midtown Lunch, Lewie's News, the bars. "Yo, Mr. Kleeve," said Sonny of Sonny's Exxon. "What ya call that hat you've got on?"

"Porkpie," Trover said, doffing it. He got a tankful of diesel and a bag of unshelled peanuts.

Then into Lum's he strolled. He cracked a shell into the bag, which he then offered to the two salesmen as they craned out of their cubicles. Both men had slicked, thinning hair and gangled out of their Easter egg-colored sports jackets. One showed too much sock; the one whose wrists protruded wore a huge gold-tone watch and tooled white ankle boots. The men carried handfuls of nuts back to their cubicles and let Trover poke around the showroom pretty much as he pleased.

"What's new in the lot?" he inquired generally.

A yawning mouthful said, "Coupla Dashers. A Vanagon."

"Vanagon?" The updraft in Trover's tone seemed to lift both men from their seats. They came to their adjacent doorways.

"Gas or diesel?"

"Diesel," said the one with the socks. "Take a spin?"

"Wife would kill me." He paused. "How many passengers?"

"All of youse, plus."

"I need new wheels like I need . . . instant glow plugs?"

"Instant chicken soup, if you want it."

But something had caught Trover's eye. He walked across the floor to a model that looked disturbingly familiar. Yes, there it was, all spruced up, added racing stripe, new mud flaps, listed as "next thing to new," the price a shave away from new. It was one he'd owned for four intolerable months before trading it in at a hefty loss. The Scirocco was a sourball from day one. The electric system was so bollixed up if you wanted heat, the wipers wobbled. Music threw the vehicle into arhythmia. Half the time he couldn't come home after dark for want of headlights. He circled the car, cracking nuts to make his interest appear casual, impersonal, but once, when he glanced up, he thought he saw an exchange of winks flash between the two salesmen. He rubbed his eyes and pretended not to have noticed. He would die before catching grown men in their turpitudes (unless, of course, they were on the stand, in which case he would roust every worm of duplicity from every follicle and wrinkle). But here in the early hours of his own personal everyday, the spectacle of common dishonor embarrassed and immobilized him. Nor did he wish to confront the hard evidence of how well he'd played the fool for fools. He rolled the top of his bag of peanut shells and recrossed the floor and poked it into the cradle made by one of the salesmen's folded arms.

Upstairs Lum's receptionist gave him a spring-action smile, and the space around her smelled of lipstick. He responded with a crisp salute that lifted his own spirits. Maybe the men hadn't winked. A malfunctioning of his lawyerly acuity for untruth? A trick of light kissing off new chrome? Had the men done anything at all but stand there trying to hang on to the frail hopefulness of another day the worth of which rested entirely on the strength of John Q. Consumer's current appetite? Such men would sell their souls for a five-day week of Trover Kleeves. All around Trover, like the bubble of scent engulfing the secretary, was a cloud of counterfeit well-being, the same unstable prosperity he remembered feeling as a teenager driving a pretty girl around in her father's new Buick.

He stuck his head in Lum's doorway, which was as far as he could physically intrude. Lum's desk was an inner yoke running flush with a display platform that extended almost to the door and lent him the appearance of wearing the world around his waist. But it was only Lum's world: felt-covered, topographical features in papier-mâché, two mirror lakes, HO houses and motels, tar paper arteries. The layout represented the general vicinity in which Lum Motors was located and included, in fact, Lum Motors itself and the big lot, boasting row upon row of Matchbox bugs and Rabbits and vans. Larry Lum protruded from a hole behind the service bay, a most favorable position to keep an eye on his operation.

Lum squinted up, a pricier version of his sales staff. The same unsubtle hues with contrasted hand stitching. "Hey, how the hell are you?" he said. He tendered a smile generically linked somehow to the men's wink, and then his attention rolled down like a window shade, and he returned to his computations.

Trover had expected—what? Coffee break banter. Ribald tales, a dose of gladhanding. If nothing else, Lum's style was usually as comfortingly unctuous as the diner fries composting in Trover's stomach. Trover had had a minor business matter to discuss with him, but now, ignored, dismissed, looming over the miniature lot like something suddenly elephantized and hideously misplaced, he could hardly remember who he was, let alone what he had come for. He found himself stuck in Lum's milieu, and when he spoke, it was in Lum's smug and trendy *patois*. "What chup to, baby?" is what Trover said, and the words curdled his stomach.

"Love to gas with ya, Counselor, but hey, I'm up to my cotton-pickin' ears ..."

"Gotta play catch-up myself. Last week was a wash. My dad—my father departed—d-died."

"Hey, say, sorry, pal."

Having carved himself this tiny, temporary niche of dignity, Trover shot a finger at Lum. "Friend," he said, "you got a date in court. Two weeks from Thursday. Get your figures together, and buzz me downtown."

Lum dropped out of sight. Trover backed into the hallway to let him out from under the dusty green skirt around the platform. He emerged head-first on his knees. When he stood, Trover's problem with scale was immediately reversed. Lum towered a head above him, breathing warm Dentyne. He stepped closer. "You straighten that little lady out, hear?"

"Give it my best shot." Rather than offer Lum another opportunity to dismiss him, he said, "Gotta run, Lar."

"Ciao," said Lum, now gone again. He crawled under the platform, and as he bumped around beneath, Trover took off.

He managed to hit the highway light sequence the wrong way, so there was plenty of time for shims of humiliation to cark and fester. Ample opportunity to ask himself why he wanted in any way to abet a slug like Larry Lum against some disgruntled customer. Why did he go to the car lot in the first place? Did he enjoy finding himself adrift in impotence against lesser men? Idiots in skimpy suits. Incurable dolts. Their ill-manneredness was like armor plate; their stupidity, impenetrable. Not only had they openly mocked him, but he was quite certain, at this very moment, the service department was plotting against his fleet. If degradation had the power to power Trover, his tank was full. He could run for days on low-grade rancor.

It was nearly eleven when he arrived at the office. The door was locked, the phone screaming. Where the devil was Debbie?

He flipped unhurriedly through his keys. The person on the other end would never hang up; the phone would drill away at lifeless space till the end of days. Even at odd hours they called. Sleeping it off one night on the library sofa, he'd been awakened at 4:00 A.M. by a woman with a perfectly clearheaded question about an action in equity. Another time, after a winter storm had all but paralyzed the East Coast, a client commandeered a giant Caterpillar to keep his appointment. He was outraged that Trover wasn't in when he arrived.

The caller was Mildred Gaugler. Trover could not recall a time when there hadn't been at least one Mildred Gaugler in his active files. He was almost afraid to ask. "What can I do for you, Mildred?"

"Why, did you get that there teapot offa my sister, Doris, yet?"

"Uh—"

"The *peacock* teapot I told you abott. The one she grabbed outa Mama's chelly cupboard the day, the *very* day, mindt, Mama died."

"Frankly, Mildred, I haven't had a chance to look into the matter yet."

"And so long's you're at it, there was such a nice little slaw cutter—"

"OK, let me get this down. You want the peacock and the slaw—"

"The peacock *teapot.* And Great-grammy Vogel's slaw cutter with the heart decorations."

He hoped the matter could be settled out of court. He had no wish to get ugly or eloquent over a slaw cutter. But he would if he had to. Over the years he'd recovered an array of oddments for assorted Gauglers: a log splitter wrongly repossessed (or rightly, but he got it back, that's what mattered); a plastic Christmas tree and a box of baby teeth from an estranged spouse; a set of Tupperware from the neighbors; treble damages for a stolen butternut tree. What was another teapot, more or less?

"Give me a buzz next week, Mildred."

"Ay, Lawyer Kleeve, anymore you always say that."

"Mildred . . ."

"You tell Doris I didn't forget neither the time she give away my harmonica to the hobo used to come round."

"When was that, Mildred?"

"Ay-yi-yi, now you got me. 'Thirty-four, was it? 'Thirty-five?"

"Mildred, I've got a call on the other line." He waited several moments, listening to the sturdy surf of Mrs. Gaugler's sighs before punching the button that lopped her off his morning.

The truth was he bore a special fondness for Mildred Gaugler and the cousinage of like clients who had been with him from the beginning, sixth-seventh-generation locals who saw fit to trust him despite his almost abject outsiderness. He would never adjust to their strange hybrid tongue, never relish their pasty suppers. They got a kick out of him when he tried. They could be pesky, quarrelsome, stubborn, intolerant, tendentious, unforgiving, ludicrously shrewd. Their laughter was round, their jokes were bawdy, they didn't let down their guard or relax their scrutiny for a second, and their final word on you was something they reserved until the day they spaded you under.

He settled their multiplicitous boundary disputes, represented their drag-racing sons, their disgraced daughters. He drew up endlessly particularizing wills in which, for instance, a peacock teapot is bequeathed to one

Mildred Gaugler. In the meantime, the teapot vanishes and Mildred raises cain and sues the estate, along with a dozen other heirs missing celery dishes and chocolate sets, copper boilers, sausage stuffers. He got their divorces and effected, sometimes with disastrous results, their reconciliations. He bought them drinks in the village hotels after magistrate hearings for traffic and game law violations. He danced at their weddings, and eventually they forgave him for avoiding their funerals. Sometimes out of shopping bags stuffed with cash, other times in dribs and drabs, they paid their bills, and they paid to the penny.

They brought him cider, summer bologna, and blocks of tongue souse. They paid him with art. Above the Xerox, they'd hung his portrait; he looked like he had a plug of Red Man in his cheek. Mildred Gaugler had quilted a nice plump cushion for his chair. They were good and loyal people. Still, he was not looking forward to doing battle over a teapot, peacock or otherwise.

He checked the mail. Several of those relentless five- and ten-dollar checks. J. C. Penney Insurance reminding him that he will turn forty-four soon and shouldn't he stock up on whole-life while he still can? His Winter Early Winters catalog. A lower-court appeal on behalf of the Uniontown Bookstore—denied. At this level he always lost. Obscenity cases had to be appealed practically to heaven. The higher you took them, the easier they were to win. But as often as he suffered these early-stage setbacks, they were never palatable. He had only to close his eyes to envision that solid block of black-clad men saying "Absolutely no" to him.

Debbie whirled into the office in that short, fat furry jacket that made her look like a wig stand. She laid the piece lovingly over the library table. She looked at her watch. "Wow. Sorry about that. Got my period this morning," she said. "Can't know what a bummer that is."

"Don't worry about it," Trover said quickly.

Now she was flying at him, yelling, "Quick, get up. You're on my Mocha Chews."

He jumped up from her desk, turned, and made an effort to fluff up the crumpled box. "Hey, I didn't see them, OK?" He shoved in and out of his pocket. "Here, get yourself some more." He handed her a twenty.

"Hmmmm, thanks," she said.

"Did we get that checkbook straightened away yet?" "We" he said and shouldn't have. It split the blame down the middle.

"Not really," she said. Month after month he'd watched her labor over the client accounts to the detriment of every other duty. As it turned out, at no point had she actually brought the books into balance. When he finally caught on, she said, "Look, it's just paper craziness. Don't act like it's real."

Now she tossed her curls and said, "If it's any comfort to you, my aunt Sue in Chicago said if I sent them out there, she'd let my cousin work on them. He's real good with numbers." She smiled beatifically and crossed to the Mr. Coffee, tottering on three-inch heels.

He imagined his books bouncing all over the cargo hold of the eight-ten to Chicago. Mrs. Reeser was right. The runway *was* far too short, and the pilot a maniac, a frustrated stuntman. "Please don't do that," he said.

"Suit yourself," Debbie replied, as if with that suggestion she'd now exhausted all remedy.

Trover's very skin seemed to shrink around a sense of diminishing reserves. He held up a finger. "One minute, Deb." But he'd already sabotaged his tone with the diminutive. *Deb.* She stood in the doorway staring at him with that look of affronted puzzlement. *What could he possibly want now?*

"Hey, maybe it's not such a hot idea either to let the phones go unmanned during regular business hours. Looks unprofessional."

"They always call back," she said curtly. "Anyhow, I thought I explained about this morning. I got my—"

"I know," he said, staying her with the flat of his hand. Then he waved her out, and she went clacking down the hall, going out no doubt while her coffee made itself, to replace the ruined cookies. It mystified him why a woman emancipated enough to go yelling around about her period would remain in bondage to a pair of uncaring shoes. "Ribbet," he said to himself, and picked up his catalog and went into his own office and closed the door.

It was not a large office. Size would have deprived this room, attenuated its textures, slackened the tone and tension, the quiet vibrancy of it, the aura of deep asylum. It had been Drum Drummond's office, the years when Trover was the hired hand working out of the library.

Without outside intervention, the character of this room would doubtlessly have undergone convulsions of vulgar renewal when Trover moved in: new tubular furnishings, a jam of ceramics and other forms of client art, a thoughtless random filling in. It was the IRS that had interceded, acting incidentally on the room's behalf, the same time it moved with unmistakable, unshakable purpose to crush its occupant.

When they finished with Drum Drummond, he was a cartoon casualty, flat broke, a federal eye on every future dime. And whatever his assets, they changed hands, ironically enough, with little appreciable gain to the government. Trover bought his office appurtenances, the whole shebang, at sheriff's sale (cannibals would fillet a man for forty-two dollars). Now Trover never balked at the chance to dismantle them. The IRS, FBI, the SEC and LCB, PENNDOT, HUD, whole armies of initials and acronyms backed by endless payrolls of pitiless men. They made juries choose between a man taken in evasion and "America," hinting that a wrong decision would come down so hard on the side of the man that "America" would be immediately and irretrievably slung into the ionosphere.

And nobody had a prayer against them. Not in the slab-solid form they presented to the public. What you had to do was pry just one guy loose from the pack and go after him. One apple-cheeked mama's boy at a time. One knife-creased knee and his gentleman lawyer. Trover loved to lure them into court and wipe the goodness off their cheeks with their own immaculate hankies. Get just one, and you've shaken the system's faith in itself, for a day anyhow. Two men, two days. You had to keep the power loose and negotiable. In the name of another, Trover would challenge the pope, OPEC, anybody. But behind the unshakable professional verve there was always the mocking specter of personal impotence, semiliterates smirking in doorways, Larry Lum snubbing him. And Trover had never in his life pursued a delinquent account beyond a second billing.

Trover came to the courage of his calling too late to untangle Drum Drummond. He'd bought his mentor's office fixtures with the idea of turning them over to Drum when he got back on his feet. But Drum was forty-six, several years past a trial lawyer's effective life. He was spending his afternoons in the slot car parlors and wandering the malls with the pensioners and bag ladies. Nights he drank and shot pathetically unsteady pool. He could no longer walk into court without retching first. He grew fuzzy and tearful. Clients with funds caught in his multiform foreclosures lodged complaints with the bar association. His wife left; his skin yellowed; his eyes dulled; he died.

So today Trover sat behind the desk Drum's parents had given him when he entered private practice. In the patinaed surface glow, his endlessly vehement, gesticulating hands flickered like another man mimicking him. Trover had made no major changes, but the quirks of his personality had encroached like the leavings of time and climate. There was the photo of Michael in wrestling gear, his body articulating its angles of menace in painful awkwardness; the trophies of countless shopping sprees—the lifesize carved Don Quixote; a ceramic kangaroo planter, its pouch full of pennies and Hershey kisses, the bags of underwear he didn't dare take home yet, an Irish tweed cap. On the radiator sat a nine-foot cloth gorilla, a gift from a grateful client for whom he'd taken on Exxon and, in effect, won for him a free gas station. It wore a necklace of sleigh bells, a gift to the creature from Mr. Kleeve.

Taking up his catalog, he turned to the tents, and that made him feel closer to the tent locked in his car. He pored over pages of shelters that were hardly more than spirits, pastel, weightless, bearing names like Angelskin,

Divine Light, Cathedral. All of them, claimed the copy, "breathed." A far cry from the smelly green canvas thing he and his dad had taken to the mountains. He'd been impatient with his father's ponderous ways, his need to teach. His father tapping in the stakes. "Like so, Bud. Always take the time to do it right. Like so." His dad wore a little button on his scoutmaster's cap that said "THIMK."

And later, at National Guard summer camp. Weekend bivouac. Saturday night he'd gone off into the woods to tie one on with some of the guys. Coming back very late and very drunk, he'd stumbled among hundreds of identical pup tents in search of his own. At one point he tripped over a stake and went crashing into one. He heard the tent pole snap, and inside the collapse ensued a churning jumble of cursing and thrashing around. He staggered off before the guy inside could catch him. It seemed then that he wandered in circles for hours before finding his way home. When he poked his head inside, his tentmate was up. "Man, oh man," he said, using his arm as a prop, "you shoulda been here Kleeve. Some asshole drunk dropped in and broke up our little home."

He admired a catalog tent the translucent blue of a blown bubble. *But, Trover, can you trust such a tent not to rise in the dead of night, with you in it?*

Debbie buzzed him. "Len DeTurk," she said.

He rose and opened the door and let the man in. DeTurk came quickly toward him. He took Trover squarely by the shoulders in a funereal commingling of kinship and affection. In his business there was always tragedy.

"What'd they hit?"

"The Ringtown store." DeTurk sank despondently into one of Drum Drummond's tan leather chairs. Trover sat on the edge of his desk and waited. It had taken him awhile to adjust to the overriding ordinariness of his porn people. Waiting for the first guy to show up three, four years ago, he'd all but held his breath against whatever noxious miasma might be steaming off his skin.

He would be unwashed, uncombed and wear his pants low. Thick-lipped and heavy-lidded and stinking of countless layers of plain debauchery, oily, avid, alert, the man would slither in. How would he get the guy past Debbie or Sue or Marsha or whoever presided over the office at the time? What if her parents found out?

Len DeTurk had been his first case, and he sat before him now in his customary bleached jeans and sneakers. Trover had taken on his case mainly because nobody else would touch it. He'd built his practice on white-glove rejects, cases thrown his way by guys who took only sure shots and jackpots; never anything tinged, touchy, or, heaven forbid, malodorous.

"Grab stuff?" Trover asked.

"Tons. No warrant. No nothing."

"Bastards never heard of illegal search and seizure."

"Stay tuned for the bad news."

Trover waited.

"Judge What's 'is face . . ."

"Bogpother."

"Yeah, him. DA's office claims he's granting their injunction request this afternoon. Close us down, you think?"

Trover stood, then sat back down in his swivel chair and swung his feet up. He shook his head like a wet retriever.

"Can he do that?"

All day long people asked him that question. Can he divorce me, sue me, steal my wife, call me names, put out my lights? As if the law were prophylactic. The law was an aftershock. You had to get murdered in your bed first and then go looking to be made whole. "He's doing it, isn't he?"

DeTurk stared at him uncomprehendingly. It was that maybe, the expression of dumb, befuddled helplessness, that made him want to rend the heavens (or at least raise some hell) for people caught in the rusty wheels of justice, and nobody was lonelier than the man accused. He shoved back from his desk, rolling off his chair pad. He propelled himself back and picked up the yellow phone. "Debbie, get Judge Bogpother out in Shippen County."

"What's the number?"

"Chrissakes, girl, that's *your* job. Look it up." Now he was humming. He could feel all his parts pulling together, his limbs lengthening, his spirit turning light, boisterous as white water. Come spring, he'd have to get himself a kayak.

"Sorry," chimed the sanguine voice on the other end. "His Honor is still in Motion Court. Miss Woodruff here. Can I help you?"

He covered the receiver. "Bogpother isn't in," he said to his client. "We'll have to make do.

"Well, now, perhaps you can," he said, encrusting his tone with grumpy rustic, a little Dutch-country grit, even though Lackawanna, where he'd grown up, wasn't fifteen miles from Ringtown. "Correct me if I'm wrong, miss, but the word I got is the learned judge is fixing to slap my people with an injunction."

"I believe His Honor is seeing the DA this very afternoon."

"Ay-yi-yi," he said, "you just stop me when I get off the track, but are we talking your basic one-sided, ex parte, illegal-as-DDT *preliminary* injunction?"

"Mr. Kleeve, *sir,* would you care to leave a message for His Honor?"

"Hmmmmm, now maybe I'll do that."

"Fire away, sir."

"Tell Hizzoner I dare him. I'd bloody well like to see him try."

"Righ-toe," she said.

"Holy geez," said DeTurk when Trover hung up. He slid down in his chair and drew his shoulders up around his ears. "Now he's really going to be pissed."

Trover grinned. "Is he ever! Dumb bunny's going to land on that paper with all four paws muddy. Action is so flagrant it stinks. Tomorrow we ask the Superior Court for an immediate hearing. Guys have no choice under the law but to stay the order. What's more, Bogpother's going to get his can kicked for civil rights violations. We got him just where we've always wanted him, on the Superior Court shitlist."

"You're the boss," said DeTurk uncertainly.

When he was gone, Trover sat back and let the dense quiet surround him like soft packing material. One day soon somebody would expect a brief or a form filled out, making him restive and testy. He'd have to punch the gorilla or go for a walk or repair to the john with a book. He remembered one winter night when he'd come home drunk and crying the blues. He was inadequate, he whined. And no good. A lousy husband, father, human being. And Louise said that for everybody there was a place, an arena, a task, talent, a single impulse that lifted him high above his best self-estimates. A "good room," she called it. And Louise, at that moment, was better than herself.

Instead of buzzing, he called for his secretary. "Debbie! Come in here, hurry!" She moseyed in, fur jacket slung over her arm. He patted the leather chair DeTurk had just vacated. "Sit, please."

The girl plunked down, working her mouth into a wan facsimile of a patient smile. She sighed and waited.

He strode briskly back behind his desk. Leaning forward, he rested the tips of his fingers on the desktop. "I want your honest opinion. What do you think of this room?"

She shrugged. "The venetian blinds are cruddy." She pushed at a cuticle, then looked up. "It'll do."

"Thank you."

"If it's all the same to you then, I'm going to lunch." She jiggled into the jacket and, with a beleaguered backward glance, wobbled out of the room.

"But, Louise," Trover had said to his wife that winter night, "even if there is something all that wonderful about me, what's it to you? You don't get much of it."

She nodded then and turned thoughtful; he'd wished he hadn't been so quick to point out the one crimp in her system.

CHAPTER

7

Trover's Rabbit completed the fleet. Now all the cars were in: the Jeep truck, the Hornet, the red bug, plus one—the saucy little Triumph belonging to Gideon McThee. Trover slammed the car door, took two steps, and all but fell over the mass of yellow rubber lying like something that had been slopped over the porch, the stoop, the driveway and left to harden there. His impulse was to kick up a fuss, but experience silenced him.

With what zestful and devilish invention family members went about mining the world for one another. Even the most seemingly incontestible evidence of misfeasance could pan out false, a red herring, a trap. If, for instance, you were to point out that the string beans were rubbery, well, then weren't they the very ones *your* mother taught Louise to freeze in that imbecilic new way, in blocks of water or mint tea or whatever? And on the way to the concert didn't the question always come up and didn't you always say, "Shoot, I forgot them!"? Just so the ensuing snit could be vanquished with a smug look and a waving of two crisp tickets under the tantrum taker's nose.

So despite being at a loss as to how he could possibly be implicated in the matter of the rubber raft, Trover remained wary. He decided to ignore it.

He managed to overlook as well the sunken pumpkin and deliquescent summer squash moldering on a common pile and the broom chewed down to an inch of bristle. Lord only knew he could not honestly accuse Louise of being hard on cleaning supplies.

Instinctively he glanced back over his shoulder: he could feel the pull of the long day, like a road he dragged behind him. The road was familiar and simple, but as often as he entered his own kitchen, well, that was never simple. This house he approached again and again as uncharted, variously treacherous terrain. If he could wrap that road around his face, he would do just that. Each day, when he came home, he was naked and unready, and each day he felt afraid of the people living there. The crooks and creeps of Lum's, at least, could take nothing from him that he couldn't live without.

His house swaddled him in its air. Their mingled personal scents made a single animal closeness that held, despite the daily introduction of variables (which in themselves averaged out over time): cooking odors; an occasional dead mouse caught in the refrigerator fan; Louise's habit of letting a crusty skillet soak in the oven until, forgotten, it formed a white putrefaction. Home all day, enclosed, Louise had become desensitized. But Trover had noticed her coming in from a day away, how she'd sniff, sniff, sniff, her chin uplifted, leery as of a strange lair, hesitant to enter. Every house they'd ever owned developed the same smell, just as every kitchen took on Louise's look of a lick and a promise.

Through the dining room dark his wife moved toward him. His heartbeat raced. Her eyes fixed somewhere beyond him, Louise seemed to float and not know he was there until they came face-to-face in the hallway. "Oh! It's you," she said. Their eyes blinked together uncertainly. "You're early," she said, a little shaky on the word "early." And rightly so, for the term implied arrival by custom or appointment or fixed schedule, none of which herein applied. Trover worked hard to keep his homecomings open-ended, random-seeming, accidents of whim and weather. A headwind alone could delay him by a good three hours.

"I'm running tonight," he said. "I'm going up to change."

"It'll soon be dark."

"I'm not going anywhere. Just around the pool and the rose garden." She grimaced. "How can you stand to run in circles?"

"It's easier to keep track when you count laps."

"You're always counting something, calories, reps, heartbeats."

God, he thought. Unmasked again. She kept summing him up in ever-shorter sentences. *You're always counting something.* Four words. He'd have to change, reshuffle himself, burrow deeper into his own mystery. He brushed past his wife and slipped gratefully into the deepening dark beyond her. She had been right about the workshop's blocking off light.

As he warmed up in the dim splash-off from the porch light, he wished his wife's eyes on him. He had nice legs, plump, rounded calves: Louise had said so. He ran vigorously in place, nice plump legs pumping like pistons. She'd be shaking her head affectionately, seeing him the way he'd seen himself the morning they'd gone to Lackawanna, when he was popping around the house, spoiling for trouble. She'd think of him as something smallish and unaccountable and beguiling. Another creature of the earth all itchy and astir with itself. Six more jumping jacks and off he went around the far side of the garden.

He ran a course shaped vaguely like a pair of spectacles. Two circles, the loop around the pool and the smaller one around the rose garden connected by the short, straight climb past the gazebo. Around and around and around until the sameness became unguent to him, and now, after completing several courses, he no longer seemed to be trying at all. He began to move mindlessly, mechanically as a toy train through a Christmas tree town.

He slipped into rhythm; he tried to elide also with thoughts of his father. Out here, moving in the cold, he could dwell dangerously yet keep his distance, keep ahead, keep going.

He found himself remembering, instead, an old, old woman. He hadn't thought about his great-grandmother in years. The vision was bleached, blurred. It was more the rhythm he remembered, the rocking, the all-day bumping against the braided rug. Her eyes carried no light; he used to imagine her head rattling like a burnt-out bulb. He was afraid of the dead eyes in the guest room, the rocking after the mind was gone. Every day his mother pinned a pretty ribbon to the wobbly head.

Bright ribbons, starched aprons. Now he was thinking of a girl he'd asked out the first year he had his own car. When he went to her house, she was all dolled up but tying an apron around her waist, with the cool, aloof efficiency of his mother. The apron was covered with happy-faced cupcakes. "One sec," she'd said, punching through a swinging door with a box of squeaking newborn kittens. At the first sound of running tap water he'd fled. And though he could no longer recall the girl's name, he never forgot the apron, the reassuring hominess of it, the killer crispness. Women wore aprons to hide their true capabilities. They bore watching.

Last night he'd dreamed of his father building a room inside his basement room. Another inside that and on through a nest of rooms to one the size of a jeweler's box which held a lapel pin nestled in cotton. The pin said "Good Scout."

Now at last he had a fix on his father himself. He is sitting on the handsome slatted swing glider purchased for his retirement ease. At dusk a boy comes moping across the lawn, but as he draws near the porch, the old man closes his eyes and nods off much too abruptly. The boy turns and starts back the way he came, no less a poseur, for quite suddenly he whirls around, catching Banfer Kleeve with his eyes wide open. Found out, the man quickly slumps and begins to snore. So affecting is this memory, so devastating the rejection that Trover believes for a moment that the boy is himself, and breathing comes hard. The vision immediately self-corrects, and Trover knows with certainty that it had happened not to him but to Michael years ago during one of the children's annual two-week stays in Lackawanna. It was the same summer Banfer Kleeve had upbraided his grandson for eating all the lemon slices out of the iced tea pitcher, and Maddy had quietly sliced a whole platterful and set them defiantly under the boy's nose. It was the summer Michael had horrified the old man by throwing away a nickel's change. Banfer Kleeve had called the boy a hooligan and a wastrel. When Michael told Trover the story of the swing glider, Trover had been as heartsore as if it had happened to him. His son, himself. But when Michael asked, in genuine hurt and consternation, "Why do you think Pap pretended to be asleep?" Trover had told him the truth. "He was hiding from you. You never stop coming."

Somebody switched on the outside lights. Long shadow strings crisscrossed the roadway, making his feet nervous at first. He leapt over the shadow of the small spruce by the pool; in the distance the Blue Mountains melted blurrily into the sky and night. Like chilled picnickers, the deck furniture huddled on the pavilion. Sprecher had neglected to store them away for the cold months. Trover felt the winter on his skin, but he was a long train with all its lights burning, shabby warmth within. He withdrew inside the train, and now the windows were black with night.

He is six, and the box of brightness that contains him contains his father as well. They have come from a small town to the South, where they have made burial arrangements for his father's father. They are a thoughtful pair but not sad. Banfer Kleeve sits with a bag on his lap. The bag bulges with popcorn balls and sundry wax novelties, lips and mustaches and milk bottles holding colored syrup. JuJubes and bubble gum, all things Maddy would have vetoed out of hand. His father is a staunch practitioner of domestic unity, but tonight is different; tonight is an island, father and son and dark all around.

He opens his Fleer's fortune: "Steer clear of get-rich-quick schemes."

The train does not rock and sway in the jaunty, unserious style of trolley cars. So smooth, in fact, is the ride that the light seems the vehicle; they are traveling in troughs of light, and the boy thinks of the pneumatic tubes that ferry money around the store where his father works. Though it is late, the boy is saucer-eyed. His father tries to explain the principles that keep the train tracking; Bud's father is always showing and teaching. He demonstrates how to knot a necktie. Bud catches on right away; he is a skilled knotsman, his father says, a clever boy.

Then they sit silently for a long time, and the sound of their travel floods silver between the boy's ears; he feels liquid, uncontained, and shoves nearer the substantive bulk of the larger body. The seats have a dense, musty smell like the inside of those plump green-tomato cars driven by old men.

"That dead guy was my grandpap, wasn't he?"

"Yup." His father hikes him tight against his chest. The smell of loose tobacco in the shirt pocket.

"What was his name?"

"Banfer Kleeve, same as ours."

After a bit his father says, "See, it's not like I ever knew the man. He took off before I could get a good look, before I could identify him." He laughed almost fondly. "That was right after I was born, I guess, over thirty years ago."

The boy says nothing, lost as he is in the notion, the ocean of time that makes thirty years. His father says, "Doubt anybody would have found him but for Mrs. Bowman wanting her room and board." He rolled a cigarette, moistened the paper, and sealed it lovingly. "Son, you always square it with the landlady and you bury your dead."

The boy watches his father's smoke rise and form a large blue saucer under the lights, and the dark outside is the world.

Trover bounded soundlessly now beneath the row of shivering pines; he had neither substance nor will. The tiny light-filled compartment he occupied kept shrinking like the window in a lengthening perspective; under his feet needles thick as field sod. An apple dropped through darkness in the orchard below. Across the main lawn between the road and his house, shadows grappled and clasped. His house, too, seemed to hold him; in each of the pale yellow windows of the long new room he saw himself, sitting stiffly, a polite but melancholy traveler.

His relationship to the moment was peculiar. He was both acutely attuned and, embedded as he was in his distances, oddly detached. He felt the eyes of small creatures hidden in brown grasses, deer huddled on the hillside. An old man's vexed regard, how he had caught his father not that long ago watching him, Trover, in the plate glass mirror above the TV, the eyes full of dark and sorrow and disappointment.

The sound of the train brushes through his bones. Tapping the boy's knee, the man points to the radio tower blinking pink and green on the indiscernible mountain, he raises his voice over the *chicka-choo* of the wheels to say, "Now, Bud, why do you suppose a covered bridge is covered? Where did the Conemaugh River get its name?" In his painful meticulousness, he loosens the end of a roll of Necco wafers and offers the pack in a ritual of communion between men.... And now what if Trover would, in the course of this run, come over the hump in the roadway and the full moon slip suddenly out from behind the tree line? Would he not be startled into weeping? He would sweat and weep, and the cold air slap his wet face, and still, he would ride in the tiny light inside himself, weightless and strange as the self will become on a train traveling in the dark through nameless places.

And when headlights appeared before him at the crest of the driveway, he went unhaltingly on. Drawing close, he saw that it was Spot Grayrain and, in the seat next to him, Michael. Trover nodded and loped out of the headlight funnel and off again into darkness. And what if his face shone luminous with tears in those few pellucid seconds? Did he know that Michael, from that hour on, was condemned to the vision of his father's sorrowing face forever?

When he had showered and dressed in Banfer Kleeve's blue velour bathrobe, Trover went to the table. He looked up from his plate to see not just Mighty, who was always tough, but Louise and Michael and Gideon McThee suspending dinner to watch him with long-suffering stares. Mighty claimed he did something with food against the soft palate that produced a "disgusting suction cup sound." With a slick, unnoticeable shift (he would never openly yield to public pressure) he eliminated the more viscous textures and made his chewing somehow less monstrous. "What are you up to these days?" he asked Gideon, by way of deflecting their censure.

"SOS," the boy said. "Same old, uh, *stuff.*" Gideon had dropped out of school the year before. Trover was hard put to figure how the boy supported himself, that is, once he'd run through profits from the marijuana plants Trover found out he'd grown in the fields last summer. Trover also wondered where he called home. Most mornings he could be found either in the guest room or on the foldout couch. But despite the obvious, Trover was not yet prepared to admit that Gideon lived right there, with them.

"SOS, huh?"

"Dad," said Mighty, "Gideon's in antiques."

Trover cocked his head, then nodded once. *Why not?*

"It takes time to get a business off the ground," said Gideon.

"Where do you work out of?" Trover asked.

"Our garage," Louise said flatly. His wife, he knew, half believed that

Gideon's long-term designs included a plan to marry Mighty and murder them all so he could take over the Knoll.

"Oh, speaking of the garage," said Mighty, "know the VW bug?"

The skin drew tight across Trover's skull. "Like my own son."

"Stupid thing's still gummed up."

"Get it fixed."

"Dad," said Michael, "that's throwing good money after bad."

"Fine, don't get it fixed."

Mighty's eyes flashed. "Jerks at Lum's don't know fuel injection from kidney dialysis. The car bucks and stalls, and then we take it in. They call, and we pick it up, and two hours later—guess what—it bucks and stalls."

Trover forced air out his nose. "I wanted to trade the Jeep in on something more reliable months ago."

"Stop him!" cried Louise, as if her husband had actually tried to bolt and run instead of merely attempt his customary leap out of logic.

"Yeah, Dad," said Michael. "What's that got to do with the VW convertible?"

"Then you handle it, wise guy."

Gideon ladled more stew into his bowl. "It's my guess there's dirt in the fuel lines."

"Anymore," Trover said, "you have to expect to spend a little time getting the kinks ironed out of a thing."

And Mighty poked a crust of bread in her mouth. "You ask me," she garbled, "those scumwads probably sabotage our engines so we get fed up and buy another car."

"Well," said her father, "the bug *is*—how old now?"

"Oh, six, eight months at least," said Louise, letting her tone lollygag over the scorn in which she held his calculations.

"More significantly, how many *miles* on the thing, Louise? We do use the hell out of our vehicles."

"Dad," Michael interjected, "knock it off. A new car is not the solution. Isn't a car supposed to be fit to drive six months later?"

"What kind of new car did you have in mind?" Gideon posed the question with almost lubricious interest. "Have you checked out the Porsche turbos?"

As one stumbling upon a surprising new ally, Trover brightened and addressed Gideon man to man. "Lum's just got in a terrific little Vanagon I wouldn't mind taking a look at."

Mighty shot Gideon a look. "Will you can it with the new car jazz? Dad, stick to the subject!"

Trover finished chewing. He shook his head. "Somebody come out with a book I don't know about, one that says dump on Trover Kleeve? Chrissakes, I don't even *drive* that red bug."

"You want us to *hire* a lawyer?" From Mighty with punch.

"Hell, no, I'll take a month off work and handle it. Just like I'm the only one around here can replace a light bulb. When was the last time your mother took the trouble to put the toilet paper roll on the holder? Did your brother set those mouse traps yet?"

Louise drew herself tall, a stanchion of self-restraint.

"I'm the only one who can pick up a newspaper, empty an ashtray." He'd wanted to avoid it, but now he was desperate. He went for the raft like a drowning man. "And let me ask you this, little missy—how long's that hunk of yellow junk going to lay out front? Till it rots?"

Mighty drummed the table with her knuckle. "Stick to the subject, dammit. If you're scared of assface Larry Lum, *I'll* tell him what to do with his—"

Trover let his fork drop onto his plate. "No, no, little Miss Wiseacre, now don't *you* change the subject. I want some hard answers here. Who's the incredible slob that said, 'Fiddlee-dee, think I'll just dump this big filthy raft right here where somebody can break their neck on it'?" His eyes bore down on her, and hers drilled right back. "That's a pig's trick, girlie."

"Pig's trick, pig's trick. Do you have to *spit* when you say it?"

"Was it you, missy? Yes or no?"

"Hey, I'm not on the witness stand!"

"Did you leave the raft on the porch?" He was smiling his now-I-gotcha smile.

"I don't know jackshit about that raft."

He turned to Louise. "Your daughter has a maggot mouth. Or didn't you know that?" He watched his wife brace herself. She knew him too well, that he was now in the process of remanding all hostilities to her because he could not bear to fight with his children, especially not the girl child who accused him with his own face.

"Louise," he said then, switching to the paternalistic diction he knew she abhorred, "you're home all day. Why can't you take charge of these loose ends that appear to be all that's standing between this family and paradise?"

"That car's been in and out of the shop six times in the last two weeks. Excuse me if I seem reluctant to spend the rest of my allotted time on earth running back and forth to Lum Motors, your headquarters for sleaze and idiocy."

Trover shoved back from the table.

"Dad," Michael said placatingly, "you shouldn't take an attack on Lum

VW so personally. Nobody holds you directly responsible for their jerki-ness."

"The hell we don't," Mighty snapped. "Why should he give people carte blanche to kick us around? Don't worry, gang, it's just my dumb old fam-ily."

"The shoemaker's children have no shoes," Gideon said sagely.

"Let's get back to the boat," Trover said to Louise. He clung to the raft, even knowing instinctively it was as dangerous to him as the red car. The yellow boat, the red car. Once they'd fought an entire weekend over a slice of green bread in his sweater drawer.

"OK, know-it-all," Mighty said, "you want the lowdown?"

So here was where the trap was sprung. He recoiled from the full wallop of the triumphant eyes she trained on him.

"Last week, while we were at *your* father's funeral, Sprecher attacked it with a knife."

The coils of his brain writhed and tightened, and wasn't he supposed to avoid stress at his age? "Lot of Mickey Mouse," he said. "It's clear as day what happened. Nobody in this household can be bothered putting any-thing away. Then, when things spring a leak, they're all upset. Boo-hoo, somebody ruined my little boat. Lackaday, lackaday!" He aimed a scornful glance at his son. "Everything around here turns into a piece of junk."

"Go look, Dad," Michael urged peaceably. "That's all I ask."

Trover dismissed him with a mirthless guffaw. "You're a bullshitter, boy!"

"You son of a . . ." the boy said as his eyes filled. "One of these days—"

"Ooooooooo-weeeeeee! Threats from a guy who let some bozo chump beat him out at states. *Give* me a break!"

"I think you owe these guys an apology." Louise's efforts to control her tone converted mildness into medium-range stridency.

"Perhaps I can throw some light on the subject." Gideon presided with the suave avuncularity of a family therapist. "I saw the vessel in question, Mr. Kleeve. There was a foot-long cut along the side. Very clean. Cold-blooded. It was *no* accident."

"And what am I supposed to do about it?"

"Not a goddamned thing," said Louise, skipping into high range. "It's your sacred duty to leave us at the mercy of evildoers and lunatics."

"How the hell do you know who did it? Sprecher leave a calling card?"

"Come on, who else would bother?"

"You have a short memory, Louise. When it comes to vandalism, your son here is no slouch. Used to be every time he'd get a bug up his butt, he'd beat hell out of something. Walls. Books. His sister. Hell, I went to court once in a shirt that said 'Daddy Eats Boogers' on both sleeves."

"Dad," said Mighty, "that was eight years ago."

"Let me alone."

"Sure, now that you've got us hooked up practically for life with con men and *murderers,* you'd rather not be consulted. What kind of lawyer are you anyhow?"

"Do . . . not . . . criticize . . . me," he said menacingly calm. As a caveat it was clear, if not timely given.

Once she got going, Louise was as unstoppable as he. She phrased this next like a high school debater, as if it were nothing more than standard forensics: "And how would you advise a paying client in a like situation? Answer me that, and I promise I'll drop the subject."

"I'd tell them to keep their goddamn mouth shut and let me eat."

"Ooooooooooo!" cried Mighty.

Filling his cheeks with air and deflating slowly, Gideon introduced himself as a cooling wind of last resort. "As I see it, what we need is a clarification of—"

"Oh, bull, it's just him." In her pale face Mighty's pupils showed hard and sharp as prune pits. "It's always him."

And when his daughter was through, Trover burned slowly at Louise, his eyes wailing the ritual lament: *You've turned my children against me. I won't forgive you for that.*

"If you want to fight, fight with Mighty," Louise said. "I'll not be held accountable for every dirty look in your life. Stand up and fight your own battles."

"Coward!" Mighty said under her breath.

It had to happen because it always did, because habit is the widest channel: The quickest way out for Trover was on a spume of steam out the top of his head. *Errrrrrrrr-rfffff.* First he roared, and the next thing he did was grab up the butter dish, the motion not unlike a preschooler's two-handed squatting launch of a Frisbee. Half the butter stayed on the ceiling tiles; the dish came back down to smash the bowl of white mums Maddy had insisted they keep out of the funeral bouquets. The pepper mill sailed through lattice-patterned glass and went on to decimate the rank-and-file glassware stored in the cupboard. He threw his stew plate into the same cupboard, gravy and vegetable debris spattering everywhere. Planting his feet apart, he ripped his father's bathrobe down the back seam with one grunting tug. He stood staring down at himself in amazement, that such a simple stroke should expose him so completely. Nakedness and rage—as contiguous realities, they were a terrible match, mutually mocking, wholly incompatible. No way out now but to drum up a diversion. He dashed his chair up and down until the rungs and spindles were a pile of sticks, and then he ran upstairs and got dressed and went out.

*   *   *

The house was dark and the quiet within like the bitter residue of a burning when he came swaying home. He switched on the lights and peered blearily around the kitchen. It was posted again. Index cards marked with a felt-tip pen pressed wickedly hard. One was secured by a magnetic cow to the refrigerator door. Another taped to the wall, another tucked between mirror and frame. All bore the same somehow breathless memo: "I must remember to hate my husband, Trover Kleeve."

CHAPTER

8

"Good morning, good morning," Trover sang out first thing. "Morning, My. Morning, Mike."

Face screwed up in stagy perplexity, Michael searched the kitchen. "Aw right!" he cried when he found his wallet in the lazy Susan. "Aw right!" he repeated, less elatedly, for his father's benefit. Hadn't they agreed to ignore the man no matter how hard he tried?

Trover bussed over to Louise. Auburn forelocks still slick from the shower bounced on his brow as he walked. "Take a look," he said trying to swivel her face toward the window. "It's winny out there today." Standard family baby talk. "Winny" for "windy", as he tried to gust himself back into the fold.

Louise held her neck rigid while Mighty and Michael eyed their father obliquely. They exchanged cautioning glances. *Look out! He's pouring it on. Don't let him be nice.* With all their practice, they had never quite learned to adjust fast enough to the feeling of sudden severe dislocation as, with one congenial yank, he jerked them up from the bitter depths to ordinary air. It made the stomach draw, the head spin, the skin prickle; psychologically, he gave them all the bends.

With unsettling good cheer, he shook out his own cereal, sliced his bananas wafer-thin, humming, tapping his toe, and as he toiled, the sullen tableau dissolved and each body began moving out into the normal morning currents.

Louise could not entirely discount her complicity in these eradications. Not a trace of debris from his blowup remained. Every jagged shard had been picked from the cupboard door; everything else was scraped, scrubbed, or swept up. Louise was anything but a tidier, yet there it was, whatever had been, whisked away. She'd risen early so he wouldn't catch her on her knees. She gave him such gifts like offerings from high-minded mortals to some nuisance deity, and he accepted them as if they were his due. She'd done her part, and now she had every right to a long face, and she'd be damned if she was taking down the signs or acting civil to a savage.

It was the running that got her. That he excused himself from the brunt of his own aftermaths. Michael choking, heaving, sobbing in anger and self-blame. Mighty's silence as he drove away, that resolute control a more lacerating spectacle even than her brother's coming undone. Did Trover know that nights he ran off like a wild dog, his wife slept in a cocoon of cold wire and her sleep was another word for dread? Those nights her dark angel always played for her the same unspeakable dream: She is looking out a wide window toward some distant city. The sky over the serried rooftops, dead-still, gritty white, suggests a blank home movie screen. A smudge, hardly more than a thumbprint, appears on the screen. By now she knows what to expect, watches helplessly as the bit of fluff begins to rise in a dark column, begins to flare into its final unmistakable mushroom form. The cloud begins to bleed along the edges, stains the sky red. She watches the city fall, street by street, house by house. Suddenly she is no longer observing from some remote outpost but from the shattering center of things. And her house is next.

"Use a few bucks?" he said to Louise when he'd finished eating.

She shook her head. *Not that easy, mister.*

"Kids need money?"

"Ask them."

Mighty said, "No!"

"Michael?"

He glanced from mother to sister. "Uh, well, I'm supposed to hand in my hoagie sale money today."

"You gotta be kidding," said Mighty. "If you sold hoagies, you must have collected money. Where is it?"

Michael shrugged. "Lotta guys said they'd pay me later, and—"

"A twenty cover it?" asked Trover, a bill tucked between two fingers.

"I owe eleven-fifty."

"Buy yourself a good book."

"Thanks," Michael said sheepishly, under his sister's shaming stare.

"How 'bout you, My? Got any loan sharks after you? You want hoagie money?"

She drew her lips tight, as if her need might escape unawares. Mighty was incorruptible.

Trover turned again to Louise. "If it's not too much trouble, Bibs, could you maybe make basghetti with clam sauce tonight?" More baby talk and *Bibs,* the pet name they called each other. "Need something from the market, Bibs?"

She muttered back.

"Beg pardon," he said.

"Clams," she snapped.

"How many?"

"Just get canned." If she didn't enunciate, if she averted her gaze, but it turned out to be nigh impossible to say, "Two cans of whole clams," nastily.

"Well, I'm off," he said. "Bye, My. Bye, boy." With the high panache of someone leading a Daisy Day parade, he blew them all kisses, showing not a drop of remorse, whistling in his preposterous white bucks and balloon red jacket. His snappy red and white person seemed to whoosh past, a magic vanishing wand, erasing whatever bad traces Louise's mop had missed. He was surely the most ridiculous man she'd ever met, adjusting his poplin hat, stepping off the porch, his popinjay walk, strolling off with the worst of it, stealing their hard-earned anger.

The day she first laid eyes on this man, at a Lackawanna trolley stop, he was a day-old lawyer in a nervy homburg, gripping a briefcase like a spanking new book bag on the first day of school. Something had summoned her, something alive in the air around his tense young body. Even that day she'd known what it was. It was her, the dizzy spin of her future, and she was in it now, wasn't she, tumbling dumb as a ninepin in the hypnotic arc above the juggler's head.

The children left, and she saw for herself how the Volkswagen bucked its way uphill on the way out. Gideon got up and left without breakfast. Louise started back to her room to work on a piece recently commissioned by a wealthy old man. His original request had been for a grouping comprised of three brothers and their father in stiff collars, standing with one foot on the dashboard of a Model T. She'd had to explain that she didn't do cars. She'd developed an almost Pavlovian aversion to them and was certain, besides, that hers would turn out looking like the Flintstones' family roadster. Moreover, she'd fairly well demonstrated her inability to give people the sort of life they deserved. He'd settled in the end for a standard pose, three men standing, one sitting (chairs she could manage). But he wanted it yesterday. He phoned regularly to hurry her. Louise liked to think that this old man could not possibly die until he'd seen with her hands.

Each session began with a search. Where were her glasses, the slip jar, her elephant-ear sponges? She'd barely begun to look when she heard the unmistakable rumble of Sprecher's truck outside. She ran to the front window and watched the old Ford bounce down the lane to the shed. Throwing on a coat, she jogged out and headed downhill after him.

It was clear, cold, and the wind drove brittle leaves down from the upper lawn, and slapped rotting quince off the boughs onto the roadway. Although she entered the shed disheveled and out of breath, Sprecher appeared not to have noticed. He was bent over a cluttered workbench, his back to her, and the last thing she wanted was to give him a start. She waited quietly in the blue-gray dimness, white pinpoints of late-autumn light sieving through the perforated tin star under the roof at the far end. The heavy-duty smells of axle grease, old metal, burlap; the perfumy sweetness of worn wooden grips. An ancient scythe hung on a nail, the splendidly counterpoised curves of blade and handle as beautiful as anything, and it seemed no leap at all to the polished knob of Sprecher's cheekbone as he turned, catching the frail light from the witch's window.

When he was wholly around, he looked at Louise with not a twitch of surprise, leading her to think he knew she was there all along. He rested a narrow gaze on her for a second before turning wordlessly toward the wall where the short-handled tools hung in a row.

"Mr. Sprecher," she called, in her nervousness rushing him from behind, "I . . . uh, *Mr.* Kleeve would prefer you didn't mow again now till spring. What with all this rain, the ground is so very wet and—"

He said something that sounded like "Nackyack." His tones might have come from a sheet metal foundry deep inside him. Everything came out jagged-edged and flat. Sometimes he honked and sometimes quacked. Maybe he had cursed her in Dutch; she wouldn't have put it past him.

She tried again. "Mr. Sprecher—"

He came around heavily as a trolley turning at the end of the line. He stared at her. "I chust come donn to fetch some nails, a rake, and hammah."

"Oh."

He shook his head. "I must fix up my chickenhoss before it comes all to chunk."

She wasn't about to question his use of the possessive "my." Nor argue that the building was too far gone for patchwork. She drew a breath. "By the way," she said then, cagily, "when you were up last week mowing, did you happen to notice anything amiss—prowlers or anything?"

He cupped his ear, and she repeated for him. He studied her face for a moment, then squared his shoulders and said, "Didn't see nothing."

"Thing is"—she pressed on—"somebody damaged the kids' boat, cut it with a sharp knife, a razor blade maybe."

"I toldt you," he barked. "I didn't see nothing."

"You sure?"

A flat black finger wagged in her face, and he was yelling at her.

"But, Mr. Sprecher—"

His voice had risen alarmingly fast to where words become splinters in the shutter-banging racket of pure wrath. *Kacknack, yacknick, raptrap. Quack, quack.* His skin seemed to brighten the way the skies in this part of the world seemed to irradiate just before the hardest rain. She took two steps back. He rammed both hands straight at his sides and cranked his body a half turn, back to his purposes.

Starting back up to the house, she felt a kind of relief to know for sure. The grudges of an old curmudgeon could be gotten around. The raft business was no worse than any other senile slip from middle ground, examples of which abounded anymore. He had stopped eating almost everything but oatmeal, convinced as he was that the woolly bulk provided a kind of insulation for his cold stomach. On several occasions last summer she'd caught him off the tractor, jumping around, cursing and yelling like Trover on a tear. Then, just like that, he'd stop and climb back up and continue cutting his peaceable, if imperfect, swaths. When he was done, the missed grass stood in ragged cowlicks, and the untrimmed borders made the Knoll look badly chewed around the edges. Either out of absentmindedness or spite, he neglected certain critical duties, such as turning off the outside spigots before the pipes froze. He performed hateful surgeries in her garden; forbade them, the owners, access to certain tools and storage areas. He did basically whatever he pleased. And what he'd prefer not to do, nobody could make him. Trover called him Bartleby the Sprecher.

He was not their doing; they'd never hired him in the first place. They'd simply bought a piece of property hiding a Cracker Jack prize, a strange little man on a rusty tractor. One day he was there, that's all, no handshake or hello, and at the end of that first week he gave them a scrap of tablet paper with his hours marked in pencil. They paid him without question, and then the next week he was back.

Now, after twelve years, his rhythms and sounds somehow bound them. The landscape had adopted his hard, gnarled presence, as one more tree or rock. That he was old, more trouble than help anymore, seemed irrelevant. Despite what she'd said last night, he certainly could not be blamed on Trover. Which of them would dare interfere with this pact between a man and a few sweet acres? They might as well try to dismiss him from his own thighbone. So they closed their eyes and left him to the vagaries of his years and temperament.

Returning to the house, Louise looked askance at her I-must-remember signs, silly now in the tranquilized house. What if Sprecher stopped by and saw them? And if the Jehovah's Witnesses came with their smiles and pamphlets, how would they take to hate placards? She stacked the cards and sighed as one who had lost still another battle against alcohol or fat. She would put them away for the next time, bring them out like seasonal accessories, the next time Trover erupted.

She went to her old rolltop desk and removed a box marked "Important Papers." It was as impossible to get right in and out of this box as it was to sort through magazines without reading them all first. She opened the lid and started to poke inside.

These were not, in any conventional sense, important papers. Trover kept deeds and insurance policies and such in his office. Mostly they were scraps of this and that significant only to her. Often the items were not even paper. There was a linotype of a group of Victorian picnickers whose dreamy faces had helped unloose her one good idea. There were holy pictures from way back to Mount Mercy on through to Geggo's funeral. The first ones bore inscriptions like "God preserve you in your vocation. In Mary. In Christ. R. M. A. Love, Frank."

A piece of brown corduroy from Geggo's last pair of Keds.

A bundle of Trover's sister's letters tied up with a bootlace. Louise read excerpts, lines she'd underscored in chartreuse. "We had you pegged from the start, Louise. Stupid we are not. . . . A lawyer's wife is expected to entertain clients, and you don't even seem to have friends. . . . Take the children to church, Louise. They'll thank you for it. . . . Granted, my brother is no angel, but *remember,* behind every good man there's a better woman. . . . We notice your daughter received at mass last week. Did she make her first holy communion? I doubt it. . . . Bleach is cheap, Louise."

Rita had never upbraided Louise publicly or to her face, so the letters retained an interesting underground just-between-us intimacy, like a furtive dirty look. From time to time Louise consulted the catalog for clues, as if from these random fragments she might piece a being, even a feckless, negligent, slatternly apostate recognizable as her own indivisible self.

Trover's one love letter, sent from National Guard summer camp where he was doing time as a clerk-typist shortly before they were married: He had some warmish words for her, but there was a typo in the very first line. "Dear *Louse*," it said.

She pulled out a theme Mighty had done for Problems of Democracy and then refused to turn in, probably because it was not in her to carry tales. Louise had grabbed it out of Mighty's trash basket. In the event of a divorce, should Louise begin to forget his finer points, she would always have this for reference: Trover succinctly put, as Rita would say, pegged. Down pat.

MY FATHER'S GIFTS

By "gifts" I mean he brings stuff home, but I guess you could also say that he's a talented man. He's clever and smart and comical when he wants to be. He knows more than he should about cassowaries and windmills and where things got their names. He knows everything there is about the Civil War, though he was not in it. Olduvai Gorge, though he was never there. Hang gliding, ice climbing, beekeeping, though he has never done any of these things. He can read in the bathtub without getting the book wet. My mother is jealous of that. That and the fact he puts things together from directions and gets away with stuff she can't. That our dog loves him best.

If you want to talk to him about anything mushy or personal, he has the power to disappear or at least fall asleep on the spot. He is good at eight ball. On skis he thinks he's hot, but everyone knows he does nolts (nice old lady turns) and he wears weird clothes. He's good at starting and quitting. Every week he takes up something new and in my lifetime I've seen him give up plenty: smoking, sweets, boxer shorts, Ban–Lon sweaters, white bread, network TV. He will never never give up ice cream or wine. When he's plastered, he wants to tell you every deep thought he's ever had and expresses himself with feeling.

But mainly this is about bringing stuff home. He is the kind that will say he's going out for pizza and come home with an Italian car. It makes my mother nervous to have so many things. That's probably why he keeps bringing stuff home. She would make an excellent poor person, which is good, because at the rate my father spends, it's a cinch she'll have her chance someday.

The other things he brings home regularly are things that tell time. Watches, pen watches, little clock faces you stick up on things. Tiny alarm clocks, massive alarm clocks. My mother resents being told how to tell time when she does it so well by the sun or whatever. She is proud that she has never owned a watch yet is seldom late. On the other hand, he has never been on time in his life.

He brings her games that she's no good at, things where you have to get BBs through a maze or into six holes at the same time. These are not proper gifts for somebody with no patience. He brings her things you're supposed to take apart and put back together, if you're a genius. After two days with Rubik's Cube she broke down and bawled. "I don't deserve to coexist with intelligent life," she said. Then he zipped it into shape in about thirty seconds. His secretary told me later that he had the solution book in the office and had been boning up for weeks.

He brings books home. For my mother, books on war heroes and isometric exercises, *Winning Through Intimidation.* She does not appreciate any of these. For my brother, wrestling books and more wrestling books and field guides to everything that ever sprouted or walked or crawled. *The Wonderful World of Knots.* All you need do is express a speck of curiosity about something and, presto, a book. You can't say, for example, "Do peanuts grow in Pennsylvania?" unless you want a book on George Washington Carver. Once I was looking for a litle box to keep my barrettes in. Well, instead of finding me a box, he bought me a book on how to make a box: *Advanced Origami.* When I was younger, he bought me the entire set of Nancy Drew. He'd read them in his office before bringing them home and leave notes in the margins like "Quick thinking, Nance." Or, "My, don't you ever pull a stunt like this." And that's how we kept in touch then.

The rattle of bags—that's the sound my father makes. It's a sound that makes my mother cringe because it means More, More, More. He brings articles of clothes four at a time. Flour fleece jackets, one for each of us. Four rabbit fur hats my brother calls Grand Poobahs. Only Dad will wear this dumb-looking hat. My mother refuses to wear any of it. She will not be made a quadruplet of, she says. Give mine to the Rescue Mission. Sometimes she really knows how to ruin things.

He brings stuff home to make up for acting like a jerk. But probably my favorite thing is a big ceramic Volkswagen convertible he bought for no reason at all except it looked like the car I drive. The only difference is it's sand-colored instead of red. Well, it's next to my favorite thing, I'd say. At least it never breaks down and we never have to take it into sleazy Lum Motors for repairs.

My favorite thing happened like this. One night he came home a little late, with that sappy look he gets after a couple of drinks. "Guess what I have?" he said. The way he said it we could tell it was something alive. "A dog," my brother said, looking around. Dad walked over to the table. He took his hat off and set it carefully down. "A hat?" my mother said. "You bought a new hat? Big deal." He bought lots of hats. "Yep," he said. "You're very observant. This hat is called a fedora," he added, looking from Michael to me. "But that's not it, nope, that's not the surprise. Come here," he said, holding his finger to his lips, like he was afraid we'd wake up his hat or something. He leaned over the table with his hands behind his back. "Look real close now," he said. We followed his eyes and there between the two ridges that made the crown was a ladybug. "She's been with me all day," he said proudly. "Isn't she purty?" My brother smiled and reached out to pet the bug. "Take it easy," my dad said softly. "Don't get too rough with her."

He gives what he can, and we take what we can get.

Louise carefully refolded the lined sheets. Mighty's voice pinged behind each word, rang in her ears. Even her literary style was clipped, styptic, decisive. Mighty, her pungent child. What could become of the little scallion?

Louise tried to imagine her settling in somewhere, the one room she would do proud, her "good room." Already the child was working wonders in the high school darkroom, turning out startlingly surreal portraits of herself and Gideon McThee, nocturnal shots in which they seemed to the stark, stubbled landscapes as alien as moon walkers. She might be doing good work, but who would hold her to it? Louise could picture her leaping sparklike from the cool darkroom, landing where? In a room with a typewriter and stacks of clean paper because she was pretty good with words. Onto the dry boards of some recital hall stage because she was, from the start, an electrifying dancer. A law office, a boardroom, a nursery. Regardless of what place Louise's mind might prepare for her, the girl was in and out of it in a flash. Very soon, Louise understood, Mighty would graduate, and she wouldn't waste much time trying to narrow things down. Louise could see her setting off down the road with a very small suitcase and sturdy shoes. The room Mighty would be burning to try would start out, at least, as wide as the world.

Louise was aware of something trying to surface, and whatever it was made her merely uneasy at first, and then it hurt to remember: Trover's face the day he'd brought the clay VW home and Louise had waited until Mighty went to bed before confronting him. "I wish you'd stop trying to buy your children," she'd said, trying to pass herself off as a wise and virtuous person. She'd watched that tenuous pleasure rush like a startled flock from every ledge of his face. And all the time she pontificated Mighty slept the easy sleep of the unquestioning heart, as wise as she was tough, her soft, plump arm around that hard car. *People give what they have to give.* If not hugs and praise and bedtime stories, then the contents of bags and boxes. Did Louise have to believe that? Damn! She stuffed Mighty's pages back in the box, slapping them down, as if such frisky testimony had the power to slap back. Then she packed away the hate signs.

An hour later the telephone rang. It was him, reassuring himself. "Now let me get this straight, Bibs. You want two cans of canned clams tonight?"

"You'd better pick up a bunch of parsley, too," she said agreeably.

"Don't start loading me down," he said.

CHAPTER

9

The summer of Louise's fourteenth year Geggo dragged her off to visit foreign-talking relatives who lived in a damp house by a muddy lake. Louise had begged to be left behind. Not to consort with boys or troublemakers but to pray. She wanted to set out Father Dugan's vestments at dusk and go to mass at dawn and drift through steamy afternoons playing nun. That was her life then, and she had felt indescribably bereft at the lake place. Dead pike floating on the water, the teenage grandson finding reasons to touch her knee. Large, laughing birds she'd never heard before. Loons and mildewed rugs: She could not believe in God there.

The Knoll turned out to be another "lake place," a summer residence down to its latticed skirt and whimsical heating system. Its natty greens and whites suggested nothing if not beanbags and hammocks and picnic suppers, tall drinks and stuporous moods and all things shiftless and unserious and flimsy.

Such a dark old house, a collar of boxwood and black pine holding the dampness in, Sprecher treating her like a nervy guest, the heavy hum of isolation. Was this the stuff of a permanent address? She could not shake the sojourner's sense of living lightly on the surface of things, of casting out and away, always. This sense of exile was heavily buttressed by the sequence of events that led her here.

The year she turned twenty-six Louise took a genuine Latin lover. Julio was wild-eyed, possessive, perpetually anguished over her. He made startling declarations; "Ju are my wooman, *sí o no?*" He gave her bold, smoldering looks, and he gave them in public. Out of loverly frustration he pounded walls and tabletops, and once he punched out a ponytailed young man for trying to pin a Flower Power button on her lapel. And even as she threw in with the first brave feminists and rational thinkers were popping up everywhere, calling for order between the sexes, Louise secretly loved every minute of her wild man's rage for her. *Sí,* she answered. *Sí, sí, sí!*

Julio was a man no husband in his right mind could miss. Trover had little choice but to catch her. He grilled her for days, releasing her only to go tearing around like some mad-dog prosecutor, interviewing witnesses against her, filling at least three legal pads. She could not bear to see how concave he'd become. Her power over him embarrassed her. His outcries broke her heart: "You were supposed to be better than me!" Broke her heart and edified her at the same time. In the end, though, racked by remorse, she could not remember a single hurtful thing he'd ever done. It was a kind of baptism by betrayal. Trover got to begin life anew with a laundered soul.

Two months went by. Trover left and came back. Wooed and abused her. Ordered her out, begged her to stay. Every night after supper he would hold her hand and interrogate her about Julio. "Yes, but were they Jockey shorts or Fruit of the Loom or what?" *I don't remember.* "Of course you remember. Think! I've *got* to know."

One day Trover came home early from the office. They were living then in a nice center-hall colonial in a small Neisstown subdivision. He said, "Come with me. I want to show you something." He drove her a great distance, far beyond the city. Thinking that maybe he planned to bludgeon her to death and throw her body into the woods, she considered whether or not to allow this. Julio once explained why men committed such atrocities. "Then eet ees at last feenished." He was smiling when he said that. Trover took her on a whirlwind tour of the Knoll that day. Two weeks later he moved her and the children in, and they went without a whimper.

In the beginning she dealt with her sense of displacement by going out every day. She prowled the malls and visited friends or drove up and down the Neisstown streets, counting fat men with black umbrellas. When the snows came hard and deep, blurring even the memory of the road out, she was panicstricken, chilled to the soul; those times she paced before the drafty windows and thought of Rudolf Hess in his echoing tower.

Some years later she would become a stolid defender of Patty Hearst. Was it so hard to understand how Patty had come to take up arms and develop unseemly attachments? Hadn't Louise herself ended up following the course of the many women spirited off to the country before her? Unconsciously or not, she began to shape a radical new identity from the alien clay. More and more of her was vanishing into the dirt. She maintained existing gardens and dug new ones. She got on the lists of the best seed houses. Her heart quickened at the sight of good German pruners, dandelion pullers, leaf shredders.

Still, her life was not a life exactly but a loose harmonic of optional jobs. She strung up chicken wire fences and built compost heaps, searched the countryside for specialty manures. She dug an adam-and-eve plant out of the woods and tucked it in with her Canterbury bells and painted daisies. Though it sent out runners and headed home, she always caught it in time and set it back.

She owned entire wardrobes of work boots and baggy overalls; her hands coarsened from continuous truck with loam growing richer by the year. Once, as she knelt over the turnip rows, Trover drove right on by, mistaking her for Sprecher.

Sometimes now, when she went to town, her city friends might remark, "Oh, I could never stand the quiet or the bugs. Aren't you afraid out there at night?" Their dismay began to delight her, for they located her life somewhere beyond the nerves of most mortals. Her life was an outback, a frontier settlement, another Churchill, Manitoba, where twice a year implacable polar bears lumbered through town.

No question but that the country queered women. Louise saw it happen again and again. There were women brought here forty years back you wouldn't try to get near today. They kept a full complement of cats, and their gaunt faces floated behind dusty windows, and you just knew they communicated with beings you didn't want to know about. When Alice Buttonworth went out, she wore three sweaters and at least as many wigs. Cat Lady, Wig Woman, that's what happened to the wives while the men worked in town.

Native women, it seemed, escaped such fates. They'd developed special immunities, stabilizers that kept their phases in steady balance. But Louise and other transplants were taken unawares, swept under by abundance, and quiet took them by surprise. Seasons, more beautiful here, more emphatic, more reckless, threw them off-balance. They were seduced equally by the delicate spring blooms as by the rank entanglements of late August. They began to feel that fatal Oneness with Nature; the sight of a plowed field made their mouths water. They were the ones who would eventually stand at the property line with a shotgun. They were the ones who would kill to protect a tree.

Leaving the Knoll grew more and more difficult. Louise worried about the house burning. She was afraid the hunters would come and try to remove a rabbit or squirrel from her custody. City traffic gave her headaches; ordinary human commerce unnerved her. Her last protracted venture to the outside happened almost four years ago. It was the ski year, and there were two men, one of whom wanted to become her third lover.

She waits for Osberg at the top of Sky Dive. The light is bad in the shadow of the promontory rising above her, and Louise squints to help define the terrain. Glancing up toward the chair lift, she watches the passengers disembark and finally spots Osberg in a new electric blue ball-tassel cap.

She's been skiing with Osberg every Wednesday for weeks. Wednesday is, in Osberg's idiom, the day he "gives himself." Meaning it's his day off. Osberg is a poet and student of the self. His analysts are a married couple named Myra and Bill. Perhaps because of his habit of biweekly unburdening, he is too quick with his secrets, and Louise knows far more about this man than vice versa.

He is wearing new snow pants that match the cap and a fat parka in plucky, no, self-assertive green. He shuffles toward her across the flat. He lowers his goggles and tugs down his cap and pokes his fists through leather pole straps. Louise never troubles to do the same; as a result, her own straps are always flapping behind, lending her, she's been told, a "willy-nilly look," an aspect of waywardness and laxity. Louise always leaves some particular unattended, so that she never appears quite turned out. A smashing new dress and run-down shoes. A button hanging by a thread. Why does she have such a fear of the finishing touch? Why does she always stop fussing too soon?

When Osberg gives her the sign, Louise skates off toward the steep. Despite her disconnected look, she is by far the better skier, as well she should be, the way she goes at it, dragging up there every day, as if the slopes were her place of business, working, polishing, shunning all human comfort to concentrate on knee cant, pole plant, edging. Anyhow, Osberg has made it clear he does not want to go first.

Her skis make a harsh, scraping sound across the crusty early-morning surface, but Louise holds her form, making pretty S's along the edge of the trail. It is a small mountain, and there have been times when, taken by sheer deviltry, she's astounded Osberg by letting it rip from the top, straight over the crests of the three humps that constitute Sky Dive, airborne onto the broad beginner slope below, flat-out to the finish, her legs two bones of burning. Each stop at the bottom a screaming miracle.

Today, though, she holds to a careful rhythm, giving Osberg not a thought until he bolts hot-doggingly past, nearly clipping the backs of her skis. In his heavy-footed way he tries to turn against a pile of loose snow, catches an outside edge, and does an eggbeater roll that leaves him sprawled in her path. Louise skis down, retrieving his bird-bright hat. She hands it back, chagrined for him. The snow wadded under his collar, under his cuffs, makes it appear that his stuffing is coming out, and his poles dangle like mittens on a string. "I'll meet you at the lift," she says, leaving him to reenter his bindings alone. He nods dispiritedly.

The other man appears suddenly from behind a scrawny young hemlock at the first plateau. He never seems to offend anybody but Louise, so others don't wonder much about him, and thus far Louise has been unsuccessful in learning who he is or where he has come from. Sharp-featured and scissor-limbed, he wears a Lenten-colored jumpsuit and rides smoothly on long wooden skis. He smiles as she glides by, smiles and shakes his head, as if to say, "Hopeless, hopeless. You'll never get it right." She returns a stylized smile and continues down onto flatter ground. Glancing at her skis, she discovers how he's spoiled her form. Her stance is wide now and infantile, tails sliding.

On the chair she rides next to Osberg in silence. She removes one mitten, shoves it between her knees, then hunches out of the wind to light a cigarette. When the chair has finished rocking through the rough links at the triple tower, the part that always alarms Osberg, he gives Louise a wounded look and mumbles into his lap, "Why do you race on ahead of me?"

"I don't know how to ski slow," she says. "I never learned to finish my turns properly." She tries to force her smoke into outer space, but it keeps doubling back on Osberg. "Scat," she says to her fumes. To Osberg she says, "Did you have a good week?"

"Excellent," he says, aligning his poles across both their thighs. "I had a major breakthrough."

"Does that mean your poetry is perfect now?" she asks—too gaily, his offended glance tells her.

He waits for her face to recompose itself. "I'm nuts about Myra," he says then. "And I told her as much!"

Louise looks at him. "Phewwwww!" he says, shaking his head, staring gravely into the distance, as if pondering something achieved in the nick of time.

"Osberg," says Louise, finally, "how does *Bill* feel about that?"

"You kidding?" He raises his goggles, exposing eyes round with disbelief and cannily triumphant. "He's tickled pink, of course. I'm *supposed* to have these feelings." He smiles, pleased with himself. "It's crucial to the process. If you're wondering what to say, say, 'Way to go, good buddy, now on to the next plateau.' "

But Louise is thinking of the plateau between Sky Dive and Peter Cotton Trail, the narrow-faced man assessing her. She glances away, then cautiously back. "I like your new outfit," she says.

"How's that for progress? Two breakthroughs in one week."

"Is that outfit a *plateau*, too?"

"Sure. It means I'm learning to give myself things."

"Where do the plateaus lead? What happens when you get to the top?"

Turning nervously away, he nibbles his mitten.

"I'm sorry. Did I say something wrong?"

"It's OK," he says. "The suit is probably premature anyhow. Did I look stupid back there? Did I look like a dolt wiping out in my new threads?"

"Don't be silly."

"Look, I'm not the kind to need a lot of stroking. Tell me the truth."

She looks hard at him. "Osberg," she says, "you *will* make a fool out of that suit for a while, but you'll see, pretty soon, they'll be saying, 'Holy smokes, there's that poet fellow again. Look at him book. What style. What grace. What a goooooorgeous suit.' "

"You're making fun of me."

"You don't give me that many choices."

"You could have said, 'No, you don't look stupid.' "

"How could I have said that? It never even crossed my mind."

"You think poet is funny, too. I could tell the way you said 'poet fellow.' Say it again."

She bows her head, squirming as if he'd just asked her to sing from *Aïda*.

"Go ahead."

"Poet fellow," she mumbles.

"See," he says.

"Stop!" she cries, turning on him. "Stop! I *don't* think poet is a joke. Honest!" She has read his work. It is surprisingly strong and wise and free, as if it had come from some well too pure for self-pity, too deep for the reach of Myra and Bill. It is also quite possible his poetry is the only thing Louise likes about him.

"Look," he says, "you don't have to be tactful, not on that score. I never wanted to be a poet anyhow. Poems are just something I do to kill time until I'm man enough to attack the novel. Poems are pennies, and in case you haven't noticed, I've always been damn tight with myself."

She draws slightly back from him, but his logic pursues her. "One of the reasons I went into analysis twelve years ago was to kick the habit. And, guess what, since breaking through to those sexual feelings last week—"

"For Myra?"

"Yes, once I allowed myself that, I haven't had to write a single poem. I've been clean now for five days."

The chair is bumping across a rock-filled ravine, the highest point along the chair line. Osberg closes his eyes and holds tight to his poles. When they are riding closer to earth, she says, "I shouldn't tease you. I do that sometimes when I'm nervous."

"Oh, are you nervous?" he says hopefully. "Hey, could I ask you something?" He produces a grin fraught with the sudden disarming artfulness of a small boy whose smile has won contests. "Remember the first time you saw me?"

"Of course," she said. "At your reading for Friends of the Library."

"Well, what did you think?" The smile cranking higher.

"You were brilliant," she replies honestly. "Breathtaking."

In a flash his face has turned dark and prayerful. "But did you think I was—cute?"

As she considers what to say, he snaps sideways to kiss her, his cool lips on her cold cheek. The stirring inside reminds her of the sudden satiny rustle of pigeons against an attic window. Not far below, thin scrub pines sway in the wind, the smell of pine tar and cold rushing up at them.

Cute? Osberg is short, balding, with a round pale face. His poems had made him glow that night; she had not noticed that he was not beautiful. Was that the same as thinking him "cute"? Now it turns out that the part of him she likes best he has despised for years. The conjunction makes her feel sneaky and collusive, the two of them in league to strip him down to common unloveliness. "I thought you were charming," she says. As if to give weight to her words, she tips her head onto his shoulder even as she fears the burden of her thoughts might buckle him. Overhead the cable thrums consolingly. Her mitten works loose and tumbles out, and when she leans out to look for it, she sees him, the man who spies on her. He is skimming darkly through the glade, his skis on edge, his trail spiraling behind, the endless parings of a large white apple.

He appears to her that night, not the poet, but the man who skis wickedly well and can hide himself entirely behind an elm sapling. He tells her that she will soon die, of some disease unique to the unforgiving heart. It's a form of recurrent dream, but always before the messenger has been her father, burned a week before she was born, in a mine fire. He always tells her the news regretfully, and there's a dark spot, like an Ash Wednesday smudge, on his young brow. But this man is gleeful, smirking, and she wakes cobbled with grief, groping for Trover.

Whimpering, she molds herself around the curve of her husband's spine. Instead of waking, Trover tightens his left arm over the one she's thrust around his middle. A very long time later, when the dream has leached away, she tries to turn back to her own sleep. When she attempts to reclaim her arm, Trover tightens his grip, relaxing only when she stops trying to get away. A second time she attempts to slip out; again he clamps down hard. She will have to explode out of this hold; only an act of violence will free her.

It's a trick of intimacy. No, the intimacy is real. The trick is Trover, the myriad methods he's devised to keep her near without confessing need. Maybe he is not really sleeping, but as long as he believes she believes he is, he will feel safe in her embrace. Soon he will roll over and make love to her, considering himself anonymous.

The first two times Trover tried to make love to Louise, *she* was the one to go into a trance. Trover probed and worried her inert flesh for long minutes before giving up. Finally he stopped and shook her. They were in his friend's apartment, on the sofa where she'd willingly let him lead her. He propped her up with throw pillows. He shook her by the shoulders until she blinked awake. "Louise," he said, "I just want you to know that if we're going to see each other—and I sincerely hope that will be the case—that you will have to stay awake and we *will* make love."

He said this with such authority that Louise figured if he said it, then it must be so. And so on the very next day, while his parents walked to the shopping center to buy some bibs for Rita's baby, they slept together on the single bed of his boyhood room. Their lovemaking smelled of Johnson's paste wax because they'd just washed and shined his first car, a Volkswagen, in the days when Volkswagens were simple and cheap and did not gather in the driveway like dust bunnies. They started calling each other "Bibs." Trover was freckled on his face and back, and already she was addicted to the raisiny smell of his hair, to the hair that shone red-gold on his wrists, to the sound she heard when she put her ear to his heart. He'd had rheumatic fever as a boy. It left him with a light murmur, a tiny sibilance. His heartbeat said "husband, husband, husband." Louise puts her head to his chest now. She has forgotten the man in the dream and the man who would, if he could bring himself to ask, be her lover. The murmur has sealed over the years. The heartbeat says "night day night day night day." Soon they both sleep for real.

By mid-February Louise's legs are wonders of created form. In the bathtub she caresses them with hands getting their first feel for sculpting. She can ski now from top to bottom without testing the limits of human endurance. She has honed her edges and thrust deep. There's a fire at the heart of cold, she's found, and a cold, clear silence at the heart of her own heat. And joy inside that. What is joy but a blue-white thing, the soul of a soul?

Trover skis on another, bigger mountain, so they rarely see one another fall, never know who's better.

The thaw comes on a Wednesday in mid-March, comes so abruptly that this hardest of diamond-cut days is by noon oozing spring. After lunch she leaves her parka behind over Osberg's protests. "Fooler weather," he insists, adding another layer to himself. She clips her gloves onto her belt loop so they can fly with the straps of her poles and the hair freed from its cap. Feeling unalterably young and lissome and unfettered now, she is beyond the pull of anything bundled up or earthbound. Even the man in purple has no power over her today.

She stands at the top of Sky Dive in a cobalt sweater bound to turn her eyes into two trumpets blasting blue. Below, the sweep of bottomland, its billowing terrain divided into tiny, tidy farms, brown fields still snow-slubbed, strips of winter wheat already greening the land. "God, that's nice," says Osberg. "Think what I might have written if I'd been brought up in a lyrical place instead of the Bronx." He looks at her burningly. "Would you believe I never had a dog. Not even a gerbil . . ."

She nods, itching to run.

"I never even had a birthday party." His eyes search hers as though she might be hiding what it would take to save him.

He drops his gaze for a second, and when he looks up, it is gashed through with that smile of dazzled bashfulness. "I like your sweater," he says, then something she hears as "You have lovely breasts," the line erased in places by wind and timidity. When she inclines her head uncertainly, he says, "You heard me the first time," and christies off in confusion.

"You have lovely breasts." The words enter her blood like pale wine. Her body warms, fills with formless yearning. Sun drenches the meadows, and when she skis through shade, it is like diving through cool currents far below the surface, and then, with a bursting urgency, she makes a run again for light. If days spent in white cold have delineated the spirit, today she is all lawlessness, a sweet undoing. She wants to encompass everything she sees.

Louise skis carelessly now, gawking everywhere, watching squadrons of geese, their staffs of scratchy music high overhead. Spotting Osberg, she raises a pole in an overenthusiastic salute. A second later she is airborne, then dumped, a clatter of paraphernalia everywhere, sharp pain in the knee; now she is trying not to cry.

On her knees she believes the man holding her poles out to her is Osberg, but when she looks up in sheepish gratitude, she sees it is her bugbear man, his eyes shiny as mica. He wears his goggles like beetle eyes against his brow, and for one long instant she is utterly transfixed by her twin reflections there. This is one of three times in her life when she is, by light and the burning inside her, made beautiful. Her hair is radiance around her face. So smitten is she that she has forgotten the insolent little man until he says, "In love again?"

Rebuked, she averts her gaze, giving up both good faces. The man stands idly by, smiling, watching her struggle to her feet. "You still don't know," he says. Then, after plunging his poles into the grainy snow, with a movement as dark and emphatic as an exclamation point, he snaps his skis together and slashes off down the fall line.

Her hands are bleeding, the knuckles abraded from snow crystals as though she'd drawn them across stucco. As once, indeed, she had. At Mount Mercy, when she was crazy for holiness and partial to pain, it became her practice to bark her knuckles across the rough walls of the aspirancy library. Her hands always bore a line of scabs in varying stages of healing or fester, and she kept it up for weeks until the nuns found out and charged her with misuse of convent property and pride of a particularly nasty order.

At the base of the hill Osberg is waiting. He takes one look at her hands. "First rule of spring skiing," he says, shaking his head. "Keep your gloves on."

"Thank you."

"Call it a day?"

"No."

After three more runs the wounded knee tweaking in her jeans refuses to go farther. But the day goes on living wildly, demandingly inside her. This is not something you take home to a dusty house. When Osberg suggests they go for a drive in the country, she allows herself to consider this a natural extension of light and desire.

Already old men gather on the stoops of country garages. Somewhere, too, she imagines, clusters of wasps are crisping to life. She and Osberg travel south into a wide valley. Louise rides near the window, looking out, quiet, holding on to things. She rolls her window down partway to taste the air.

The rise and fall of farm country, flying miles of it on either side of the road; she counts ninety-four barns in five minutes. Then the landscape closes. North again over a road that moves under them like waves. They are silent through domes of crosshatching hemlock branches, the glistening salad of light and shade. "Hey!" says Osberg. "Hey!" He's smiling at her, and she watches him warily, imagining his narrative as lariat, in motion already, looping hungrily above her head.

He manages to hold off for another three or four miles before saying, "Don't get me wrong, Louise. Bill is damn competent. Hey, I dedicated my first book to him. But dammit, it was quiet little Myra who got to the root of my trouble."

Louise draws a breath. "Which is?"

"God!" He looks at her wonderingly. "Why do I find it so damn easy to open up to you?"

"I can't imagine," she says.

"OK, here's it," he says, so happily it harms Louise. "When I was eight, my mother started to push me away."

"But I thought the real troublemakers were the clinging types."

He shook his head emphatically. "Not this time. One fine day, just like that, it was: 'Go out and play, enough with the grabbing and hanging, take a hike, kid.' "

"Isn't a mother supposed to start drawing the line ... I mean—*weaning*—"

"Maybe so," he said, "but see"—that head-on, high-beam grin—"*I* never got over it."

"Oh."

He was smiling now in nudging increments, boosting her over the top of something forbiddingly difficult. "That's why having a case on Myra is such a critical synapse in my emotional development. You follow me?"

How can she tell him that she is deathly afraid of the moment when she might follow him? "And Bill, is he still—"

"Very proud of me, of course."

"Good," she says. "Uh, good."

"You keep fixing on that. Do you have a personal reason for asking? Does your husband play around?"

It's a long story, which Louise believes is the best revenge. She tells him about a phone call some years earlier. It was from a woman unfortunate enough to have been on the other side of one of Trover's domestic cases. "I saw your old man last Friday night," she said. "And he wasn't alone." She described the girlfriend: young; brunette; wearing a yellow summer dress. "They looked pretty chummy, if you ask me," the woman added. Heart racing, Louise thanked her politely and hung up. When Trover came home, she confronted him, demanding to know the other woman's name, and he told her. The woman had been wearing a black wig and Louise's best dress. The woman was Louise. In her panic she'd not recognized herself.

Louise laughs, tapping her breastbone, squealing, "Me! It was me, *me!*"
But Osberg gives her a long, disappointed look, as if she'd deliberately
tricked him. Louise would not go on to tell him now that the woman she'd
admired in the purple man's goggles was also Louise. Louise lovelied by a
trick of fooler weather. And tomorrow she would be jealous of her, too. Osberg would not appreciate this twist any more than she could imagine plateaus and synapses. They would not forgive each other for not being each
other. Lovers need at least one solid bridge to start with. They will not be
lovers. Is this a sound decision? Or just one bright day trying to stay out of
dark places, cheap rooms?

Egypt, Yellow House. New Jerusalem, Vera Cruz. They have circled the
county outskirts and are coming up the back way from Lorraine, northeast
toward home. Up Kauffman's Hill and around that double curve and now
they have to slow behind a school bus. They follow the bus for miles. And
the break in pace opens like a crack in the high-ceilinged day, and there
comes that breathy pressing on them, that sudden downdraft of sadness.

"They claim it's haunted," she tells Osberg, pointing to a derelict building set back from the road to the right. It has a pretentious wrought-iron
balcony, shutters swinging by a hinge, stately proportions. "Local lore has
it the ironmaster's wife lost all her children to diphtheria. They say she
wanders all night looking for them." The slow afternoon light coats the
windowpanes, making the old glass dimple and wink. Osberg has turned
very silent, his eyes working the road searchingly. Has she again said the
wrong thing? Has Osberg identified with the lost children of Sally Ann
Furnace?

The bus turns off at a Y intersection. They pass through a town comprised of five cabbage green houses in a row. All five yards have choruses of
clothes billowing on high, taut lines: sheets and shirts and flowered dresses,
red towels blowing together in a bright cantata to broken weather. Louise
wants to feel windy and open again, but Osberg's hand has just landed
with the cold, meaty thump of a toad on her left knee.

Without a word she tucks the hand into his coat pocket. "Don't be hard
on me," he says. *"I'm* not."

A friendship that has gone as far as it can go is the corpse kept over the
winter, the dark thing on the porch, begging to be taken. The dark thing is
with them, and they are still four or five miles from her car.

Osberg pulls off the road in front of another stone building. The yard
around this house is full of living children, in sweaters and rubber boots,
preschoolers punching each other and playing tag. Osberg watches them in
silence, then turns to Louise. "Someday I'm coming back here with my
bride," he tells her. "I'm going to buy that house, and we're going to pack it

to the rafters with kids"—he gestures toward the children—"just as goddamn nice as those."

"How old are you, Osberg?" she asks.

"Forty-eight." He grabs her hand. "Is it getting late, Louise?" She understands this is not a rhetorical question.

Closing her eyes, she has a sudden picture of Osberg in the wide front seat of a new-smelling Mercedes. He is sitting happily between Bill, who is drawing on a good pipe, driving, and Myra, who can't stop fussing, tucking his mittens, picking lint and loose threads from his snowsuit. "It's OK," Louise tells him now, touching his pained face. "You'll be all right. You have a nice little family."

Two swans glide across the gold and green beaded surface of a small pond not far from where the children play. Moving slowly onto the road now, Osberg's car seems to float in amberina light. The swans swim without effort, serenely separate, their shadows wrangling and twisting near the water's edge.

By the weekend the Pinnacle has closed down for the year. Louise follows the snow north through the Poconos, the Catskills, the Adirondacks, then into New England, each time fleeing slopes savaged by sweet weather. The pursuit is manic, ruinous, the blue-white magic gone. She has chased a season past its natural life. When her ski runs away on Mount Mansfield, she lets the mountain have it. She understands about offerings. Hadn't she left her small pearl ring behind when she left Mount Mercy for good? She has driven deep into both worlds, gone as far as is permitted to go, and then there is nowhere to go but home.

Spring has come to the Knoll in earnest. Emperor tulips line up on either side of the lane. The great cloudlike red maple tints the air pink. Lace defines the limits of the far perspective—apple blossom froth and pear blossom tatting. The flowering almond and quince have never shown such brio. But Louise will not go botanically haywire this year. The ski season has carried her a great distance but will not snap her all the way back to where she was. She will never root so deep again. Between polar extremes is that pale green mapmaker's band of temperate intentions. Louise welcomes middle ground as only one can who has never been at home there, who has lived life in traversals, zig to zag. Nobody has to settle on middle ground, but you have to touch it at least in passing, plant your plum tree, and go on.

Louise plants a damson plum and one crimson tree peony. At Trover's behest she transfers a cactus he bought her years before to a larger pot. She plants a ring of pink and white begonias in medium shade. The adam-

and-eve plants have escaped the garden and returned to the woods for good. Her trowel is smooth as a convent banister, her life showing wear, but nicely. It is May 26 of a year to be reckoned with.

From that day on Louise's life was not a vacation anymore, not a hobby or habit, not a vestibule to the future. She had come to discover what had been true all along: Her life was her life, and now, when she left the Knoll, it was not with rage or trepidation but with a long list—the trips a countrywoman makes into town for supplies.

And her house was her house, even as it stood, in both fact and imagination, fragile and impermanent as the summer place it inescapably was.

CHAPTER

10

"Listen very carefully, Mr. Hendershot," said Trover. "I don't want you to expose the prosecutor as a lush and a fat cat. Mouth off like that on the stand, the jury will think you're some kind of nut. Do you follow me, Mr. Hendershot? Mr. Hender—"

Trover shrugged and hung up. Between Hendershot and Mildred Gaugler he'd spent two out of the last three hours on the phone. Now he was wanted again. "Yeah, Deb."

"Guy won't give his name."

"What can I do for you, sir?" he said into the phone.

"They're harvesting God's trees for you. They're making dirty pages from the tree of life. Ever think of that, Mr. Quick Thinker?"

He buzzed his secretary. She came to the doorway.

"What gets into people?"

"Beats me," she said, yawning. She returned to her desk.

Trover put his feet up and tilted back. So, this was the practice he'd asked for, shaped from scratch? Years ago already he'd started turning down the low-key, lucrative stuff—probate, property, tax law. When a new client came in, he needn't have cash, but his story had to be a grabber. Trover looked for tension, adventure, a traceable plot, a tangible foe. The ideal case came in with a hue and cry behind it. He liked nothing better than to lean on people leaning on people, so defending his merchants had been stirring and fun at first. But the business kept coming; cases poured in from all over the state. In two years obscenity work had come to constitute a lopsided forty percent of his practice. Around and around with the same rebuttals, the same paper odysseys up through the courts; the scandalized tone on either side had achieved a numbing equilibrium. Outrage was habit, bad acting. It was getting harder and harder to sit still, field the phone calls, dictate briefs tense with the effort of translating the language of smut into hard legalese. Hell would be the endless reenactment of the same battle for a bad cause. War was boring.

He circled his desk three times, ate an apple, a granola bar. He took his pulse and blood pressure. Normal was boring. He set up the projector and put on his favorite reel, Michael taking the regional championship last year. Debbie came right away when he buzzed. She sat down facing the screen, foot tapping the practiced beat of her tedium.

"Watch this, Deb . . . watch him pussyfoot out of this one . . . you're not going to believe this pancake. . . . What a whizzer . . . ever see a granby roll into a Peterson? Hold on—Christ, was that nice! Hey, don't go, semifinals coming up."

"Phone's ringing," she said.

"Let it."

After Michael had pinned in the finals, he flicked the switch quickly, before the film moved on to the fiasco at states. He checked his watch. "I'm going for a walk," he said.

"Suit yourself."

It was not an ideal day for a stroll. Outside the building he stopped for a second to watch Nimson Ickus, the oldest member of the bar, trying to traverse the windy corner at Sixth and Widcombe, all but spinning across. Now Trover stepped out himself, head battering into the wind, shoulders rolled forward, like wings. It was in the body lean, possibly, or in the buffeting, that he forgot who he was and became, for a moment, his father, the day they did Dog Jaw Mountain. Through high winds and hailstones, hard into the laurel thickets, Banfer Kleeve had led Troop 34, stepping high and lively long after it was clear he'd led them wrong. What Trover remembered most about the hours they were lost was how his father saved face manually, tugging up from the mouth, supporting that image of a leader of men, even as his eyes reddened with the terrible strain of bravery.

Neither would he admit to better retail than Pincus Brothers, a higher good than the quality shoes he sold there. Less flexible than his product, he preached Life Strides for wise women and had nothing but scorn for the mother who would shoe her babe in less than Buster Brown. But what happened when faith failed, when he didn't believe any of it? Monday nights and dollar days and the slow damp letdown of every January. What did he think then, varicose veins at eye level? How did he bear leading one more clubwoman to the machine that showed if the feet were pinched, his doubts as crowded as the tiny white toebones.

Trover was astonished to see that he'd already walked far beyond the business section of town. He was passing large Victorian showplaces turned into studios and offices, a renovated house with windows like phone booths. Freezing, he hailed a cab to shuttle him back down to Sixth Street. Instead of going to the office, he took his car out of the lot and drove to the mall. He phoned and told Debbie not to expect him in the rest of the day. "I'm at the law library," he told her.

"Come off it," she said, "That's what *I* tell eye-rate clients. But that's *never* where you are."

"OK," he said, "I'm at the mall. I'm goofing off."

First thing he did was go to Sears for a humane rodent trap. They'd finally got Michael to set the spring-action traps at home, but the very first catch had been a bad one, the mouse struggling to unpin his little leg. Michael let him go, then sprang all the other traps and threw them out.

At Radio Shack Trover bought earphones for jogging and a little electronic box named Boris. Boris could beat experts at chess. Then he bought the companion book on how to beat Boris.

When he ran out of quarters, he left the space game arcade and drove out to Lum's VW. Larry Lum said, "Jeez, baby, Vanagon's gone. Why the hell didn't you say you wanted it?"

"I didn't know I did until this very minute."

"Nice sunroof diesel in the front lot."

The car was exactly like the one he'd driven up in, but brown, a rectangle cut in the roof. The small purchases he'd made lay like a handful of millet at the bottom of his bereavement. He was still sucking hunger. It might take a full-size car to fill him up, but a compact would go a long way. "If I can take it with me," he said.

"No sweat," said Larry Lum. "I'll put the boys on it right away. Tell you what. I'll even have them drive the old one out to the house tomorrow. Or did you plan on trading it in?"

"Oh, no," he said quickly. "I want them both." His Dad had got a kick out of women who put their new shoes on and carried the old pair home in a box, like a coffin.

On then to the Improper. It was only four. Before the cocktail hour a lounge was a woeful thing, naked, bereft, its cracks and shabbiness laid open, cigarette burns in the Leatherette, that pissy smell that cushiony, pretentious places take on after a decade or so in the same foam rubber. Always at least one boozy housewife, trying to read her watch in the dark, muttering about supper. Waitresses standing around, still tired from the night before, always getting over somebody named Rick.

At the end of the bar stood Kilray, the dining room host, in his cerulean cutaway and frilly white shirt. The man looked bored, stalled, as if his life could not possibly resume until the dinner crowd began to dribble in. Avoiding Kilray's eyes, Trover hunched low over his lambrusco.

When Kilray shambled over anyhow, Trover gave him a taut sidelong look, a curt nod. The man had dank, pouched cheeks and small, insolent eyes. He put his hand on Trover's shoulder and brought his face too close.

"Liar game must be slow, you're cutting out this early."

Trover shrugged, waiting for the inevitable "trouble with you guys" number, which, in due course, came. Stiffly polite, he endured the smug aggression masquerading as a friendly ribbing between equals. "Just as a for-instance," Kilray was saying, "what if the person on the other side is some poor orphan kid and your client's trying to grub his last dime? Whatcha gonna do, Counselor?"

"Punt," said Trover.

"What if your client's up for murder and says to you, 'Kleeve, ol' boy, I did it. Sure as God made popcorn, I stabbed her eighty-nine times and buried her out back.' Whatcha tellin' this clown, Counselor?"

"Ribbet," said Trover, winking at the bartender.

"Who you for anyhow?" the man said, openly belligerent now. "The criminal or the victim?"

Trover met the man's eyes head on. "Simple," he said. "Before the crime I'm on the victim's side. After the crime I'm for my client." He paid for the drink and left, Kilray's breath still wet on his neck.

The way home was long but handily subdivided. If he drove straight out the old highway, there were still five or six reasonably congenial way stations en route. His last regular stop within the city proper was a place called the Office. Dark hardwoods and a dignified, dyspeptic bartender helped sustain its clubby atmosphere. The Office catered to a primarily professional crowd, journalists, lawyers stopping for a respectable two drinks before heading out to the suburbs, where civic-minded women waited in gleaming kitchens. Their counters would not be cluttered or stained from bleeding green stamps. They would have definite opinions on real subjects and keep their shoelaces tied.

Or they would arrive from offices of their own, their lunchtime purchases in stiff bags from toney shops. Trover had nothing against these women, but he'd never wanted any of them. Why did he shame his wife because she was a mite irregular? Louise asleep in her choir gown, Louise coming back from a flea market wearing all her new old things at once. Should Louise reform tomorrow, he would then set that new Louise against ever-rarer expectations, the ideal forever revisable. She would never be right. He would never have the right wife. If he did, he would probably lose her.

Chip McLaird stood with C. R. Briggs, one foot on the rung of the latter's stool. He watched two others approach. No, Trover did not want their women; and he did not want their practices. The lawyers acknowledged Trover obliquely and went on with their conversation.

They were the legal gentry, and Trover knew whatever scorn he bore them was returned a hundredfold with a disdain more confident than his own. He knew these men saw him as unbridled and eccentric, disgracefully got up, vulgar. They viewed his criminal clientele as the company he kept, defense work as tantamount to accessory-after-the-fact. Representing adult shops and Mildred Gaugler types made him practically casteless. He ordered another lambrusco. What did he care what they thought?

Something in the air brought Michael to mind. Michael, only twice in his life his father's son. When he was a baby, his eyes were round and bright, and sometimes when you held him, he would wedge his head under your chin and drive up until you cried uncle. And later—was he nine, ten?—when he set his whole self against the world. He made his teachers weep and his sister beg for clemency. He saw to it his feet stank. Still, for all that independent spirit, the boy could hardly bear the precariousness of the outlaw life. He would not be cast out! Trover picked up his drink and went to crash the clique of gentlemen specialists.

"Chip," he said. "C.R." To the other two he gave a genial nod and raised his glass. They were young, young men. There were so many new lawyers anymore Trover could hardly keep track. "Kleeve," said Trover.

"Oh, wow, hi," said the smaller of the two, thrusting out a hand. "How are you, sir? Wow, you're practically a legend. A courtroom gorer. Grrr!" He was eager, clean, shiny as the buttons on his blazer. Waves of thick, burnished hair, neat-fitting suit, a lawyer doll.

The other young man was eager to get on with his hypothesis. "So anyhow, these two couples have a verbal agreement about the two houses, but nothing on paper, when party number one—"

Taking tiny, thoughtful sips, the shiny young man mulled the question while the two older lawyers nodded in false attentiveness, their eyes watching the secretaries straggle in. Trover said, "Gotta run. It's a long way out to God's country."

"Yeah, take it easy, Kleeve," said Chip McLaird, the questioning way you say good-bye when you haven't bothered yet to say hello.

Trover carried his drink out with him.

At the Hessian Inn he spotted a former secretary. Her name was Cathy Koolbaugh, and she was dining with a young man. Hoping to avoid her, he waved offhandedly from the foyer, pretending he'd just dashed in to buy a pack of cigarettes from the vending machine. Outside, he tossed the L & Ms into the hedges. There was no rational cause for his discomfiture; the girl hadn't the faintest notion how he'd misused her name.

Once after one of his friskier rampages Louise and the kids had turned into a chorus of hissing indignation, ordering him to leave forever. "Get out! Get out!" they shrieked. "I'm splitting this pigpen," he answered, "and don't try to stop me." Sleeping on his office couch, he'd awakened in the early hours sodden with the incomparable grief of the spirit not yet hardened to exile. He could not survive another second without hearing their voices. Yet penitence was out of the question. Stupidly he phoned without rehearsing first. When Louise answered, to his horror, he started to cry. Humiliated, he had to think fast. "Remember Cathy Koolbaugh?" He sobbed. "I must have been crazy to let her go. I'm heartsick, heartsick. I think I'm in love with the girl." "Oh, you liar," Louise said softly, and hung up.

Trover stayed on the old road that ran parallel to the interstate. It would carry him to within a half mile of his front door. The bars were spaced farther apart now. The inns that contained them were eighteenth-century wayfarers' stops, one in each country village. It was very lonely between towns, and the tavern lights drew Trover as lines thrown to him in darkness. The places had names like the Womelsdorf Tavern, the Drovers and Farmers Hotel, Lavina and Pete's Place. They smelled of stale beer and dry rot and frying, the damp stone walls covered in damp blond paneling. In one of those places Trover shot a game of baseball darts against a guy named Ron whose tiny daughter sat on the stool munching Slim Jims and calling Trover a "poophead" every time he scored. The men talked about upkeep, on cars and beards. "Must you cut it much?" Ron wanted to know.

"I pretty much let 'er rip," Trover said, caressing his red bonfire of a beard.

"Now me, I get the wife to trim it good Saturday night. Makes it nice for church." Trover left feeling vaguely chastened.

The lot outside the next place was parked solid. Big farmer cars—Pontiacs, Impalas, a goodly number of four-wheelers and pickups. Country music floated in the damp air, and the moon was a snippet of skin adrift in the mottled dark. The jangle of noise when he opened the door felt like getting hit in the ear with a wire brush.

Not a seat in the house to be had. Not at the bar, not at the oilcloth-draped tables laden with platters of ring bologna and American cheese cubes and sweating pitchers of dark beer. Trover had almost forgotten how it was on ladies' night at the Longswamp Hotel.

The noise grew, aggressive, excruciating and eased off only as the din from the *boom-bas* blunted the hearing. Trover looked for a chink in the wall of bodies pressing the bar. Even the nine or ten *boom-bas* players had to fight for space on the narrow strip of floor allotted them. Dozens of like instruments hung from hooks on the wall behind them or leaned against tables and laps, awaiting their owners' turns on the floor.

The players pumped and pounded and drummed to "Slap Her Down Again, Pa," and then "The More Beer Polka." The jukebox jumped, and the floor shook; the sound hummed, like blood in the bones. Several bangers wore the look of serious musicians and appeared to be refining fancy mannerisms. One very tall man described a high, elegant flourish after each strike of the cymbal. Another, younger man hunched over his stick like a bass player, eyes closed, the tip of his tongue lolling.

The *boom-bas* itself was not unlike a pogo stick in size or function. Its heavy spring base gave it bounce, and the wealth of attached noisemakers turned it into a kind of compound percussion instrument. A band-on-a-stick. You might find bolted along its length a tambourine, a cowbell, a bicycle bell, and a musical block. More often than not a strap of sleigh bells and a Good Humor bell and maybe now and again, on the deluxe model, *double* cowbells and a shiny brass Model T horn. Like a coolie hat on top was a set of cymbals, and above that, covering the tip of the stick, was something akin to a hood ornament, a personal totem—maybe a beer tap handle, a Mack bulldog, a Kiwanis *K*.

Two players staggered, exhausted, to their seats; two more took their places. The reconstituted crew battered through "Chattanooga Choochoo," rallied, it seemed, around the rowdiest among them, a damp dumpling of a woman, playing with crashing abandon, all parts invested, from the flying elbows to the liquid ripple and shift of breast and belly. She had lively little foam-soled feet, and her slacks were too short, overstuffed peach polyesters that rode up and down as she stretched and flexed, a face florid with enjoyment. Onlookers stood by with tiny, undecided smiles that reminded Trover of screen doors cocked partway open. He found himself bopping in place, pumping his shoulders in ragged counterpoint to the woman's looser rhythms, the flesh of her upper arms swinging, jiggling like sleeves.

The music stopped, and Trover's woman came off the floor, sweat-soaked, a plump hand calming her heart. When she came abreast of him, he was disappointed to see how common she was offstage. Common as Mildred Gaugler. Good God, it *was* Mildred Gaugler!

And now it was too late to look away because she'd already spotted him. "Ay, don't tell me!" she cried. She pinched his cheek and led him by the elbow to a table taken up with four equally vivacious late-middle-aged women. Somebody handed him a glass of beer, and Mildred Gaugler introduced him. "And this here's my ladies' night recklers," she said. "Myrt, Verna, Vi, and Irene."

The women had either blond or blue or pewter-toned very short perms you could see through in the light coming from the kitchen. They wore earrings in shiny plastics and startling circles of rouge drawn low on their large German faces. Each time he finished his beer, somebody replaced it, and then they all sat grinning from him to one another. He might have been a kid they'd agreed to take for the day only to find themselves at a loss as to how best they might keep him entertained.

When the music started up again, Mildred hooked his arm and yanked him out of his seat. "Loan us your stick once," she said to Irene. "For Lawyer Kleeve here."

By the time they edged their way out, the floor trembled again at full capacity. Mildred bumped a coatrack out of the way and set him up at the very edge of the players' area. She showed him how to hold the stick, then zipped around, taking a firm grip on him from behind. "Now that there's your tempo," she said, demonstrating. He felt the heavy tides of her flesh against his as she pumped him up and down from the armpits. "Move!" she cried. "Don't be so darn *pokey!*"

"Bounce from the knees, mister." Verna, having joined them, was trying to make herself authoritative over the din. "Now bounce!" She was wearing a short-sleeved rayon shirt that said "Zieglersville Grange Auxiliary" across the back. While Mildred operated his body from behind, Verna made his arm go, ringing here, clacking there, honking to "Knock three times on the ceiling if you wa-ant me." After a while somebody yelled, "Ease up once. Now let him go," and they released him as tenderly as they might a kid on his first bike.

The women took up their own instruments and positioned themselves on either side of him. He began to move, woodenly at first, not bouncing so much as pitching from the waist, and when he poked his butt out too far, one of the women whacked it back with her stick. What an ingenious device it was. The more you drank, the faster you learned. He began to warm to his art. In the frenzied heat his muscles loosened, turned fluid. The women's boisterous enjoyment splashed him like sparks from an arc welder. They were a tiny world of one-person bands, and he imagined he could hear the jolly rattle of the skeleton inside his clothes.

When the record changed, he took a break and bought his table another pitcher. Then, to the grave and stately opening strains of the *1812 Overture,* he sashayed back out to the floor. The players' faces turned immediately serious, then solemn, then rhapsodic as the sound behind them swelled with fife and violin and then guns and cannons and fireworks and extra shots of passion and madness. Trover hammered and bashed and went crashing into crescendo with the rest; the *boom-bas* line was one human musical fever that broke in concert, and then they all stood slightly dazed in dripping skin, dazed and luminous and a little self-conscious, when the music stopped.

Trover stayed for two more considerably less affecting numbers. He began to add his own dips and furbelows; he danced around the stick. How quickly the alien way became a way of life. Then he and Verna and Vi and Myrt followed Mildred Gaugler around the room in a raucous, wobbly congo line, hammering between tables, banging the tabletops like drums as they snaked in and out.

The quiet hit hard. Looking up, he saw that the place had emptied out and a burly bartender was pulling the plug on the jukebox. Trover's party returned to their table, where Irene was waiting with her arms crossed, her lower lip shoved out. Trover handed her *boom-bas* back.

"Don't do me no favors," she said.

"Un-oh," he said. "Seems I've been a bad boy again."

But Mrs. Gaugler stopped him. "Ach!" she said, turning in cheery disbelief to the others. "Bad boy maybe, but he's a good *man*, not?"

Myrt and Verna eagerly agreed.

"Well, hey, bring us the best you've got," Trover said, addressing the waitress wiping the adjacent table.

"Last call was fifteen minutes ago," she said without looking up.

He hunched his shoulders and turned up his palms. "Oooooooch," he said. Then he bowed from the waist to the petulant one. "Good night, Irene," he said. He kissed her hand.

She pushed at her curls. "Night," she said coyly.

He turned to the others. "And good night, ladies."

"Don't do nothin' I wouldn't do," Mildred called after him.

He pulled up in front of the Kemp Hotel, the last hope this side of home. The phosphorescent clock face in the window of Groff's garage said 2:46. Resting his brow on the hotel door, he pounded and pounded. A starving rag of a cat joined him on the stoop, slunk against his ankles. Finally he stepped down and squinted up at the windows. Even the Budweiser neon had been extinguished. Cold dark on Dog Jaw Mountain. Dark was endemic now. Stooping to the cat, he peered out into the somehow forlorn, somehow seductive murk of the last leg home.

CHAPTER

11

Louise dreaming her dream of houses. This time the house is opalescent gray, a pearl of Victorian absurdity. The dream becomes a realtor of sorts guiding her through the endless articulation of cubbyholes and porches and corridors, and she never wants the dream or the house to stop. She could ride the cutting edge of her interest forever.

She awoke when he called her. Her name entered the dream like a lummox, crashing through rooms, battering plaster. "La-weeeeeze! La-weeeeeze!" In the lingering dust of the demolished dream, she tried to rise, wooden legs tangling with the flannel sheets. She staggered to the top of the stairs and stopped, heart thundering, clutching the newel-post. Trembling, she followed his voice downstairs, to the kitchen.

He was on his haunches before the closed broom closet, his back to Louise. "What's wrong? You OK? Trover?"

Swaying on his heels, he brought his arm back to beckon her closer. "Come look," he said gluily. "Not so loud. *Molliter.*"

She was standing about ten feet behind him, his back blocking her view. "What is it?" she asked, still leery. Creeping closer, she peeked timidly over his shoulder and saw the cat, a scrawny, battle-scarred calico. Bagel, crouched low, was looking from the cat to Louise, incredulous, disgusted.

"Watch this," said Trover. "Watch this cat lap milk."

When her mouth dropped open, he put a finger to his lips. "Shhhhhhhh," he said. *"Molliter. Molliter."*

"You got me out of bed to watch a cat lap milk and shut me up in Latin?"

Apparently sated, the animal slunk away from the bowl, batted a paw at Bagel, leaped onto the countertop, where she remained, studying them all with no special fondness.

"You missed most of it," said Trover lugubriously.

She stared at him. "Hey, you think it's easy, you try it, see how much supper you get just using your tongue."

Louise was still viscous with sleep. Her muscles ached from the hard waking. "Wait a minute," she said. "We don't have a cat! Where did that animal *come* from?"

He held up one finger and cracked a lopsidedly prankish grin and walked over to the counter and picked up the scabby cat. "That's our little secret, right, Caroline?"

"She already has a name?"

Holding the cat close, Trover approached Louise and bussed her cheek. "Bibs," he said, "you're my beautiful girl, but—God bless you—you're dumb when it comes to function. Tell me everything you know about how a cat's tongue works."

She gave him a dumb, faintly hostile stare.

"Ahhhhhhhh," he said. "The cat's got your tongue."

Now he'd made her laugh when she didn't want to. Nobody but an idiot would stay up a second longer to take instructions in animal anatomy from a drunk. Yet there she was, rooted to the spot, attending this facetious person, as if he were somehow as wondrous as the lapping cat.

She watched him attempt to demonstrate the precise twist and flick that turned a tongue into a spoon. Somewhere he'd read just how many tiny muscles it took to make a cat's tongue. But then he wasn't sure he hadn't confused the figures with the flavor buds in a wild strawberry. Tongues and strawberries were similar, didn't she think?

Trover had always been an affable enough lush, but Louise hadn't always been so easy. She was thinking how he used to come in at three, singing "Sweet Caroline," so obliviously wistful she believed he deserved to die on the spot. Unwilling to let him fall asleep happy, she would whip him into a state easier to work with, and then they'd fight to some spectacular conclusion.

Once after she'd needled him long and hard, he chased her out into the snow. He tackled her, and she bit his wrist. He looked at her with that expression he had, of immeasurable affliction, and said, "I know I'm a trying man, but couldn't you for once just be glad I'm home?" And she thought it was the most reprehensible statement ever made. She would have to leave him, go back to the convent, join the circus, do something great and slay him with fame, but she could not decide between the former, and fame took time, and time passed quickly as Trover went on getting away with himself.

Now she stood with Bagel and the strange cat, watching him make a sandwich, his movements slow, stilted, imprecise. He who required paper-thin sliced his cheese into ragged slabs. He dropped sprouts like forkfuls of hay on top, and then red radishes hacked in half, fat as acorns. She poured him a glass of milk and carried his sandwich to the table. Trover patted a chair seat. "Sit," he said.

She demurred grumpily.

"Stay a spell," he said. "Keep an old war-horse company."

She sat uncommittedly on the very edge of the chair opposite his, trying not to see how he wolfed his sandwich in crumbling bites, stringing garlands of mustard through his beard in the process. He looked up, creating the impression of having considered long and hard, "*I* love you, Bibs," he said, as if in response to some sniveling wifely lament, as if she'd said only moments before, "Nobody loves me, nobody cares."

She gave him a narrow look.

Leaning close, he held up a finger. "Client of mine," he began. "Guy named Bryfogle. Had a terrible fight with his wife. The wife jumped in her car and took off. She didn't get very far when she noticed all the neighbors hopping around, hollering, trying to get her attention. Finally the cops pulled her over. God, there was Bryfogle, hell of a mess, all bruised and bleeding from clinging to her bumper. Guy got charged with following too close."

"A lunatic," Louise said.

But Trover hadn't taken his eyes from hers for a second. "Bibs," he said, "I'd do that. Yep, I would, you ever leave me, I'd scrape my ass from here to Toledo over you."

Louise thought about this. "And if I don't leave?"

Now it was his turn to consider. "Then you'll just have to take your chances."

She sighed and slid back in her chair. Say what you want, there was gold in drunk talk, even if you had to pan for it. Even if it was only dust and dribs of Polish mustard. Still, it irked her that he could have her at so small a cost. For anybody else the price of her good offices at this hour would have been prohibitive.

And if he was not quite as drunk as he let on, she was not about to call him on it either. Trover needed these small sabbaticals, needed a sabbath, in fact, a day of rest from the strain of supporting an impossible self. And Louise needed relief from him and from the unalterable workaday dynamics of them, that tense competitive dance that was the way they were married to each other. In this tiny buffer zone made of hours few others can use, they were good friends and playful lovers, secret, protected from their daylight selves. Tomorrow they would officially remember none of this, and even now Louise knew not to press for more.

"So," she said, "what's up with the late-night crowd?"

"That's something else you missed," he said. "Yours truly and the Morsells."

"*Morsells?* You mean morsels. As in chocolate chips."

He explained about Mildred, Myrt, Verna, Vi, and Irene. "Those Morsells are hardly morsels," he said. "But, man, do they have talent."

Louise shook her head. "Why do I love thee?"

Trover spoke with a straight face. "Because you think I'm adorable."

"But what in heaven's name have you done to deserve it?"

"No damn good if you have to *earn* it," he said sternly.

A hitch in tone and he could be a whiner, a crier, one of the chronic insufferable. Louise thought of Osberg. Poor Osberg. Was it possible Trover's saving grace was shamelessness?

Now he was collecting all the chunky things that had rolled out of his bread, examining each find. When he looked up from his gleanings, he seemed surprised to see her. "Louise," he said, "nobody would call my dad a great man."

"But?"

"Not buts. He was not a great man, I'm telling you."

"A common deficiency."

Trover rotated his mouth in that way he had that suggested a warm-up drill for discourse. "True story," he said, raising his right hand. "One spring morning my dad woke me very early. Christ, it was still dark. Early dark's a lot scarier than night dark. I felt sneaky, unreal, like my own ghost."

"Was he taking you fishing or what?"

"Well, hell, I didn't know what was coming off. First he made us a couple of soft-boiled eggs. I got some shells in mine but didn't let on. No, ma'am. Would have spoiled things. When it turned light, he got the binoculars out. Guess what we saw out there."

"A pileated woodpecker," she blurted, the words surprising even her.

Trover's eyes flew open. "Louise, you *witch,* how did you know that? We'd never seen a pileated before. How did you *know?* My God, there it was out back in that little wooded lot my dad liked to think was the bloomin' wilds of Borneo. And . . . it . . . was . . . a . . . beaut, drilling away, that furious little head. . . . Anyhow, whole time Dad kept checking his watch. Then he said, 'OK, Bud, it's seven. You come with me. It's time I taught my son the proper way to wake a lady.'

"Now try to picture this: Mum is still sound asleep. He motions me to wait while he tiptoes toward the bed—God, his face is sweet, kind of Simple Simon sweet. 'Watch this,' he says to me. He bends down. He plants a big one on her forehead, one on each cheek. Then he comes back for me. He lifts me up, flying me over her bed, dipping my face close to hers. I kiss her on the forehead. Hell, I felt so sacramental I could have canonized myself."

"What a lovely thing to do," Louise said.

Trover scowled at the sentiment. "No question about it," he said then, "the kiss brought her around. She opened her eyes and sat up blinking. She had heaps of thick red hair then, all fluffed out, like her face lived in a pink cloud. Prettiest damn thing I've ever seen. There she sat, blinking and rubbing her eyes, pretending not to know where she was or who we were, and then she started twisting her fingers—you know how she does. Then guess what, Louise—that woman started scrubbing at her face. By God, she wiped them all off!"

In typical rash, undercalculated fashion, Louise, wishing to be an instant comfort, tried to occupy the chair beside his before she had vacated her own. She dropped hard into the chair at the head of the table. Trover, staring sadly off somewhere, did not seem to notice the shortfall. Louise rose once again, clambered in next to him. She reached for his hand, which he gave gravely, eyes cast down, his beard creeping under his collar. When, many minutes later, he spoke, she could barely make out the words.

"Did you say something, Bibs?" she said.

"What kind of ice cream we got?" he asked anemically.

She could not resist. "Pileated vanilla."

"Don't joke around right now, OK?"

"Plain old vanilla."

"I'll have some," he said. "With wet walnuts, if it's not too much bother."

After giving hefty dollops to Bagel and Caroline, she brought him his order. "Correct me if I'm wrong," she said, "but I think you're asking me to spend the rest of my life making up for a rejected kiss."

He stopped with his spoon inches from his mouth, his eyes large and troubled. "Would that be asking too much?" he said.

"Trover," she said, "you're an ass."

"That's right," he said, perfectly sober now. "And I intend to be loved anyhow."

CHAPTER

12

Mighty came to the foot of the attic steps and yelled up to Michael's room. "Ten seconds!" Then: "Nine, eight . . . I'm warning you!"

"Hold your horses. I'm tying my shoe."

She paced the upstairs hall. He was always making her late. Last June she'd had to keep coming a full week after classes let out to discharge a massive detention deficit. Thirty hours' worth, every second accountable to him. And if that weren't sufficiently galling, Michael himself consistently passed unharmed through the snares of the system. Nobody sent *him* to the office to sign in late; nobody tallied up *his* crimes at the end of the week. Having his wrestling coach for homeroom certainly didn't hurt but fell far short of explaining the blanket immunities he enjoyed as a matter of course. He'd been getting the same happy shake for years.

She considered his foggy blond looks. Eyes the color of tap water tinctured with a single drop of midnight blue ink. Mistaking him for smoke or some oddly familiar aroma, maybe teachers didn't notice him come in. Or, as one was tempted to suspect, he really was an angel and everybody had come to expect him to slip in and out of focus, to arrive and depart with hardly more than a fluttering page to mark where he parted the air. Angel, shit! They didn't have to live with the little derelict.

"What *are* you doing up there? Playing with yourself?"

"I'm tying my *other* shoe."

From the bedroom across the hall came Louise's strangulated voice. "Why does everybody have to yell around first thing?"

Mighty poked her head in. "I give up, Ma. Why do they?"

Whump! Whump! Whump! "Oh, piss," Mighty said to her mother. "Your boyfriend's rattling his cage." Trover was in the shower beating on the tiles. "Who's using the wah-der?" Mighty intoned, waving her arm like a magic wand.

"WHO'S USING THE WATER?" her father bellowed on cue.

Ignored, he pounded again, and Mighty opened the bathroom door. "Your son, the village idiot. That's who's using the water." She kicked the door shut and went humping back to the attic stairway. "Michael, you using HIS water?" No answer. When the thumping struck again, she tore back through her parents' room and hurled herself at the bathroom door and ripped it open with both hands. "Come out of there!" she yelled. "You're clean enough!" She slammed the door so hard that the antique dolls atop her mother's dresser shivered in their summer dresses.

Back to the stairs. "Listen carefully, Michael," she said, waxing wickedly sweet. "The next sound you hear will be my little departing feet." And down the steps she went, stomping to give him one last warning.

She had hoped not only to avoid a tardy mark but to get off in time to use the school darkroom before classes started. Gideon was staying the night with a married sister (he and Mighty had agreed that he should break up his residencies with an occasional night away). Otherwise he would have gladly given her a lift to school. Her chauffeuring duties were unenforceable when the participating car was not one of their own. Nobody could make her wait for Michael then. She laid on the horn and started to back out (they were always *pretending* to leave without Michael). She was faking forward, muttering, when he came flying off the porch with his jacket hooked over his head, a scramble of books and tablets clutched to his chest, gym bag dragging. He was wearing a kind of sweatshirt, slate blue with dingy white ribbing at the waist and cuffs and a crumpled white collar. It did not bother Michael that his favorite shirt had shrunk several sizes. His constant yanking it down at the waist created the illusion of fit, while the resultant skimpiness in back bared a goodly crescent of moon-pale flesh. Like their mother, who sometimes neglected to comb the back of her hair, he remained happily innocent of the hidden discrepancies.

Mighty had photographed him in that shirt. The camera never missed what the eye caught only now and again, and fleetingly at that: the unsettling sweetness he had; that dreamy and somehow luminous appreciation in his light, light eyes; how fragile he looked for a weight lifter. Years from now a gaunt figure in that shirt would haunt the avenues of her adulthood,

and good would always have for her a human shape, as real and knowable
as the dark and bloody shapes of bad. Oh, he did tug at her, as relentlessly
as he tugged at that shrunken shirt. Damn him anyhow. She preferred not
to anticipate a future goodwill when right this minute she wanted to iso-
merize him.

Tossing books and gym bag in back, Michael swung into the passenger
seat. "Ooooops!" He raised arm to face in a posture of self-defense.

"What now?" she asked.

"I forgot my homework."

In an effort to show good faith, he managed to make more noise than
time as he went clattering across the porch, throwing superfluous motion
into the struggle to open a simple door. "God," she said aloud, "I can't take
it anymore." At any given moment, somewhere in the house, somebody
was saying that: "I can't take it anymore." Yet they went on taking it,
whatever the current or cumulative "it" was. Why did they? Why was she
waiting in the cold for some dipsy doodle when she could as easily be halfway there?

When he returned, she slammed the car into first and took off in earnest.
At the very first curve, the hard left at the lower end of the rose garden, the
car got the shakes. Mighty tried everything she knew to humor the engine,
a steady but delicate pressure on the accelerator, pumping the cold start,
rocking, grunting, sweet talk. But the trouble dug in, and by the time they
reached the iron gate, the little car was bucking and lurching and stalling
out every several feet.

"Trash bucket! Bloody heap! We're not going diddly in this thing. Lum
incompetents oughta be shot."

"What are you going to do?" her brother asked, so mild and composed it
was all she could do to keep from shaking him. "Wanna take the Hornet?"

"*Your* mother lost the keys, remember?"

Mighty went upstairs and asked Louise if they could take the Jeep.
Half-asleep, Louise muttered that she was picking somebody up at the bus
depot.

She appealed to her father. "Is it cool if we take the new diesel?"

"It's not broken in yet," he said. "Besides, if I know my kids, you'll go
right out and drive it over a pile of rocks or something."

"Fine," she said. "Let Mom take the new diesel. We'll take the Jeep."

"Your mother is boycotting the new diesel," he said. "Didn't you know
that?"

"Goddamn, with all the possible combinations . . . How 'bout you take
the new diesel, we'll take the old."

"New one doesn't have a tape deck yet. Please don't confiscate one of the
few creature comforts I can count on in this life."

The man could be had, of course. He'd exhaust her first and then hand over the keys to the vehicle of her choice. But she'd gone as far as she was willing with this one. She pumped the air out of her cheeks slowly. "Forget it," she said. "Keep your precious fleet."

Sometimes the grade school bus was late. "Run for it," she told her brother outside. "Maybe if we're lucky, we can catch a farting contest."

They took off down the lane in a sprint. It was mild for early December, desultorily sunny. At the bottom of the gradient they left the road and walked several yards and spread the branches where the hole in the box-wood hedge had grown together. They dived through the breach, and the branches sprang back and nudged them into the woods. Years ago, when she and Michael were in the grades, they'd loved this route. Those days the footpath was still intact, and the steep, rooty terrain seething with sur-prises, especially in the spring, when the bulb flowers came in their suc-cessive stages. First the snowdrops, in a broad band running from top to bottom, a floral carpet for the royal kids. A week later the same swath turned yellow with jonquils, then frothy white again with bloodroot, the stems of which leaked red when you tried to pick them.

Now the trek was a blooming pain. Some of the larger stepstones had been undermined by runoff and frost heave. Deadfall lay across their path, and winter introduced hazards they were not eager to challenge anymore, certainly not since renouncing the school bus and its abominations forever.

Driven by the fitful energy of the vastly put-upon, Mighty pressed forward, Michael picking his way and trailing. At the bottom she crossed the log bridge over the creek and glanced out toward the lean-to-shelter under which, if luck was with them, local urchins would be waiting for the bus. The shelter was deserted. Michael straggled up and stood next to her with his head bowed, conspicuously remorseful. "Let's go over to Sprecher's and call Ma," she said tightly.

"She'll kill us."

"We'll get over it."

Walking single file, they skirted the base of the Knoll, then set off on a tangent the several hundred yards to Sprecher's place. His tiny vinyl house was perched precariously on a steep bank, enjoying at the same time the protective hunch of the hump of land rising directly behind it. Up a piece from the house there stood a long, low planing mill, out of which spilled a mountain of delectably rotten sawdust. His road clawed its way up a lesser but still formidable grade just beyond the house, then split immediately, sending one offshoot up the hill to Tumbling Run; Mighty and Michael took the left prong of the road down into Sprecher's rutted, tummocky yard. They heard the cries immediately.

"Gawd," Mighty said, looking out toward the mill. "The saw must of got him. What if he's getting sliced into boards?" There were squawks and grunts and full-bodied howls and, every few seconds, one savagely ragged, resonating bellow.

Michael swayed, draining color. His lips turned the whitish gray of worms washed out of the garden.

"Go see," she said wickedly.

Taking his sister's hand, he said, "Come with. Please."

"Oh, for crying out loud, let's go." And even as she spoke, his hand went limp in hers, and after a halfhearted attempt to support his slumping body, she let her brother go. She stared down, disgusted, stuck with the dirty work again. Everybody had a vanishing point, and saints faded fast when the subject was blood.

She dumped her purse alongside her brother's books. "You'll just have to bring yourself around when you're up to it," she said, setting off across the muddy lot. Michael was always passing out. On the mat when his nose bled. When his opponent's nose bled. Last year she'd driven him to the doctor for a tetanus shot which the doctor stupidly administered as Michael stood in the hall outside the treatment room. Eyes rolling, Michael slid slowly down the wall, flopping sideways like a rag doll. Mighty went after the doctor with both fists. "Bastard!" she cried. "You murdered my brother!" The nurse brought Michael around with ammonia pellets, and when he opened his eyes, Mighty, heart pounding, mortified, whispered into his ashen, uncomprehending face, "You dope, you're not dead!"

Mighty strode past a small unpainted shed to which Sprecher's sleeping shepherd Joe, was tethered. The dog opened one eye and thumped his tail and went back to sleep. Inside the shed chunks of furry green meat hung from rusted hooks.

She spotted Sprecher behind a waist-high stack of rough-cut lumber at the lower end of the mill. The ancient, monstrously involved, and awkward belt-driven equipment stood eerily still. The only thing running was Sprecher. It amazed her an old man could jump so high. He pogoed up and down, then proceeded to execute a series of vehement stomps. Terrible inhuman sounds issued from him. It occurred to her that there might be a person beneath his feet getting stomped to death. Maybe he'd finally caught one of those hyperactive campers. Maybe he had finally, irrevocably, spectacularly popped his cork. She was about to back discreetly away when he caught sight of her. He made three more grunting jumps and stopped. He came toward Mighty with his jaw upthrust, peering at her, all his suspicions framed narrowly in the wet fish-gill slits of his eyes.

"We need to use your phone," she said. "My brother, uh ..." She pointed to the spot where she'd left him. On his haunches now, he was brushing off her purse, and she had to cough to dislodge the pitying thing all but closing her throat.

"Phone's in the hoss," said Sprecher, almost challengingly, as if Mighty would find it peculiar that he kept his phone indoors, but not at all odd that he spent his mornings hopping around like a nut.

Sprecher started stiffly toward the house, his thumbs hooked under the straps of his bib. There were old scores to settle from Michael's uncouth days. "Brat!" Sprecher used to shout. "Brat!" Sprecher used to shout. "Brat. Quack." "Sprecherduck!" Michael would taunt, provoking the caretaker to a fresh round of "brats" and "quacks."

"Come on," Mighty said to her brother as she passed by on Sprecher's heels. "You big, squeamish baby. You talk to her. She'd do anything for *you.*"

They followed Sprecher into his gloomy kitchen. A dented aluminum saucepan wobbled on the burner, a gobbet of cold oatmeal stuck to its side. Mighty figured the old man subsisted almost entirely on oatmeal and that evil green meat in the shed. And horseradish. Once, when she and Michael came to drop off his paycheck, he'd gone in the back for something, and while he was gone, she'd stolen a peek inside his old Philco: a jug of water, an uncovered dish of chowchow, and three tall jars of horseradish.

He was stinting, too, with electricity, the kitchen cold and dark in the shadow of Tumbling Run. They followed him through a faded chenille curtain into a tiny parlor busy with knickknacks, Perma's things, and smelling mostly of dust and old mohair. Sprecher pointed at the basic black phone. "Chust see you don't make no pay calls," he said, careful not to honor Michael through direct address. He left the room.

Mighty dialed and handed her brother the phone, and when seconds later, he hung up, she said, "Well, what'd she say?"

"Users, manipulators, irresponsible snots."

"She'll come," said Mighty.

Sprecher had returned, with a card in his hand. He was tapping it importantly with the flat of his black pointer nail. Clearly he wanted Mighty to look. It was a penny postcard with a glossy black-and-white photo of five identical curly-haired little girls. "Chust two times we went away, Perma and me," he was saying. "Once to the ocean. Didn't come to much," he added dismissively. His hands made ups and downs in the air. "Put me in mind of right arond here, only them waves wass a sight wetter." His grin was sudden blue and toothless, and his eyes probed theirs until they smiled with him, whereupon he turned immediately stern again.

"The other time we went on a Greyhond bus up Canada ways, to see them there kinktuplets. Ay, such a long line we wait on, and in pourin'-

down rain yet, and then we come past this big winduh, and there they set. Them fife yungksters all alike, playin' with fife dolls all alike. Ay-yi-yi, now that there was something."

Then Sprecher went through the curtain, letting it flap back in Mighty's face. He stopped in the kitchen and spun around, fixing her squarely. "The missus, she sez to me, 'Now, Earl, if Gott makes fife the same, how is it he don't divide them up nicer, so's it's fair?' See," he added confidingly, "her insides wass all *ferhuddled,* so she couldn't have no kitts."

Now he clamped his lips and shot Mighty a look with red-hot lead behind it. "She wass settin' right here when it come," he said, indicating an arrow-back chair at one end of his breakfast table.

"Who's that, Mr. Sprecher?" Michael asked.

"Perma! Who d'ya think?" said Mighty impatiently, relishing her favoredness, that Sprecher spoke only to her.

The old man slapped his hands together. "Chust like that, she wass on the floor. Her eyes was shut tight, but she wanted so to get up. Ay, such a rutching and thrashing arond. *'My Gott,* Earl,' she says, 'what will happen to me?' " He stops, letting the size of it all surround them.

"And what did *you* say?" Mighty said, not wanting to know.

"Well, I sez, 'Perma, I chust don't know what to tell ya'."

After a long silence Michael said, "Mr. Sprecher, you did everything you could."

Sprecher waited out the condolences with prickly impatience. "Know what kilt her?"

"Wasn't it a stroke?" said Mighty. "Or a heart attack. One of those things."

He chased her ignorance out of the space between them, and two hanks of dirty gray hair lashed across his eyes, eyes burning like small flames behind black glass. *"Gotts bitte noch ah mol."* he clacked. "Trouble put her under. Trouble and worry."

"What was she worried about?" Michael inquired, round-eyed, deterred not at all by the shunning.

"Why, them hippies," he said. "And dope pushers. Goddamn govermint buttin' in, killin' chickens. White sugar at fife dollahs a pond. Nukler pawr and all them mud dams about to bust . . ." He squinted in close to Mighty. "Them Russians are nutzed, ain't?"

Mighty backed off from the sour rag of his breath. "Perma always struck *me* as a laid-back type," she said cautiously.

But he had moved to the window. "Worst thing was them city nickers," he said, pointing into the base of the hill that would be crowned come summer with Camp Tumbling Run. "Ay, it spites me to think how they bust loose and come down here. Such a loud, rowdy bunch, mouthin' off, stompin' the missus flahr betts. And she had blood pressure s'wonderful bad, ain't?" He turned around and wagged his finger at them. "I believe them camp teachers learn them kitts to stapp people."

Mighty drew back, dipping her chin sharply. "Stapp?"

Ramming a fist into his own middle, Sprecher reiterated. "Stapp! With a knife. Stapp and leave ya for det."

From her room in the trees, Mighty had often seen the glow from those fires, and the camp songs rode the damp summer breezes over the dip between hills, shimmering across the pool, strumming the pine boughs, drifting through open windows like tiny, tinkly bells. She opened her mouth to enlighten him, but Sprecher's black fingernail was on the move again. "Them type got no business here."

"But you don't think anybody belongs here. Not me, not my brother, not anybody who doesn't look and talk and think just like you."

The old man had grown so agitated he could barely get the words out. "*Schwetz nott so dumm,*" he spat. "All them fools come ott from town, lookin to buy themselves a farm. Think they're schmart riding them little tractors, putzin' around, getting their pitchers taken with a bunch a punkins."

"So?" said Mighty. "Where's it say they're not allowed to grow pumpkins? It's a free country."

"But them type don't stick with nothing. Next think you know they're fet up with the work, let everything go to pots." He stepped forward, scrutinizing her face. "It wonders me now," he said cagily. "When's your pop get off his behind to mend the henhoss?"

The horn sounding outside saved Mighty having to explain when no explanation on earth would satisfy. "Well, thanks heaps," she said.

"Have a happy and prosperous day, sir," Michael said, his leave-taking lavishly bumbling and uncertain.

Outside, Mighty knuckled his skull. "Why didn't you tell him you'll write? Jesus crackers, you always get sooo attached."

Michael lowered his gaze in some kind of regret she did not wish to partake of. Long dark lashes curled neatly into the hollow beneath his eyes. Mighty traced a finger along the rim of that hollow. "Lay you odds Ma's still in her jammies," she said softly.

"She was sleeping," he said.

"Some law against dressing for the road?"

"You know Mom. She doesn't think clearly first thing, especially not when you rush her."

There was a trick to opening the passenger door of the Jeep, a trick to everything they owned. Mighty jiggled the handle, at the same time rapid-battering the door with her hip. She enjoyed the crisp, efficient air she kept about herself while her muscle-bound brother stood gawking on the sidelines. The catch yielded with a rusty screech.

Except for waiting until all their parts were aboard before lurching out onto the roadway, their mother made no effort to acknowledge them. Staring straight ahead, mouth clenched, she was wearing a fake-fur Russian hat so far down that her bangs were plunged into her eyes. Where her robe fell open, the pilled red flannel of her nightgown showed, and the robe itself was black velour covered with hairs from Bagel and that cat their dad had dragged home. Over that she wore the hunched bulk of a plaid Woolrich jacket Trover had bought for a hunting career that lasted all of twenty-five minutes, from 6:55 to 7:20 one opening day of deer season their first December on the Knoll. Mighty suspected her father had never intended to shoot anything in the first place. She thought now of Sprecher's impatience with city people and their fickle interests: the farmers-for-a-month; the pretend hunters; suburban housewives bumming around in a big truck. Mighty nudged her brother. "Check out the footwear," she said. Louise's accelerator foot was sheathed in a sleek cordovan boot; the other wore an argyle mukluk.

Michael gave her a cautioning glance and said nothing. Under the circumstances it was folly to antagonize the woman. Shaking her head, Mighty watched Louise, how she goose-necked forward, her grip on the wheel sweaty, tenacious, eyes searching the distance in the squinting, suspicious scrutiny of a schizoid or a severe myopic. When she had allowed her mother sufficient time to adjust to the conscious world, Mighty said, "And what if you have an accident?"

"Then I'd have them all in stitches down at the morgue, wouldn't I?"

"I was thinking more in terms of *hospital*, Ma. Must you always be so—so radical?"

But Louise was craning past her children into a patch of marshland off to the right. "Pampas grass looks glorious this season. I've never seen such luxuriant plumes. Oh, let's come down someday soon."

Mighty laughed. "One of these days, lady, someone's going to blast you out of their weed patch."

And after what she interpreted as a fierce inner struggle, Michael said, "If we don't have practice Saturday, maybe I'll help you get some."

"Better pack the smelling salts," she told her mother. "Macho man took the vapors in Sprecher's yard."

Louise's long white fingers drifted past Mighty, alighting weightlessly on her son's sleeve.

"Just because he had this picture of Sprecher getting carved into steaks and chops." When her mother darted her a look, she explained what happened. "And there he was, jumping a mile off the ground."

"Yes," said Louise. "He does it frequently."

"All the rage with the older set, eh?"

"I do believe the man is within his rights."

"Sprecher's spiteful and soft in the head. When I'm his age, I hope somebody has the good sense to cancel my show."

"Mighty, that's enough!"

Once she got her mother going, it was hard not to keep giving her another spin. "Take him to the vet's, Ma. I heard it's perfectly civilized and painless—"

"Well, I do hope when I get a little old and squirrely, you'll remember these mad morning dashes. . . . I'm counting on you to feel guilty and obligated. . . ."

Louise old and squirrely? Mighty swallowed, and the wind left her voice. "Oh, Ma, you'll probably just be a little dizzier than you are right now. You and Michelangelo here—it's like a bus dropped you off on earth last night and you're still trying to get your bearings. You still think air travel's miraculous. Something can happen a thousand times, and it still surprises you. You're both sort of adorable in a perfectly maddening way."

She watched their mouths, the near-identical twitches of self-conscious pleasure. Mighty shared that baffling knack with her father, the faculty for pleasing far out of proportion to the gift. The smallest, even left-handed compliment from them was taken up like a chicken neck in the hands of the poor, bones sucked clean. Their "true feelings" were sniffed out, snooped for, scrabbled after. They were continuously solicited, perpetually wooed. And she and Trover tried to work the same powers on each other, but neither was willing to grovel or be grateful.

"Poor old Perma," Michael was saying. "There she was, dying on the linoleum, and when she wanted to know what would become of her, the best Sprecher could come up with was an honest answer."

"That's the trouble with the Dutchies," said Mighty, carding skeins of hair around her hand. "They're so damn literal. What's wrong with 'You'll be fine, dearie'?"

"Hey," said Michael, "maybe Sprecher just wanted her to reassure *him*. After all, Perma was the one causing all the trouble."

"Just like a man," said Mighty. "Trying to squeeze some comfort for himself out of a woman's dying breath."

"Probably ended in a draw," Michael said, sighing. "Those two never budged an inch."

Leaning over the wheel, Louise caught her son's eye. "Why, that can't be so. Perma budged. She *left* him, didn't she?"

Now that her brain and limbs and tongue had loosened up, and the road, too, had uncoiled to form a rare stretch of straightaway, Louise started to burn rubber. As the needle shivered past sixty-five, the chronic shimmy kicked in. Her hat jiggled off, and her cigarette danced against the wheel, but nothing in her soft, thoughtful expression indicated that she'd yet noticed anything untoward.

"Mom!" Michael shouted above the racket. "Cut us a break, will ya?"

Easing back, Louise said, "I better get this thing aligned before your dad picks up on it."

"He'll say you drove over a pile of rocks," Mighty said. "By jingo, ain't easy finding decent rock piles to drive over these days."

Michael's laugh was cool and frictionless and reminded Mighty of the handful of marbles she and some friends had once bowled under the feet of the VFW marchers in the King Frost Parade. Every time Michael tried to talk, he fell back in hysterics, slipping on his own giggles. "How 'bout," he finally managed to say, "how 'bout when something happens—just *happens*—like the tail pipe rusts off or the tie rod snaps from metal fatigue and you practically get killed and Dad gives you one of those disgusted looks and"—Michael worked his arms like a conductor—"what does the man say?"

In shrieking unison, they said it: "EVERYTHING WE OWN TURNS INTO A PIECE OF JUNK!"

Louise was shaking and rocking so hard the truck went wild and left the road and came back several times, and they laughed all the harder for the needless risk of it, for the sheer sudsy delight of nonsense and frivolity, and when Louise had halfway collected herself, she, too, chimed in. "Louise, what did you do with my three thirty-second-inch drill bit?" she mimicked.

Mighty stopped smiling. "You guys make him like that."

A bright silverfish of a giggle turned into a squeak of disbelief. "Huh?" said Michael, mouth dropping. "What guys?"

"You and *her*. You don't take care of anything. She leaves the groceries in the Acme parking lot. You forget you rode your bike and walk home. How many gallons of ice cream have been lost because one of you flubdubs put the carton back in the bread drawer instead of the freezer?"

"Come off it, My. If you think it's all us, then how come you're always ragging on the poor guy? You're harder on Dad than anybody."

Mighty sucked in her lower lip and reached up to her eyes, and Louise said, "Hey, you promised to quit pulling your lashes out."

"And you told Dad you'd stop smoking," Mighty snapped.

In a voice at once burly and palliative, Michael said, "Never let it be said a Kleeve quit." He flexed his muscles.

And Mighty crossed her arms high. "Shut up, jerko," she said.

They were coming into Lorraine now, traveling between the river and a row of jumbled zoning, two-family dwellings and T-shirt mills and small new businesses. "By the way," said Michael, "who you picking up at the depot?"

"Her name is Frank."

"Sure it is," said Mighty.

"Frances Jane. Sister Innocent to you. We went to school together."

"That holy roller place?"

Louise nodded. "Mount Mercy, among others. From first grade on she was my best friend—and worst enemy, of course."

"What's she look like?"

"Well, I'm not sure."

"She getting the guest room?"

"Did you think I'd toss her a sleeping bag?"

"Where's Gideon supposed to sleep?"

"There's lots of sofas. Anyhow, who said he could stay?"

"Hope she doesn't mind living in squalor."

"Who?" asked Michael.

"That nun person."

Louise grimaced. "Oh, dear," she said, "Frank's immaculate. I'd forgotten." Louise looked around, as if for help and saw Hen's Heap Big Clean go by. She turned to Mighty. "Ever try one of those coin-operated places?"

"Of course," said Mighty. "I'm neat, remember?"

"This truck is a mess. Quick, tell me how it works. Anything in there could maim me for life? Is it a hundred percent automated? I don't want anyone to catch me running around like this."

"Ma, what you need is a crash course in neighborhood services," Mighty said, riding the lilt of a superior tone. "Here's . . . what . . . you . . . do," she sang out. "First you find the little slot that says, 'Insert correct change.' Then you read the posted die-rections. Drop in your little coinies—"

"Mighty, our mother is not retarded."

"Where do you two bums want dropped off?"

"South lobby," Mighty said. "You picking us up after school?"

"Take the bus, Won't hurt you once in a blue moon."

"I'll barf. Hey, look, Gideon doesn't really mind the couch." She knew how to play her mother. Take a refusal, force a guilty concession. "Maybe he'll come by and pick me up. If he does, can he stay over?"

Louise raked under her hat and sighed.

"Don't worry about me," said Michael. "I'll get a ride back with Spot after practice."

"Or maybe he'll just astral-travel home."

CHAPTER

13

Louise watched her children mount the school steps, one on either side of the rust-colored railing. Inexplicably, at the top, Michael stopped and let Mighty cross in front of him. Michael, as though directed to finish the figure, then angled off to the right, paused once again in front of the door his sister would more logically have entered, turned, waved to Louise, and went in.

As she pulled away from the curb, that deft, symmetrical, and ostensibly random maneuver remained as afterimage, a deeply scribed X in the wax of Louise's formless morning mind. And by the time she hit the last bump strip in the lot, it struck her that this was the shape of how her children had changed. At some point over the years they had somehow traded lanes, switched temperaments, and only now did she miss those original selves.

Ransacking the past was best done in the garden or in bed, on terra firma, but driving seemed much the same as sleeping to Louise. She could cover enormous ground without once surfacing from the subconscious. And so, as she rattled on out Noble Road, she was registering not Noble Road and the quiet life of a one-horse town but Mighty when she was still Mary Ann.

The child had begun life delicate and colicky, creeping into early toddlerhood, shy, complaisant, addicted to everything that could be clung to or suckled. She made crayon drawings of meek creatures, fish and box turtles, and she never pressed down. An incorrigible mama's girl, she rejected all other custody, and so, for a long time, Louise left home only by breaking her baby's heart.

Michael was born with so much dark, unruly hair, that he resembled nothing if not a miniature rock star. Large and lusty, he tyrannized not with tears but with the relentless surf of high spirits. It was years before he would sleep through the night. When finally he went off the breast, he woke chirping for a *glass* of milk. Eyes laughing, a bony part of him always digging a bony part of her, he held her to a maternal bounty she never bargained for, kept her barefoot and thin, a washerwoman in a river of milk.

In early photos a certain prim straightforwardness undercut the full scope of Mary Ann's precociously sensuous beauty. "Goodness!" people were moved to remark. "What has such a pretty little girl to be so serious about?" On the other hand, most of Michael's early pictures suffered some central comedic distortion, his mouth crumpled like that of a ruined cartoon cad or sprung wide enough to expose a glistening obscenity of fat pink tonsil.

Michael courted all comers, chased strangers down the street, begging to be kidnapped. Louise could not recall his ever crying for her or reaching out, as had Mary Ann, with pale, achingly fragile arms. With him, nothing was escapeproof, not fences or bars or folding gates or any other kind of barrier they might contrive to seal off the porches, the stairs, the yard. Later, in the Neisstown suburbs, when he was two or three, he would slip out of the locked house before dawn to knock on doors and beg her neighbors for pennies or lemons.

From the start Mary Ann was the soul of tact and decorum. She knew instinctively that certain words were not good usage when the priest came by to ask where you'd been. But they lived in dread of Michael's potential. "Shits" and "tits," "goddamns" everywhere. When Maddy had a headache, he presented her with Louise's birth control pack. "Hey, mister," he said to an elderly census taker, "don't croak in *our* kitchen, OK?"

Louise had gone several hundred yards past the Heap Big Clean before remembering. She made a U-turn and circled back, her mind racing, tracing the unaccountable twists of another track. How had those two children got *here* from there? Reconstructing these early versions was like finding a couple of lost relatives. If she could sort it all out, find the key to these transpositions, the precise turning point, well, then, couldn't she sit back and relax in the hardy comforts of the informed and orderly life?

The facility had a single bay, a flat roof and towering sign of the tepee mounted on the roof. Pulling up to the treadle gate, Louise peered out at the instructions, scanning the way she usually did when her mind was occupied elsewhere. How complicated could it be anyway? She deposited eight quarters, and when the gate arm jerked creakily upward, she pulled into the building.

Doors! How Michael had hated them. He and Mary Ann had occupied cribs in the same room for a while. Michael wanted the door left ajar at all times, to facilitate the procedures whereby he made demands and kept surveillance on them. If someone shut it, he would cry, "Lie, lie," meaning "light, light," like a voice from the grave. One night they ignored him. It was a lovely surprise how quickly he settled down. As best as they could figure later, the child must have rocked his crib across the hardwood to the door, which he then opened by turning the knob. The next step would have been to work the door back and forth, thereby loosening the hinges. He would have used his thumbnail then to remove the screws. Sheer conjecture, but was there any other way to explain how it happened that when Trover came up to check later, the door was leaning against his crib and Mary Ann sat with the stunned look of someone who'd witnessed a dismembering and expected to be next?

Poor Mary Ann. In the same way, another day, he rode his crib over to hers. She must have watched in silence, weighted with dread, ripping at her lashes. Watched as he proceeded with journeymanlike purpose to turn the nuts and bolts, remove the rods, and shake the ends away from the sides. Hearing the crash, Louise and Trover came running, and there was their tiny pink-clad girl, kneeling on the mattress, on the floor, her safe nest in shambles around her. Face in hands, she was sobbing softly, despairingly, shamingly. She would not look at her parents or the tiny, smug barbarian with whom they'd forced her to cohabit.

The car wash was cozy and dark as a dreary day. A zippy mechanical thing with busy arms whirled around and around the truck. Louise laughed out loud to see the thing come around front and hammer heavy rain onto her windshield and then, like some fun-loving, larking dervish, go banging off, only to come back and douse her again. She loved the dense privacy, the water coursing down over all the windows now, splashing the roof, then the dim rhythmic scrub-glub of the brushes. What an unexpected pleasure. God bless and keep the technocracy. She sat back and closed her eyes.

As for Michael, no crib, of course, could hold him after that. They were afraid they'd have to buy him one with solid sides and a lid. "Call Tupperware," Trover joked. "Have them custom-make something."

The boy devised masterly spite campaigns that grew even more inventive as he matured. At three, when Louise refused to take him along shopping, he took all the air out of her tires. He drew Magic Marker sea creatures on her bathroom curtains. Punched holes in the plaster and gouged tabletops and kept his sister in line with a full range of subtle torments, invisible pressures. She sat when he said "sit." Played games she hated and hated even more having to let him win. She fetched for him and tidied up his room. It seemed Mary Ann hardly grew at all; year after year she was like a fine doll, fragile, endangered.

She was a perennial classroom favorite. By contrast, Michael's teachers were always "appalled," "distressed," and "horrified." Michael wanted to be the teacher; he wanted to be chief interlocutor and stump the teacher; he wanted to sing and build things at workbook time. "Mrs. Kleeve," a gray, tic-ridden man whispered in her ear at conference time, "your son is wrecking my life."

Whole faculties denounced her son, forcing Louise into the error of assuming a reciprocal disaffection. Time after time he amazed her. He wrote these same implacable teachers praiseful verses. He'd discover among them a certain penchant for pralines or sourballs and beg a bewildered Louise to procure these items. There was neither irony nor guile in these efforts. He liked his teachers, no, loved them. Weekends he missed and prayed for them.

As time passed, he grew the way a storm gathers, sucking up darkness and dirt and ferocity, every day a shade more menacing. Once, watching him strum a vegetable grater with a rasp, Louise had asked facetiously, "And what number is that on the nuisance list?" "Nineteen," he replied happily. He ran upstairs and returned with a handwritten sheet. "Buggers" he called them, and the list included whole subsections devoted to mouth sounds alone, tongue clucks and lip smacks, gurglings, slurpings, six kinds of burp.

And demure Mary Ann had no such tactical catalog, though she did keep on her nightstand an old biscuit tin in which Louise discovered a small miscellany of her own. "They're parts of me," explained Mary Ann. She pointed out a root from her first molar extraction. A bashful scattering of eyelashes. "This callus came off my heel," she said. "And this is just a common toenail paring." She begged her mother not to betray this cache to Michael. "He'll eat them," she said.

Considering the extent of her son's bluster, the riskiness of his villainies, it always amazed Louise that he did not suffer repercussions gladly. Not even with the sardonic acceptance of the true roué. Spanked, scolded, he would fly into a state of thrashing bewilderment, savage desperation, his eyes anguished behind great shimmering sheets of tears.

The child was unsnubbable. Rebuked, he might hound his victim for days, building a case for himself, rebutting the grudge, as if it were that, not his crime, that should be subject to review, to binding arbitration. "Try to remember," he'd say, "I'm just a little kid. Come on now, kiss me. KISS ME!" And when he was in the process of suing for peace, Mary Ann was no match for her brother. "All right, I love you!" she'd scream in the end. "Now go to bed!" And that would suffice for his purposes. "God, thanks," he said once, swinging around the newel-post, taking the steps two at a time, in sweet, unburdened bounds.

When Geggo was still alive, the year before she died, in fact, and she was all bone, bituminous eyes, and white fluff, she'd come to the Knoll for what turned out to be her last visit. One Saturday afternoon Louise drove Geggo and the children into Neisstown for a matinee. On the way home Michael ordered her to stop for a Mr. Chock-o-Pop. In the clammy grip of late August Louise, feeling wretched and faint and hardly amenable to the hard sell, wanted only to rush home and drive them all into the purple-blue bliss of the swimming pool. "There's ice cream in the freezer," she said, letting the frosty words cool her tongue, her temper.

With demonic volition, Michael kept up a needling that was like intricate tattoowork on Louise's brain. He was also pressing too close to his sister in the back seat. It was all Louise could do to ignore him, and then finally, quite miraculously, the car fell into stuporous, humid silence.

Moments later, stopped for a red light, Louise glanced behind her in time to spot Mary Ann all folded into herself and whimpering. "What's going on back there?" Louise demanded.

"Nothing," Mary Ann said in a faint disenfranchised voice.

"Like da dickens," Geggo cried. "I am witness. He iss digging wit elbow."

"Please give him what he wants," Mary Ann said, sobbing.

He was holding his sister for ransom and Louise was appalled. "Not on your life," she said. "Louise Pegeen Kleeve does not capitulate to terrorism." She looked to her grandmother. "Hasn't history adequately demonstrated the folly of that?"

Geggo stared at her. "Better ve stop for Pop Chock."

"Never! Now listen, you goon, get away from your sister. Get over on your own side."

"OK, I'm over. Is this really my side? Do I own it now? Is this my side forever and ever?"

Louise snapped on the radio. The Vandellas shouted Michael down. But when they had gone several more miles, just as Louise was pulling onto the interstate, Geggo turned the radio off with a vengeance. "He is up to old tricks again. I catch him stab little ribs with beeg Crayon."

"It is not! It's a green Pez."

"I saw dat! He geev poor little leg nasty pinch."

With her free hand Louise reached back and grabbed a gobbet of fat cheek, a move she learned from the nuns. "Wait'll we get home," she shrieked. "You're a dead man!"

"Holly modder!" Geggo wailed. "Stop machine. Dis ees best vay in vorld to have accident." She thrust hands ridged like topography maps under Louise's nose. "See how I shake. You vant feel my heart?" She scrabbled in her handbag and fished out a pack of Luckies. Years before, some quack had recommended cigarettes to her for "nerves," and once a year she felt the need to take the cure. Louise punched in the lighter, but it took three times—Geggo was trembling so—until the cigarette was lit. Her grandmother never inhaled. The smoke came out in round mouthfuls, thick, terse spurts. From the back seat came Michael's gristled voice: "Put out that cigarette, croneface!"

Geggo obeyed without question, stubbing the butt so hard that one half snapped into her lap and melted a hole in the rayon before Louise could retrieve it. Geggo started to curse and pray in Slovenian. Tossing the cigarette out the window, Louise cut the wheel viciously to the right, swerved over the berm, and bounced them into somebody's rye field.

The three victims seemed to come into joint possession then of some profound primal know-how on coping with bullies. Tiny, dry Geggo turned around and grabbed Michael's hair the way, when pressed, she used to manhandle little Louise. Louise, grown up now, ran around to the back door, flung it open, and wrangled down both arms as he rushed to protect his face. Mary Ann pummeled and pushed from behind. Persuaded thus, he eventually tumbled out on the grass, where they set on him like a pack of she-wolves. They were all three catchers in the rye that day, and he was conclusively caught. They were deaf to every plea and threat and act of contrition, and the way he shrieked and howled, it was surely a miracle, a true measure of heaven's blessing, that nobody stopped to rescue the child from their clutches.

Pulling out onto the highway again, Louise looked back and saw the nest their skirmish had made in the sea of ripe grain. A cup of struggle, she thought. Salt glazed her lips and tasted somehow sweet, for it was the height of the feminist movement. But Michael had also noted the matted area. "See," he said, sobbing. "God saw you jerks trying to kill me. He marked the spot."

A year passed, maybe two. One summer evening, out of sheer rambunctiousness, Michael shot a young rabbit with his BB gun. So stunned and heart-stricken was the child that he carried the wounded creature to the house, where it died in his arms. A long time later, when he stopped trembling, he buried it under the rhododendron, marking the spot with a roofing slate on which he printed, in solemn parody of the canine grave near the pool, "Socks was a fine American Rabbit."

What was Louise to make of this? Had some wildness in him died with the last thump of that small wild heart? Could the course of a life turn on the quiet passing of a spotted rabbit? By what logic did the gentle child who was Michael come from that spawn of early rapacity? Had he been getting all his lawlessness in before he could be held responsible? Or had he foreseen the future, the peaceable thing he would become, and was he sowing his wild oats before marrying himself to himself forever?

And Mighty. What had she been up to all those years as Mary Ann? Giving them a breather before lowering the boom? Tricking them with whimpers, so they would not assay the strength of her mettle, would not marshal against her? Louise saw her children then, and she saw them now. The days between carried too much muddy weather to see through. Things changed as you slept. While you were digging dirt out of grooves and flirting with poets and botany, your children traded natures like baseball cards, and then one day, when you had better be minding the matter at hand, you said, "Well, fancy that!"

Louise looked out upon her dripping hood and for several moments sat disjointed and confused. Where was she? A garage of some sort. The smell of disinfectant and dirty water, the chicken feather reek of wet cement. Oh, the Heap Big Clean, of course!

Well, she'd done it. The truck was gleaming, and she sitting high up and delighted with herself. She turned the key and let the comforting bloom of ignition surround her. Throwing the stick into drive, she started to ease forward. When the truck appeared to balk, she checked the emergency brake. But that had already been released. Perhaps it was stuck in some mechanistic limbo between gears. She jammed the selector back as far as it would go. This time when she gave it gas, the Jeep coughed forward and settled back again. What was that? Louise turned off the ignition and listened, certain she'd heard something dragging across her roof. But whatever it was seemed to be gone now.

She tried again, giving it a timid, coddling shot of gas. More scrapings, a sound like the soft crumpling of aluminum cans. Leaning forward, she squinted up through the windshield. Was it her imagination or did the Heap Big Clean have a particularly squat roof? She sighed and stepped down from the cab.

Faced with the range of copper joints and bushings and elbows crimping the soft fiberglass of her cap, Louise could no longer deny the size of her predicament. She was pinched in by plumbing, and it was clear now there was no honorable way out of the Heap Big Clean. She returned to the cab and lit a cigarette. She smoked another, three more after that. Geggo had been right about dressing well for accidents. Got up as she was, how could she go romping about in search of a phone? Who would she call anyhow? A service station? The fire department? She certainly didn't want Trover to know.

Maybe she'd just wait it out. She hardly ever went to doctors, and nothing had yet taken her. And Louise had rare powers of her own, not the least of which involved the ability to clear small spaces, incongruously sane and green and melodious in the midst of chaos. So there, in her fabricated springtime, she sat now, hardly discomposed at all, dreaming of mystical deliverance, remembering better times, or thinking nothing whatsoever. Thinking nothing, nothing, just smoking and humming. Sometimes she just hummed, like a bee in the sweet hollow tree of her skull.

Only when another vehicle pulled up behind did the situation take on the sting of immediacy. A small foreign car, it gave off a vague familiarity she did not feel pressed to investigate. Any second now the driver would meander up to see what was keeping her. He would peer in and observe at close range her pasty face and deranged attire. He would think she'd come from somewhere scarier than sleep. Panic blew out her brain; the engine boomed to life. She jammed the pedal to the floor, and like something huge and prehistoric and pea-brained, the Jeep leapt stupidly out of its stall.

Despite the harsh effects—the shearings and scrapings, the clink of fittings hitting the cement—in those few brief seconds of breaking out, Louise felt wondrously sprung, disencumbered, high above strife. Bits of debris rained down behind her, and then, thundering over the tarmac, she spotted a large metal sign in the rearview mirrow. It was dangling from a chain, by one corner, over the exit ramp. WRONG WAY, it said. *Wrong way. Wrong way.* It struck up a chant beneath the giddy tension that held her rigid behind the wheel and kept the Jeep tracking, over the curb, across the street, up over another curb, on two wheels. For an instant, she fully expected to plow into the Fotomat in front of LaVolsi's Beer and Soda, but the truck chose to clear it by inches and then shot off at a hard angle, back into the street, west toward Trexler Avenue.

At the intersection she hung a right and rumbled down to Main, the shimmy under her skin more pronounced than the Jeep's. Taking the turn wide, she also ran the red light and saw with horror how quickly her crimes were piling up.

It would be unwise, she realized, to drive by borough headquarters, and she could not possibly turn right off Main up Elm toward home without confronting the Heap Big Clean, where already neighbors would be assembling to sight-see the damages. At Elm she hung a right and headed out Stony Lonesome Road, into the hinterlands. To mask the inevitable siren wail, she turned on the radio. When no sound seemed forthcoming, she looked up and saw that her antenna was gone, detached, no doubt, in the clash of her escape. She avoided checking the rear and side mirrors to keep the law out of her life as long as possible.

Deep in the feed corn and dairy country now, she coveted nothing more substantial or less bounteous than miles, miles of miles between her and Lorraine. She and Osberg had passed through these same hamlets so many springs ago: New Jerusalem, Huffs Church, Windsor Castle, East Texas, Persia, Goshenhoppen, Bath. Fourteen miles to King of Prussia. Two to Vera Cruz. The world would swallow her up, and nobody would think to look for her in places with such remote and ghostly names.

In a town called Yellow House the sight of a wide housewife with a full-bristled broom made Louise remember tormentingly her own unswept porches. When they came to get her, would they notice and would they "talk"? A ring of pensioners stood watching them sandblast the hotel, abraded brick blazing in the sun like the walls of a lost city. GEE, AIN'T GOD GOOD? said the man-size letters on the side of Elmer's Autobody Barn. The butcher crossed to the palmist's house in a bloody apron. Like a flea in the cotton wool of dailiness, Louise snuggled into the spirit of this town, feeling progressively more secure. But then she remembered the one other time in her life she'd physically fled the law.

"Here comes Bruno!" somebody yelled as she and Frank and several others stood on the forbidden novitiate steps, not going anywhere, just standing there, testing. The warning scattered them like grackles. On the naïve assumption that toilets were private and inviolable, Louise had raced all the way to the day school "kimmy," slipped into one of the booths and sat down. Even when Sister Bruno's square black toes appeared on the gray tiles, Louise clung to the illusion of sanctuary. So convinced was she of this most fundamental of human immunities that when her door flew open, the scream she unleashed was more in startlement than terror. Then Bruno yanked her off the hopper, worked her over, and slammed her back into the seat. Louise still dreamed about that incident. From that day on she knew there were no good hiding places left. In the dreams no matter where she went, even deep in the earth, Bruno still sniffed her out and shook her off, like a buried bone.

Again she remembered herself. What time could it be? Moments like these Louise repented her routine dismissal of Trover's watches. Normally her own sense of time was more than reliable, but today was already deranged beyond her small knack; even the light looked incalculable to her. With some relief she remembered the clock on the dash; it said nine-ten. She did some hasty figuring. The bus would arrive in Neisstown at ten-twelve. Louise was still two longish legs of a triangle from the depot. Many miles south of Lorraine now, she had to be at least forty-five minutes from home. Another half an hour from there into Neisstown. That made an hour and quarter right there, not even counting the time she needed to change. Frank would panic if alighting from the bus, she didn't spot Louise immediately. Indeed, if Louise were even a little late, it would mean her having to search the depot building dressed for bed, and that was out of the question.

So Louise proceeded in the keenness of many necessities and evasions. By now the entire borough would be alerted and looking for her. What, she wondered, would they finally charge her with? Entering and breaking? Leaving the scene too abruptly? She trained her sights on the rising sun and tended generally northeast. Eventually she came out on the Neisstown road, safely down country from Lorraine.

She hit the terminal at exactly ten-ten. Slouching behind the wheel, she waited like something lurksome and unsavory. As soon as she spotted Frank, she would lie on the horn until the nun spotted her. But by ten-fifteen the bus hadn't yet arrived.

There was another clock within view, this on the peeling cupola of the depot building. Louise kept an idle eye on it; to her grave annoyance, the bus was now fifteen minutes late, twenty. She built up a massive resentment of Trailways while she waited. It was perverse, inhuman, unfair. She sat up and looked at the clock harder. Was she seeing things, or did it say *nine*, not *ten*-forty? A wave of disorientation swayed her. Then she was just plain outraged. Why would a bus station try to mislead suffering humanity with a false show of time?

It took her another thirty seconds to figure it out. It was the Jeep clock that was off. Typically she'd not troubled to turn it back when the rest of the country returned to standard time. She was living in a floating hour. The thought made her feel infinitely marooned, past rescue, like a stranded astronaut. See what happened when you consulted with clocks: waste; chaos; alienation.

She crumpled deeper into her big coat and lit a cigarette. She hummed and thought of summer. She hummed the smoke slowly. What was there, after all, but to abide, to wait quietly in the trickiness of space and time while the world took its sweet time catching up with her?

CHAPTER

14

"What do we do first? Cake mixes or bakery?" Spot leaped onto the electric mat and bowed to the door as to a lively dance partner. Michael followed him inside. At this hour the supermarket was nearly deserted. A single checker stood leaning against her register. Spot pointed to the dainty pink cursive over her hefty bosom. "I keep telling you, Dotty, you should put your weight right up there next to your name." He spun Michael around so she could see the hard facts on the back of his all-star jacket. "Just like Mr. Kleeve here."

"Bite your tongue," she said. "Hey, Russell, it's the boys from hunger again." A white-haired, whey-faced man in a paper hat waved to them from his office window.

"Hi, Mr. Reichard," they said.

"We got a lot of folks coming in here just to peek at the magazines, but you're the only ones come to look at the food." The manager presented his realm to them with a flourish. "Help yourself," he said. "Anything for team morale."

The boys exchanged grins.

"Hey," said Dotty, "we got a new line in this week. Canned raspberries, blueberries, gooseberries. Great pictures on the labels, real lifelike."

"No thanks," said Spot. "Last time we looked at a lot of fruit on an empty stomach, I got the runs."

"Anyhow," said Michael, "we go more or less for the heavy-duty stuff—fudge sauce, bear claws, Polar Bars . . ." He made his voice viscous. "Peanut buther!"

Mr. Reichard laughed. "Aisle three," he said. "But then you gentlemen know your way around by now, say?"

"Blindfolded," said Spot, and the boys play-pushed each other out of the way to be the first into the aisle.

Arranging his face in assorted raptures, Michael cradled a forty-ounce Skippy. He tried to smell it through the glass. "Oh, chunky," he crooned, "my life is nothing without you."

Spot picked up a tiny jar, ribbons of grape jelly artfully swirled in with the peanut butter. He held it to the light like a rare jewel. "Here's one for the connoisseur," he said. "Throw some chocolate chips on top; stick the whole shebang under the broiler. Tastes just like a Reese's peanut butter and jelly cup."

"Reese's doesn't make a peanut butter and jelly cup."

"Well, they're crazy not to," said Spot, skipping off.

"Wait up," said Michael. "Think I'll get a small-size Skippy. For the mouse."

Spot retraced his steps backward, squinted at Michael over his shoulder. "For the what?"

"The mouse. *My* mouse. Dad got me a humane trap last month, and the first time I set it up, it worked like a charm. Only thing was, I didn't know what to do with the mouse once we had him."

"Easy. Drive him out about ten miles and kiss his little buns good-bye."

Michael shook his head vehemently. "It's cold out there. He'd freeze. I mean, what's the point in a humane trap if you're just going to . . ."

"So what's the peanut butter for?"

"He has to eat, doesn't he? I mean, what's the point of a humane trap—"

"I know," said Spot, "if you're just going to starve him to death."

"Exactly," said Michael. "He loves peanut butter, and besides, it's easy to squeeze through the wire mesh."

"Right," said Spot.

At the deli case they stood several moments in reverential awe. Among the heartier concoctions a tray of ambrosia shimmered and quivered, as sparkly and ephemeral-looking as a mound of spring snow. "Maybe I could just get a quarter pound of creamed herring," Michael finally said.

"You hate the stuff, Kleevinsky."

"I know, but if I don't enjoy it so much, I wouldn't have to feel so guilty, would I?"

"Man, you are twisted. I had calories to burn, I'd shoot the works on the pineapple cheesecake. My dad makes one called the Big Cheese Cheesecake. It takes six packs of cream cheese, eight eggs, a tub of heavy cream." Spot licked the words as they left his lips.

"I thought your dad was into whole earth and stuff?"

Spot shrugged. "Nobody's airtight. Anyhow, I think he puts buckwheat groats in the crust or something."

"OK, tell me again what's in the cake. Slower."

"Coming right up." As they walked on to processed meats, Spot recited the recipe again, this time upping the proportions, like a good host dishing out extra. Michael thought of the pastry cookbook he'd bought his mother for Christmas two years earlier. The next month he was laid up with water on the knee. Supine, inactive, he could afford even fewer calories than before. At his request, instead of bringing him dinner every night, Louise read to him out of the cookbook.

"I used to hate this junk," Spot said, holding his cheek against the smart-looking Oscar Meyer see-through pack that said "Minced bologna." "How could I have been such a fool?"

"Jumbo baloney!" Michael cried, as one encountering a childhood friend. "My dad goes on these kicks, see. He'll go months munching out on nothing but one thing. One time it was jumbo and Mr. Mustard sandwiches. Another time it was Limburger and onion. Lox and bagels. It's been Mini-Wheats, bananas, and milk every morning now for about six years."

"Put sugar on them?"

"On what?"

"Them Mini-Wheats?"

Michael smiled. "Once he was into these fifteen-dollar freak-out pies from Larger-Than-Life Bakery. He was trying to quit drinking, and my mom said he needed the sugar. Man, those babies were humongous, and he kept them coming in for about a month. We couldn't keep up with the suckers. That's all we had room for. No meat. No potatoes, just strawberry wallow."

"God!" Spot was breathing hard. "I mean, what'd they look like, them pies?"

"Clouds nine and ten."

Spot stood rapt before him. Michael might have been recounting tales of untold riches—fourteen-karat bowling balls, galleons leaking ducats.

"Know what I've been thinking about a lot lately?"

"What?" said Spot, eyes still shining.

"One time we went to this smorgasbord place. Awesome pigout. Lobster bisque, shrimp, spareribs, ham with raisin sauce. The works. I went back three times. Kept shoveling it in until there was just one thing left on my plate."

Spot egged him on with lascivious eyes. But Michael said, "No way, man. I was bloatus to the maxus." He gave his friend a doleful glance. "Now I can't seem to forgive myself for leaving it on my plate."

"What the heck was it? A sand tart. A butterscotch brownie?"

Michael opened his mouth and then snapped it shut cagily. "Tell you tomorrow, Raindance. Give you something to look forward to."

"Asshole!" Spot drove Michael before him with whisking blows from his leather gloves. Michael paid for his peanut butter, and they left.

Once back in the cab of the Leper, boxed for travel, the boys always slumped into sudden exhaustion. It seemed to Michael that some false bottom dropped away then and he'd find himself somehow under things, the day's thump and tread dimly audible overhead, his and Spot's laughter still ringing in the aisles, but remote, disembodied, like the campfire ditties drifting home from Tumbling Run. He could still feel the slap of Spot's glove on his satin back as he sank through layers of the day's echoing.

They headed out of town, the chalky hieroglyph moon bouncing back and forth across the road. It was the road, of course, not the moon, that skittered so, as if the engineers, in their whimsical fondness for loops and twists and switchbacks, cared not a fig whether or not their project eventually saw people home.

Sometimes, riding like this in the chilly dark, they talked quietly about serious concerns. How it felt to lose, to win, to appear less or more than another man. Parents, divorce, *real* hunger, nuclear dreams. Was there life after wrestling, life after death? Life! Even the word was strange, rootless, in the rolling dark, the dug-in silence under the darting moon. Sometimes they talked about girls, confronting the subject with similar wistfulness but deeper caution than when bandying menu items.

Girls would turn you to fat, too. The time you gave them always came out of your commitment to discipline, to a good night's sleep. Girls expected to be taken out weekends, but having starved for days, the Saturday night match out of the way—weak, wrecked—you wanted nothing more than to binge out privately, disgustingly, then crash in your own sweet bed. He could hardly blame Emma Jean Hontz for pouting. Wasn't much of a deal, going out with a guy whose matches you felt obligated to attend, and then after collecting another pin, the jerk pats you on the head and splits for home.

He didn't know quite what to make of her either, this sturdy German girl with the heart-shaped face and hands larger than his own. Emma Jean was lively and goodhearted, but there was, in her eyes and on her mouth, a certain set, the look of a face in front of a mind made up, made up as neatly as the quilt-covered bed she would someday occupy with some steady type named Dreisbach, or Sprecher.

And there Michael was, never as much as the present moment in hand: how dazedly he followed his homework into another day, the wrestling schedule into the next week's match, always a little surprised to arrive, to be him, to be. Holding Emma Jean's hand was somehow the same as pressing bedrock or scrimmaging the Pack boys. Together they were—yes, he thought, the word was "inert."

They passed the House of Seven Sours, where among the pickups parked in front was one with a large field-dressed buck lashed to its roof, a raw red gash halving its rump where he'd been gutted. Neither boy let on that he'd seen.

From this point the road combed steadily upward through hills studded with small family farms, an occasional three-bedroom split-level or rancher. To the left, tucked among scrub growth and evergreen, just before the flume of woodland into which the road took a hooking right, was the one-room schoolhouse. Someone could buy that old building for a song, he thought, fix it up for his wife. Once the kids started coming, though, they'd have to move; the house sat too close to the road. Just yards from the wide front door stood a bare oak, its trunk thick as an oil tank. It would have been there, then, when German-speaking children came down from Sally Ann Furnace, came out of the hills and off the farms, with their slates and copybooks.

Spot geared down, and the old V-8 engine dragged and the truck pulled through the serried hills, the moon like the moving dot on sing-along lyrics. But something had come between the two boys, something with icy breath, and Michael was afraid to look at his friend, humming quietly beside him. His thoughts went white, and he had no thought of the ones waiting at home, no memory of touching or hurting or of feeling invincible. It was as though he had fallen into step with the German schoolchildren, single file, woolly white, lost in awful time. When they passed the ancient gristmill, he thought he heard the millrace rushing between his ears and, farther on, set back in its hull of creaking timbers, was the Ironmaster's House, itself a ghost ship against the gremlin moon.

A sudden vision of Erica Lavender rescued him. It was along this stretch, he remembered, that she and Yoder kept their daily trysts. He closed his eyes, and if it isn't summer, her presence makes it seem that way. Her face shining in the early dark, her scent suffusing the air. She wears a yellow dress of some soft, filmy material; her sleeves flutter like curtains at the car window. Tears on her cheeks are rain on marble. A strand of soaked hair undercuts her pretty cheekbone.

It goes without saying her jerkwad husband has been up to his old tricks, staying out, yelling around and smashing her treasures: the dresser set from her grandmother and the peach-colored jar sitting on her sill filling with fire; other things, nice things she's made with her own dainty hands.

Erica Lavender does not get out of the car but meets his concern with brimming eyes. Not knowing how else to help, he offers to wrestle off the bum she's married to. She shakes her head no, in a miserable, despairing way. He feels strapped and absurd, utterly useless. In his excruciating inarticulateness, he cannot explain that his impulse has something to do with loving her, also to do with turning back a person's power when it's outstripped his good sense.

But now old Ox would probably weigh three hundred pounds. All that beer and tongue souse at the Legion Hall, football muscle run to blubber. And wouldn't they all look like dolts, even Underdonk, for taking on a wimpy schoolboy not half his size? Compromise a man like that, and there's no telling what he'd do.

He looked up to see Spot leaning over the wheel, eyeing him insinuatingly. "Hey, no wet dreams in my limo here."

"Shut the hell up," he said, and his friend gave him a puzzled glance and withdrew. "Just drive, OK?"

Spot had a heavy foot, and the truck, with its worn shocks and throaty motor, seemed to gobble up turns out of its own belching, backfiring desire. From the crest of Kauffman's Hill they plunged blindly into the full velvet of the valley. They were really cruising now, letting the hills lift them up and ease them down. It was always a temptation to cut loose over so sportive a landscape, ride inches above the seat, limbs gone liquid, stomach rising, wild travel. In the spring the roads would be running like streams with small lives, raccoons, possums, rabbits, young creatures in the gleaming bewilderment of their first weeks as whatever they were. The shiny fur and tiny pumping hearts, the eyes still-burning with eternity. So from April through August he made Mighty and his friends hold their speed on the back roads. Sometimes he felt like some kind of shepherd, a husband. He'd read somewhere that "husband" meant one who manages and protects. He was not yet sixteen. He was too young to be saddled with the welfare of women and wild things.

Spot slowed as they approached his place, a rusty Silver Streak trailer between Upper Black Eddy and Kemp. He lived there with his father, a man so possessed by the one American Indian buried deep in his lineage that he'd changed his name to Grayrain. Mr. Grayrain described himself as the "Champion of the green world." He wore blue jeans and T-shirts put out by the herbal tea companies. Spot called him Steve, and Steve called himself Spot's best friend. They did grass together after meals, and when Spot asked his father's permission for things, Steve rebuked him. "Hey, man, it's your life," Michael heard him say. But Spot, ruled mainly by his sport, hardly had the time or the energy to take advantage of a liberal up-bringing. It seemed to Michael that Steve had no force in his limbs or fire in his eyes. His thick hair was solid white now, and Michael wondered if it hadn't all started with one spot, hatching itself daily, feather by feather.

"Trailer's dark," Michael said.

"Steve went down to Jersey, that antinuke caucus. Guess he'll be gone another day or so."

"Hey, you're welcome to stay with us."

Spot grimaced. "Nah, best stick around and keep an eye on the coffee can."

To foil the crooks and creeps and marauders of this world, the lower section of the Kleeve driveway had been left uninvitingly rough. Spot and Michael rumbled onto the stretch of hard yellow dirt. Over the small cement bridge now, around the first curve where the macadam began, pulling around the wide bend, skimming past the lone red oak, sharp against the dark fields, the mountains looming grayly beyond that, the loose swag of purpled sky. And then the road shot straight and away, the grade easy, and both boys gasped as the moon leapt out from behind the fantail of white pine where the ground crested. The moon was polished silver now, pulsing light, and a stiff wind shivered the pines, trembling the seed heads in the border garden, raking curled leaves like dry little skulls across the tarmac. On the gazebo, last summer's deck chairs. Widows rocking, thinking, waiting in the wind.

The kitchen window carried the same wallop as the moon. Coin-bright, sharply struck. The background blur would be his mother by the stove. The figure up front, just behind the glass, was motionless. Solid black against the bright fluorescence, and the countless values of black outside were pressing in. The shadows and pines, the gray hulk of the house, the tangle of dark through the yard where the nun seemed to be looking. From where she stood, Michael wondered, could she see the moon? Raising her arm, she sipped something crimson from a jelly glass.

"Who the heck is that?" Spot asked.

"Don't know," said Michael, not wanting to say "Frank," not wanting to go into it.

CHAPTER
15

"I had a dream," said Louise. "About rabbits."

"Your nun still sleeping?" Trover replied.

"What a funny dream," she said.

"You know I don't like listening to people's dreams. Too long, and they never add up."

"This one does."

"DeTurk's picking me up"—he checked his watch—"in about *two* seconds."

"In the beginning," she began, "there's only one rabbit, a nice polite white one. Time passes, and then there are two." Drawing a breath, she gauged his mood, then hurried the words out. "Both diesels, both featuring four on the floor and mud flaps. One white, one brown."

He peered into his cereal.

"Well, naturally, they multiply. Two becomes three, four, five . . ."

"Naturally," he said, sipping the meniscus of milk from his bowl.

"The dream keeps filling up with rabbits, in shades of buff and tan and ecru."

"God bless ecru."

"Winter comes; the night is bitter cold. There they are, all huddled together, noses nuzzling the porch, plugged in with those fat extension cords we buy them for when the temperature drops below ten. So many bunnies at the dugs. Spring rolls around. They're constantly sick and disabled. I have to exercise them to keep the tail pipes from rusting, the seals from drying out. Seems it's always state inspection time. Oh, those endless rotations. Drop one off, pick one up, drop one off, pick one up. Well, you know how it goes. Gets so I can't cope anymore. One day I drive the whole lot of them so far into the sticks they'll never find their way back. I park them in front of monasteries and barns, hoping kindhearted people will take them in."

"What do you call that, Louise—a disgruntled mother fable?"

"As I said, it was a dream. A *dream.*"

"Dream, my foot. Dreams don't work like that. You made it up."

"So what if I did?"

"Is this another way of saying that you resent your own children?"

"Trover, I'm talking cars. We have too many. They drive *us.* Our life is cars," Despite the strain of increasing pique, Louise's tone retained a surface evenness, plastic but fragile, like the skin on scalded milk. If she raised her voice, he would double the ante, and there were guests to consider. Gideon, who'd heard it all before, and then Frank, behind the white door of the guest room, before whom they had yet to expose themselves as a tribe of louts and lowbrows.

"Bottom line, Louise: Maybe raising a family is just too much trouble for you?"

"Forget it, Leopold. I'm not biting." Once she would have danced on the end of his line for an hour, frantically defending herself, as a sentient creature, as a model of American motherhood, as a deep thinker. To go on living was impossible lest she be squarely, certifiably in the right. "I'm trying to be fair," she'd sniffle, fairness the sweet open sea she longed for, the only fair way out.

But what did *he* care for fairness? He was a lawyer. He could not afford the luxury of justice, not when he was pledged to prevail. The pool he had to swim in was called the winner's circle. Without winning, he would dehydrate and die writhing. It became clear he would never, never concede her a noble thought, a virtuous episode, would let her neither die nor off the hook. Louise had had to learn to live without convincing him.

"I rest my case," he said.

"Boob."

"I said, I rest my—"

"Consumer!"

"Fine," he said, his voice a bad seed soaked in sarcasm, swelling, sending tendrils up the stairs after the sleepers. Nudge them awake. The one thing will cramp her style is a witness. "Tell you what," he said. "You go out and bust your hump for a buck and I'll squawk every time you buy some little doodad. I'll stay home and invent bogus dreams and morality plays."

She hit him with a forcible whisper. "The gross feeder is man in the larva state."

"Thoreau," he said. "So?"

She ironized her smile.

"Goddamn worm metaphors for breakfast," he grumbled.

"What Thoreau was trying to say was you need too much."

Trover stared at her. "He meant *me?*"

DeTurk had pulled up outside, and Louise knew she was home free. She could say almost anything now in the reasonable certainty that Trover was not about to rip his clothes off in front of a client.

"Name a grosser feeder; I dare you. You're omnivorous, insatiable. You imbibe, you buy, you—you're going to be too hot in that hat," she said suddenly.

Someday the guests would be gone, she was thinking, and the kids off to wherever kids go, and no Len DeTurk riding up in the nick of time. Who would stop them then? It was with a measure of relief that she remembered the summers the children went to visit their grandparents, leaving Trover and Louise to their own devices. How idyllic those weeks, how judicious their disagreements. She and Trover had an intuitive grasp of the squabble launched in solitude, nothing at all standing between them and an infinity of distances. By sheer force of contumely and temper—and will!—they would be flung a million miles from each other, into orbits irrevocably separate. They would be lost to each other for all time. Alone, they knew better than to incite. They never fought outside the range of rescue.

Hand on the doorknob, Trover paused. "Don't get the new car all junked up inside," he said.

"Sleep easy on that score," she said. "I'll *never* drive that car."

"If it's such a burdensome thing, a late-model item, clean, paid for, don't bother driving it at all." Gathering his gear, he gave her a look like an old bruise. Eyes of a spurned suitor.

As if he were likely to poke her one and run, Louise hugged her ribs protectively. Then she lurched forward, her lips resting but only resting, on his cheek, for it had dawned on her that he might be gone for a while.

His arms were weighted with briefcase, duffel bag, and a navy-blue garrison cap. His chin was at half-mast. Just before leaving, he said, "Look, you can drive my car if you want. Just don't smoke in it."

* * *

"No regular milk?" Gideon was saying.

"Just two percent," Louise replied without looking up from the glossies. They were eight-by-ten prints Mighty had taken and developed herself. Rare finds. It was not Mighty's wont to leave things about, to expose what was fragile or valued to the family. Somebody might spill molasses on the prints or ruin them with cigarette burns or spoil them emotionally with a stupid question.

Gideon returned his cinnamon Life to the box. To avoid having to hob nob, she lost herself in the glossies. Wasn't that Gideon on the high dive, a spritelike thing, glowing in the dark? Gideon again, in tights, legs apart, his body lines as stark as the wand of broken light leaping from his fingers.

"What an extraordinary effect!" she said. "However did she do that?"

"Easy," said Gideon. "She gave me a penlight to use. It lets you write with light in the dark."

She gazed at him in amazement. This light-writing wizard, intermediary between her and the riddle that was Mighty Kleeve. She indicated a second picture, this one looking into a greenhouse, the girl inside strikingly disjunctive, her shoulders on one plane, her head quite plainly on another. Mighty's look of chary hauteur. "And this," she said. "Now how did the head get way over there?"

"Beats me," he said, buttering a doughnut.

Vaguely annoyed with the boy for exhausting his powers so soon, Louise returned to her perusals.

"What are you up to today?" he asked.

"Me?" she said. "What are *you* up to?"

"I'm hoping to get some serious picking in today."

She thought of potatoes, peppers, guitars. "Picking?"

"You know, knocking on doors, asking people if they have anything to sell."

"Such as?"

"You never come right out and say 'antiques.' Be dumb to educate the masses. Old stuff, I say. Junk. Once they let me in, I'm home free. Work my way down cellar, up in the attic. Pay dirt, man. Dry sinks, redware, Boston rockers."

How pretty he was, with his agate green eyes and long brown hair and dimpled chin. Old women would flit about, feeding him even as he stripped their plates from the rail, the rail from the wall, even as he made off with the mantelpiece.

"Junk," he repeated, his grin wired with cunning.

"Hey!" Louise cried. "Leave some doughnuts. Frank—Sister Innocent— my friend hasn't had breakfast yet." Gideon rolled the last doughnut back in the bag.

"Here's my problem," he said, as though she'd asked. "Can't get any real *meaty* pieces in the Triumph." He paused. "Mind if I bum the Jeep offa you today?"

"Sister Inn—Frances—Frank . . ." For her life she could not settle what to call her guest. "We're going into town. *We* need it."

"No, you don't. Trover's new Rabbit's out front. In a pinch, you can use *my* wheels. I'll show you how to hit the solenoid to get it started."

It rankled that Gideon knew more about the family holdings than she did. He kept score; he kept track. Knew what was tied up, what available. When Louise mislaid something, Gideon could locate it in seconds. With dazzling virtuosity, his mind worked to compute from the contents of her closets and drawers the precise mode and degree of their advantage to him. Doubtless, with no time lost, the new diesel had been translated into terms of availability of the vehicle most useful to him, the lowly Jeep.

Well, the bug was sitting out front awaiting Lum's wrecker; the Hornet was keyless. She had no intention of tapping Gideon's solenoid. Nor was she inclined toward trying to justify to him her continuing repudiation of the new diesel. Sometimes Louise had to remind herself that it was not always necessary to provide supplicants with itemized refusals. Sometimes you could just say no and be done with it. "No," she said.

"Wow!" he said. "You musta really did a number on the Jeep."

She raised her eyes slowly. His smile was small and tight, she thought, a twist of secret knowledge on the lip of his glass. She watched him pour what was left in the juice carton. Louise stood and walked to the window, affecting a thoughtful posture. Furtively she looked for his car. There it was, under the defoliated maple. Except to brood a little over its unsafe appearance, she'd never paid much attention to this vehicle. It was a tiny thing, low and roguish. Young in feeling, but old in years and decrepitude. Teal green, with orange rust paint, it rattled and coughed, and something in her unconscious coughed, too, and up came this solid fact from yesterday. There was no question about it; it was the same car that had pulled up behind her as she sat trapped in the Heap Big Clean. And no doubt but that the driver had been this shrewd young businessman, who would someday be master of all she surveyed and who swindled spinsters and widows out of their heirlooms.

"Cap's a little crumpled and the antenna's broken," she said (as if he hadn't already checked for himself).

"Smellin' like a rose," he said, shaking his head. "*Car wash* is totaled, man."

"Wow," she said softly. *Wow.* He had her where he wanted her, in his language. Blackmail was making them the same, full partners in a fowl business. *Wow?* He'd changed his mind about the milk and was filling his cereal bowl full, submerging what she took to be miscreant glee beneath a healthy adolescent appetite.

"Next time let a little air out," he said, swiping milk from his mouth.

"Out of what?"

"The *tires!* I was going to give you a hand, but psssssshewwwww—you were out of there like a shot."

Let the air out? What a perfectly elegant idea! Nothing difficult about that. So why had it been beyond her? Why did she have to meet her demons head-on, bash her way in and out of predicaments, as if every tight spot on earth had to be a hard birth to be worth it. Slowly she let the air out of her lungs. "Keys are in the truck," she said. "But of course, you know that. Tailgate sticks."

"Nothing around here works right, say not?"

"Say not" was one of the quainter localisms. No more "Dutch" than her own children, Gideon, unlike them, seemed to know instinctively what of the dialect was charming and what not. What was valuable about the homely local artifacts and what not. That a peacock teapot, say, was worth twelve tulip butter molds. According to Mighty, the boy was the youngest of eight and sometime around his sixteenth birthday his parents had declared themselves independent and taken to the open road in a Winnebago. For nearly two years Gideon had been shuttling back and forth between his married sisters, as each in her turn tired of having him around, of feeding him. Last year, shortly before he dropped out, two weeks after she'd rescued Bagel from the Acme dumpster, Mighty brought Gideon home from school and gave him a bowl of Life. The next time he requested cinnamon. Now when the boy was around, Louise felt pursued, in a way she was hard put to explain, and when he left, she checked her small collections, her graniteware and china dolls, and sometimes she counted the silver.

"Say not," he repeated.

"Not as a rule," she said obediently.

Louise left the door to the Room open so the nun would find her when she came downstairs. When at last she appeared in the doorway, she was wearing the skirt of her habit and a shirt that said "This Body Climbed Kilimanjaro."

"It was draped over the upstairs banister," Frank said sheepishly, "I couldn't resist."

"That's Trover's," Louise said, "and it's all a lie. He never climbed beans." Louise felt uneasy staring at the nun's chest. "Well," she said quickly, "I have a feeling, though, he's working up to it. Reading and buying stuff and eating his heart out. One day he'll up and go to Tanzania and legitimize his ice ax and that show-off shirt."

"You two don't worry much over the normal order of things."

"No, not much, I guess."

The nun caught her looking again. And Louise blushed. "Don't worry," said Frank. "I'll change again when we go out." Hands on hips, she gazed out over the little hamlet of plaster families. "What's all this?"

"My work," said Louise. "You know. Capital *M.* Capital *W.*"

"They remind me of—"

"I work from old photographs. Tintypes, daguerreotypes, or whatever. I keep the same basic sepias and add some sharp white accents. A little lace at the throat, a bow. White stockings are nice, don't you think?"

Frank hiked her skirt, danced out a black leg, laughing.

Smiling uneasily, Louise went on. "It's a certain quality I'm after, something the early camera, with its interminable exposure time, captured, well, without tryng (I won't, *can't* say 'by accident'). The sweet, sad, comic faces. They're *all* so unsure, even paterfamilias there, trying to be fierce, formidable. See how he's betrayed by the shadings of his inner life." She was pointing to a linotype in a gutta-percha frame. "Look at this man. The yearning and puzzlement, something holy and unquenchable in those eyes. The sense is not of time stopped, but of time tapped into. It's as though he saw beyond the camera and all the way through to us, strangers gazing upon his likeness a hundred years hence, as if he were saying, 'Oh, friends, I was and am. I'm caught in the common clay. Find my edges. *Shape* me!' "

The way Frank was staring, Louise knew she'd been a little unquenchable herself in the telling, that her cheeks were carmine with ardor. She slowed down and allowed some doubt to cool her tone, so as not to frighten her friend right off. "Well, what I mean is, it's as though the man were already mourning himself. And maybe his wife and those flap-eared offspring of his. These are the Harkins, by the way. Mary, Joseph, Sarah, Beatrice, and Luke, of New Bottle, England."

"Charmed," said Frank, and her pebbly laugh made Louise lean close, as if hearing something she'd needed to mark this woman as her old friend Frances Jane Gahagan. The giggle was almost as old as they were. Louise grinned in appreciation.

Frank curtsied to the Harkins family, then turned to Louise. "They're marvelous, I suppose, but don't you ever work from *new* pictures?"

"I tried that," Louise told her, "but instead of those heartbreakingly stiff spines I got calcified spirits, layer upon layer of obligatory good cheer, professional happiness. A lacquering so thick nothing shines through. Ask people to pose, and right away they want to do a Burger King commercial."

"But then you're limited to doing people's forebears."

"I'll do anybody," Louise said, "as long as they're seasoned first."

She explained how she'd found a photographer who specialized in antique folios. When her clients arrived, he dressed them in authentic period costume—Victorian, Edwardian, muttonchop sleeves, middy waists for the women; the men in stiff pointed collars, suspenders, bowler hats in their hands. Children in knickers and dropped waists. His studio had been the parlor of a great mansard-roofed, many-turreted turn-of-the-century mansion. The woodwork in mahogany and walnut, very somber, fragile ladies' chairs, a patriarch louring from every wall. "It's a house," Louise said, "impossible to be bubbly in."

Frank looked puzzled or troubled or bored, Louise had forgotten which. She hurried on, to cover all contingencies. "Honestly, you'd be surprised how it goes, how instinctively clients bend to my expectations. With minimal coaching, out of the sheer weight of ambience—from those dark details—the entire composition makes itself, everybody stumbling into place, a man's hand flying to his wife's shoulder, Vaseline smiles drying. And all without any technological gimcrackery beyond the use of those antiquated film processes." She pointed to the man in the gutta-percha frame. "See how he burns still."

Frank tapped the side of her nose and opened one eye wide, and another piece of her chinked into place. It might take awhile, but an old friend returned to you like a rusty skill. "Whooooaaaaa," Frank said. "Who *are* these people? I mean, if you remove them from their time, impose on them a false milieu, deck them out in granddad's pants, Louise, who in heaven's name are they?"

Louise shrugged and for a second looked at a loss. Then she rapped the piece she was working on, emphatically. "They're the ones I want!" she said.

"And that's that!" said Frank. "The way you're looking at me, I'm reminded of the time Bruno called you out of chapel line for wearing a rumpled blouse. You were so sweet and pathetic and defenseless, right before you hopped up on your old high horse. Then you told her in no uncertain terms how you'd put that blouse in the clothes *press,* pushed everything tight, and you couldn't imagine why the blouse hadn't come out ironed. You were *much* put-out over it. Bruno said, 'Louise, Louise, you're a natural enemy of the natural law!' "

"Then she made me iron all the prep blouses, until I figured out what it took to make the wrinkles relax."

When Frank laughed, she pressed in, letting each successive wave lap closer to your face, holding your eyes. "You dope," she said. "You scorched all the collars. Because of you, we looked positively *muddy* for months."

Louise grinned.

But Frank was looking elsewhere. "Oh!" she said. "Those people there. That's you, isn't it? And Trover. The kids . . ."

"I call them the Landers, short for *ausländers,* which is what our man Sprecher calls us under his breath."

"And the odd one, isn't that the young man I met last night?"

"That's Gideon all right. He rode over with us to the photographers, and it wasn't until the proofs came back that anybody noticed he'd sat in on the picture."

"But you could have ruled him out of the art."

"I did. But when Mighty saw what I'd done, she accused me of trying to exterminate him—an apt term, I must say."

"So doting mom that you are, you put him back."

"Like a stolen cookie," Louise said. "But it meant I had to start over from scratch. I've redone this piece a half dozen times. Just as I think I've got it, something awful happens." She pointed to Mighty's chipped breton.

"How'd that happen?"

Louise considered a moment before blurting, "Trover did it!"

Frank peered at her quizzically but did not pursue, disappointing Louise's sudden desire to tell the whole story (*oh, you don't know what it's been like all these years*). How she had to prepare for battle by hiding her pretty dolls, her grandmother's bisque, the graniteware coffeepots. Secrete them out of the animal's reach. Tell her how the Landers were too cumbersome to be readily moved, so that's where he headed when he needed heavy damages, finishing off a tantrum like the grand finale of a country kitchen band. Whack it with a skillet, throw a soup bowl at its most salient features. Lunatic! Beast! But Frank didn't ask. "Hmmmmmm," she said. "I would have suspected you instead. You were always so, uh, provocable."

Even the prickliness was coming back. A bit put-out, Louise said, "Somehow this is the one place in the world where I'm restrained as I have to be, as neat and meticulous as you, almost. As if this thing, this *art*, were the one I'd been saving myself for."

"Here," said Frank, proudly, handing Louise the shard she'd just found on the floor. It was from Mighty's hat.

"No!" she snapped. "I want it whole, not pieced. Is that too much to ask?"

Now it was Frank's turn to look stumped and uncertain. She twisted her wedding band. "Hey!" she said then. "Let's go to K Mart and buy something cheap. Cheap and trendy. I'm sick to death of quality—good shoes and durable cloth. Down with things that last and last! I haven't had anything really shoddy since eighth grade."

"Poor baby." Louise winked, or tried to.

"Still can't wink," Frank said teasingly, "not without scrunching up your face."

"Never learned to whistle either or make my tongue curl up like a little canoe."

Frank smiled and held it, and something in that beaming presence made Louise strange again, and shy. She bent quickly to her work, whisking plaster bits out of pinafore folds and wrinkles. She blew them away. "We could do the outlets, too, if you'd like," she said.

"You call it."

"Just let me clean up here," Louise said, realizing she hadn't accomplished a thing, feeling encroached upon, dislodged. "I'll be with you in a shake."

Louise watched her friend slip into the perpetual dusk of the dining room. She'd grown a little since Louise had last seen her, the September morning Frank left for good. Louise could still see Mrs. Gahagan, a big puffing ship of Sicilian piosity, hurrying her daughter out to the car where Mr. Gahagan waited impassively behind the wheel, reading *Grit*. Once Mrs. Gahagan had considered Louise a model Catholic teen, but when it became clear that she would not be going to Mount Mercy after all, the woman's goodwill turned to glittery suspicion. Louise was a secular influence now, a "bad companion." The flesh pads under Mrs. Gahagan's eyes were always damp and liverish. In the bright autumn light her black mustache and convergent brows showed almost dashingly. "You musn't stand by the car and wave goodbye," she told Louise. "Frances Jane will pray for the return of your desire to serve Christ, won't you, dear? Say hello to your grandmother for me. Does she still embroider those lovely altar linens? Good. Good. Run along, dear."

Frank wore a flat straw hat with a little rolled brim, a paper mum at her neckline, blue anklets. After Louise hugged her good-bye, Mrs. Gahagan shifted from nervous vigilance to simpering benignity. "God love you, dear," she called after Louise, who wished her skirt longer as she shuffled up Arbor Street. Overhead the elms had grown together, their ribs curved in such a way as to form a tapering perspective of Gothic arches. Shafts of sunlight burned through the boughs; medallions of light scattered at her feet. She ducked into the rhododendrons in front of Freeburn's house. Five minutes later the Gahagans' Packard floated by, Mom and Dad, and Frank ramrod straight between them.

Louise watched her friend's sassy little hat until it was black against the sunlight pouring into the notch at the top of Arbor, at which point the car blazed red-gold and was gone. Frank was gone. The Gahagans had finally closed the door on what had been for Louise a long siege of divided allegiance, the end of an era. Under the cathedral elms Louise walked home, gliding like a bride, and, despite her renunciations, felt processional and solemn and chosen. Humming "Adoro Te Devote," she went gladly to her life, a life as suddenly open and boundless as the fields that ran from behind Geggo's little house to the horizon. She walked another block, and then she began to run.

It had started in eighth grade. Frank and Louise had barely begun to notice boys when they were taken by convent fever. A dreamy young nun named Sister Serena had turned their heads to herself, then to higher things. They fought for her favor, for the privilege of dusting her desk, of hemming her dustrags. Of course, they wanted to be humble and good instead of blond and popular. Together, the next fall, they entered the prep school of the Sisters of the Sacred Mysteries.

Finding themselves miles from home, shod in black oxfords and subject to proscriptions against, say, running down to Walgreen's for a cherry Coke, their first reaction was panic. They stole pudding from the pantry at night, prowled the cellar, the forbidden attic, jimmied the novitiate door.

They were afraid of Sister Cook. Ruddy, corpulent and foul-tempered, she said "hell" and "damn" and went around calling people "nutbuckets." Old Sister Maude kept wandering over from the professed quarters; they'd find her grunting in the prep "kimmy," with the door wide open. A fellow freshman named Bonnie Bobinski gnawed the meat from her pork chop, then threw the bone under the table. Her tablemates looked at one another and shrugged, then followed suit to the girl. Even as Louise reeled with the shock of it all, Sister Bruno, the prep mistress, insisted upon saying, again and again, "Madam Louise, I'm surprised at *you!*"

A month or two into it, both sides, still bewildered, settled for one another regardless. Sister Bruno changed the name of the place from prep school to aspirancy. ("Make no mistake why we're all here.") Louise changed her tune, too, turning, almost overnight, deadly earnest. She observed to the letter the junior rules of silence and of use. She ate every scrap on her plate and never hogged the shower. She kept her spiritual life as tucked and white as the small bed on which she practiced over and over, against every instinct, the godly craft of the squared corner.

Even at fourteen, Louise sniffed something specious in her substance. "Substance" was what the nuns said authentic vocations were made of. She understood how the love of romance could seduce one into a premature or false commitment. And wasn't Louise in thrall to the music and poetry, high on the haze of incense and mysticism, addicted to her own postures, full-blown, fiery, heroic? Preferring prie-dieu to pew now, she would kneel in line with the tabernacle, cruciform, holding out until her arms twitched with unwillingness, wanting no less than to outsuffer Christ.

Soon she began to jettison her worldly goods, as ballast. She ate sparingly; her breasts melted off like lard. She developed anemia, and this impoverishment, too, she welcomed with all her iron-poor heart. Dwindling was not a project she'd been assigned, not standard aspirancy practice, and Sister Bruno began to steal nervous glances at Louise over her teacup.

By contrast, pragmatic Frank husbanded her vigor, pursued a far more sensible path to her groom, ate what pleased her, in life-sustaining shares, prayed with her arms folded instead of flung, and had the wit to keep what she needed. And while she prospered, Louise soon palled; after two and a half years of scruples and striving, she took to her bed with the shakes. Sick and empty, she received visiting sisters, who took her hand and looked down at her wan face in helpless perplexity. Sister Bruno explained that her approach had been wrong. *Trying* to be nothing was making *something* of it. You couldn't be nothing and proud of it. "But I'm nothing anyhow," Louise argued.

Sister Bruno nodded wholeheartedly. "Being nothing is a snap," she said. "Living it is the real challenge."

By now Louise begrudged everything she'd destroyed or given away in search of self-denial. A snapshot burned because she looked pretty in it; a blouse Geggo had smocked for her in ice cream colors, cut to ribbons. In trouble, the heart narrows its demands to one long undeniable burn. All her regret came to concentrate in one spot: the half pound Mount Mercy chocolate bar she'd won at the community bazaar and given to one of the day students for her invalid mother. She began to yearn for that candy. Morning after morning she awoke with the heat of chocolate on her tongue. The taste lingered, like a last bite, sweet spit. She could have wept for wanting it back.

She tried to explain to Frank about the candy as a prelude to saying good-bye. Frank didn't get the connection, but the message hit her hard. She covered her face, and her hands filled with tears. Louise saw herself as weak and disappointing, a runaway mother. Rashly she vowed to rejoin Frank after graduation. They'd enter the postulancy together. As security, she left her pearl ring at the feet of St. Stephen in the quadrangle. It was the last good thing she owned. Then she tried to bring Frank around with kidding, tweaking the corners of her mouth into brave little smiles. Frank's smile was a jumble of wayward, difficult teeth. Where else would you take a smile like that but to a nunnery? she thought. Louise was shocked. How could she think such a thing? Thoughts like that came out of a mind that would not be nothing, a contrary heart untouched by a good friend's grief.

People like Louise had abortions and sold national secrets and denied Christ for a chocolate bar. She did not expect her life to go easy on her or anybody else.

Yesterday, at the bus depot, the first thing Louise had noticed about Frank was her abbreviated habit. She had not seen her friend in the early years, in the old medieval garb, the flowing robes with which they had draped their adolescent passions. Stepping off the bus in her calf-length skirt and pert little cape, Frank looked more like an early nurse.

The second thing was the straight line of icy white teeth. It was a stunning smile, a forgery. Grotesque in the way an impersonator, even more beautiful than the original, can be grotesque. A contextual trauma, jarring to the eye.

The smile skewed their reunion. Twenty years did not drop away at a glance. They'd embraced awkwardly, and Frank had backed off and looked Louise over—Louise in her many layers and towering hat. It would have been a mercy had she laughed and said, "Same old any-which-way Louise."

In the truck she handed Louise a gift across the block of silence between them. "Oh, please open it for me," Louise said. Fastidiously Frank undid the seal and slipped off the wrapper. She showed Louise a half pound bar of almond-studded chocolate, a picture of the motherhouse on the label. Louise smiled. She would have preferred the pearl ring.

On the long ride home, in fits and starts, Frank tried to fill in between the lines of their spotty correspondence. She summarized her life, Louise noticed, in terms of needs and issues: wars on poverty and tyranny and illiteracy; wars on nuclear weapons; wars on war. When she wasn't teaching wealthy girls from the Pittsburgh suburbs, she organized marches and consolidated food giveaways. Her black Irish-Italian eyes, though earnest and determined, lacked the fire from the aspirancy days when the only permissible cause was the Son of God.

Oh, but Louise had encountered this breed before. These neoreligious played banjos and carried placards and confessed impure thoughts to talk show hosts. They made demands for higher pay and greater latitude, and for two cents they'd give the pope a public dressing-down.

They kept moving farther from the motherhouse. They lived in halfway houses and homes for the unwed and unregenerate and unwanted; sat on school boards and city councils; stood in line like everybody else. Frank talked on. Her habit of crushing her vowels into that Lackawanna twang seemed at odds with the crisp, articulate woman she'd become. Louise listened in silence for a clue to what they both had come to.

*   *   *

They took off for K Mart in the new diesel. They had not gone as far as the highway ramp when Frank dipped into one of her capacious black pockets and produced a pack of Virginia Slims. As Louise watched the car clog with a whopping lungful, she remembered Trover's parting injuction. She turned to her friend abruptly. The subject was smoking, but she heard herself say, "You guys still believe in God?"

Louise passed a fourteen-wheeler laboring to gain the hill. She passed a convoy of pink Mary Kay cosmetics trucks in the time it took for Frank to think it over. Frank expelled her smoke in thoughtful jets like blank white comic strip balloons. *Puh. Puh. Puh.* Wasn't she supposed to say, "What kind of question is that?"

Louise had not meant the question snidely. Indeed, she had hardly meant to ask. Panic had slapped the words out of her. Louise might never have visited with Frank over the years, but the nun had been with her nonetheless, moving quietly behind her letters, with all the others Louise had left behind at Mercy. Unassuming but diligent souls, like the monks who'd kept alive the light of learning through the Dark Ages. She'd left the faith of her grandmother in their hands, entrusted it to them, and now their hands smoked and wrote slogans and made funny seesaw gestures when you mentioned God.

"Yes," said Frank, finally. "Most of us accept some aspect of the concept."

"Aspect of the what?" Louise said.

Frank dropped her hand onto Louise's shoulder and gave a quick squeeze. She stubbed her butt in Trover's spotless new ashtray, and Louise began to fear for her home. "This is lovely country," the nun said. "What are those gorgeous strips of green, and so late in the year?"

"Winter wheat," Louise replied stiffly. Pantheism. Nature worship. A pagan sensibility. Who was keeping an eye on the beyond? They sped east on the interstate. From the crest of a small rise the hazy buildings of Neisstown loomed into view. Frank lit up again and smoked with her forehead pressing the window, as though clamping down thoughts she could not possibly part with.

When she was back in Lackawanna for Banfer Kleeve's funeral, Louise had found a Show Biz Pizza on the site where Geggo raised her. The little pink house and the white hydrangea bush at the doorstop had been paved over and parked on. Was everything, then, erased and nullified? She couldn't let go of this thread. "You still go to mass?" she asked thinly.

Frank's eyes sparkled, and she hitched closer and blew out smoke and said, "Act your age, Louise."

CHAPTER

16

They rode out to Ringtown in the same van they'd taken to wrestling tournaments the summer before with Michael and DeTurk's son, Levi, named after the jeans. Levi was Michael's age but two weights up. The boys would sprawl in the back of the van, using stacks of plastic-wrapped "publications" as pillows, and sometimes they'd sing, "Oh, we're going to heaven in a smutmobile."

From May to late August, up and down the coast, they'd courted glory. As far south as Atlanta, north to a wrestling camp contest in Maine which both boys lost first round, so Trover made them all go out to Mount Desert Island to look for puffins. Mighty called her father and brother Chicken George and his Fine Fighting Cock.

The men made the trips go faster by focusing on the boys: asking after their health every ten seconds; counseling about cradles and takedowns; pushing vitamins and electrolytes; taping elbows. Still, it was a festive kind of fussbudgetry, untainted by bad press, and DeTurk's face would reflect the tense, tenuous pleasure of Trover's own. They were healthy men, their own bosses, with leisure time and two fine boys, and the air slapping through open windows echoed their own air of raggedly happy expectation.

But those days seemed far away. The man next to Trover now was De-Turk, the transgressor, speeding to judgment. A troubled man with captive counsel. The trip promised endless hours of pyramiding panic and anxiety. DeTurk had eleven and a half bookstores (one partially razed by a civic-minded wrecking crew) and seemed loath to deny any one of them its pro rata share of paranoia. What's more, the man smoked like a bad motor.

"I mean, hey," DeTurk was saying, "take Alsace. Did we win in the courts only to have the zoning board take a whack at us? No adult shop within two hundred yards of a place of worship? Just answer me one thing." He looked over at Trover. "Can they really claim Girl Scout head-quarters is a *convent*?"

"Cloistered order."

"You serious?"

"No." Trover cracked the spine of his book so it would lay flat. He'd been on a solid Hardy diet for weeks. He was midway through *The Mayor of Casterbridge.* Between Henchard, the grain merchant, and DeTurk, the dirt broker, he was getting the tales of woe deliciously mixed.

DeTurk blathered on. It was the state cops that had burned down the King of Prussia store. He'd lay odds on it. And how could he force the landlord in Fogeldorf to turn the heat back on? Hell, it was winter. And by what right was the Goshenhoppen vice squad keeping an illegal seizure? He knew for a fact they'd donated a mess of videos to the county, for when things got dull down at the row offices.

"Great names," interjected Trover.

"What's that?"

"Guy's got a genius for names. Eustacia Vye. Farmer Oak. Bathsheba Everdene."

"Do I look like a 'scumbag' to you? Cripes, some lady claimed she saw my name in a dream, written in dung, in the *Book of the Damned.*"

Trover marked his place on the page with his thumbnail and looked up. "Tell you what," he said, "if the law library carries the *Book of the Damned,* I'll check it out, see if you're listed." He batted fumes away. "Look, friend, if you have to smoke, crack your window."

The road was no place to battle conscience. Later in the motel lounge they'd quaff a few and put all questions to bed properly. Once again they'd denounce their accusers as hypocritical fools, reassert how sex cases brought out the crazies and crowded the courtrooms. They'd damn the politicians for damning pornography only in election years. Examining the issues meant reasoning backward, easing themselves gently into the pleasant scald of victimhood, where hunkering low, they hid from born agains and feminists.

Once Trover had received a contingent from the Neisstown NOW. They asked him to add his name to a list of lawyers refusing to represent book-store owners. He looked. And laughed out loud. There wasn't a single *trial* lawyer on that roster; not one of those high-minded signers had ever de-fended as much as a menu snatcher. "Do you folks mind if I go on repre-senting murderers and molesters?" he'd asked.

"Certainly not," their leader said unblinkingly. "It's your sworn duty."

These women, he knew, were right and wrong. He had no choice but to believe they were more wrong than right, led afoul the mark by the not so unreasonable human need to fix the root of rage and violation outside themselves, where it might be nicely got at and excised whole. It made life look curable.

Trover saw nothing uplifting or indispensable in porn operations. In this he and the women concurred. The art was bad; the paper, cheap. He'd thrown up his arms. "I hope the demand dries up," he said. Far be it from me to drum up interest in dirty books. The shops go belly up on their own, don't look at me, I won't lift a finger to save them.

"BUT"—and he'd pounded a stack of files so hard a paper clip flew across the room—"don't ask me to strong-arm them down or help you ladies do it or let the state use thumbscrews. And don't you gals ever, *ever* ask one man to sign away the rights of another. Don't ever ask *me* to sign anything. Pe-riod." Some of the huskier women had names for him. But several others looked nervous and defeated. For their sakes, he wished the powers they wanted to confer on him were real. He wanted to say, "Yes, I'll sign this sheet, and nothing will touch you again. You will never be leered at, never taken in lovelessness, or loved and left. Never die."

Oh, but he was sick of his arguments, weighing bad against worse, spending precious breath on behalf of panderers. Shouting down grand-mothers, other men's daughters. The subject tasted bad anymore, like a piece of meat from between your teeth. End of subject. DeTurk would have to discuss something else tonight. What? Michael was racking up a banner year. Three pins in a row. They'd talk their sport, of course. Trade bravest moments, smartest moves, the palaver itself a free-style struggle for the best boy.

"Well, Counselor," said DeTurk, "what's our battle plan? Whatcha got up your sleeve this time?"

"State secret." Trover hadn't a clue to what he would do tomorrow. "Relax," he said, turning a page.

His major worries ignored, DeTurk took up with his highway chant the way some people might pick up worry beads. "Shop Harrisburg," he said. "Deer Xing. Water beds. Free Coke with every fill-up. Copper Rock Ca-verns. Jesus loves you. Wide load."

"Mother Cuxsom. Benjamin Brownlet."

"What?"

"Vintage Hardy."

"Rivets."

"Ribbet."

DeTurk swerved sharply onto the access lane. At the edge of the Howard Johnson's parking lot he jammed on the brakes and hopped out. "Gotta use the little boys' room," he said.

Thirty seconds later Trover, tired of waiting for DeTurk to return, left the van, went into the building, and wandered around until he chanced upon the gift shop. He bought some things to take west with him. A diet poster that said amusing things about string beans. A very tall beer glass called "A Yard o' Ale." A hamster wheel. Trundling outside with his purchases, he saw right off that the van was gone. For several seconds he stood, arms full, regarding in detachment the distant band of vanishing highway. He pictured the van roaring obliviously westward, DeTurk nattering his way toward the Allegheny tunnels. "Remove sunglasses. Reduce speed. Rivets." Trover counted on one full exit out and one back. Thirty miles twice. He'd need some reading material since presumably Hardy had skipped out with DeTurk. He shrugged and lugged his things back in and bought a paperback called *You Can Canoe and Kayak Too.*

He spread out at a table for six and ordered all the life-threatening menu items he refused to accept from his wife. A double cheeseburger, steak fries, shoofly pie. By now Hardy was cruising the dark under the mountains, so Trover read up on strokes and sweeps and, while he ate, practiced his paddling.

When the better part of an hour had passed, he peeked out from his books and spotted DeTurk inquiring at the register. He was talking too loud, and his face was red and tic-ridden, the desperate look of a man who'd mislaid his lawyer. Trover ducked back behind his boat book and stayed there for another minute or two. It was uplifting to be missed, to be panicked after. Then, gathering up his possessions, rattling his bags, he scraped away from the table.

DeTurk came running. Trover doffed a fictional hat (he'd left his garrison cap in the car) and handed him the giant beer glass to carry. He ordered two rocky road ice cream cones. One for the lost and one for the finder. Something cold to numb his client's tongue. Something sweet to cut the drone of dread under the hum of travel.

The motel was located between Bargainland and World of Wallpaper on a gawdy commercial strip called Miracle Mile. What happened to places with names like Pincus Brothers and those sweet old men who knew so

much about good suits? And quality shoes? DeTurk picked up the keys to
two rooms. Dropping Trover off, he said, "Sack out, Counselor. Nap'll do
you good." Trover imagined DeTurk imagining him, his advocate's head
set importantly on a clean pillow, recharging in dark and solitude. DeTurk
gladly paid the freight for separate rooms.

The bed was covered in a ribbed pink fabric that reminded him of icing.
He sat down gingerly, half expecting to sink through to the spongy sums of
all the fatigue and sin and despair deposited there. His bed at home, a simple snug double, suggested a different brand of obscenity, the raw dishevelment of an escaped grave. "Why make the bed," she argued, "if we're only
going to mess it up again?" "Why bother to live," he said, "if we're only
going to die?"

Trover never unpacked in motel rooms. Such an act would mimic moving in too closely, presage the day when Louise finally found a way to unload him. Not that she'd never evicted him in the past. She had. But he
actually left only when he believed her to be bluffing, testing him. For the
times he feared she might mean it, he had a ready antidote. He said NO.
Then he went to bed and locked the door behind him. He was *never* going to
be sent to a place like this. Let some other guy personify twentieth-century
alienation.

She'd colored their room brown, then cut the gloom with sepia and
white, and, like the elm outside the window, let her leavings lie where they
fell. Consequently the room always looked provoked, stopped in the middle
of things but ready to start up again any minute. Nights he didn't roam the
bars, he barricaded himself up there, with his books and her books and all
the bits of strewn minutiae, scarves and buttons, socks, bras, dog collars,
Bagel herself curled up on Louise's bathrobe. A woolly brown burrow, perfect for groundhogs and wombats.

He'd do sit-ups on the floor or read in bed, his wife beside him reduced to
little more than psychic phenomena, a shadow, a soft glissando up and
down his spine. Should she insist upon material form and full rights, should
she speak of the neighbors or ponder aloud the Great Secrets, soliciting his
vision, eyeing his body, he had the power to dive even deeper into his interests, deeper still, if need be, into the mossy quarries of sleep.

Later, much later, he would rise through all his substrata, taking the
sleeping body of his good wife to his own, making twilight love to her,
making his need abstract, the wordless yearning of a dead man turned up
in a dream. It was his dead man act, and it was a crime. For the entire time
his pipes would be vibrating with a specific, conscious, twenty-one-gun desire. He wanted her. He knew her name. It was Louise.

Other men might spend their passion quick and be rid of it. But in his miserliness, his endless furtive hoarding, he was stuck with this messy person. To keep her from knowing how he felt, knowing he was mostly true to her, he had to hold himself close under his coat. He could never remove such a coat, and his arms were never free. He would wear his coat to court and wear it home. He would wear his hat and coat to bed if he had to.

Removing only his hat now, he stretched out full length, wadded a pillow around his head. He closed his eyes, and just as he began to drift off, the phone yanked him back again. "Have a nice snooze?" said DeTurk. "Super. Hey, meet me downstairs in twenty minutes. We gotta talk. I won't sleep until I know where we're headed with this."

Trover scowled at the handset. Then he said, "Check." He hung up and went to the john to think. Defense. The man wanted a defense. Well, dammit, how many times did he have to explain? Only a fool could try to argue these cases on the merits. Plain dealing here meant disaster. How did you argue "redeeming social value," for instance, to a panel of retirees? It was all the elderly could handle adjusting to "unwed" and "androgynous"; what were they supposed to do with "Tea for Three"?

Second criterion. Did the said material offend community standards? A sea of ambiguity if ever there was one. And from what pool was Trover supposed to draw his respectability experts? What Sunday schoolteacher was likely to step up and say, "Hard core might have its detractors elsewhere, but Ringtown needs it!"

The third point was prurient interest. The obvious strategy was to soft-pedal the indecency factor. Lately, though, out of desperation, Trover had been letting the evidence ride, the more graphic the better. Then, after the prosecution had run the film, he'd approach the red-faced, excruciatingly engorged jury. "You're shocked and disgusted," he'd say. "My sentiments exactly. This stuff sure doesn't appeal to *my* prurient interest. Tell you what, ladies and gentlemen of the jury, deal. This crud turns you on, go ahead, find my client guilty." It had turned out to be one of his most effective rebuttals yet.

Well, he'd play it by ear, as he always did, pretending, in the meantime, for DeTurk's sake, to have everything perfectly worked out. He glanced around for his hat, plucked it off the bedside lamp. His fingers were cold. And bare. Louise kept buying him wedding rings; he kept shedding them. The last one, he complained, was too small, gave him headaches. He had rings mixed up with Jockey shorts, she said, in her customary tone of sly sanguinity. Her own rings typified the way anything of hers, once laid, stayed. It didn't occur to her to remove them for filthy jobs; hence, her diamond usually carried paint flecks or dried pie dough or manure under its prongs. God!

The heat went on with a bone-cracking snap. Room key in hand, Trover popped on his cap, opened the door, and let the cold, clear night hit him.

Tall and stripling thin, the barmaid looked uncomfortable dressed as a wench. She remembered Trover from the last time. "Hi-uh," she said, giving him a lambrusco on the rocks. "I thought you lost your case and went home months ago."

"They asked me back for an encore," he said. He went on to explain the way the deck was stacked, grumbling that the DA was free to bring separate indictments on every piece of merchandise in the shop. Theoretically he could try Trover's client nine thousand times, if the mood moved him. "Supreme Court knocks out one conviction, they trot out a different picture book and"—Trover danced two swizzle sticks around his glass—"here we go loop-de-lu again."

She nodded with the prim, imprecise sympathy of the professional listener.

"Picket still going strong?"

"Sure is," she said. "They bring their kids and make a day of it."

"Well, it's illegal," he said sharply (as if she were complicit in this). "They plunk right down on my guy's front stoop. Let him holler till his teeth rot, law looks the other way." He drank fast and nudged his glass forward for more.

Refilling him carefully, she said. "So, what's the big deal?"

The girl was young, scrubbed, arms delicate as daisy stems. It did not seem proper to pursue these wherefores with her.

She wiped the bar and went on chattering matter-of-factly. "Sometimes they have me work the banquet room downstairs. I was on last summer for the annual fire fighters' stag night. Mucho adolescent, if you know what I mean." She rolled her eyes for him. "Some girl popped out of a stack of pancakes. And the movies? Well, sir, they were *not* Disney." She paused importantly. "Guess who came to dinner?"

The nostrils of Trover's trained nose quivered.

"Keynote speaker no less. The Honorable Bert Bogpother."

Loath to give away his appetite, Trover held his face to a polite interest. "Got up and walked right out, did he?" he asked, taking the drift from the girl's cigarette without a single consumptive gasp.

Giggling, she said, "You nuts? He loved it. And the guys loved him loving it. You know how it is when the preacher tells a raunchy joke or something, like wow, he's just a regular guy and all."

"No kidding." Trover ground ice between his molars. "Don't suppose you'd care to testify about that?"

"About what?"

"Forget it," he said.

She knitted her brow, and he watched her forehead furrow the other way as it dawned on her. "Oh," she said, "I didn't mean to imply . . ."

"I know," he said, sighing. "I put you on the stand, you'll say the guy took one look at those flicks and whipped out his hymnal. Right?"

The girl's shoulders slumped, forcing her front to go not flat but hollow. She stood like a canoe on end, chagrined the length of her. "Would you . . . you wouldn't. Would you make me say that in *court*?"

Trover crumpled up his face like an idea not worth saving. "Relax," he said, giving his glass another nudge.

When DeTurk came in, Trover led him off to a corner table. "Did your people rent any flicks to the city firemen?" he whispered.

DeTurk smelled clean. He'd showered and put on soap colors, pink and green Lacoste. "Why d'ya ask?"

"Can you find out?"

"I'd have to call the store," DeTurk said grudgingly, as though reluctant to get dirty.

"Do it."

DeTurk wasn't gone but a minute. He returned to the table and wrote *Ladies in Waiting* and *Tea for Three* on a cocktail napkin. Their furtive manner was not so tactical as it was aesthetic. DeTurk's business was somehow mollified by whispers. Secrecy airbrushed an aura of intrigue, like a halo around his affairs. "Now what?" he asked softly.

"Pay dirt, that's what." Trover stabbed an emphatic finger at *Ladies in Waiting*. This is one of the ones they're introducing into evidence tomorrow."

"So?"

"So?" he echoed. "Bogpother was there." He related the story without disclosing its source, leaving the impression that the good judge was the sweet he'd been saving up, the mystery trump in his magic pocket.

"We're going to have him arrested?"

"Don't be ridiculous," he said. "Bert Bogpother's going to be star witness for the *defense.*"

"Get serious."

"Thimk!" Trover said, tapping his skull, leaning low across the table. "Remember our old friend community standards?"

DeTurk remained at a loss.

"I'm trying to tell you we've got an expert now. A genuine touchstone of ward morality. If your product stands approved by the respected judge, who's to gainsay it?"

DeTurk's lower lip hung inside out and doubtful. "Bogpother's gonna flip. I only hope he doesn't figure *me* for the brains behind this little caper."

"I wouldn't worry I were you."

"We got witnesses?"

"Nobody willing to come forward." Trover grinned. "But *he* doesn't know that."

"He'll kill us."

"Not this round he won't."

DeTurk grimaced like a schoolboy seconds after throwing in with the ringleader. Or so, Trover, feeling every inch the ringleader, interpreted the man. Shenanigans, Banfer Kleeve would have said. Monkeyshines. Well, how else did you answer a mischievous prosecution but with trickier mischief? Maybe it was that, the high jinks and fun, that kept him going, sustained him through the murky spells and gray areas, the losses of heart and hope and passion, the times he forgot what amendment it was he was supposed to be defending. Authority baiting, rule testing, the tweaking of pious pink jowls: maybe even great men kept the long, cold march of their causes alive with the heat of petty conflict, the intermittent glee of devilish invention.

After dinner Trover located a process server and had a nervous DeTurk deliver the subpoena to his home. At eight forty-five the next morning Judge Bogpother was served just outside his chambers, as he arrived for the day's business. Advised of this, Trover grabbed his battered briefcase and went buoyantly on to Call of the List. "Ready, Your Honor!" he belted out when his case was called.

Bogpother called him up to the side bar. Peering coldly over Trover's shoulder, he said, "Be in chambers in ten minutes." Then he fixed Trover hard. "Two seconds late you're in contempt."

When Trover emerged from conferring with the judge, he interrupted DeTurk's pacing outside chambers to ask for a ride back to the motel. He let his client stew for several blocks while he savored his triumph in private. DeTurk kept glancing over. At last Trover said, "Looks like the learned judge has a middleweight at home."

"Huh? Wha' ya talking about?"

"Got the kid's portrait hanging in chambers. Full color no less, red, white, and blue singlet. Star-studded frame. Got him right up there next to the governor. Only twice as big, by God. And twice as cocky."

"Great, great. But what'd he say about *me*?"

"Bogpother sent us home," he said laconically. "He called me a ragabash."

"What the hell's that?"

"Lowlife," he said, grinning. "Rabble."

"But what's the bottom line?"

Trover turned to him incredulously. "Bottom? What makes you think your life has a bottom? We're off the hook for a while, that's all. Call it a breather, and enjoy it."

DeTurk nodded and pondered quietly with his cheeks sucked in. Trover waited for him to sight in the next crisis. "I just thought of something awful," he said at last. "What if they legalize this business? They can do that, can't they?"

"Anything's possible," Trover said.

"They'll be pushing porn in the convenience stores," he said. "*Tea for Three* right out there with *TV Guide*. They'll flood the market . . ."

"A smut glut, sure, why not?"

"Then the day the heat's off, I'm cooked."

"That's pretty much how it works."

"What a bummer," he said.

"Hey, where you taking me?"

DeTurk sighed. "I gotta stop by the store a minute. Sign some checks. Mind?"

"What I mind is your stinking up the car."

"Sorry." DeTurk took one last drag and stubbed his butt. "By the way, were you really going to put Bogpother on the stand?"

The truth was Trover had no wish to humiliate the man. He knew, moreover, that once he'd got over the initial shock, Bogpother would have deferred to one or another judicial immunity. But not without taking a Sunday punch from the press first. Trover would not have wanted to follow through, but driven to the wire, he would have pressed, and Bogpother knew it. That's why you needed a reputation. That's what a bad name was good for. It spoke louder than the lawyer. Trover looked at DeTurk. "I'll never tell," he said, and winked.

The bookstore was a former Arthur Treacher's with stove-blacked windows, a glimpse of the grimly forbidden on that Miracle Mile between Dinette City and Sneaker Kingdom. With the case on the docket and publicity running high, the straggly ranks of righteousness had filled out considerably. Easing onto the gravel lot, like a jaded priest making his weary kyries, DeTurk read the shibboleths aloud. SIN MERCHANTS. TENTS OF WICKEDNESS. BLOCK MOTHERS AGAINST SICKOS. "Holy crap," he said, his voice rising shrewishly. "Now they're *importing* crackpots."

He was referring to the fleet of pugnacious snub-nosed buses abutting the rear wall, most still running, the drivers snoozing behind the wheels. Trover disembarked and took a better look at the one closest to him. Did it say what he thought it did? "Holy Redeemer Middle School, Lackawanna, PA."

"That's my old grade school," Trover said, moving away quickly, lest he be set upon by a squadron of the same nuns he remembered for their sharp knuckles and pretty calligraphy, who taught first-grade girls to sit with their knees together. "Keep walking," Trover advised his client as they shouldered through the clots of demonstrators. "Don't show fear."

Surrounded now by detractors, they were the cynosure of a hundred pairs of glaring or, worse, pitying eyes. Nobody spoke, not even to curse them. Mainly the punishment was the crush of bodies and silence.

Trover spun his client forward again, and they continued their choppy course toward the rear entrance of the shop. As though moved by intermittent winds, the crowd murmured and settled, rose and fell, the men bobbing like small skiffs in the surf of judgment. It was hard not to be swayed by public opinion when it was bumping into you. Trover felt like an archdebaucher; he felt smelly, and that was far worse than being scared.

At first, he thought the hand belonged to Len DeTurk, that it had been laid on his shoulder in encouragement and friendship. Then the hand clamped down, and there was a mouth near his ear, a breathy message that sounded final. "Job one: six. Revelation eighteen: three."

Coming about awkwardly, Trover found himself inches from a round florid face ballooning out of a cleric's collar.

"I beg your pardon," Trover said imperiously, his free hand coming up between them.

"So," the man said, "Mr. Quick Thinker."

"Down, boy," said Trover, applying a slight pressure against the minister's chest with his spread fingertips.

It happened very fast then, the iron grip on his other shoulder and he drawn forward in something not unlike a gentlemanly embrace. Indeed, for a moment his fear was that the man would kiss him: *Nice going, Mr. Thinker, thanks.* But then both black arms pistoned out, and Trover was released like a line drive, bodies parting to let him stagger backward, unimpeded. He had little choice but to come down hard on his tailbone.

A bladelike pain knifed up his spine. Head hammering with hurt, he was afraid he would be sick. It took some time then, as the nausea ebbed, to locate himself in the chaos of his predicament. There he was, sitting on peastone, legs sprawled, papers strewn, hat gone. Unfriendly eyes inspecting his person. His arms formed a protective tepee over his delicate pink pate. One shoe had come off and lay in the submissive position, facedown. His sole had a hole in it.

On his knees DeTurk scrambled after the papers, stuffing them back into Trover's briefcase. There was a smattering of hesitant applause, and several bystanders instinctively popped forward; then, catching themselves about to abet the oppressor, drifted awkwardly back. But some Samaritan type had managed to get behind him. Wiry fingers tugged on his coat collar. "Git up, Bud!" he heard through the spin of insult and diminishing pain. Someone was pushing his shoe on, tying it. Then his hat was back.

It couldn't be. She was in mourning, wasn't she? But it could be and was. Now she was standing in the V made by his splayed legs. Her arms were folded high across her chest, and her scrappy little hat, a maroon pillbox with a short veil, slipped askew as she clapped at him. "Up and at 'em!" snapped Maddy Kleeve.

"Mum?" he said miserably, his face pinched from squinting, for in the scuffle he had also lost his bifocals.

With one quick stroke, she hooked his glasses over his ears, stepped back, chin tipped, studying him. Her son looked back at her through two cracked lenses, then, mortified, shied away, preferring to face the mob. The people seemed almost indifferent to him now. Some were chatting; children cried, and a large, energetic woman was doling out sandwiches and apples from a straw hamper. The burly minister was nowhere to be seen. Trover took DeTurk's arm and hoisted himself to his feet.

Slung low in pain and embarrassment, he hobbled several tentative steps before being sure that he would make it.

DeTurk introduced himself to his lawyer's mother.

"How do," she said crisply. They were but inches from the store, but how could Trover invite her in? How could he not?

"Can I give you a lift home?" he asked lamely.

She had come out of nowhere, so it seemed reasonable to assume that she was, by her own legerdemain, stranded. But she shook her head no. "Thank you," she said, "I'm with the bus." Pointing her nose toward the one marked "Holy Redeemer," she went ticking off in its direction. Trover toddled helplessly behind. Just before stepping up, she turned to him, her mouth twitching, nibbling it seemed, at crumbs of lingering question. "I seen the whole thing in the paper," she said. "I seen yer name. Obscene lawyer, Banfer C. Kleeve."

"That's *obscenity*, Mum. Obscenity lawyer."

She ignored the distinction. "Then boys, oh, boys, I seen in the Sunday *Bulletin* how the Rosary Altar gals is bringing this bunch down to raise heck."

First he watched his own toes turn in, and then he watched hers wiggle like mice inside her Life Strides. They were both dying of this. "Anyways," she said, twisting the strap of her small pink bag. Her eyes darted from him to the crowd, fallen, since his fall, into dishevelment and aimlessness. "Ticket includes a box lunch plus a tour of Charlie Schwab's birthplace. Lotta nothin!" she said, sharpening her gaze against the demonstrators.

"Well, get along home now, Bud." She gave him the once-over. "You should have popped him one back. Them Protestants been runnin' the country long enough." She paused. "He hurt you any?"

But before he could reassure her, she'd wheeled around and scampered up the steps into the empty bus. She walked toward the rear, took a seat by the window. When her right shoulder began to roll in a way he remembered as the rhythm of her innermost distress, he knew she was doing crewel or crochet. With a vengeance. How many toilet paper dolls had humiliation made? How much bitterness in those black and orange and purple afghans? He knocked on her window and fluttered his fingers in uncertain farewell.

She grimaced back, her arms working furiously, her lips making a mute spectacle of counting stitches.

CHAPTER
17

At K Mart Louise helped her friend unload the cart: six paperback mysteries, extra-hold hair spray; a box of tampons. "You didn't offer me coffee," Frank said, setting a jar of instant Savarin on the counter rather smartly.

"Oh, dear, I forgot. *Adults* drink coffee. I suppose Trover and I have been fighting off coffee for years. Here," she said quickly, "let me pay for those." It panged her to see Frank dip into her little black coin purse, that worn pocket of poverty. "You're poor, aren't you?"

"Poor but not dumb." Frank had the flashing sass of the black Irish. Her lips clamped down on the *m* of "dumb," and she held Louise with her smart dark eyes. "When Dad died, I managed to keep a fraction of my inheritance, and I've been salting away small change ever since."

"Knocking down on God?"

"Cash or charge?" the checker asked peevishly. Her plastic bar pin said, "D. Glogowski."

"*I* steal, too," Louise said brightly, leaping for common ground. "You never know when you'll have to make a fast break in the dead of night. I've got a wad fat enough to choke a leaf shredder. Trouble is they're all singles." She smiled. "Our consciences have been tooled for only small crimes, you know."

"Or big ones in increments." Frank turned to the impatient checker. "Cash," she said.

"Well, I should say so!" D. Glogowski took the bill by one corner, holding it out from her like scandal.

A major discount center, Neisstown attracted buyers by the busload from as far away as Boston and Atlanta. If Louise had sounded blithe and proprietary in suggesting this part of the trip, if she seemed to include herself among those crisp, deliberate seekers of truth in torn labels, unfailing discerners of the one dream dress on a rack of purple horrors, she soon set the record straight. After an hour of driving around a city billed as the Outlet Capital of the World, she was unable to locate a single discount house. It was Frank who finally spotted the lingerie place.

It was called Dream Fair, and it was an armory-size hall filled with row upon row of the softest software imaginable, colors so silky and pale they threatened to slip off the spectrum. Nightgowns, camisoles, teddies; merry widows in apricot and dusty rose, the air holding the hues tenuously as clouds of bath powder. Entire phalanxes of floaty robes arranged according to shade, black ones dancing wickedly at the edge of the whites. Panties on parade and squadrons of bras on tiny hangers. By zagging from rack to rack, you could find items to match, a completely coordinated underlife. Aqua overlaid with ecru lace, creamy prints, green sea-foam. Everything doubly delectable at half price.

Louise was overwhelmed. How had she lived half a lifetime, almost, in darkest ignorance of this place? How had she lived at all outside the state of graceful underwear? The room seemed to flow on and on, like the house in her dreams, and she found herself drifting happily among and between the rows, touching velvet, stroking the satinet, floating weightless as lace, Frank ecstatic beside her. People turned to smile at the sight of a nun and countrywoman running amok among the product line.

"Oh, Weeze, look!" cried Frank. The wrap was flamingo pink and trimmed in maribou. She tossed it around Louise's shoulders and spun her around.

Louise ducked under the hood. "Remember the time," she said, blowing feathers away from her face. "Remember the time they threw us out of McCrory's for laughing at the underpants."

Frank shrieked. "Oh, those big pink Pechglos."

When Louise laughed, the feathers that framed her fluttered and fell. Their eyes, glinting with devilment, met, and they laughed again. Louise's breath snagged in her chest. Only at this moment did she know how much she'd missed this friend over the years. If she had dared mourn her properly, how would she have borne the sorrow?

Today she knew again what it was to have someone to run with. How sanguinely they had once worried the world, tested the fabric of things. "Being a brat was bliss," she said.

"And how." Frank quickly agreed.

Louise could almost smell that sooty, almost savory Lackawanna air. Nearly every Saturday, the summer between seventh and eighth grades, they'd take a trolley downtown. First they'd go to Glazer Brothers, to buy red-skinned peanuts and giggle at the immigrant women, with their bags of greasy meats, their garters rolled around their ankles. Peasant women, like their own grandmothers. Louise and Frank were laughing at exactly half their own histories.

Then they'd cruise the aisles of the five-and-dime, bearing their special knowledge of things: that only colored people used Blue Waltz perfume; that nice girls didn't wear ankle bracelets or nylons with butterfly designs. They knew not to swear or shoplift, and they didn't. They inspected the bins, alert to any hint of titillation: male trusses; "Modess because" in the plain blue wrapper; massive underpants. It was the fifties equivalent of reading the dirty parts. Then outside again to the dingy street, with their peanuts and vague cravings. They were buoyant as fish balls in their full skirts, the floats of ruffled crinoline that was lingerie then.

Because all the cubicles were occupied, both women had to squeeze into one tiny dressing room. Louise needed bras. But she could not bring herself to undress in front of Frank. Instead of bras then, she tried on peignoir sets over her clothes. She looked like the same benighted creature of yesterday, only in reverse.

When Frank removed her habit, Louise stole furtive glances. The cellulite surprised her. The skin under her upper arms was beginning to shine, laxity at the waist. It didn't seem right, a woman under wraps all these years. Like a Sunday sofa, shouldn't she still be good as new?

Frank shimmied into something red and black, in bias-cut satin. "Well?" she said.

"Well, shades of Gracie McCake!"

"Who? Oh, Louise, I *do* remember. Gracie *Lee* McCake."

Early in their freshman year Gracie McCake, a full-bodied, irrepressible redhead, managed to smuggle a mail order out with one of the day students. The package was intercepted on the way in. It was a flame red baby doll pajama set from Frederick's. Gracie was sent home the same weekend as Bonnie "The Bone" Bobinski.

"You never, *never* saw anybody go," Louise said. "You'd get up one day, and they wouldn't be there, that's all." She looked away, remembering those skinless mornings, for whoever it was, however disliked or improbable, was missed. The thinnings diminished everyone, turned them into a sort of lump sum, a corps of uniformity from which all texture had been planed away.

"I know," Frank said quietly. "Now how do I *look*?"

"Gorgeous," Louise said. "Scarlet makes your skin glow. Unless you happen to be blushing."

"I don't blush."

"You used to."

"Ladies, ladies!" cried a voice from outside. "Count your items."

"Pardon?"

"Three apiece is the absolute limit."

"Oh, sorry."

"And these," said the unseen enforcer, a manicured hand tapping the merchandise they'd draped over the curtain rod. "You must remove them this instant."

"But why?" Louise asked. "What harm could they possibly do there?"

"You're flouting the law, ma'am. We cannot permit . . . oh, dear, let's not have an episode, don't force me to do something we'll *all* regret."

"Whose law?" Louise pressed, as if it were something she had to get to the bottom of.

"We'll remove them immediately," said Frank, and to Louise she whispered harshly, "This is neither the time nor the place for a moral stand."

The woman seemed to be gone. "If I'm *flouting* the law," said Louise, "I'd like to know where it's written. Is that so unreasonable?"

"Well, smarty, she probably went after the store detective. Listen, sometimes it's a luxury to be wrong. Look how easy. You pull down the items in question, toss them in the corner, and everybody's happy."

"But . . ."

"No buts. I'm not going to fight with you, Louise."

"You always used to."

"I've changed. And you should, too. . . ."

Louise lowered her eyes. Frank sounded like Trover, right after he quit smoking or upon having done something nice for his body. *You should, too.* But Louise still smoked and avoided exercise and argued with clerks and car washes. Her teachers called her unteachable. Her teachers, it seemed, were legion. She looked up to see Frank shaking a bundle of black cloth at her. "Here," she was saying. "Just out of curiosity, you be me for a minute. I'll be you."

Louise drew back. "Oh, I couldn't."

"They're only clothes, Louise. Woven fiber."

Louise hugged her shoulders, hoarding her shirt, a sweat that Trover had brought her from Mount Snow. The front design was a standard ski trail symbol, a large black diamond that stood for "Most Difficult." "I don't know," she said, "I just don't know. Oh, here!" Stripping the shirt off, she quickly covered herself with Frank's white rayon blouse and little black cape. They they traded the black gabardine skirt for brushed denim pants.

"These legs have a slight bell," Frank said. "Were you aware of that?"

"So?"

"Bells have been out for ages."

"Oh," she said stupidly, vaguely annoyed. Frank Gahagan always had a way of making you feel untutored. And Louise noticed that on Frank her jeans were far too long and did not zip all the way. Mrs. Gahagan's hips. She noticed but said nothing. The whole affair made her very edgy, and so she began to rattle on about midday traffic and where they would lunch and what they would have. "On me, of course," she insisted.

"Good," Frank said, "I hate to pay for food."

Then they both stopped talking to look each other over, and Louise drew close to the mirror, peering at herself for a long time. She made room in the mirror for Frank, and then they glanced from reflection to reflection, and together, quietly, they said, "My. Oh, my." Then they cracked up, laughing nervously at first, then uproariously, then they were sliding as one down the wall.

"Ladies! Ladies!" The voice was back.

"It's Bruno," Louise whispered. "How did she find us here?"

"I wonder what it's like for sex change people, the first time out in their new parts," Louise said, safe in her own clothes now. They were drinking discount spritzers at the Outlet Town Tavern.

"How do you imagine they feel?"

"Like assassins."

"My dear child, it's a wonder you ever made a decision in your life."

"Oh, Frank," she said. "I dream about Mercy sometimes. I leave there again and again, and each time I do I come awake grieving. Other times I dream that I leave my husband and go back to Mercy, and guess what! I wake up grieving." She did not tell her that in some fundamental way the habit had seemed absolutely right, overdue, in fact, as if her life had been but a long tending to the quiet flow of plain wool, the cool brackens of silence. As if at some subterranean point all yearning merged and flowed in the same direction. "And how did *you* feel?" she asked.

Frank said, "Indefinite. The habit pretty well limits your identity. Without it, I could be, well, anybody almost. Even Gracie McCake."

"Isn't Gracie McCake something one should work up to?" But then Louise remembered her first year away from the aspirancy, how she had gone right out the next week and used Light and Bright on her hair and stood with her hip slung out at the Teen Canteen. "Yes, Gracie McCake," she said, retasting the name.

Frank smiled. "And what was that funny religious name you wanted?"

"If it were mine to choose, I would have taken a name like a freight train, a veritable litany of saints. Virgin, martyr, mystic, thinker. I really believed I could pull all that."

"We have a way of dealing with you ambitious types. We'd have given you something we call 'pimply.' "

"Like what?" Louise studied her friend's face in the flattering tavern light. A delicate oval, still smooth, pale against the dusky hair. Tiny black dots where she'd plucked above the bridge of her nose. She had her mother's abundance of brow as well as hip.

"Like Polycarp. Or Cuthbert."

"I would have felt like a fish. Or a frog."

"Exactly."

"Ribbett."

They ordered a second drink. Alcohol and laughter dissolved years, blurred the borders between them. In the fullness of their renewed intimacy Louise felt free to say, "Your smile. It's stunning."

Frank set down her glass, her eyes shining with story and fortune. "Well, let me tell you," she said. "One day I went to a new dentist to have a tooth filled. When he was done, he said, "You could be perfect, Sister." He took my case right to Mother, presenting it as a matter of, well, rectitude rather than vanity. He kept referring to my malocclusion. You know how nuns mistrust words with 'mal' in them. It worked like a charm. The order sprang for braces. And now"—she presented her corrected grin—"as the man predicted, I'm perfect!"

"Quite," said Louise.

Now Frank tossed her head and regarded Louise archly. "I wasn't going to bring it up, Louise, but as long as we're touching upon *things,* how come you were traipsing around in your nightgown yesterday?"

"Oh, that." Fire raced along her jawline, spread to her neck and chest.

"Yes, that, Louise." *Yes, that, young lady.* Echoes of a dozen nuns before her, and Louise felt like those times when she'd been asked in class to repeat a whispered wisecrack, and there was never any decent way out of it.

* * *

When Trover came home the next day, he was walking like a pregnant woman, tilting back on his heels and holding his back. "I'm hurt," he said, depositing his booty on the dining room table, groping his way to rest. "And depressed," he added.

They were nearing the shortest day, and already shadows waited between the arms of the sofa, and Louise watched the dark finger him. She covered her husband with a black and purple and orange afghan.

Frank tiptoed in with a pillow.

Mighty gave him light.

"Hey!" he cried. "Turn that off. I'm trying to sleep."

"Dad, this is the living room. People *live* here. People need light to live."

"Come on, Rita. Get off my back."

"Rita?" Mighty was horrified. "*Aunt* Rita?"

He cuffed at the air. "I had a bad day," he said. "I was confused there for a minute. Anyhow, you bossy types are all alike."

"Thanks a lot."

"Mighty," Louise said. "go check the potatoes."

Trover's lips were working, a sign that he meant to say something weighty. "A man of the cloth beat me up today," he said.

"Beat you up?"

"Well, pushed me down."

"Really?"

Mighty sidled in next to her mother and bent to her ear. "Don't baby him!" she whispered.

"Who I baby is *my* business!"

"Chump!" Mighty left the room, and Frank slipped out with her.

"Yo, Mr. Kleeve," Gideon called then from the doorway. "What's this hamster wheel for? We don't have a hamster."

Trover propped himself up on his elbows. "It's for Michael's mouse," he said. "Poor little sucker doesn't get enough exercise in that cage. Think he'll like it?"

"He'll be delighted," Gideon said dryly. Then: "Who's that Yard o' Ale for? Bring *me* anything? He grinned as if he were kidding.

Trover stared at him for a second and settled back with a tiny moan. "I brought *you* guys something. It's in the kitchen."

"Oh?" said Louise.

"Why don't you just let it out?" Gideon asked.

"What?"

"The mouse. Let it fend for itself. This way you'll have to provide for it the rest of its life."

"It'll get caught in the refrigerator fan," Trover said. "It'll crap all over the cupboards."

Gideon scratched his head. "Shoot, you'll end up needing a zillion cages. And a zillion hamster balls to keep them all happy."

"The system's not fool-proof," Louise said. "But we do what we can."

When Gideon was gone, Trover indicated the spot where he wanted Louise to sit abreast of him. Closing his eyes, he appeared to settle snugly into the sheltering embrace of the kindly wife Louise believed herself to be at the moment. "Poor lamb," she whispered. "I know how hard it's been for you. Life never looks the same to a man once he's lost his father."

"What's for dinner?" he asked.

"Short ribs with horseradish sauce."

"Red meat?"

"You can have a peanut butter banana."

"I guess meat wouldn't hurt me just this once."

"No, I don't suppose."

"As you were saying," he said, "life is short. Damn short."

"What brought all this on?" she asked, in cautious good humor.

"Shhhh, let me finish," he said, brows knitted, tone groping as though for the precise slant to slice all the way through to his true meaning. And Louise held her breath on the cusp of the occasion where surely now, at last, after nineteen years, he would reveal himself. Now he will say what he wants most, loves best. Without his wife, life would be ice, lice, dirt, dreck. Detestable!

She'd forgotten how easy it was to love this man. She knew now she'd never seriously considered leaving him. Gently she rested her hand on her husband's chest.

"Oooooooo! ow!" he cried. "My back! You're hurting me."

Whisking her hand away, she smiled gently and said, "Sorry."

"That's OK," he said, patting her arm.

Again she rose to go, but he tapped her shoulder down the way he once tapped a Camel back in the pack. "Maybe I'm not making a hell of a lot of sense, Bibs, but what I'm trying to tell you, well, look, when I'm up and around again, let's take a little run into Lum's. He's got a tangerine Vanagon that'll knock your wig off."

"I thought the subject was the transience of life."

"Honey, life is too damn short not to take what you can while you still have the strength."

Under her incredulous gaze, he seemed to pale. "Let me get this straight," she said stiffly. "Your answer to the brevity of life is—is . . . another car?"

He pulled his mouth tight. "I should have known better than try to discuss anything with you."

"Yes, you should have," she said. "But you don't. You don't know me at all."

His eyes, tiny creatures peeking out of dimness, gazed far away, presumably through to a better world. "You suck all the life out of things," he said gravely.

She got to her feet. "If I said, 'Fine, we could really use a Vanagon around here,' you'd run right out and buy a dune buggy, a troop transport, because you're going to get to me if it breaks you. You want me to be the guardian of sanity around here, so you can be some magnanimous nut. *I* want to be the one with all the crazy hats and irregular hours. I want to be memorable! I hate it that you think of me as steady and dependable, the voice of reason—"

"Wrong," he said. "I never thought of you as anything but a pill."

She'd been on her way to the kitchen in a huff, and now she turned back. She wanted to say something terse and blistering, though safely finite, limited to the matter at hand. Instead, she did what she always did when driven to unspeakable rage. She spoke too much. "Get another car," she said, "and I'm divorcing you."

"Fine," he said, reciting from heart. "Hit the pike."

"You go."

"I'm disabled."

"Far be it from me to push a cripple out into the night. You have till tomorrow."

"Louise, get the phone."

It was a neighbor, Minnie Grimm, the one who always called when there was death or trouble. "It's Sprecher," Louise told Trover when she'd hung up. "He had an attack of some kind in the lot outside the broom works. They just took him down to Neisstown General."

"What are you waiting for?" Trover said. "Do something. Call the florist."

In the dark of the dining room, Louise stopped to light up. With the smoke rose the smoky image of Earl Sprecher. He was behind the wheel of the old Ford one glorious day last fall. He was hauling a load of leaves that she'd offered to help burn. She'd not been to the burning circle, in the lower meadow, for years. She stopped short when she caught sight of the three metal incineration drums. Having steadily rusted away from the bottom, they now stood a third of their original size. Sensing her dismay, Sprecher turned to her, his face as unforgiving as the gray cliffs carved in the high far distance. "Missus," he said, "everything that comes on the earth leaves the earth. *Old man,* she thought. *Dwindler yourself.* But he was looking at *her* feet, and when she glanced down, she almost cried out. Her shoes were covered with rust and ashes.

Louise drew smoke so deep her chest ached. Tomorrow she would call the hospital. Tomorrow was soon enough to know where she had to go to find Sprecher.

"Let me have a drag off that," Frank said when Louise came into the kitchen. The nun was slicing lettuce into a bowl, and Louise deemed it too soon in their renewed acquaintance to correct her, to suggest that she tear it. "Gideon," she said instead, "whatever are you doing up there?" Standing on a kitchen chair, he appeared to be rearranging the bric-a-brac shelf above the windows.

"Just be patient," Mighty sang out. It was the voice she might have used on Mother's Day, were she the sort to bring breakfast in bed. She was sipping something of delicate hue from a stemmed glass.

"Mighty, is that *champagne?*"

"We didn't think you'd mind."

That too inclusive "we" again. Louise cast a glance toward Gideon, and couldn't she just hear him prompting the girl, nudging her toward the cupboard he had to know like the back of his hand to locate the champagne among the Borateem and flea powders?

Gideon hopped down now, and together he and Mighty presented the prize. "Ta-da!"

Louise followed their upswept arms to the top shelf. There in the very center of her small agateware display was the loveliest miniature she'd ever seen. A rare ivory and lavender-speckled coffeepot with a pewter lid. It was crowned with a finial as handsome as a Prussian helmet ornament.

"Oh!" she cried, her hands clasped to her breast, and the sight of the exquisite vessel seemed to release every dog of sorrow in her heart: Trover tormenting her again, Sprecher dead or dying, rust on all their shoes. Tears of anger and grief and gratitude built up in her eyes, then toppled like towers.

"It's lovely," she said, collecting herself. She allowed herself to believe it was not stolen, though she supposed it was too much to hope Gideon hadn't fast-talked some pensioner out of it.

"Fine a piece as you'll ever come across," he said.

Mighty set to wiping her mother's eyes, smiling indulgently, saying, "Oh, Ma." But Louise was deep in the crawl space beneath this gift, questioning the motives, wondering how long one must wait after the gift to evict the giver. First blackmail, now bribery. Stymied, uncomfortable, she asked Mighty to set the table.

"I have to mash the potatoes," she said.

Gideon leaped forward. "I will!" he said, racing for the silverware drawer.

Louise drew herself to full height. "Mighty will do it," she said. "This is *her* house."

Gideon stood with his helping hand frozen in the act. Her house. The "her," like some territorial growl, hung in the air with the smell of garlic and meat. Most houses were, in a way, women's houses, and Gideon stood there blinking away hurt, like the eternally dispossessed.

Not six hours ago, over lunch, Louise had told Frank the fateful tale about racing the kids to school and about the car wash. At the same time it had seemed a stroke of genius, sharing the details with another party, the crime divided, Gideon McThee reduced to a three-way partnership. Dilution of equity. If she told a million people, the boy would be wiped out, destitute. Maybe this knowledge was all the capital he had in the world. A zipper of pity stitched across her chest and oddly seemed to close some terrible wound that had opened in her. She stretched to claim the coffeepot. How swiftly the wealth of nations and men changed hands.

CHAPTER
18

"So how come Michael doesn't have to go?" Mighty was about to leave for school with Gideon and a steaming cup of Frank's Savarin.

"He's exhausted," Louise said. Then, defensively confessional, she added, "*I* told him to stay in bed."

"Little angel needs his goodness sleep."

"Your brother works very hard and on practically *no* nourishment."

"So, who says he has to do that?"

A spot of raised pink marked the girl's chin, the beginning of a pimple. Against the pale, perfect firmament of Mighty's face, the spot shone like the sun trying to come out. If perfection antagonized the eye as infinity the mind, then the flaw seemed to Louise a safe place to rest her gaze. "Nobody *says*," she said. "But as long as he lives as he does, I'll not have him die in the process."

Mighty set her coffee down too hard. "*Die?* Oh, brother, you know what the trouble with this place is?"

"What place?" For a moment Louise thought she was speaking of life, of travail, of the common lot of humankind, but then the girl drew a small, tight circle, presumably describing a more compact unit.

"This one!" she cried. "Louise and Trover's place!" As if they were a country pub she was getting the hell out of. "There's nothing standard here. Nothing you can depend on, like the music scale or the metric system. You jump right from 'working hard' to 'die'." She grabbed up her coffee again, sucking down a mouthful.

Louise's giggle seemed to soften the set of Mighty's jaw. "I mean it, Ma," she said. "You really shouldn't encourage Michael to hock out of school. It's against the law. You could go to jail."

"Oh?"

Mighty bit back a smile, and did Louise imagine that she and Gideon exchanged glances too well informed to be affectionately meant?

"Hey, OK if I borrow your Zuni bracelet?" Mighty shot a sleeve and exposed the turquoise of the already appropriated bangle.

With a surge similar to the thrill of getting, Louise leaped at the chance to give. Oh, anything to deflect the merciless searchlight of Mighty's scrutiny. Endless debt was emptying Louise's drawers. Even if Mighty deigned to return things without being asked, they were never much good anymore. They were objects subverted by youth and beauty. It was months, for instance, before the shape of the better body left a sweater for good. The flawless curve of Mighty's cheek calmed the wrong color of things. This bangle, set off by the daughter's uncreased wrist, was already spoiled for the mother. "Take it," said Louise. "Please." And the girl came through with a smile as bountiful as a blessing.

"Thanks," she said, and Gideon seconded her gratitude. But Mighty's free hand was on its way to her face, frisking her chin. "Oh . . . damn," she said. "I have a big zit!"

So the grace the bracelet bought flowed among them for all of fifteen seconds, and Mighty left disgruntled, daubing her chin with alcohol, Gideon in attendance. They were gone then, except for their ghosts. How inconsiderately people lingered; Mighty's face kept teasing Louise with disapproval. Mighty, that fragile, fastidious, doll-like child. What comic God had commended her to the care of someone like Louise, who'd wrecked every doll she'd ever owned? How had this careful creature been set among the clutter and glut of consumers, strewers, and slobs? Even their affects offended her. Finding foreign objects in her room—scarves and hairpins left behind, Michael's Frisbee, odd socks turned up in drawers—Mighty wasted no time considering gentler methods. Sometimes she tossed them out in the hall, sometimes out the window, where things smashed on the tarmac or caught in the trees and didn't come down for years. The sign incised in her door said, NO ADMITTANCE, YO YO.

When Mighty was four, a neighborhood ruffian touched a stick first in

hot tar and then to her fine yellow hair. For days Louise stared at the lico-
rice-sticky nest as it gathered more and more of Mighty to itself. Louise
could not think through such a snarl. She told the tormented child she
thought it would have to *grow* out. In the supermarket several days later a
woman came up to Louise and advised her to try gasoline. Louise considered this, even after it occurred to her, the chance of fire. As it turned out,
that night Mighty took matters into her own skillful hands, cutting the hideous wad away with paper scissors. Louise suspected that some of the re-
proach lingering in her daughter's eyes went back that far, to tar and
scissors and a flirtation with combustible measures. Someday Mighty
would have to pay her back.

Louise carried her tea back to the Room. Clearing a space for herself, she
stood for a moment, sipping tea and soaking in the smell of slip and plaster,
the odor of her only holiness. She was good back here, and she was true,
and however it unnerved her, this work was the steel rod through her spine;
it supported an entire family of inadequacies. Back here she would be equal
to pitch, solvent with remedy.

Today she attended to small odd jobs. She painted all the chocolate
brown on the family men that the old man had ordered. She dabbed
white on another. She'd been losing sleep over the broken Landers and just
last night resolved to recast the piece, in a new plasticized compound she
hoped would increase the resilience of the final form, better absorb the
blows.

In a small Tupperware bowl she mixed the melding agent, a fumy chemical bath that burned her nostrils, but without which the piece would dry
too fast and too brittle.

When the phone rang, she leapt over the habiliments of her trade,
vaulted the pressing bench, and ran to get it. Someday her art would also
save her from curiosity. Someday she would have the mettle to ignore a
screaming phone.

"Good morning, Louise."

"Uh, good morning."

"Ardith Budner here. How's Louise today?"

"Very well, thank you. And you?"

"Couldn't be better, Louise."

"Sorry. I didn't quite catch your name."

"Ardith Budner. From Good Forever."

"Where's that?"

"All ready for Christmas, Louise?"

"Do I know you, Ardith?"

"No doubt you've already ordered the Christmas portraits."

"Christmas portraits?"

"The ones you generously provide for the aunties and grandmothers."

"Well, no, we've never made it a point . . . anyhow, my eldest is, well, she's a killer with that camera of hers."

Ardith Budner laughed. "You can't count on her, though. I got that right, didn't I?"

"Well, no, you can't count on her at all."

"Young people are so flighty and self-absorbed these days, if you know what I mean."

"I do. And besides, she more or less specializes in high-tech and surreal."

"We come to the house, of course."

"Gosh, Ms. Budner, I really don't think so. I—" The children were immortalized in scores of pictures. Even Trover was regularly done by the bar association. But Louise hadn't posed for a full-face since high school. One day she would show her grandchildren the family album and be unable to explain how she went from seventeen to seventy in the flutter of an album page. Not a single proof of this, her prime, nobody to say her life had a middle. "To the house?" she repeated meekly.

"You betcha. Been our policy since one-nine-six-two. And for the next ten days we are offering our eight-by-ten half price, your choice of backdrops. Painted Desert, Great Pyramids. Home library's our most popular."

"And when can you come?"

"Name it, Louise. We'll be there with bells on."

"Tomorrow?" she asked. *Hurry. Catch me quick.*

"How's about Friday?"

"I suppose that would do," she said, vaguely disappointed.

"Now how do we find you, Lou?"

"We're RD two, Kemp, on the north side of the Maiden Creek."

"Awrighty. A quick check of my field map here tells me—ooops, I'm afraid we've hit a bit of a snag. . . ."

"Actually you could come next week. Monday would be fine." Louise would blow-dry her hair and wear aquamarine eye shadow, a streak of Indian earth to emphasize her cheekbones.

"My dear, I'm afraid it's quite out of the question. Our photo van doesn't go out your way. The territory stops on the opposite side of the creek. We *never* pass beyond that point."

"Well, what would it hurt? Just tell them to cross at the iron bridge, make a left—we're talking a quarter mile here at best."

"You have to draw the line somewhere. I really am sorry, Mrs. Kleeve."

"But, Ardith, you called *me.* I was extremely busy, and you interrupted me at a critical moment and said—"

"Mrs. Kleeve, answering the phone is optional. Look, I am sorry. If it were up to me . . . my hands are tied."

"But listen . . ." The woman was escaping with the last blush of Louise's youth. Now nobody would believe she had lived and worked and loved at thirty-nine. Time was dissolving her, blurring nose into cheeks, into chin, into clavicle. Clay. "Oh, Ardith, sure you won't change your mind?"

"You could go somewhere and have it done. Sears would be happy to take you. You don't even need an appointment."

"No," she said dejectedly. "It's too far. It's not the sort of thing I'd go out of my way for."

"What can I say, ma'am?"

"Ma'am? What happened to *Lou?*"

"Not every relationship pans out, ma'am."

"I'll pay full price."

"I have other calls to make. I'm hanging up now, OK?"

"Ardith?"

"Bye now." The woman from Good Forever was gone in the tenderest of disconnections, a barely audible click, and in the flow of dial tone the face Louise would weep for someday was ferried away. Now time would run with her, and she would age quickly and die, oh, dear, oh, dear . . .

When she returned to work, she discovered that it was now too late to add the slowing agent, and her miracle compound had set up too far to be poured, and the chemicals had eaten the mixing bowl and ulcerated the floorboards. Today the elements were working overtime, even back here, where *she* made the rules.

She carried the batch of slurry out back and dumped it in the woods. She rinsed out the pan. Her face might be past saving, but there were still the various consolations of the Room, not the least of which was this: Nobody could take her failures and display them. If nothing else, her mistakes were hers, and tomorrow, maybe, when she was older, she would know better. Tomorrow she would fix it.

One minute she was on her way to the kitchen, feet on the ground, the next she was pedaling space. Strong arms girded her rib cage, lifting, turning her in the air, dropping her gently to the carpet. She rolled to one side immediately, keeping one shoulder raised, for the instinct to go unpinned was supreme now in all of them. "Michael," she said, "it's not polite to wrestle your mother."

Driving for an arm-and-leg lock, he stopped, dropped back to his knees. He brushed his palms together, pretending she was done for, duck soup. Then he helped her up. "Mama," he said, "how many times do I have to tell you? Never, never walk around the house like that. Never let down your guard. Look, lady, I'll give it to you one more time." Burlesquing her, he started to mince around the room, arms floating like a dancer's. "Keep your elbows tucked," he said, demonstrating. "Don't let *anything* stick out. Your legs should form a solid base at all times. Be prepared for the unexpected."

"Gotcha," she said. Feigning an intention to continue kitchenward, Louise wheeled back instead, going at him the only way she knew how. She lunged for his head, and when her arm was securely hooked around the thick stalk that was his neck, she dragged hard, getting leverage by coming off the ground herself. Michael let himself be felled, dropping beneath her only to roll slickly on through the move so that, with a small *whump*, Louise landed flat on her back.

Michael howled. He brushed the hair out of his eyes. "That was the dumbest, stupidest move I've ever seen in my life." Laughing loosened his hold, enabling her to crank upward several notches. Then she turned into him, pushing on his chest in a muscle move so singularly inept that Michael fell back in hysterics. The more ridiculous her methods, the harder he laughed, and thus it was that her most useless moves—always some form of brute force—were also her most effective. And every time he came close to nailing her, she'd yell, "Ow! My arm! My leg!" knowing he'd never have the heart to test her sincerity. It was a ploy she considered doubly funny, and once she had him in stitches, then she'd go after his ribs.

"That tickles!" he yelled.

"Who's the champ?" she said.

He grinned. "Me!"

She stepped up the treatment, striking with agonizing randomness, singing, as she had when he was two, "I'm going to drill a hole. . . ." Somewhere she'd read that tickling was a civilized form of torture. "*Who?*" she said. "I didn't hear you, Rotweiler."

"I give up," he cried. "It's you. You're the champ."

"Who?"

"You."

"Champion of what?"

"Peru." He giggled.

"Come again, McNertny?"

"National champion!" he shrieked.

"Wrong again," she said. "World champion. Say it. World."

"World champion."

"Champion of the universe."

"Intergalactic champion."

She thought of Ardith Budner. "Champion of Forever." And leapfrogging then from dimension to dimension, when there was no time or space left untested, she let up on him, her smile abashed now and foolish. "From now on," she said, "you don't scrimmage your mother. I mean it."

Scrambling to his feet, Michael shook his hand at her to show that his fingers were crossed.

"Anyhow," she was saying. "You're supposed to be sick." Working over the cutting board, she handed him half a grapefruit, which he examined and handed back.

"You do look a little peaked," she said.

"I'm feeling much better actually."

"What am I supposed to do with this?" she asked, tapping the grapefruit.

"If you really love me, you'll section it for me."

"Like fun," she said, spinning it onto the board. He was kidding, but he meant it, too. How was it that men so easily sniffed out that willingness of even undomestic women to serve in matters of food and nutrition? "You'd better eat a little more than that."

"Gimme a lemon."

She tilted back to regard him. "How bright your eyes are, Cotswold." The deprivations of the past weeks had turned his complexion grayly radiant; light furred his surface, a riveting translucence. "I could advertise you and get a monthly check from Paul Newman."

He caught her eyes coaxingly, the corners of his mouth turned down. It was the kind of vulnerability you'd show only to a pretend enemy.

"Uh-oh," she said. "What is it now, Rotweiler?"

"Promise you won't get mad."

"You broke your bed."

"No."

"Lost your retainer."

"Haven't worn a retainer since ninth grade."

She straightened her shoulders and blinked hard. So the boy with the retainer was gone, too, with his mother's youth. She looked at him closely now, as though snapping a more recent picture. "Well, then, let's have it."

"I want to get to school in time for practice."

Now she had to get tough. "Too sick for class but fit for a good stiff workout? No dice, Clyde."

He put his arm around her, his wide smile mocking her outright.

"And what if the principal would catch us waltzing in at three?"

"He won't," Michael said, looking askance at her, watching for her inevitable collapse into his agenda.

She took him by the shoulders. "Now listen," she said. "This is important. You cannot keep your own hours. Not in this world you can't. A major aim of your education is to acquaint you with the various terms of the 'social contract.'" (What the hell was she talking about?) "You give something, you get something. You learn calculus, they let you use the wrestling room."

"I get straight A's."

She had hoped he wouldn't, as he always did, force her deeper. She would have to explain the interplay of ritual, faith, and public compliance, the duty of each of us to participate in the common theaters of experience and learning. She could make an equation of love, of solidarity with fellow seekers, even the teachers, who knew so little they wept at night for want of a vocabulary word. We paid for peace with a piece of ourselves. The coin was us, our time, heart, will, intellect, even flesh if necessary.

One night Trover came home from the bars disconsolate. "I want my fingerprints back," he'd told her. The U.S. Army had them. They'd taken his prints at basic training, and he had not known better. He gave Louise a woeful look. "I should have clenched my fists," he said, demonstrating. "I should have made them pry the suckers open." One by one he'd unfurled his fingers. He stared despairingly at his fingertips as if they were all rings missing their emeralds, and the fool was weeping, weeping.

As Louise grappled with the great issues, attempted to mediate between society's demands and the rights of the common man, Michael moved in. He was circling, crouching low, fingers spread, his eyes searching for purchase. "Dammit," she said, slapping at his hands. "Now knock it off."

He was dancing at her, pincering in. She was back stepping fast. Now he had her against the refrigerator. He read aloud from the note just above her right ear. "Self, if you can't find your good coat, it's at the cleaners." She had the refrigerator door to push off from, yet when she tried to shove Michael back, he stood firm, smiling at her. It frightened her some, the powerlessness of her female limbs, even against this good son, benevolent contender. Her dutiful pique over the boy's truancy then took on even greater freight, that vague panic you feel when they won't let you be angry.

With his curved fingers he formed a vise. "Did you say, 'Go in peace, my son'?" he said.

"I did not!"

Against her throat his hands were icy. Starvation, no doubt, was keeping the blood from his extremities. He tightened the circle, a choker of bones.

"Michael, stop it!"

He made a ferocious underbite. "What was that?" he said. "I didn't hear you."

"Come on, let go. I have work to do."

"Repeat after me."

She grunted and shoved.

"Repeat after me, 'I will be honored to take my beloved son to work out with the team.' " She loved the way he laughed when he was trying not to. In little snips and scissorings.

And she was laughing, too, in that unwilling way, with hands on her throat, and the sounds coming out not round but notched and broken, as if she were laughing up shale. It didn't matter whose hands; it made her very nervous to have her throat worried.

"Repeat after me, 'I will be honored to cut my son's grapefruit into little bite-size portions.' "

She was licked, she knew, the instant she'd relinquished her rightful tone. The second she smiled, he had her. "OK, you win. Now unhand me, you ape." And when he eased up on her, she ducked under his arms, waving two sets of crossed fingers. She sprinted off and went upstairs. Then she came back down to section his grapefruit.

And she also agreed to take him to practice. To mollify the almost obscene ease of her surrender, she added conditions, saw to it he would have to go far out of his way before arriving where he most wanted to be. He would not get a free day of it. "We're going to visit Sprecher," she said. "You aren't ready right after lunch, I'm leaving without you. And if you expect not to be able to find your wallet, you'd best not be able to find it right now while there's still time to look."

He began to look for his wallet just as she was shooing him out the door. He found it twenty minutes later. Then Louise mislaid her purse, and as she searched the house, his gym bag disappeared. "It couldn't have walked away!" he wailed. And then when they seemed to have everything, she looked at him and couldn't remember when he didn't have that grimy stringed bag slung over his shoulder, that he wasn't wearing something stretched out and highly absorbent with a hood. She pulled up the hood and stood back. How his eyes burned back at her, clear and blue, like tunnels you could follow out of time.

As was their practice, Louise allowed the unlicensed boy to drive a piece, the length of their road and then as far as the four-lane. This was also despite the fact that Michael was as hard on cars as he was on human nerves. Not that he deliberately mistreated them or even drove recklessly. He was, after all, a gentle boy. Under his control, though, vehicles behaved like children in the hands of a substitute teacher; they went crazy with blowing tires, and parts fell off, and mufflers sprang gaping holes, and hoses leaked.

After five minutes they'd be riding in billows of smoke and commotion. Now, when he reached for the radio, the knob twisted off in his hand.

"Try not to touch anything you don't absolutely have to," Louise pleaded.

"Yes, ma'am," he said. He hit the seam between macadam and clay too hard. They popped up in unison and settled back without another word. They bounced over the tiny concrete bridge that spanned the tunnel passing beneath the roadway.

Louise said, "How's your heart, Polycarp?"

"Good."

"Good."

Across their path lay a broad pink board the barn had shucked off. Michael stopped the truck and got out. He tossed the board back to the barn and stood for a moment, taking in the broken, bloated hulk of the old farm buildings.

"First good wind," he said sadly, getting back in. At the foot of the road he made a left. He stopped at the next intersection. "Hey," he said, brightening again, "what's the gross national product of Japan?"

"Who cares?"

"Just give me an answer."

"Forty-five billion dollars."

He shook his head, giving her his egglike pedantic look. "Spam Orientale," he said smugly.

"I don't get it."

"A *gross* national product."

"You just made that up."

"Could you tell? Come on, you couldn't tell. I thought it was pretty good."

"You would, cornball."

"OK," he said, pulling out. "Try this one. There are five apples. I take away three. How many do I have?"

She gave him a look of stylized suspicion. "Trick question, right? Ah, three. You have three. Right, angelfat?"

"Very good, Mama."

At the next stop sign they switched seats. Louise made the wide sweeping turn around Sweetfern Horse Farm. Three Arabians stood at pretty angles to one another and seemed to be listening toward the bony woods. They passed through a grove of pine and rhododenron. When they emerged from the bottle-colored dark, Michael quietly said, "Is there a heaven, Mom?"

"That's a joke, right? Some sort of riddle?"

"No," he replied. "I just want to know."

She cast him a quick sidewise glance and saw the caught breath, the sweaty grip he had on the question. He actually expected an answer. A wave of resentment washed over her, the kind she hadn't felt since her children were small and her world soaked with their piss and fragility. She felt unbearably burdened. She had given this child life, and now an eternity was required of her. What was she supposed to say? She wanted to punch him.

"We'll discuss this later," she snapped, as if he'd just made some spoiled brat demand. Someday, doubt on the downswing, hope rising, faith flowing like milk, she'd come stumbling at him with the news, even if such a copious moment should come, as it often did, in the dead of night. Yes, she'd come up with something. If there weren't already a heaven, for such a child they would have to invent one.

When they came in, Sprecher was sitting in a chair next to the windowsill holding the chrysanthemums they'd sent him, his pajamas on the floor. He peered out through the flower heads and then fixed his gaze upon some point well beyond them. Even more alarming, Michael's appearance provoked in him no more than a brief but dying spark across the eyes. Louise and Michael then set the flowers on the window ledge, helped him on with his clothes, only to have him, in his methodical way, strip again to skin. He reached for the flowers, which he planted again over his defeated blue genitals.

Flowers had seemed a ridiculous gift for a man who showed them such relentless contempt. Who hacked down tulips and scythed columbines at the height of their season. Sprecher was tender only to food crops. Once Louise might have been silly enough to send him a bag of carrots or a pound of seed potatoes. She remembered what she had brought to the Sprechers' fiftieth anniversary party, not long before Perma died. It was a time when sugar was scarce and expensive. Perma, she knew, was doing without. "White gold" the media was calling it, so sugar seemed doubly apt for a golden occasion. When Perma opened the ungainly package (five five-pound bags), she cast Louise a speculative glance and set the gift aside. She went on to marvel over subsequent offerings, a dozen or so assorted commemorative vessels—cups and bowls and brandy snifters—bearing tacky happy anniversary letters, all from Hottensteins' Gifts in Lorraine. Watching Perma rejoice over the resolutely useless, Louise knew she'd never be quite forgiven for her gift of common sugar. Maybe she was learning these Germans at last. Maybe the sugar business was the only lesson she'd ever learned, and that is why she sent Sprecher mums instead of seed potatoes.

Louise went out to the nurses' station. In order to wrest from the duty nurse the scantiest data, she had to pass herself off as Sprecher's niece, his next of kin. "For your information, they brought him in in a straitjacket," the woman told her, in a voice that really said, "That's what you get for asking." She read from the report: ". . . patient observed by broom factory foreman behaving in crazed, erratic, hyperactive manner. Incoherent. Possibly violent. Patient responded inappropriately when approached."

"But I spoke to him not three days ago," Louise said. "He recognized me then. Now he's practically catatonic. My God, what's wrong with the man?"

"Your uncle's getting on there," she said. "These seizures are not uncommon in a man his age. Believe me, I've seen worse."

"When might you expect to have a diagnosis?"

"That's hard to say. He's not one bit cooperative. Half the time he's not even . . . decent."

Back in Sprecher's room, Louise spotted his vacated coveralls and three yellowed union suits hanging like a brace of farmhands. Underneath stood his cracked black clodhoppers, mere shells still holding the churlish curl of the ancient, angry feet that had given them vigor and shape and transported a half ton of manure into parlors and general stores over a lifetime. The solid heft of his cast-off clothes made Sprecher seem even barer, raw as plowed ground. She ripped the top sheet off his bed.

"Michael, take an end," she said, and together they draped the sheet over his shoulders, tucking it under his chin and under the base of the plant. Michael let his hand hover a second or two above Sprecher before giving the silvery head an affectionate pat. And Sprecher managed to muster enough strength to reach up and whisk him away.

They left the hospital then, and Louise headed west to Lorraine. They were quiet and thoughtful and halfway there Louise realized that she was unwittingly taking the highly recogizable Jeep back to the scene of the crime. But how else was she to get Michael to school? The problem, she figured, hinged simply enough on her lack of practice. She was not used to thinking like a felon, maneuvering her affairs around the snares and sinkholes of a less than rectitudinous life.

But that was sloppy thinking, she saw. Worse, it was untrue. She lied a little every day and salted Trover's money away along with her own. And Julio—hadn't she schemed to see him and schemed not to be seen? How many times had she slipped beef broth in the soup, letting Trover think it was meatless? But it was equally fair to say that her evasions were not lies so much as small capsules of diverted truth that like the stashed money, sooner or later she'd turn in. Trover would use the money to equip his retirement, with T-shirts and gadgets. With the truth, she would buy little more than trouble, yet it would burn a hole in her possession, and it would out. How could it not, with all those eyes on her?

A grandmother who said, "pardon me," to tables and chairs, when she bumped their legs with the vacuum cleaner.

Sister Bruno, who upon seeing Louise with a blue towel over her shampooed head, gushed, "Oh, Louise, you look just like the Virgin Mary. My, quite an image to live up to."

Trover, who for all his calumnies, believed her to be far better than he was. And she'd never troubled to correct him.

The narrow man on the long wooden skis. Or was she thinking here of Christ? Christ? The thought surprised her. But yes, once they put Him into you, how did you remove so deep a burn without dying in the process?

But today was claimed, taken up with practical matters; she would stay in hiding, skirt this crime the way her art circumvented her worst deficiencies. They had plenty of time until three. Her best bet was to enter Lorraine at the southwest corner, from the grid of small towns and patchwork farmland to which she'd escaped the day of the mishap. She'd drop Michael off, then continue down far east of town, where she would cut across the Neisstown road and take another off-the-beaten path home.

Off somewhere, that lost look in his eye, Michael did not seem to notice that she'd left the thoroughfare. He was absently chewing on the radio knob, and just as absently Louise took it from him. A sulfurous sun dissolved into a powdery glow before her. Into that dying light she continued to angle, ever west on roads that never stopped to give her bearings but looped and turned with exquisite abandon, like a ball of yarn given infinite slack. She was not afraid of getting lost; eventually she always came out at a K Mart or Hardee's.

From the crest of a small rise the Jeep took a sudden plunge. The valley was deep and weakly green. Then they were soaring upward again, into open land patched with stubbled squares and stripes of soft green seedlings, like baby hair. Now down through a rugged landscape strewn with giant blue boulders. They clattered past a cider mill, a meadow edged with brown lace, down still farther, to soggy bottomland.

"Whoa!" Michael called out, and his mother swerved off to the berm. He came around and helped Louise down out of the driver's seat. He escorted her like a lady of rank to the lip of a vetch-covered drop. "Lo!" he said. They were looking out over a wide swale, at the edge of which wagged a patch of cattails popping their yellow stuffing. The rest of it, all the way out to where the terrain began to rise again to dry ground, was an ocean of pampas grass, its opulent plumes alive in the light wind, and the earth seemed to sway all in the same direction.

She looked at him questioningly. He said, "You want weeds, woman, do we got weeds." And so he took her hand, and they scrambled down the bank, catching Spanish needles as they descended. At the bottom they stepped in ooze up to their shoelaces, and Louise thought she had never seen anything so lovely as the pampas feathering together, that liquid rippling shimmer, and the closer view, each curled frond studded with little seed stars that puffed away at the touch. Michael's pale fingers were shy along the spines, and then he blew the dust from his hand.

It was growing late; they gathered quickly without speaking. Michael carried the stalks to the truck and set off down the road, disappearing around the first curve. He returned minutes later with an armful of something wild and stiff and grumpy-looking, a red-brown shrub with gnarled joints and hard, barky, erratic branches.

"Sprecher plant," he said.

And Louise could hardly laugh at this because the giddiness had struck up and bonded with something else working inside her, something like Ping-Pong balls or wind chimes, a raucous pandemonium of sorrow and gladdening that was close to the tyranny of tickling. So that nothing bright or good might escape, she clapped her hand over her mouth. She watched Michael lay the disgruntled plant next to the bundle of pampas grass; then they boarded the Jeep with muddy feet and took off uphill out of the swag.

When they were moving through gentler country, the crazed elation subsided to something closer to the quiet land swell billowing out and around them. And neither was faith a steady thing. It waxed and waned, came and went. Faith took rhythm and thrust from its tidal encounters with doubt. Faith, like the sea, the land, the cycles of life and dying and every story ever told, washed in and out. *Now* was her time to know what she knew. "Yes," she said, "the answer to your question is yes."

"Good," he said, "That's what I figured," and they continued around the same dairy farm twice before finding the road they knew would take them to New Jerusalem, where they would pick up the spur leading to Eckville and then down the long straightaway past the Farmers' Market and the Old Smoke Church, and then they were at the school where a line of yellow buses waited out front. Running toward their cars, departing classmates waved to arriving Michael. She deposited him at the door of the wrestling room, waited until he was safely inside, then fell into line with the outbound buses and headed home.

CHAPTER
19

Trover Kleeve gave his family to believe that whether or not he arrived on time was entirely the doing of factors beyond his control: loquacious clients; traffic jams; the guys he was forever bumping into, faceless Jims and Jakes and Rons who bought him drinks obligating him to untold cycles of reciprocity. But wrestling nights betrayed his best excuses. Wrestling nights, unfailingly, he was home before dark. And he was home happy, expansive, his Irish side alive without a single drink in him. Tonight he came in singing "Waltzing Matilda." Trover knew all the verses. When he came to "Here's the jolly jambock I put in my tuckerbag," he swung the day's take onto the counter.

Gingerly Louise poked into the first bag. In silent scorn she removed four portly tomes, textbooks to be exact. *Algebra I* and *II, Calculus of One Variable, Advanced Calculus.* "Why?" she asked, looking stricken. "Why, Trover, why?"

"Use your imagination, Louise. Supposing one of us develops an urge to learn something for certain. Trig could provide that."

"We could sign up for night school. Anyhow, what are libraries for?"

Trover smiled. "We have our own library, Louise."

"But we don't have a mathematics section."

"We do now."

"There's no shelf space."

Now he was rolling. "We'll make more shelves."

"Where?"

"We'll add rooms."

"Oh, yeah. How?"

"We'll add another porch," he said. "All around the house. Then we'll wall it up, just like we did with the first one. Then, if I feel the urge to expand my reference section or something, we'll tack on another porch and enclose it and then another, and so on, as long as we both shall live."

"Help!" she said.

"Here." He handed her the second bag, as if material gain were just the thing to appease her.

Peeking inside, she brightened. "Mmmmm, something good to eat." She fished out Greek olives, Russian rye bread, and Jarlsberg cheese. "What's this?"

"Gourmet bean salad."

"Oh, what makes it gourmet?"

Trover flipped back the plastic lid and looked. "The corn," he said matter-of-factly.

"I see," she said. "You want some for dinner?"

"I don't eat bean salad," he said. "Or didn't you know that?"

"What can I get you then?"

"I'll just nibble," he said. Wrestling nights he was so full of hope there was hardly room for food. And Louise didn't eat much either. For religious reasons, he presumed. In Michael's name, a sacrifice of calories.

"Where's the Ant King?" he asked.

"Up in his room. Can't you hear?" she said, cupping her ear, turning, whisking the delicate drift toward Trover. "He's taking a music appreciation minicourse this quarter. Guess how they're teaching kids these days to recognize Mozart's fortieth."

"I give up."

"OK," she said, waiting for the right phrase. "Now listen." Her finger danced lively little arabesques in the air as she belted out the words "Mozart's in the clawwwwwwwset." The finger stopped and then parried thrice. "Let him out, let him out, let him out." She was watching Trover expectantly, her face tensed on the brink of enjoyment, brow faintly quizzical. Her pleasure apparently hinged on his participation. His laugh would crack her wide open. He studied her face. That's how a girl would look waiting for a man to propose. Trover had never actually done that, proposed. He'd just nudged and spun her toward the altar as one might dance a date into a darkened garden. He'd kept waiting for Louise to say, "Whoooaaaa, Trover, where do you think you're taking me?" But she hadn't. Despite the limited discourse, they'd married anyhow, and here it was almost twenty years later and he had a woman on his hands still waiting to be asked. Would a laugh do it? If he laughed with her now, would it ratify their union?

He said, "Ribbet," and, "Ribbet," again and ate a black olive. "Open up, sis." He fed her a yellow bean, then left her there, as ever, just inches shy of winning him.

Now he set about performing the small chores that constituted a biweekly rite. He examined his sound camera, new last season. Fastidiously he dusted the casing and polished the lens. He saw to it the film was fresh and the supply sufficient to last as long as Michael's opponent. Where three packs were more than ample, Trover stuffed his camera bag with three dozen. Then he bounded upstairs to check out Michael.

He found him turning at full tilt, a metallic burr in the storm the music made in the slanting attic room. Sealed in a silver rubber suit, he alternated running in place with gyrating from the waist. "Mozart's in the clawwwww-set," Trover sang to himself, quite helplessly: The teaching aid had taken over the symphony and the notes would never be themselves again. The music seemed to pick up heat from the mustard-colored walls and Michael's frenzy; the air shimmered, dripping with sweat and arpeggios. "How far over?" Trover hollered above the classical racket.

"Two pounds," Michael said. He was flushed, puffing. He tucked wisps of dripping hair under his hood, then returned to his rotations.

Trover turned down the sound system. He wagged his head. No need to explain. They both knew you couldn't suck weight right before a match without risking a critical loss of strength. Trover made as if to leave in disgust, then thought better of it. He strode over to Michael and pulled his arms out of the air and held them down. Catching the sky-colored eyes, he bore down with his hard dark ones. "On second thought, Son," he said, "how can you lose? You're one of the great ones."

Michael dropped his gaze and waited politely for Trover to release his limbs to their propeller work. "Do me a favor, Dad," he said. "Don't believe in me so much. Mighty's doing some real exciting things with color. Can't you get interested in *her?*"

"Forget I said anything." He gave his son that droopy look that pegged the boy ungrateful. And none too bright. Didn't the kid understand, just the sound of the word "winning" was a boon to Trover, the ring of silver, solid coin. A mat victory was a kind of clear Lucite in which all of them were preserved whole and untouchable, forever excellent, invulnerable to muggers or mad dogs or age.

Once his own triumphs had been enough, each win dipping him in glitter, even as he was plunged into multiple dungeons by each defeat. It used to be a good verdict would last him awhile. Not anymore. As he got older and the age more dangerous, it seemed he required more and bigger boys behind him. He needed not just Michael, but the entire Panther bench to win. He needed many teams these days: the Lackawanna Loggers and Nittany Lions, the Pirates and Steelers of his western Pennsylvania past. When the teams of his youth and bachelorhood slumped, he switched to the local heroes. The Seventy-sixers, Phillies, Flyers. Bullpens, kickoff squads, off-ense, de-fense, whole armies mustered in front of him.

He went downstairs and changed into a pair of cross-country knickers, some hiking boots he'd been wanting to break in. It was vaguely disheartening that nobody winced, not even his daughter, always on the watch for oddity.

At the meet he took his customary place in the stands, bottom tier, just to the right of the statistician's table, a spot affording him an unimpeded field for filming Michael's match. From there he could also establish a rapport with the scorekeeper. "Smarten up," he told the boy when the wrong total flashed on the board during one of the jayvee bouts. "Give the kid his back points, *please.*"

"Boo!" he yelled routinely to the ref, a fine-boned black man who moved around the mat like a dancer. "Boo! Boo!" when the ref called pins—depending on which team was at risk—too fast or too slow. Somewhere in the upper bleachers were Mighty and Gideon, standoffishly off with their friends. The nun had come in mufti. In Louise's loden kilt and knee socks, she could pass for a girl, a fifties teen. Single women always seemed to him less finished somehow, better able to assume new forms than married ones. The nun, he thought, was trying on lives as frantically as a shopper, just as the store was closing.

Louise would be up there, too, next to the sister, girding herself for Michael's time. Were his opponent of greater repute, she would have stayed at home. "In another age," she once said, "I'd have been the mother of a gladiator. You think I don't know what the fall really *means?*"

Little Jeff Kern led off for the varsity. "Locked hands," Trover informed the young referee, who replied at first with a cryptic smile. Then he flung out his arms as if to say, "Hey, take it easy. Boys will be boys."

"Locked hands!" Trover insisted, and this time the ref shrugged and reluctantly called it.

Once the Crusher opened his grip, the Panther reversed him. Into the lull that followed came the sharp tracery of Mrs. Kern's instructions to her son: "Shoot the half, Jeff. Attaboy." Then, when he threw in a cradle, her clean sirenic alert: "Too high, too high!" Her son looked up, his eyes lost in their dusky sockets. Grimacing, he searched out her face. "Ease back now," she called calmly as an air controller talking a small plane through fog. And ease back he did. As the meet progressed, Trover noticed other boys harking to her counsel, and coming as it did from a tiny graying lady hardly distinguishable in the busy plasticity of the crowd, it had an almost oracular effect.

The Panther bench was, in actuality, a crooked line of folding chairs stretched roughly the width of the mat. Over their singlets the boys wore fleecy white meet jackets. In the center slumped Coach Yoder, his face one of those wide, pliable ones that showed every crimp and dimple of emotion, a wax register of events. You could figure things out as well by scanning the lineup, know at a glance who'd gone already and been defeated. The losers occupied their space with the hopeless skew of discarded socks. Flop-limbed, sloppily folded, they stared ahead or held tiny smiles to the point of spoilage.

Up and down the bench the boys sucked cut oranges while their managers, two girls not pretty enough for cheerleading, quartered more. The citric sharpness cut the gymnasium reek in much the same way something tart relieved a meal of fatty meat and gravy.

Spot Grayrain loped onto the mat, snapping his headgear in place. Always about this time Michael, too, left his seat and walked back behind the warm-up mat, where the on-deck wrestlers were being broken in over bigger boys' backs. On the narrow strip of varnished floor he began his ceremonial walk. He paced with hands behind his back and his head pitched forward. Face perplexed, he strode and slowed, walked and stopped, with the anguished stoop of theologians muddying their minds with the great questions.

A minute to go, Grayrain dominant but down by three. He needed at least a near fall. Trover looked up. Thirty seconds. Twenty-nine. "Green's not wrestling," he informed the ref. Ignored, he craned forward. "Yoo-hoo! Wake up out there. Stalling on the bottom! Stalling on the bottom!" He'd hoped to provoke a hometown chorus, but nobody picked up his cue.

Instead, from the Crusher side, a lone baritone boomed back at him, "Stalling on *top*, stupid."

Miming confusion at first, the lithe little official then spun *en pointe* and called the boy in green for stalling. He wheeled again and called Grayrain for the same. His great white smile spread jawbone to jawbone, and he bowed to both sides.

Trover didn't have to look back to know who was pounding down the bleachers. Louise squeezed in next to him. "Shove over . . . *stupid.*" Her lips were so close the *S*'s tickled the fine hairs of his ear. "Christ, you're worse than the Platz boys."

She meant the beefy simpleton siblings who always sat across the top tier, delivering a steady contumelious torrent against both contenders, home and away.

"Kid was dragging butt," Trover said.

"So, who appointed you wrestling commissioner?"

Trover filled his cheeks with air.

"And the knickers just make it worse."

"And what are you, pope of dress code?" God, they were all in quality control, inspectors every one.

But Louise's mouth had tipped, producing a crooked, experimental smile, and he felt safer now in the light of loving disapproval than if she just plain loved him, kindly, blindly. Emboldened, he said, "Here," and handed her a sealed film packet. "Have this ready in case I need it."

Trover kept a rein on himself through the next two, losing matches, though he could not seem to help making even his restraint conspicuous, lips bitten back, arms binding each other, all the agitation and unrest confined to one wildly bucking runaway knee. As the time grew near, Louise began the process of ossification. She sat almost frozen now, hands in lap, feet flat on the floor. A twist of irony lent her face interest, the look of the determinedly good-humored even unto death. Only once did she respond when he glanced at her, and that was to say, "Feel my heart," which request he declined emphatically.

The thirty-two-pounder pinned in the second period but lost a team point by shaking a triumphant fist at the opposing stands. "Dummy," Trover muttered.

Trover zoomed in as Michael strode onto the mat where the kid from Coalport waited, prancing, blowing into his fists. Michael's manner was diffident, a shade ungainly. He reminded Trover of himself as a greenhorn lawyer stepping up to the bench. With the handshake came a shy, apologetic smile, a flickering glance of dubious amusement, as if to say, "I don't know, pal. You sure this is what you want?" Next to spider-limbed Michael the shorter, wider kid looked alarmingly indestructible.

Halfway through the first period the boys were still sparring, feinting, waltzing each other back and forth across the mat. "Shoot!" Yoder yelled. "For once, *you* shoot!" But Trover knew Michael would stick with tradition, trust to the rubrics of countering. When the kid finally came in, it was a dive against the legs. Michael replied with a lizard flick of a whizzer. Side by side, arms linked, they jockeyed for balance. Dragging downward, they struggled into a hard hiplock, on the face of it a stalemate. Michael reared up, pivoting on one knee. His right arm rocketed, hooking under the other's shoulder, and with a superhuman surge he delivered the final grunting thrust of circular force that pancaked the kid over. The Crusher landed on his back, but the buzzer sounded; the round was done.

Michael drew the down position and freed himself in under ten seconds. He turned and took his man down again with a textbook ankle pick. He released the Crusher, who immediately lunged and was dumped again. Michael began to toy with this kid, to work his gifts with the slow, smooth articulation of total command. Trover's son was exquisite, classic execution, all business. No ferocious gestures or phony stylistics, not a single extraneous move.

Michael took the boy down and let him up, took him down and helped him to his feet, a salesman showcasing his samples. Who said he was weak in takedowns? "Pack 'em!" somebody shouted, as if the fall were something Michael owed his public, something he had, in the pleasure of play, selfishly lost sight of. He dropped the Crusher again, from a fireman's carry. "Pick an ankle!" called Shirley Kern. Now Michael laced a leg and began to ride hard. He tried a Jacob's, and the smooth, seedy whir of the camera seemed to be Michael's own sound, seamless, reliable.

Michael took the opponent's left arm and lifted it over his own head. He was not afraid to lie back, exposing his own shoulders to peril, and for a moment a tenuous physical pact was struck between the two young bodies; the figure they made became superb architecture, a triangular harmony of perfect balance, a moment's truce between equal and opposite, dominant and down, I and thou. Then Trover's heart started to flutter as Michael lay precariously back, the weight of his upper body now testing the equilibrium. The entire structure bent, then buckled, and the Crusher's shoulders sank closer to the mat. Trover dropped greedily to one knee, pitched forward on his elbows, his Sanyo ready to collect the fall.

"Damn!" he said. The camera sound had changed to a warning click. He reached behind him and made gimme fingers at Louise. Getting no response, he twisted around only to see that his wife was all but glazed over, eyes glued to the mat. He snapped his fingers in her face. "Yo, Louise. The film!"

Under his panicked gaze her eyes closed tight; her face drained the last of its color. Robotlike, she handed him the cartridge. "Shit," he said. It was still sealed in its wrapper.

He made a disgusted guttural sound. "I can't live with this incompetence," he muttered. Plunking down the camera, he tore away the foil, dropped the film, bobbled the clip, and recovered it. Reloaded at last, he looked up to find his subject. "You're kidding!" he said, as if the spectacle facing him were merely some implausible plot development. For the boy on the bottom was not the Coalport fish but his own invincible son. Worse, Michael lay in extremis, trying desperately to bridge out of the tightest half nelson the Crusher would ever throw on a guy. Michael raised his right shoulder, then the left, according to where the ref was. Like a springbok, the referee went about his duties, pronking back and forth across the bodies, dropping to his haunches, then to his belly, scuttling around behind their heads.

The suddenness of the upset so unhinged Trover that he forgot to raise his camera again to the fray. Stunned and sick, he watched with his own unmitigated vision as Michael's predicament deepened, and once, for a split second, the space between his shoulder blades and the mat vanished entirely. "Oh, God, he's gone," he said.

But the ref was between vantage points. He hadn't seen. *Oh, God, thank God!* Officially the pin didn't exist. The cheated Crusher stands took up an affronted thunder. "Four seconds!" Trover yelled to give the boy heart as he tried to hang on. And away people's rage traveled from their stomping feet to the bleachers to the floor boards and up and down all the long dark halls in Trover's bones.

Three. Two. One. Trover mopped his brow.

He knelt silently for several moments. Then, swallowing, he turned very slowly to the woman behind him. Louise showed no outward signs of having lived through a squeaker. She showed no signs of life at all. Her eyes were still shut, her breathing shallow, her lips dry and white. "Well," he said quietly, "I hope you're satisfied."

As it turned out, Michael survived. He played the third period close to the mat, where he was most at home, most masterly. He picked up another near fall and the final score stood, incredibly, twenty-one to nine. Cat and mouse. But the score lied. The victory had not gone uncompromised. And Trover could not let go of that moment of terrible peril. The experience offended him in a place far deeper than pride, violated much more than his sense of athletic integrity. When they got home, he took up his *Complete Guide to Body Power and Self-Defense,* which he only pretended to peruse while the powdery dread kicked up in his heart settled. Later, when Michael came home with pizza on his face, Trover shook the boy's hand. "Nice going," he said.

"Thanks," said Michael, with not a trace of self-irony.

Trover followed him into the kitchen, watched him swirl Ovaltine powder into a pint glass of milk. "You came back from the dead, Son. Or didn't you know that?"

The boy half grimaced and half grinned.

"For crying out loud, what happened there?"

"Dad, *things* happen. Planes drop out of the sky. One minute it's nice, the next rainy. Cold sneaks in and freezes things. . . ."

"Same old Michael. Ask him how come he almost got schmeared and he discusses the weather."

"Well, I'm not exactly sure how it happened. I mean, I remember thinking . . ."

Trover shook his head. "About every blooming thing but the matter at hand, I'm willing to bet."

Michael screwed up his face. "You couldn't exactly call it thinking either. Uh, see, I had this music in my head, Mozart's fortieth—you know that one, Dad? Well, it played on and on, and that kid from Coalport was like my cello or something. I could get him to do any tune I wanted. I was completely in charge and he was so darn easy I could play him in my sleep, and then I got thinking about that old composer, all these years in his dark closet and his music so bright and alive outside. For a second I could hardly breathe I felt so bad for him. . . ."

"Attaboy, blame it on Mozart."

Michael smiled. "Hey, hey. Papadog, I won, didn't I?"

Trover adjusted his glasses so he could stare at the boy more penetratingly, laser through to the real issue.

Michael pinched his father's cheek. "You're right," he said. "I acted like a ditz. I should have concentrated on what I was doing. But I am prepared to make you one final offer, right here in River City."

Trover hedged and harrumphed. Then he said, "Which is?"

"You stay as sweet as you are and I'll never get pinned."

Trover turned away in fake disdain and then came slowly around again. "Promise?"

"On Grandpap's grave."

"I'm holding you to that," Trover said.

But Louise had come in, and she was not pleased. She tossed the dirty silver into the dishwasher basket. She took a crusty skillet that had been soaking in the oven and slammed it into the sink with such vehemence that greasy water splashed out, sending man and boy leaping out of the way. They stopped talking, and when they did, she addressed them. "He blamed it on me," she said.

Michael said, "What?"

"That second-period reversal. Your father looked at me and said, 'I hope you're satisfied.' *Me?* What'd *I* do?"

"He's right here," said Trover. "Why don't you ask him?"

"All right," she said. "Let's have it."

He turned to his son, man to man. "Your mother's not herself at those matches," he said. "She thinks her little guy's going to get hurt. She's afraid some goon's going to break your face for you."

"Dad, stick to the subject. How was it Mom's fault?"

"You mother's a bright girl. Let *her* figure it out."

"You owe me an explanation!"

Oh, his wife provoked was not his wife comely. Anger tugged tiny lines around her mouth, weathered her cheek bone. She became for all the world some aging Balkan matriarch bearing up under the slings of the ancient oppressor, eyes malefic as the tips of icicles.

Well, they both knew where they were headed with this one. What did she expect from him? Did she think him crazy enough to try to describe how he'd felt when he returned to the match with his fumblingly reloaded camera? How that lag time, small lapse of his regard, had loomed like a black hole that had taken everything good and turned it inside out. And hadn't Louise been her usual disorganized, unthinking self? Hadn't she neglected a mere pittance of a charge, forcing his fixative eye away, flinging the boy into the perilous murk just beyond his vision? But he could not furnish adequate proof. Moreover, there were some points he did not wish to adjudicate. She would not honor these limits. She would pursue her innocence to the bitter end, and he could feel himself being swept away, lifted inexorably through the familiar concatenation of locks leading to the wide channel of common strife.

CHAPTER

20

Her parents had moved into the front room, and from the kitchen Mighty could feel the fight flesh out over the same old sour bones of contention. No matter how it started or who spooked whom, it always took off like a wild horse in the same direction. Not two people but one wholly integrated stampede of lunacy.

She watched Gideon inspect the inside of the refrigerator, aimlessly, the way you look when you're not really hungry. "This is the only fridge in the world where the light goes *off* when you open the door," he said.

"Grab a couple Neisstowns," she said.

"You sure?"

"They're strapped in for the ride. Sure I'm sure."

He forked the beers over, and she snapped off the tabs and handed him one. She took a mouthful, swallowing hard. "Let's get out of here." Halfway out, she glanced back at him. "Hit the outside lights, will ya?"

The grounds were wired like old-fashioned streets, with bonneted globes on tall, tarry poles. Saucers of thin illumination fanned out at wide intervals along the driveway. High-wattage floods affixed to the corners of the house swept brighter shafts across the lawns and into shrub banks, lacing the edge of the woods. Mighty bushwhacked past the overgrown junipers blocking the walkway to the gazebo. She strode onto the leaf-strewn floor. A circle of yellow bug lights fringed the edge of the hexagonal roof. When Mighty threw the switch, they all lit up at once. Gideon was waiting on the road. She caught his eye, and they smiled, but oddly, like petulant children overtaken with sudden unwelcome delight. It was an embarrassing moment to be alive.

When she came down from the gazebo, they resumed walking. "I remember the first time they brought us here," she said. "It was like they were showing off their little Christmas village or something. 'See the big house. See the pretty porches. See the trees. Look at the brook, the little bridge.' When they turned on these lights, my dad started singing 'Oooompa-pa oooooompa-pa,' " and Mighty imitated his mummer's strut, weaving back and forth between Gideon and the tree peony. She stopped short.

"It was August, crummy hot, and the orchard was full of ripe stuff. White and yellow peaches, rotten pears, purple grapes, raspberries. A slew of gardens. Even a color scheme—red, white, and blue and a huge American flag flying up at the pool."

Gideon looked around. "Where'd all the gardens go?"

"My mom promised the Hummers that she'd try to keep things up. But I guess she got tired of it, and Sprecher wouldn't help her. It was real sneaky the way she let the gardens slide, one a year, so that nobody noticed until it was all gone except for the roses and stuff that blooms every season no matter how much you don't give a shit."

Mighty spun around so that she was looking down toward the gazebo. It rose out of its cloud of bushes and shadow with an aspect of strangely stunned gaiety, a carousel suddenly come to life in an abandoned park. "My first thought when they told us we were buying this place was, wow, a person would be nuts not to be happy here. Everything shipshape the buildings painted, hedges trimmed, tools lined up in the shed. Misery was messy, it wouldn't fit in here. My dad would come home each night, and we'd have picnic suppers on the pavilion by the pool. I imagined Mom with a rake, Dad with a hoe, growing all our food and falling into bed exhausted. And then my next thought was—shee-it."

"How old were you?"

"Going on six."

"Did you think shit when you were only six?"

In reply she swigged again and quickened her pace.

As they walked, Gideon draped his arm across her back. Something flapped wings in the dark of the pump house, and straight ahead, in the distant dark wedged between Tumbling Run and the mountains, was the floating glow of some farmer harvesting his feed corn. As though powered by small explosions, she moved forward in spurts, that relentless inner force of hers pulsing her out from under Gideon's arms, at the same time they passed beneath the ancient boughs of the twin oaks flanking the roadway.

"Where we heading?" Gideon quickstepped apace with her.

"Nowhere." They continued along the roadway, past the pool, past the last of the landscaper's deft asymmetries: the stand of ornamental crab; a single silver birch in a half circle of inkberry and contoneaster bushes; the sweeping wing of white pine. They passed beyond the last arc lamp into open land, where nothing buffered the winds whickering off the mountains. Despite the cold, Mighty made no move to close her coat. "Hey, My," said Gideon, "what d'ya say? Another crop next year?"

Shrugging, she looked out toward the recess in the tree line where eight cannabis plants had grown to the height of sumacs without attracting undue notice. Prime stuff. Gideon had cleared enough cash to get his car fixed and set himself up in business. Turning to him, she stared until the coastline of his face clarified in the chalky dark. Despite its conventional grace, his profile was somehow too acute, ready, a wiliness hardly softened by the stiff cowlick lifting in the wind. He stood vibratingly quiet, stock-still, as if sniffing something he always wanted in the scrub. Maybe it was this animal sharpness, the hint of ever-present hunger, that had prompted her to plant him in her house, to keep everyone vigilant.

The marijuana operation had been nerve racking, but there were times when she had listened almost hopefully for the sound of overhead surveillance, for choppers landing in the meadow, armed men charging the house with a warrant, busting her parents.

That was crazy thinking, she'd conceded that. Still, right at this moment, she would welcome such intervention as the desperate measure required by desperate times. There they were, the two assholes, gearing up for another stupid brawl. Somebody had to stop them, cite them—for what? Well, their crimes were obvious, weren't they? His twisted intellect and supple evasions. That temper. Toenail clippings, yellow and horny all over the house. The way he could never find the *TV Guide* and expected someone else to look.

And her mother's clutter, dust. Once a nasty knot of tar. She made you finish her thoughts for her. Everything she owned chipped and sticky. Gardens grassed over, gone. Wet laundry rotting in the washer. The way she never got used to the way things were but went into a state of shock every time people pulled what they'd been pulling on a regular basis for years. The way she forgave the unforgivable.

A commendable tendency, she'd heard. The Christian way. But Mighty was beginning to see how virtue worked. Once it had passed a certain point on the curve, it began to turn into something else. Louise, in extreme, was nothing but mush. And Mighty suspected she'd once had a lover. Then, too, she'd wanted to call the cops, but there was no stopping her mother, no stopping anybody without a gun. Though she did try to keep her camera handy.

She didn't really want to see her parents in jail. Maybe just in court. Let some judge decide who was upright and who was unjust, who stupid, who lazy, who using whom. Let somebody else do it. Out here she could keep safely out of things that concerned her and aloof from that moment when her father would go roaring off in his car. Each time he left she feared it was for good. She yearned for the law, stern, implacable, armed. "Get back in the house, buddy. Now!"

At the place where the road swept around and down toward the bridge and the foot of the lane, Mighty gave Gideon a tug, turning him back. They sliced across the low meadow, a great hump of land that dropped to a sheltering dell. It was a fairly clear night, a sliver of citron moon and a rubbing of stars. She plunged cold hands deep in her pockets.

Briskly now, they moved along the upper tier of the orchard. Below was a tangle of naked black branches; chinkapin nuts cracked under their feet. They entered the apple orchard. The trees here were huge, unpruned, their crowns interlocked. Coming to an abrupt halt under the dome of dark fretwork, they held each other back. Shhhhhhhhhh, they said. But the deer had vaulted their feeding station under the Northern Spies. A doe and a fawn, the flow of their flight like smoke as they made for cover.

"Listen," Mighty said. She was shivering now, but there was something she wanted to tell him. Gideon drew her close. Men were always shutting you up with hugs. And they were the *nice* ones! She allowed herself a tingle of warmth before wriggling free. "I want to tell you something!"

He threw up his arms as though to show himself weaponless. "What? What?" he said. "I'm listening."

"One summer me and my brother spotted a whole slew of them up there. Ten, maybe twelve whitetail." She gestured vaguely toward the mountains. "Way, way up in the fields. The sun was just going down, and the deer just seemed to be floating in this reddish amber glow. But the really weird part was how the two of us turned without a word and started up there after them.

"They were in that field, over there, but we kept just this side of the tree line. We were very careful where we stepped, and we didn't talk at all. We had to hurry because night was coming on very fast."

"And the deer didn't split?"

She shook her head. "They seemed to be waiting for us. They were getting harder to make out, but you could tell they were turned our way, taking us in, listening. Gid, I swear I felt their breath on my face. It was warm. It smelled like tansy and mint and clover."

"You always get wind up here. *Hot* wind in the dead of summer."

"Breath!" she said fiercely. "I said breath!" She leaped up and snapped off a piece of dead twig. She leaped again against the grip of remembering how it was when they knew for sure that dusk would outrun them. The closer they came, the dimmer the creatures grew, all watery and unreal. And still, they had hurried on, hoping. Hoping what? And now she saw that she had bolted off from Gideon again. She waited for the boy to catch up.

"What'd you want them for anyhow? *Meat?*" he said.

She would have punched him if she hadn't caught the panic in his eye just before he said it. She'd been dragging him with her, leading him to shadows and futility when he, like her, wanted something to touch—handfuls, mouthfuls. "Meat?" she said. "God! We didn't want to *eat* them."

Gideon shrugged.

"You want to know what happened?"

"Yeah, sure."

"Well, by this time we were winded from the climb and the pace we'd kept up. They were so patient, waiting like that. The only trouble was they were still on the other side of the tree line. We couldn't cross over without making noise in the brush. We knew if we tried anything at all, they'd split on us. No way to get closer. We couldn't touch them or take them home with us or whatever it was we expected to do once we got them. The only way we could have any part of them at all was to stay where we were.

"We didn't move a muscle; it seemed like hours. My eyes began to hurt from trying to keep them separate from the dark. The tension was unbearable. Then, just as I thought I couldn't hack it another second, Michael— God, he scared the hell out of me—yelled at the top of his lungs, 'Greetings, beasts!' "

"They took off?"

"Suddenly we just knew they weren't there anymore. At first it was such a relief, and then, well, I felt empty and sad for a long time afterward."

Gideon dropped his gaze. "Yeah," he said. "Sometimes you just want them to take off and be done with it."

She touched his arm. For a moment it seemed that it had been the two of them in the field instead of her and Michael. But when Gideon looked up again, his mouth was bitter.

Now it was he who broke away from her. He went sliding and stumbling downhill over the stones and apple rot, and then he sprang onto a low hanging branch. He heaved himself into the crotch of a large Baldwin. He climbed higher, taking solid footholds on opposite limbs. Hugging the trunk, he began to rock and bounce, and the tree responded with a small, unsupple creak and barely budged. Bringing one foot around so that both feet were tandem on the same branch, he grabbed the bough overhead. Now he began to pump, riding the branch as a surfer would a wave, big frost-mushed apples raining down, splatting on the grass. "Hey, beasts," he yelled, "free apples!"

His face, partially silhouetted against the crescent moon, hair streaming behind him, reminded Mighty of a racing greyhound or a hood ornament. More fruit fell. Now on the downswing, the long bare branch, instead of flexing back, cracked and groaned earthward. Gideon pitched forward and hung on. Fortunately the limb did not snap off at the break, and he scampered down its length and hopped off. "Oooooops," he said.

She helped scrape apple pulp off his back and out of his hair. "Sprecher'll kill you," she said. "That was a good-size branch."

Gideon ripped off the broken branch and swung at an imaginary bad boy. "*My Gott,* you ruint my tree. You rascal you. Take that and that and that. Quack, quack, quack."

Mighty laughed, then reminded of the skirmishing down at the house, cut herself short. "Come on, let's go."

They set off again, Gideon dragging his branch. "Two bits she's still trying to get an apology out of him. I mean, when's she gonna get wise?"

Gideon's mouth went tight and prim, suggesting someone set in his ways, a person ill equipped to explain the ways of fools.

On second thought, her father was too smart not to have turned the tables by now. By now Louise would be on the run, fleeing an inquisitional blizzard. "When are you getting a job?" he'd boom. "You go out and make a living, and I'll sit home analyzing every nuance." At a loss for excuses, he could always maintain that he needed none. His earning power was just that, power he'd earned, the ultimate rebuttal, protection from scrutiny.

Thinking he had her, he'd clamp down. Bully in tight, smirkful, puffy with the smug, ugly menace of the crack interrogator. Had she sewn the button on his blazer yet, called the man to service the furnace before they all burned in their beds? Speaking of beds, SPEAKING OF BEDS, well, never mind, he'd send his *secretary* out to make *his.* And why did she butter his broccoli when she knew he was watching his fat intake? Was she trying to kill him. YES OR NO?

And sometimes he'd get her so rattled she'd actually answer those questions, with tears in her eyes. "Why would I want to kill you? You're my husband. I love you."

"Ha!" he'd crack, and then, in a wee, seething voice, she'd say, "Oh, God, what's taking so long? Why *doesn't* he die?'"

Then he'd trot out that look: family dog dying. *Well, finally, the truth comes out.*

And knowing she hadn't a prayer against this master obfuscator, Louise would soon cry divorce, and he was at great pains to hide how he hated that part. Spittle beading his lip, he'd tell her to go right ahead and file; wasn't she in for the shock of her life? As if the courts of the land had spent the past two centuries cooking up something hideous just for her. And having made such an insupportable claim, he'd order her off the subject. "You're not going to drop it, are you?" he'd say when it was obvious she couldn't possibly.

He'd grab something she liked very much—a doll, a salt shaker—or a favorite thing of his own, because he knew in either case she'd feel equally bad. "One more word out of you . . ." And she always had at least that. She gave him no choice but to throw it, and the act would so appall him that he would have to smash a second thing to baffle the sound of the first, and when he was done, he'd leave in a hurry, a dirty little squirt taking off after he'd smashed all the cookies.

Mighty sent her beer can spinning into the woods. "Well, maybe that nun hanging around will help keep a lid on things."

"Watch it," Gideon said. "Don't junk up the place." He walked to the house and neatly laid his branch beside the trash cans. "Want another beer?" he asked.

"Sure. This time get me a St. Pauli Girl."

From where Mighty and Gideon stood just yards away, they were all clear as day in the bright side window. Apparently the war-horse had repaired to the kitchen. Trover with his back turned, Louise facing him from behind the counter, and Michael angled behind her: an artfully balanced diorama. So tranquil, in fact, was the scene through the double plate glass that when Mighty opened the door, she was stunned to be met with invective. "Pickpocket, pickpocket, pickpocket!" As Mighty approached, Trover addressed her directly. "Young lady, did you know your mother's a thief?"

Mighty looked to Michael, who sighed and said, "He got her to admit she has a little money set aside."

Trover's eyes opened like windows on his innocence. "All she ever had to do was ask. Have I ever denied your mother anything? Yes or no?"

"Idiot," Mighty said. She helped herself openly to two St. Pauli Girls, and there was more haranguing behind her, and when she turned, her father was fixing on her with a kind of maniacal delight.

"That's it!" he marveled. "It just dawned on me. That's what's wrong with my life. My wife is a piece of junk."

Michael's arm shot out in front of his mother the way hers did to protect her children from a sudden jolt in the car. Trover was bopping around now like a holy roller. "Piece a junk, piece a junk, piece a junk," he chanted, in the same bullying tone he'd used earlier to boo the ref.

Spotting his car keys on the counter, Mighty scooped them up. "One more 'piece a junk' out of you, buck-o, and you can kiss these babies goodbye."

"See here, missy," he said, when he saw what she'd taken, "I'd watch your step I were you." He thrust out his palm. "My keys, please."

Michael said, "Dad, let's sit down like adults and talk about it."

Trover ignored him. "The keys," he repeated. "You have no legal right keeping me prisoner in this house, young lady."

"So, sue me."

"Dad," Michael said imploringly, "you always leave, and nothing ever gets settled."

"I thought it was settled. I thought we'd agreed. Your mother's a piece of junk."

"He said it!" Gideon rushed to point out. "He said 'piece of junk.' "

"That's it," Mighty hissed. She pulled her brother close and whispered in his ear. Leaning over the counter, she consulted with Louise. She spoke quietly to Gideon, handing him the keys.

Louise waffled, but for only a second, because as they conferred, Trover turned himself loose. He raked his arm across the counter, exploding all the condiment jars out of the rack and onto the floor. He threw the ewer of pampas grass. With a whooping lurch, he was off then. Thumps and thuds from the dining room; the telltale crunch of potted plants tossed down the cellar steps; shattering glass. Then the heavy door to the Room slammed, and Louise winced.

"That does it," said Mighty. "Let's go."

The four of them slipped out the kitchen door, and as they did, the nun came flying out the front door, which was but two feet away. "Hey, where you going?" she said, following them off the porch. "Don't leave me here with *him*." Louise took her arm and steered her toward the brown diesel.

For the moment Lum had the superbug running again, and Mighty got in it. "Keep your headlights off," she yelled out the window. One after another the family fleet came to life. With its unmistakable throaty hum, the bug started up, then the diesels with their long warm-ups and loose-screw ignition. The Jeep kicked in and stalled, started and stalled, struggling with the chill, for it responded nimbly only in forgiving weather. With its dead battery and two flat tires, the Hornet was useless. But Mighty jumped out and ran over to Gideon in the Jeep. "You got the keys to the Triumph?" He patted his coat pocket. Gideon was always one step ahead of you.

Mighty in the lead, the four cars rounded the lower curve of the rose garden, then veered off across the main lawn. The grass was stiff with frost, and Mighty feared he would be able to follow their tracks in the rime. To foil him, she hung a right when she reached the road between the lawn and orchard. She led them up along the pool and then down again over the, ruined vegetable patch and into the low meadow. Only once had she glanced back. He was standing under the porchlight, hands on hips, watching their exodus, watching his escape's escape. Now where would he go? Under the porch? Behind the furnace? What halfway place between the point where he damned them all and the point where he had to have them back? She wished she hadn't looked. She'd forgot how hard it was to take anything from a man who looked as though he wouldn't outlive the loss.

The hour was late, winter in the air. Behind her the shadowy cavalcade bumped along over rough terrain. Lit with a kind of melancholy courage, Mighty felt like a leader of doomed partisans. She led them to where the land began to slip into hard decline; to the old orchard, just at the edge of the woods. She cut the lights and motor and drifted down between the barren trees soundlessly as a boat into a slip. The others found similar slots and did the same. Louise and Michael emerged from their respective Rabbits. Gideon jumped down from the Jeep. They gravitated to where Mighty stood, arms folded, against the fender of the bug. Frank waited in the car.

Somebody said, "Now what?"

"We lay low for a while," Mighty replied.

Louise looked cold and bewildered. "Why are we doing this?"

"Because we're going to bust that sucker's cycles, that's why. Let's see how wise he is stuck without wheels."

"Yeah," said Gideon, "but he's stuck in a warm house, and we're stuck in the woods."

Now Frank emerged from the brown diesel, skittishly, as if expecting crossfire. She joined the nodding, shifting committee, arms tucked into the sleeves of her fleece bathrobe.

Michael said, "Betcha he's down there on the john reading Hardy."

Teeth clicking, the nun joined in. "Not that I follow this thing completely, but now that you've, uh, *confiscated* the vehicles, can't we just go back to the house?"

Mighty said, "Then he'll know they're still on the grounds and go looking for them."

"We have the keys," Michael said brightly.

"He'd get them away from us, and you know it. He'd mug us. He'd tackle Sister Frank here if he thought she was holding out. Anyhow, he *may* have duplicates. Mighty drew herself erect. "Let's walk," she said. "Keep moving." And for want of a better suggestion, they followed her single file along a hard climb straight up the hummock and across the orchard, up the stone steps to the pool. The boys gathered some upended deck furniture; they pushed webbed lounges and chairs into the corner concealed from view on three sides by a massive spreading juniper. Then they sat down and waited.

The pool water carried an unhealthly oily sheen in the meager light. Somewhere down in the valley a semi rumbled by. A chained dog yowled. A hoot owl. A poacher's scattershot. They waited, glumly incommunicative; they waited, watching the moon. "What are we waiting for?" the nun asked.

"I'm not sure, ma'am," Michael replied.

"Sister." Louise corrected.

Then Frank twisted around to Louise, saying, "How the hell can you live this way?"

"She gets a kick out of the guy," Mighty said tightly.

One by one they turned to Louise, accusingly, as if, after centuries of figuring, they'd finally been led to the root of all trouble.

Louise scrunched low and poked a cigarette in her mouth.

"Hey, don't light that," Gideon said.

And it occurred to Mighty that all this bitchy discomfort was probably wasted anyhow. Maybe her father had gone on foot, taken one of the paths through the woods. At this very moment he could be trooping out the township road. Midnight. No taxi service in these parts, no buses or trains, not a single motel for miles, and there he was, marching off like a man of incontestable destiny. A chill of panic shot through her. "How do we know he didn't sneak out the back?" she asked.

The moon was a cold blade rocking on the roof of the house, the house whose warmth Mighty didn't dare covet now, not with him roaming his bones through the cold night. She envisioned her dad on endless miles of unpaved road, too weary at last to go on, lying down next to chickens or the ghosts of the Ironmaster's House. The half-wit Platz boys would murder him for his new boots. Or he'd get snared in a muskrat trap and have to chew his leg off.

Louise shot out of her chair. "Maybe we'd better go look for him."

But Mighty had already aligned her back molars. "The hell we will."

"Shhhhh, what's that?"

Little frizzles of hesitant ignition, then full-throated v-rooooms. Not so close but not that far away either.

"Nobody guns an engine like that but you know who," said Gideon. He jumped up and peeked around the shrub bank. "It *is* him," he said. "Holy Jeez, here he comes!"

The others rushed to the edge of the cement apron just as he came roaring through in Gideon's Triumph. He slowed as he pulled abreast of them, and Mighty didn't have to see his face to know they were getting the jutting jaw, the look he routinely threw to motorists who in some way hindered him. Then he shot off into the night.

Gideon pulled out his keys and stared at them. "He stole my car," he said. "How would he know how to hot-wire an ignition?"

"He reads," Mighty said. She tried not to smile. They were so much alike. In his getting away with things, in his shameless endurance, she saw a future for herself.

Then the little committee filed back down to the house. They hugged their bones and tried to cover their foolishness with shivering.

"Honestly, Louise," the nun said quietly with her hand on the newel-post.

"Good night," said Louise.

"Well, good night then," Frank replied.

In rapid increments the house took on its burden of light and then—as if each room had the power to cancel light with a sigh—slipped into the uneasy guardianship of dark tarnished with absence.

CHAPTER
21

Ay, she soon comes, thought Sprecher, tipping an ear. He listened as the girl worked her way up the hall. It was a different sound from the meal wagon's slapdash clatter and occasional clang. Her smooth rubber rumble matched the grumblings in his stomach, and his mouth watered for what was turning out to be his daily Snickers bar.

He rose from his chair and went to the nightstand, where he poked through loose change, silently cursing the laborious chore it had become to isolate and extract, in pennies and nickels and dimes, the exact handful he needed. He muttered against the price. Ay, Perma. Good you didn't live to see me give fifty cents for a nickel candy.

The girl popped her head in. "Friendship Wagon, sir?" By way of reply he shuffled over and emptied his palm into hers. After she'd maneuvered her cart in, he hung low over the wares. Pretending to puzzle over the compact array of sweets and reading matter, he stole furtive glances at the candy striper. Fifteen perhaps. With red-yellow hair and strong teeth, this one wasn't sour-looking as some that came around. Such nice round busts, hard belly, wide hips, thighs solid as poplars. Hills and trees and the moist dirt crumbling in his hand. He wanted his land back! "Girlie," he said, "soon I have sweet corn. And barley too yet."

"I don't doubt that for a minute," she said pleasantly.

He grunted and snatched up his Snickers. A nest of apples caught his eye: red Delicious in crinkly blue paper. The waxy film would shine off nice with his pajama top. He envisioned the transparent sheen, the kingly streak of purple. He had half a mind to take one, but then he'd have to put his teeth back in. Anyhow, they were fancy types, not a spot on them. As a boy he'd been forbidden to take unblemished fruit from the bin. The injunction had stuck. His arm would refuse to reach for such apples. "Come back once them apples go badt," he said.

The girl sparkled when she laughed. "A man after my grammy's heart," she said. "She always picks the bruised fruit out of the bowl. Prefers broken pretzels and day-old bread."

Sprecher prickled with new interest. "Well, now, what's your grammy's name?" he asked, as if a common penchant for seconds indicated kinship.

"Ada Clauss," she said.

Ada Clauss. He knew that name from somewhere, but the only Clauss that came to him right off was Clauss the douser, and he was dead long already. He wished he could place this Ada woman. Maybe then the nice girl would set and talk a spell. "You like chokes?" he said.

"Pardon."

"Chokes. Ho-ho!"

"Oh, jokes. Sure."

He recited his favorite in a sober monotone. "Well, two stranger fellas set aside each other in a bus station. The bus comes at last. One of them oldt fellas gets up. Why, it goes wonderful hard for him. He has it so in the joints. 'Ach,' he says, 'I am suffering from arthritis.' 'Well, now, pleased to meet you,' says the second fella. 'I am Snyder from Dryville.' " Sprecher drew a breath and looked her hard in the eye. "That's a good one, ain't?"

The girl's laugh unraveled in a pretty glimmery strand. Her hand brushed his lightly. She took another second to realign the sweets. "Good luck with your corn and stuff," she called over her shoulder as she muscled the bulky cart back into the hall.

For an instant he swayed in the heady evanescence left in the girl's wake. He felt unbearably light, almost as though she'd carted off with her sweets his burden of age and anger. Something was astir in his belly and legs. His hand burned from her touch, his hand hot on the wheel of the tractor where the sun beat down. Goaded by the sudden quickening, he paced his room, all but butting its four corners, the chair, the bed, the windows fuzzing with dusk. He was all fired up, raring to go. Then he realized he had sped beyond simple excitement. He found himself moving as one pursued, with a sense of things closing in.

What was the trouble? It was not his way to bustle around. Hardly anything on the farm responded better to speed than ease; his pace had long been set by the cadence of days and weeks and seasons, the green needs of things. Something deep in his cells resisted any effort to spur him to urgency.

So what was happening now? Why was he so far off his pace? It threw him back to third grade, how he felt on the way home from school knowing Toby Absolom was lying in wait. He meant to take Sprecher's penny and push him into the jagger patch. But that was then. What could be after him now?

After ripping off the candy wrapper, he crammed the entire Snickers into his mouth at once. He stuffed the overflow back with both hands, chewing fast, licking the trickle. He half expected somebody to come busting in and snitch the sugar from under his tongue.

The goods consumed, he savored the syrup that remained, then swallowed. *Gott fadommt,* gone in a gulp. Now, what was to want? What would they fetch him for supper? He tried to recall his meal from the night before but could summon up nothing but a hazy picture of himself lifting the spoon as though it weighed like a shovel. Up and down, up and down, old man dumb to lumpy or smooth, hot or cold, bitter or sweet, the sweet, sweet difference between this dish and that. Ay, that was it, ain't? The reason to rush and gobble like a dog. Nobody was after his candy. It came to him and now he knew. It was his memory they wanted, his will, that and the clear lines dividing things. Right now his appetite was good yet; his bowels ached him like always; he knew a good apple and a pretty girl when he saw one. But he wouldn't stay so smart for long. Soon he'd be down under again, brainful of batter, arms like the weights in a cased clock. Soon, soon. Something told him the time was at hand.

What day could it be? What month? It was cold long already. Could it be it was soon spring? He had to buy scallion sets and seed peas? He was seized with fear for his outbuildings. His absence took on the terrible negative force of vacuum; it would suck down the barn and chickenhouse, swallow his world as greedily as he'd gobbled the chocolate.

Well, if the buildings went, perhaps they'd fall on the Kleeves. He grinned into the mirror, then almost as quickly rescinded the glee, winced it away. It wasn't wise to lay curses at his age. He limited his ill will to a wish for a wonderful dirty mess on the roadway. They'd call him to clean it up so they could pass by. And he'd stack the fallen timbers in the soft orchard grass and stockpile the foundation stones and fill coffee cans with square-headed nails. And soon the carpenters would come and raise studs against the sky that was his forever.

Ach du liever, now he was ticking. His reconstituted life loomed before him, distant but indestructible, deathless as Himmel's Hahn on a cloudless sky. Every ridge and cliff and notch visible, goshawks paring the air, the pocket of wild mustard like gold dust on the western slope.

And he saw that given half a chance, he would go right on clarifying, framing the scene, making ever sharper the distinctions, every line absolute as the pointing between stones. And in the same swing of lucidity he saw the seeds of trouble in this, his Germanic need for preciseness and completion: how he and his kind made themselves rigid against the flow of things, drew borders that couldn't be defended, made schedules impossible to keep, categories that strayed like sheep. It made them pigheaded and iron-jawed, and when man and wife walked, it was with the stodgy galumph of a single sack of yams. Nothing could budge this couple, but the slightest shift in routine sent them doctoring for nerves.

Yet this was but a glimpse, as of a traveler passing under a moment's illumination. And Sprecher had no words to refine the thought or desire to go beyond what simply was and so clung to his tiny, bright vision of Himmel's Hahn, even as he understood it would soon dissolve. Time was ticking toward the inevitable. His inner clock told him so, just as he'd always been able to name the hour by the color of the light on Perma's arm as she redd up the table.

Soon he would drift back into his own twilight. To sleep was to lose the precious edges of things, and to die ... to die ... He watched the darkness deepen at the window, and he never in his life loved an orange-haired woman, never ate a perfect apple.

He waited in helplessness, as though the enemy were no more substantial than a value of light. Waiting, he heard footsteps in the hall, the unmistakable smug squeak of a nurse's tread. He caught his breath. *Squeak*. He sat bolt upright. Such a squeak always preceded his drop into dazedness. Ay! His mind leaped clear of itself and sailed into cool blue, and he understood at last what they were doing to him.

"Happy tenth of December, Earl," she sang at him.

December. Still a good ways till spring. "Who toldt you to call me by my first name?" he said.

She paid him no mind. "Mrs. Tilton is gratified to see we're wearing our jammies today."

He stared past her. She wanted dumb Dutchie, she'd get Dumb Dutchie. He extended a leaden arm to accept the little paper cup. She poured his water, and he took that, too. She watched him place the pills on his tongue.

"Down the hatch, love," she said, pivoting toward his dresser, where she secured her cap in the mirror. He watched her exiting rump and thought not of broad fields but of a broodmare, meaty and twitching.

When she was safely gone, he spat the soggy tablets and pressed them into the vermiculite around the plant the Kleeves had sent. Then he gave them a shot of water from his pitcher, almost as if from these seeds something unspeakably lazy might grow.

CHAPTER

22

As Christmas crept closer, Louise washed all the Santa mugs and carried pine branches in from the woods. She hauled the crèche up from the cellar. Several years earlier, when Trover smashed the wassail bowl, Mighty fought back by breaking St. Joseph. Louise immediately closed the ranks by pushing a plaster bust down from the opposite end of the mantel; now it was Jesus, Mary, and Beethoven.

Carolers never penetrated this deep into the country, but the Jolly Good Fire Company came, eight men in a red truck, sirens shrieking until Trover silenced them with a donation. And there was no dearth of telephone solicitors, though to Louise's disappointment, Ardith Budner never called back.

She began to haunt the malls. For once giving plenitude its due, she stood humbled before mountains of beribboned beefsticks, panda pyramids, ten-foot cheddar churches. She skated to "Adeste" and even the Muzak "Ave Maria" had the power to dissolve instantly every lump of curmudgeonliness in her blood. Caught off-guard, she once thanked a mechanical Rudolf for calling her "sexy." She made many such trips, but so taken up was she with spinning in the crowd, transcending pettiness and resting from the breathless press of it all, she often forgot that she'd come to buy.

But buy she would; the day of reckoning always came. Painful hours hunting redundancy. More shirts, boots, ski poles. One day, staggering back to the car with her purchases, Louise began to understand the underlying logic of surfeit, the true mode in which Christmas upheld the family. What love couldn't preserve, cargo would. It was a fearsome wind that would carry off *their* house. A rag, a shoe, a ski pole at a time, they were weighting the nest, building a history too heavy to move. Who could face divorce when packing alone would take the better part of a decade?

And so, the accretions of nineteen years larding her heart, Louise went about the grim business of increase. Trover was by far the hardest. She might just as well get him a box of Kleenex as scour the city for something in that certain umber tone that, what with his russet beard and brown eyes, would give him the rich burnish of a Pennsylvania autumn. Whatever she might come up with would only drive him to a kind of fidgety nonchalance, as if showing delight were just one more tax levied by relation.

And Michael, who steadfastly refused to publish his pin record by wearing an equal number of diaper pins on his warm-up suit, as was the custom—well, such a boy would never say what he wanted. He'd like everything he got. How did you narrow down for someone with whom *all* offerings found favor? Good people did this to you. You asked, "What do you want?" and they led you to the plains of vagueness and possibility, where you could wander the specialty shops until you dropped. It was useless to be good for practical reasons. Virtue was no less hazardous than iniquity.

Mighty requisitioned everything months in advance, and Louise filled her order like an old-time grocer ticking down the list. And Gideon—how should Louise reward the household opportunist? A leather blackmail kit? A handy pocket diagram of all her cubbyholes and secret wishes? And thinking of Gideon led to thoughts of the car wash and yet another holiday obligation. Years ago she should have begun stretching her capacity for guilt. Small crimes just didn't do it, and now she was stuck with Gideon and this itchy bladder of a bad conscience.

Occasionally Frank went shopping with Louise. Sometimes she wore the habit, sometimes she went in disguise, and she was fussy, too, about what she would accept from Louise's closet. Nothing in black or brown, nothing in bonded polyester.

She'd been with them a week now and, to Louise's knowledge, neither made nor received a single telephone call. Louise finally asked when she had to be back. Frank answered, "Whenever." And then in a wispy voice: "They don't know where I am."

She was mending a pair of stockings at the time, and watching her thread the needle—the taut patience, that scowl of concentration she had even as a child—Louise knew if she hadn't found her way here, sooner or later, Louise would have gone looking for her.

Somewhere in mid-life, even as the future seemed to line up straight ahead to the end, you had actually begun to bend toward your beginning. Forty-year-old ex-farm boys were frantically buying up the rural country-side. The year before she died, Geggo, ancient and frail, returned to the cottage of her birth, brought Yugoslav scree back in her handbag. And Trover put on hiking boots to walk again with his father.

In the days since Frank's arrival Louise had begun to dream again about Mercy, more particularly about the green room. This room had material-ized, almost by magic, sometime during Christmas vacation her junior year. When the aspirants returned in January, there it was, three stories up, wedged between wings A and B and the main building. At the top of its column of air it sat like a stuck elevator. The floor, of some strange spongy material, ran halfway up the walls. The single window was a square of glass blocks thick as Bruno's bifocals. You couldn't see out, nor, it could be as-sumed, in.

Wednesday nights on a bimonthly basis, a contingent of professed sisters would flock over from their own quarters, and the result was what came to be famous as the Aspirancy Dance. A vintage Victrola churned out tinny renditions of show tunes, operettas, and big band. It was more prestigious to dance with a nun than another aspirant, and when you landed one, you'd put on something slow, "The Blue Danube" maybe, fluid ebullience to go with their flowing robes. They specialized in the polka, the *chardasz*, and other Catholic dances. They did jigs. All those Irish in a green room, the result was a lively and imaginative mix of the weird and lyrical. And Frank Gahagan was the resident jig instructor.

But there was something dense and indifferent about that room. Its rest-ful tones and no-wax shine concealed a cruel acoustical perversity. The clogging and stomping that had so thoroughly rattled the floorboards of the old community room raised hardly an echo in that stern, impervious chamber. At times dancing became physically painful, a laboring to enter-tain oneself. You felt weightless, thwarted, ridiculous as someone writing her name again and again in white ink. Even the nuns' hard leather heels barely registered a tap before they were subdued. They all seemed to oc-cupy some alternate dimension, a universe refusing to talk back. The harder they worked, the more thoroughly they were absorbed by the mira-cle synthetic that packaged them. This pursuit of simple pleasure quickly became exhausting.

One morning, drained from a dream about the green room, Louise tried to relate it to Frank. Her friend's eyes sprang wide. "Oh, that dreadful room. Louise, I dream about it, too."

"You do?"

"*Do* I? I used to be deathly afraid it would work its way loose and clobber old St. Stephen down in the courtyard."

"Worst community room crash in peacetime history."

Frank edged closer, making her smile intimate, knowing. "And don't think they would have shed any tears for us. That's why they kept us in a box in the first place. We were a blooming nuisance."

Louise was shocked. "We were?"

"I didn't see it either until moving up to the novitiate. They called us nunlets, you know. Imagine having all those little imitations under the same roof. Little nonworking versions of yourself. Remember how we used to run along behind the novices, snapping up any black-headed pins that fell out of their habits?"

Louise blushed.

"In contrast to the day students with their pretty clothes and ponytails and boy-girl dances, everything about us was jury-rigged, improvised, unseemly. We substituted nuns for boys and one another for nuns and tried to make black saddle shoes look like Enna Jetticks. We *trafficked* in black-headed pins, for pity sakes. We wore bone corsets. We mimicked two worlds but occupied neither. We defied category. We were spooky, Louise."

"And none too attractive."

"Yes, they cultivated plainness in us, then chose their favorites from among the pretty day students."

"We were odd ducks all right. Sometimes even nasty, but Lord, Frank, we were so full of *trying.*"

"You know, of course, that aspirancy was dissolved some years ago . . . ? Louise, why are you smiling?"

Well, what could she say? The forge that forged her had been dismantled. She was one of only a handful extant; her kind would not be seen again. She fondled that not unpleasant thought awhile longer before rousing herself to thoughts of work, and then she headed back to the room that was full of the equally febrile trying of her middle years.

"I got the Landers to where they're ready to decorate again," Louise said. Frank's arms were folded below a gaze as shrewdly inquisitive as a shop foreman's. "Maybe I'll have them finished for Christmas," Louise added.

Stepping closer, Frank stroked the raw white finish.

"I hate letting them stand around like that. Could you hand me the fine line brush?" It was a pleasure now to adorn her daughter—sandstone on the piping of her hat, a great furled tray of grapes and rosebuds tilted hoydenishly over one eye. Only Louise would know about the tar wad lurking under the floribundas.

In a silence twitching with pigment and solvent smells, with the friction of things unsaid, Frank brushed chalky palms together. "I was thinking," she said. "Louise, do you remember how we carried on over that pregnant woman?"

"What are you talking about?"

"I think it must have been Mother's Day weekend or something. The order sponsored that retreat for laywomen? Remember? We were massed in chapel for benediction when she made her grand entrance. Louise, *nobody* ever used that center aisle. Who would have dared? It was there for solemn processionals. The *bishop,* for crying out loud, entered that way. Remember the pearly wax swirls from the buffing machine—how long they stayed perfect."

Louise was smiling, shaking her head.

"And suddenly, there she was, must have been eight and a half months, all glowing and rosy and oblivious. A big pink balloon bumping down the center aisle." Frank laid her hands across her middle and arched her back, a beatific grin on her face. "And smiling to herself. I'll never forget that smile. I half expected her to continue on up to the altar and plunk down in the bishop's chair, that big carved throne of a thing."

"Mary Clare Lynch started to giggle. In two seconds she had us all going, falling in the aisles. Bruno had to herd us out of chapel like a bunch of drunks. I thought she would kill us."

"And imagine how that poor woman felt, the lot of us snickering at her sex life."

Louise dipped her brush and waited patiently for a single dark drop to form and fall back in the jar. "If I recall, the very next night there was an emergency sex education class in the green room."

"Father Meagher, poor man. He was so nervous. . . ."

Louise laughed. "He kept calling it 'congress, not to be confused with Capitol Hill.' "

"Bruno was falling asleep standing up."

"Frank, we were all nodding off."

"And we were all faking. We heard every word."

"My kids got their education on the school bus. And it was not the Douay version!" Louise looked up to find Frank staring at her, wide-eyed, prickly with interest.

"Louise . . ." she began.

"Yes?"

"Louise?"

"What?"

"What's it like?"

"What? Oh . . . what a question, Sister I!"

"No worse than 'Do you guys believe in God?' "

"Touché, Sister."

"So?"

"So—oh, the phone!" Leaping to her feet, Louise hurled herself toward the ringing with a directness hardly befitting conditions. She immediately kicked over the jar of sable paint blocking her path; brown-black splashed on the perfect white garden party frock of her own plaster counterpart. Grabbing a rag, she swiped at the spatters, turning them to smudges. "Oh!" she cried again, trying to fling her hands as far from harm as possible.

In the meantime, Frank had picked up. "For you!" she said, sounding disappointed.

It was a nervous-sounding doctor from Neisstown General. Louise was listed as next of kin and they wanted her to know that the old man had escaped at daybreak.

"Looks like Sprecher's outfoxed the AMA," she told Frank. "Trover will be delighted. Come on, let's see if he's home yet."

When they arrived at Sprecher's, the truck sat in his muddy back lot, but Joe was nowhere to be seen. She remembered then that one of the neighbors had been keeping the dog during Sprecher's hospitalization. She checked out the sawmill and stuck her head in the meat-hung shed. She walked around to the side of the house, and just as she looked in the window, a gray head sank behind the mohair sofa. Hoping that person was not some squatter, she rapped twice on the pane. "Earl Sprecher, that you? It's me, Louise Kleeve." When several minutes elapsed without further development, she pulled Frank down with her into the foundation well below, where huddling together, they stared into the cellar window: stacks of peach baskets; Perma's bean dryer; rows of horseradish jars. Louise had a sudden image of these items stuffed in boxes up in the yard, a wise-cracking auctioneer sending them off to live again among young marrieds and city collectors.

She gave the quiet another five minutes to entice him out. She popped up in time to catch his eyes periscoping just above the sofa back. Frank stayed in the well. "I can't believe people live like this," she whispered. "We're always hiding somewhere uncomfortable."

Louise stood and rapped again. "Mr. Sprecher, I'm over here."

He ducked his head and then slowly resurfaced. He straightened out and started stiffly out of the room. The women went to his kitchen entrance. Opening the door a crack, he spotted the nun and slammed it hard.

"He thinks you're from the hospital," said Louise. "Mr. Sprecher, she's a houseguest, a friend of mine. Why don't you come out and meet her?"

Five minutes went by. Shuffling and bumping inside. When he reappeared, he was wielding a stillson wrench at least three feet long, his presence slab-dark in the doorway.

"Earl Sprecher," Louise said, "Sister Innocent."

And when he didn't so much as grunt, Frank thrust out her hand like a well-bred schoolgirl. "Welcome back, sir," she said.

Ignoring the gesture, he searched her eyes.

"Well?" said Louise, stiffly cheerful. "How'd you get home?"

"The regkler way," he said. "The bus so far as Alsace. Then Schaeffer, the hardware man, fetched me home."

"You sure you can manage on your own?" Louise asked.

He turned the wrench vertical, and it trembled from the tightened grip. *"Gott fadommt!"* Them hospital men grabbed me offa public property. They mayn't do that, I tell you. That smark aleck head doctor fetch you over here?"

"He's quite worried about you."

"Worried, ach! Them's the devils *ferhext* me in the first place. Give me such pills to make a *dummkupp* out of me. Once I figgered it out, I cleared the heck otta that nuthouse and come home where I belong."

"But, sir!" Frank said. "From what I understand you were in pretty rough shape when they admitted you. Was it a seizure of some sort or—"

The old man moved on them with murder in his eyes. Years ago, the first time he'd charged her, Louise had flinched and hidden from him. Now she held her ground and let him menace her grandly. He was barking spit at her, his breath like the water in a vase after the flowers have died.

"Didn't nobody ever tell you, lady, a man has ice-coldt gas in his gut, he tries to get rid of it best he can. And ay-yi-yi, the hoodlums come and tie him up and cart him off like it was buck season."

"Gas? You mean—"

"Why, sure. Ay, it gets me. I have gas since Chon Kennedy got in." He pogoed twice on the cement slab. His face, with its poor color and patchy gray growth, resembled the furry meat in his shed. He stomped his foot. He pounded his belly. "You must beat it ott of them intesteens." He sprang up again, astonishingly high. "Achhhhh!" he hollered. "Oooooooosh!"

The same war dance Louise had witnessed so often before in the orchard.

When he ground to a stall, she said, "Are you trying to say you jump and holler to relieve, uh, digestive upset?"

He looked at her as though she were his slowest apprentice yet. "Are you deef?" he said. *"Gas!"*

"And that's why they put you in a straitjacket?"

For a second he faltered and did not seem to know where to go with his eyes. Louise had shamed him. But he wasn't unnerved for long. He pointed the wrench at her rib cage, trained it on Frank for good measure. "Next time certain indeewiduals come, I'm ready," he said matter-of-factly. "You tell them Sprecher once kilt a gypsy near to death with his bare hands. Earl Sprecher's a pahrful man yet."

Louise hastened to reassure him. "You took off, apparently, before they finished their tests. They haven't committed you. You've still got the law on your side, Mr. Sprecher."

"Law slaw!" he shot. He clomped awkwardly around before turning back, remembering something. "How's the grass grow, missus?"

It was Decemer, brown uphill and down, but she said, "Oh, would you like to mow, sir? You may if you'd like."

He pondered this, then said, "Ach, too coldt." He sounded tired, mild. "Next week perhaps," he said. Then he went in.

Louise pulled up in front of the house. They sat idling for several minutes before Frank turned to her. "That old man's a disaster. He looks unhealthy and malnourished. What do you suppose he runs on?"

Louise snapped off the ignition. "Gas," she said.

Shortly thereafter Trover phoned to request something "robust" for dinner. He would leave the specifics to her, meaning that he'd eat meat as long as it wasn't his idea. "And I'll buy you a bag of dinner rolls," he said: his part of the deal.

Louise came out of her afternoon slump like someone expecting company. She dashed out for veal medallions and bell peppers and wine. When she came back, Frank seized the ingredients, insisting it was her turn to do the cooking. Unlike Louise, she chopped her vegetables into nice tidy sums and made a federal case of cleaning as she went. From her perch atop the stepstool, Louise drew on her cigarette and observed, with mixed disgust and delight, gratitude and rancor, the checkered benevolence of a friend. Frank, God love her, loved to help. Frank, God help her, loved to work rings around Louise.

Louise settled the dilemma by reflecting fondly on the dinner rolls. She set her heart on croissants. No, tea biscuits. She'd warm them in the oven and spread their inner stuff with raspberry jam. Frank's veal smelled opulent with basil and savory, but Louise longed for dough, the goods Geggo had raised her on.

When the meal was ready, they filled a Tupperware caddy and took it to Sprecher's house. From now on Louise would have to look after him. No doubt he'd been half-starving since Perma died. This time Sprecher met them less inhospitably. He lifted the plastic lid and poked his nose inside. The look he gave Louise expressed dull disgust, as though he'd peered lasciviously into a Whitman's Sampler only to find it stuffed with postcards or mending yarn.

"Scallopine," Frank explained proudly.

He took one final sidelong glance at the foreign provender and, shaking his head, went back inside. And so the offering was borne home again and returned to the common pot.

At six Trover phoned to say he was on his way. Louise had no business believing him, but she said, "Hurry, hurry. Frank wants to know if any of those rolls happen to be croissants?"

"My lips are sealed," he teased. Oh, there were croissants!

"And tea biscuits?" she asked.

"Why should I buy tea biscuits just because my Bibs is a Crisco junkie?"

Oh, tea biscuits, too, she exulted, ignoring the tilt in his tone that said he'd been drinking.

At seven-thirty the phone rang again. "Just calling to let you know I'm halfway home."

"Why are you calling?" she wailed. "Why don't you just come?"

"I'ze acomin', Bibs."

Then Mighty came home with Gideon in tow. Louise spun two plates onto the table and stood by as Gideon raked through the solid scallopine matter. "No mushrooms?" he said offendedly.

Louise was weak from hunger and bitterly disappointed by now. No mushrooms indeed! She opened a can of stems and pieces and plunked it down by Gideon's water glass. *Voilà!*

Michael dined on a scrap of veal and all the cooked tomatoes they could spare him. He stretched a slice of bread into a twenty-minute meal by nibbling the edges around and around toward the final sad bite in the center. Then Lousie said, "Honey, call the Drovers Hotel for your dad."

"They said he left ten minutes ago," Michael reported back.

"Well," she said, "if it's true, he should be at the Womelsdorf Tavern by now."

When Michael called, they said, "He left ten minutes ago."

"We'll wait a bit, give him time to get settled," Louise told Frank. "Then we're taking matters into our own hands."

At eighty-twenty they hopped into the truck and drove down to the Kemp Hotel. "I knew it!" Louise cried. "The sunroof! There it is!" Trover's car sat two feet from the curb, the impish, impenitent thing. "I'll pull up alongside," she said. "Frank, you hop out and grab the goods."

"What if he catches me?"

"Frank, this isn't the great train robbery."

"I'm wearing the habit. . . ."

"OK, wait here." Louise jumped out. The sky over Groff's Garage was the romantic blue of the nights in Victorian parlor art, and the flaccid moon roosting on the tin roof radiated the same melting yellow as the one hotel window framing the taproom. Louise stopped with her hand on the handle of Trover's car and peeked in. The old walnut bar shone with a buttery luster, and she had never before noticed the elegant back bar with its mirrors and panels of beveled glass. Genesee Christmas neon blinked red and green. The paunchy white-aproned bartender stood looking out without seeing her. It was a room in a Gay Nineties postcard. She edged closer, increasing the angle until her husband curved into view. From what she could see, Trover was the sole patron. He stood at the far end, a man with a beard, homburg on the bar. He busied himself with fastidious sipping, pocket foraging, rotating his coaster. With shining eyes and mouth tensed wistfully, his air was of a man most pleasantly engaged. Emptying his glass, he slid some coins toward the bartender. Almost as if she'd caught her husband with his hand in somebody's blouse, Louise felt a flush come over her. Ducking quickly under the window, she slunk to his car and there removed from his possession one plump bakery bag.

"Now let's make tracks," she said to Frank, in stitches by now, doubled over against the door. Louise turned around at Groff's Garage, and passing the hotel, she slowed, checking the window once again. The light seemed diluted now to half strength, and the dark blur at the corner was her husband, gathering himself to leave.

When Trover stumbled in twenty minutes later, the women were holding glasses of pale rosé over bellies bloated with dough, their mischievous secret tickling between them. He stood in the entryway with his palms turned up to express their lamentable emptiness. "Ooooooooch," he said, "they flew the coop." His tongue was boozy with rue and lambrusco.

The women exchanged glances.

"Hey, listen." He was wearing new contacts, and his eyes burned large and red. "What I'm trying to tell you is the holy goddamn truth."

"Trover!" cried Louise.

He bowed to Frank. "Sorry, Sister." He returned to his wife. "See, I stopped at the hotel—for *one* quick one. When I came out, my rolls were gone. I even tried to get them back for you. I saw a couple kids across the street. I took off after them. I said, 'Hey, you two punks, gimme back my buns.' "

Louise and Frank were snorting into their sleeves.

"Look at me, Bibs," he said with those mendicant eyes. "Scout's honor, I bought the rolls. Two dozen, six blessed kind. Right hand up to God. Now I don't have them anymore." He lowered his head so that his brow rested on her shoulder, lightly as a teacup. "Oh, I blew it, blew it. You just say the word. Tomorrow night I'll bring home the whole damn bakery." He slapped a sticky kiss on her cheek.

As ungainly and facetious as it was, Trover's kiss wedged between the two women, hitherto in cahoots. Discomfited, Frank turned away to pour herself another drink. Louise disengaged herself from him and, reaching behind her, whipped a package out from behind the toaster. She tapped his pate with the bumps left in the bag. "Let there be bread!" she said.

Trover took the package. All drunken thumbs, he unfolded the top edge and, comically puzzled, peered in. "You got some, too!" he cried. "Why didn't you tell me? Son of a bee, your rolls are just like mine!"

"They appeared at the door not a half hour ago, crying, 'Eat me, eat me, your husband's in the tavern, letting us get stale!' "

His head drooped like a soaked tea rose. Then he peered up at her, plowing a slow smile through the flesh of his left cheek. "Pirates," he said, "I got pirates living under my roof. Couple bloody highwaymen—par'n me, ladies— highway*persons*. You two gals ripped me off." Crooking a finger, he beckoned to Frank.

Awkward as a wallflower, Frank obeyed. He threw an arm around her waist. "They teach you to steal bread in the nunnery?"

"Louise did it!" she cried in mock self-defense. "It was all her idea!"

Trover gathered Louise into the other arm, drawing them both closer. Louise thought Frank looked ridiculously, unreasonably pleased, her chin crinkled cutely. How easily certain men could reduce a grown woman to the girl she was. Then he stood the women at arm's length. He gave them each ponderous looks. "I ever tell you gals what's important in life?"

Frank stared back transfixed, and even Louise was listening. He was having some difficulty, though, with collapsing syntax. "What?" the women said as one. "What?" Oh, weren't they both suckers for a mouth struggling to encompass the truth?

But then his arms flew up and timbered to his side, as though the idea had vanished the way his rolls had. He erased the women's fixity. "Forget it," he said. "Figure it out yourself." Fumbling a biscuit out of the bag, stuffing his mug, listing badly, he left the room.

With a plate of scallopine and two more cold croissants Frank scampered after him. Louise ate her dinner standing at the sink. When she joined them in the sun room, there was Frank on the floor at his feet, buttering his roll. "Can I get you some greens?" she was saying. "Hearts of lettuce? Waldorf salad?"

Louise snapped on the TV. Merv Griffin was playing the organ while Perry Como lip-sang "Silent Night" in a snowstorm of colored sparkles.

"You must be starving." Frank pressed on, turning those rosin-rubbed, seraphic tones to the service of devotions less than liturgical.

"Nobody tells him to hole up in smelly saloons," Louise snapped. "Let him eat Slim Jims."

More television benevolence undermining Louise's pique. She snapped off the set. Several minutes later Frank went upstairs and changed into a swishy skirt Louise had given her. She turned the TV back on and coaxed Trover off the sofa and proceeded to demonstrate the jig to "Jingle Bells."

There was Mary and there was Martha. Martha went out to clear the table and load the dishwasher. Adoring Mary gave free dancing lessons. The house resounded with Trover's lumpish thumps on the sun room floor. Louise tapped her own indignant time on the toaster-oven. Christmas carols gave way to the three-quarter time of *Die Fledermaus*. Somebody was playing records. Louise remembered the day she and Frank had traded clothes. When they came home, Louise went upstairs and, using a pillowcase and black taffeta skirt, modeled the habit she'd never worn. She hiked back the flesh of each cheek to see how she would have looked as Sister Polycarp at nineteen. Then, nudging the fullness forward, she scowled. Sister P at eighty. She traversed in minutes what she'd once planned as her entire life. She wondered now if Frank hoped to compress as much into twenty minutes with a married drunk.

Louise left the dishes and hurried toward the carousers. She found them gamboling about in the wide-open center of the living room. Well, it was abundantly clear that Frank was out of practice. They whirled and lurched and turned until Trover, reeling backward, collapsed into an armchair. Frank stood over him, arms akimbo, laughing brassily, a bad actress trying to play a crapulous flirt.

"Well," Louise said. "Well, *well*. This is an odd-couple night to rival the Aspirancy Dance."

CHAPTER

At the age of six Louise stole an Esso wrecker from a neighbor boy named Augie Hudgins. It was the tag end of a short but lucrative career she would later refer to simply as "when I was stealing things."

Three years later Gegggo unearthed the wrecker in a box of junk under the cellar steps. "Return to owner, if you please," she'd said in that syrupy singsong that signified her final offer.

Louise was nearly ten and tall for her age. Two old for dolls, she was handing over a toy wrecker to a big, bewildered kid who no longer played with trucks. To make matters worse, they were tacitly sweet on each other, and when she gave it back, Augie flushed and looked down at his feet. "That's OK," he said. "Keep it." Near tears, she pressed it on him, and when he would neither hold out his hand nor look her in the eye, she sent the truck in a murderous spin across his porch, and ran.

Frank saw no reason for Louise to go back to the car wash. "Those places have a built-in break-out allowance," she argued. "They expect an occasional Louise." Situational ethics, thought Louise. What next?

When she mentioned Gideon, Frank had laughed. "He'd never squeal. What's the percentage in it?" But Louise had her doubts. Besides, he'd broached the subject again just before asking to use Trover's lathe. Then he boldly left shavings all over the floor and all the shaping tools out, and now sawdust fuzzed the bright fresh paint of the impossible Landers.

Neutralizing Gideon's position then was certainly a factor, though hardly the controlling one. Mostly it was the irrational rage to do good, to make good, to be good. Were they one and the same? She couldn't be sure. Was such a drive decent? Or was it only the lust for a kind of square-cornered tidiness that eluded her in the material world, a tight ethical tuck, no more, no less, than the arrogant, often crippling desire to be always right.

Of course she had to go back.

The Heap Big Clean was just around the bend, now rushing by on her right. She circled the block and made another pass. How serene the place seemed, amazingly so, like a patient seen for the first time since the accident. No blood. No dangling parts. No squads of investigators or reporters or repairmen. A man in gray coveralls disappeared around the side of the building. Her heart sank; she had hoped to get by with leaving a note. Oh, the place seemed now not so much tranquil as holding its breath or playing dead. She lost nerve and hurried on to Lorraine.

She went to the art supply shop for gesso and paint. At the state store she picked up her holiday wine supply. She wandered into Woolworth's and there bumped into Shirley Kern. She was all fired up, this blunderbuss of a housewife and, as usual, in a blistering hurry. But how lucky she was to have run into Louise. Had Louise heard they were organizing a group called Wrestling Mothers?

Louise clutched her breast. "Not me, Shirl. I'm in terrible shape."

She giggled. "Heavens, you wouldn't be expected to *wrestle*. We're a booster group. For the boys." She ticked off a brief list of proposed fund-raisers: a chicken-corn soup stand at the home matches; Saturday funny cake sales to provide the kids with varsity sweaters. Whipping a large bath towel out of a tote bag, she held it across her bosom. "Silk-screened these jobbies myself," she said.

Louise stared at a huge blue panther on a fluffy white background. Instinctively she reached out to touch it. The panther was so stiff with paint that it would scour a person's skin off before it sopped the wet. "Well," she finally agreed. "OK, give me some towels." She'd take them home, but she wasn't about to peddle vicious linens to her friends."

"Super," said Mrs. Kern, loading Louise up. "Pay me later."

Louise stood rapt before the round, animated, purposive face. The barely contained busyness made the woman seem to vibrate in her boots. "I bet you left your car running," Louise said.

"You said it, kid."

"Oh, I do so admire your attitude. You go about everything with such energy and dedication. And when it comes to wrestling, why, you're practically a genius. Most people don't know half—"

"Most people know what they need to, if only they knew it."

"Well, suffice it to say, I'd be grateful for a tenth of your get-up-and-go."

"You have your own gifts, Louise."

"Just the same, nothing I do serves the common good in any appreciable way. Even your chicken-corn soup is a kind of comfort to the weary spirit. It's extraordinary stuff." Louise bit her lip. Why did she go on so? Once she got started praising or damning, she couldn't stop until she'd ushered her subject into heaven or hell. It was a terrible habit, and it unsettled people. The woman was looking at her as though she could not locate herself in this blizzard of good opinion.

"I'm late, late," Shirley protested, but Louise was loath to let go.

"You must give me your recipe. For the corn soup," she said.

"I'll phone," said Shirley, groping toward the checkout. "In the meantime, you ride herd on that boy of yours. We're counting on him to be little Lorraine's first state champ."

Louise nodded, and Shirley Kern held up one finger. "Sports banquet coming up, you know. Maybe you could bake up some little clay wrestlers, as favors."

"Anything," said Louise.

Mrs. Kern left Louise blinking after her. Louise immediately resolved to work on being useful. She would use those penitential towels to rub some of Shirley's vigor and single-mindedness into her own ambivalent being. She would charge her slow blood with school spirit and involvements so plentiful and pressing and passionate that anyone would understand how such a person would have to rip the roof off a car wash now and then.

When she pulled into the Heap Big Clean, the man she'd spotted earlier was solidly ensconced on the stoop in front of the office. There was no backing out now. Alighting from the Jeep, she waited while he sawed off a piece of ring bologna with his penknife. The meat lay on a piece of butcher paper spread across his lap. He nailed her with that squinty-shrewd local look that magnified your simple existence to something over-bold, a strike against you.

"Good day," she said. "You don't know me, but . . . well, maybe you do . . . by my works, I mean. Well, there's no excuse for what I did, and I'm dreadfully sorry to be so long in owning up." As if it were still possible to appear businesslike, she tugged crisply at the tips of her gloves.

Chewing in slow, ruminant circles, he sized her up. He hacked off another hunk and dipped it in yellow mustard. So he would not make it easy for her, an *ausländer* woman, flustered, tongue-tied.

After rewrapping his meat neatly, he set it on the cement step. "Hen never said nothing about no roppers."

"Oh, I'm no robber," she said emphatically. Then: "Who's Hen?"

"Henry Stump, your perprietor here."

"Then who are you?"

He was surveying her now from various angles. "Say, this some kind of old debt or something? This time of year, don't they come out of the woodwork. Little Eyetalian kid used to swipe the crumb cake otta my lunch kettle at recess. Now this goes back a ways, late forties. Yeah, well, didn't he grow up to make a bundle in mushrooms. Every Christmas now since '58 I get a unanimous gift, a basket of mushrooms and Twinkies." He smiled slyly. "Fella don't think I know who he is."

"Just to set the record straight," she said, "I'm not a thief—exactly."

"Not here five minutes, and already she wants to change her story yet." But there was nothing unfriendly in his manner. Indeed, he seemed to like her.

"Could you just tell me where I might find Mr. Stump?"

"Sure. Down Tampa ways. Loafin'. Shoots down every year this time. I keep tabs on the operation for him."

She'd prepared a note in advance. She handed him the sheet with her name and address and phone number. "Can you see that he gets this, please?"

He said, "Come on, what could the nice little lady want with a fellow like Stump?"

She hesitated, but the momentum of truth was upon her, and she couldn't hold back another instant. "Well, I really did a job on this place," she said.

The man scratched under his cap.

"Not on purpose, you understand. It's just that I couldn't think wedged in like that ... I panicked ... I—"

He was laughing aloud now, shaking his head in hilarious recognition. He strode over to her Jeep and ran his hand along the crumpled roof. "Son of a beehive, so you was the little hoodlum." He glowed now with knowledge. He crooked his finger, and when she didn't step closer, he approached. "A couple tees," he whispered, "brass bow or two ... I should know. I'm the plumber put her back together. Came to all of thirty-four bucks, plus my time. Shoot, old Stump collected fifteen hundred clammers from Aetna. Stumpy was here, he'd kiss you."

She drew back. How was it possible? She'd acted alone, hadn't she? Yet within seconds Gideon was involved, and unbeknownst to her, she was abetting a guy named Stump against a company called Aetna. And Aetna? Why, at that very moment, they were raising rates, and soon thousands of little homeowners would be paying for her fecklessness. She saw herself pursuing a crusade of retribution to the edges of space, the ends of time, and the plumber's hand on her shoulder was like a sentence passed, a pox on her house. No wonder she stayed home most of the time. Just step outside for a second, and you're stitched into history forever.

But the man's smile was waxing more avuncular than judgmental. "Stumpy didn't make his bay high enough, say not?" He was one of those wiry types, with the whimsically geometric French face that turned up now and again among the pale Germans, the dark Alsatian ancestor poking through. There was a glint in his eye and an even broader smile brewing.

She forced a weak chuckle against what struck her as an interest too neighborly, too personal.

Nodding, nodding, nudging her, at last, he came out with it. "Don't ya recognize me?" he said.

She gave him a questioning look. And now the smile he'd been saving broke, and he thrust out his hand. "Soon's ya pulled up, I said to myself, 'Darn, don't that lady look familiar?' " He paused. "You know me, not? *Sterl LaWall!*"

She blinked, sneaking a glance at him.

"Fuzzy's pop."

"Of course!" Take a man out of his context, and he's a different man entirely. She imagined him next to his thin wife in the high school bleachers. When his boy lost, as he did consistently, both his gaze and his arms dropped between his knees, and his wife would follow suit, neat grief, like bleeding into buckets. Something about the way the woman, who was not the boy's mother, copied the father's melancholy always touched Louise. "Yes, yes," she said, dropping her hand into his like a furtively insufficient tip. "How are you, Mr. LaWall?"

He waved the question aside as someone else might dismiss flattery. "Wait up," he said, pleased, excited. He walk-ran to a panel truck. Opening the door, he rummaged inside, one foot kicked out behind him. He returned to her with his small French teeth gleaming and both hands full. "Close your eyes and open your purse," he said.

Despite substantial misgivings, Louise did as she was told, and moments later felt the pelting weight of things dropping deep into her custody. When she opened her eyes, he was holding an object up to her inspection. A brown comb in a plastic case. Bold gold letters said, "Seasons Greetings, Neighbor. LaWall's One-Shot Service."

Glancing down, she saw that her handbag overflowed with more of the same. Then LaWall knifed the final comb down with the rest. "My best to the family," he said.

By way of reply Louise scurried around to the passenger door of the Jeep. Returning seconds later, she presented him with a liter of Trover's lambrusco. "My best to yours," she said.

"Oh, shoot," he said, a tad coyly. "No darn need ... well, now chust holdt on a second." He skipped off sideways and disappeared into the building. He came out with two paper cups.

"Oh, no," she protested, "that's for you and Mrs.—"

"I insist," he said, digging into the cork with the primitive little implement on his penknife. And as he grappled with the honors, she looked out over the street. Dusk had moved in as they talked, dark scarves trailing above houses outlined in yule lights, above trees lit with silver and gold. A fine silt of ruby bumper lights flowed out the parallel streets toward the country. Two Amish buggies clopped by to the five o'clock carillons chiming uptown, and the woodsmoke was good stuff, apple and cherry and pear.

"You daren't go home till we drink a toast," he said, handing her a cup.

"I should say not," she said. "Uh—I know, let's drink to something we both care about." She raised her cup. "To the boys."

"Couldn't have said it better myself," he said, brushing her cup. "To the wrestling season."

She took a gingerly sip. It rushed everywhere at once. It lit her instantly. How lucky she was. How lucky indeed to be allowed, by dint of a single stupid act, to make this homely exchange and to send tremors both malefic and tender, great and small, through a listening universe. She felt as resolutely singular as the light-delineated houses, and as solidly connected, and that drop of red wine went on chiming inside her. She stood with her cup in the air, grinning in ridiculous friendship.

"A little tip," he whispered confidingly. "You tell that smart husband of yours, you tell Lawyer Kleeve to sue the pants off Henry Stump." He tapped the roof of the Jeep. "Least get a new cap ott of it."

She laid her finger perpendicular to her lips. "Shhhhhh," she said. "Lawyer Kleeve doesn't know a thing about this."

LaWall's accompliceship was, if anything, too eager. He nodded in wholehearted collusion. Now it appeared she was stuck to this man the way disappointment glued him to his slip of a wife.

"Merry Christmas," she said. And Merry Christmas again. "And take care."

"*Machs goot,*" he said happily, as she entered the musty darkness of her old truck.

She had only one life but many pacts with many people. To how many and in how many ways was she married again and again? The implications dizzied her. And in how many ways was she alone, the thought echoed back, as falling into line with the outbound vehicles, she entered the even rhythm of traffic moving through dying light. Out past the sewage disposal plant, the auto graveyard, up past the one-room schoolhouse, and now it was open country where finally, by the halfway point, she was alone on the road.

At the summit of the first rise she looked around. The land undulated away to her right, one stark tamarack against the purple western sky. The world of interpersonal complexity had diminished now to a spot of light inside her remote as the pulsant glow in the window of the farmhouse deep in the folds of the valley. The chill dark seemed palpable now, almost impassable, as she labored uphill past the millrace and the great Ironmaster's House at Sally Ann Furnace. She proceeded more slowly now, taking the switchbacks meticulously, a solitary woman heading home with a holiday cargo of wine and combs and nasty towels.

Louise woke that night embedded in an ache that was specifically Gideon's. How did she know whose ache it was? How did you know the man you dreamed was the father whom you never beheld, your son, though his face be a stranger's? Yet this was not a dream, exactly. Assault, visitation, seizure, whatever, Louise was apparently prone to it.

Once, several weeks earlier, she had awakened in the sullen white corpulence of Paulie Bortz, the Panther heavyweight. She hardly knew the boy, yet she awoke soaked with him, her body a sponge so heavy with torpor and despair her lungs hurt.

Another time, years ago, Louise found herself trying to breathe in the terrifying airlessness of a black woman's week-old bereavement. Louise had seen it on the news, the woman's child brought lifeless out of a lily pond. The attack came days later, Louise slamming awake, her own being thinned to a glaze over perfect emptiness. It was hours before she dared move out into her own rooms and confusions.

She had less control over these inhabitations than over pregnancy. What was going on? Was she carrying all those others around with her like the countless eggs constellating in her belly, and what was the touch that sparked them to life, raised their cries in *her* throat? Granted indefinite tenure, would we, each of us, deliver every other out of the dark improbability of our own bodies and breath?

But Gideon McThee? And why today, when she had earned the right to expunge him? Just as he'd made himself at home in her house, he'd commandeered her person, flooded her thoughts, all his cunning and calculations liquefied inside her. It tasted black; it tasted tragic! He was, in her, a causeway of pure wanting; it wetted her resolve, swept her helplessly toward morning.

So she started her day dulled. She feared these aftereffects might possess an indefinite half-life, and he would smell the clemency on her breath. Fortunately for her, like most dream remains, the residue faded fast, and by noon she was nearly clean of it. She went looking for Mighty, found her scouring the green stamp stain off the counter. Louise pottered about for several minutes before saying, "I think it's time you told Gideon to make other arrangements."

"You tell him," the girl said.

"But he's *your* friend, *your* responsibility."

"Why does he have to go? Give me one good reason."

"I could give you a dozen—without scratching the surface."

"In twenty words or less, *Muhthur.*"

"Would you like to try blackmail for starters?"

Compressing the sponge to nothing, Mighty spun around. "Oh, God! Look at you, still in your nightgown, bangs in your eyes, talking blackmail, of all things. Get with it, woman!" She scanned the room frantically. Running to the open cupboard, she grabbed a ten-pound bag of Chippewas. With the boning knife she slit the bag from top to bottom and dumped it onto the counter. She scooped one up and thrust it at Louise. "Here, woman, get hold of something real. Take it, take it, Mother. Hold it. What is it, Mother?"

Louise thrust her arm behind her back and herself recoiled from the daughter's ferocity. She had those Tatar eyes, like Geggo.

"Say it, Mother."

Louise stared at her, an alarming pulse punching out of Mighty's throat.

"Potato, Mother. Say it. Potato." The child's face was small, smooth as rage could make it, her slanted eyes shiny with malice. She went on reciting, "Potato, potato, potato," until the word stumbled out of meaning and became the clumping cadence of some primitive chant.

Louise took the tuber. "What should I do with this?" she asked.

"Ffffffffwhewwwwwwwww!" Mighty said. "You don't even know enough not to ask a question like that when someone's pissed. Oh, do what you want, throw my friends out. Throw us all out. Then you can have your little palace all to yourself." She picked up the sponge, bunched it again, and let it leap out of her hands at Louise. "Since it's your house, you *clean* it." She paused in the doorway. "I'm going to my room. Do not disturb me."

Louise waited until after supper (this last stew she'd loaded with mushrooms). When Gideon came out of the room with Trover's glue gun, she had only to say, "I'd like a word with you." Scanning her eyes, he shrugged and handed her the glue gun and without a word slouched away.

She heard his heavy tread on the stairs to Mighty's room. Then after a while he came down, leaving by the back door. Then the unmistakable phlegmy hum of his motor, then gone. Gone! That loophole of a word, noose around absence, you holding the rope. You trying to breathe relief and filling up again instead with that night sludge, that dirty grease of yearning you thought you'd shed. Gideon's misery choking you. Tough! Suffer, Louise.

In the kitchen the nun was making popcorn. How the hell much longer was *she* planning to stay?

To the Room then, with vengeance. Once she got started, she didn't want to stop. Mighty was right. She felt like getting rid of everybody, everything in the house. The ecstasy of divestiture. She lugged a crock of dried clay out to the trash. She carried out an extra set of fifty-pound weights and that giant round barometer calibrated to tell what color of ski wax to use. How had her simple life attracted such objects?

She stopped then and listened. Was she hearing things? Mighty was two floors up with her door closed; Gideon had left the stereo blasting. With all that blessed intervention, how could it be, why were Mighty's sobs sawing through her mother's bones? Louise accelerated her pace to increase the static, the racket between them.

Just once she wanted to be done with something. Wasn't there a way to lay down the law that it stayed laid? But as soon as you tried to bring the truth to earth and claim it, as soon as you stopped it dead, it died. It lied. Or at least it wasn't entirely true anymore. She could hardly remember the principle on which she'd convicted Gideon. Only the person lived on. Lingered like scent. Mighty, disconsolate in her dainty room. Louise as she worked, found herself leaning. A tree on a tugline. Timber!

Louise gave the door a hesitant tap. More warning than request. This room was the scene of all their reconciliations. Mighty always made you come to *her*. And Mighty always made you wait.

She muttered, "What?" but Louise found her facedown, head-tented. As she had done so often before, Louise pulled the blankets away gently. Mighty responded with belligerent rigidity, nose to mattress. From time to time Louise twisted the ends of her daughter's hair and waited. More min-

248 / Sharon Sheehe Stark

utes went by. And still more. Mighty twitched. She rotated her face a quarter turn so that her profile lay exposed, one eye open, dead trout style.

"Really, My, was I so wrong? Was I? It was a cheap move on his part, and it hurt that you were in on it."

More silence. Louise remembered waiting for her infant daughter to learn to roll over, the flailing feet and furious face. Now the abolescent girl was up on one elbow, more incredulous than enraged. "In on it?" she said. "Did you think we'd turn you over to the FBI?"

"I didn't know what to think."

"You never do." She sighed. "Well, you're right. Gideon did want something. He wanted you to give him something, anything, I guess. The way you give *us* things."

"Did he say that? I mean, what kind of person would say a thing like that?"

"Of course, he didn't say that. Any dipstick could figure it out. The way he keeps trying to burrow in. He wants a place here."

"But on his terms."

"So?"

"Gideon's technique is to bully his way into my house? What a peculiar notion."

"Not when you've already been as nice as you can and you've given all your gifts."

That graniteware coffeepot. So it had come with a price tag after all.

And now that she had Louise thinking, Mighty sat up. Ah, didn't she have her father's combative gifts, his flawless timing. "Besides," she added, "it's not such a peculiar notion. We all work the same scam."

"Mighty, I, for one, do not blackmail people."

"Oh, Ma, we all do. 'Behave,' we say. 'Or else.' Know what we hold over people? I figured it out."

Louise refused to answer. Another teacher. She would not be taught.

"Themselves," Mighty said smartly. "And we've seen it all. 'Behave, you slob, lazy ass, pervert, pig. I know you better than anyone else, and you're not nice.' "

And Louise thought of Geggo, those slanty eyes putting the squeeze on her: "You better be telling truth. I call fortune teller, find out."

"No wonder Dad hangs out in bars with all those strangers. He still has a chance with them. They can be *fooled*."

"I'd prefer you didn't explain your father to me," she said. "It's not your place."

"Why not?"

"Look, My, maybe it's true, maybe you do take a lot of crap from family.

But Gideon? Chrissakes, where's it say I have to take it from someone else's kids?".

"He's been on his own a long time."

"He's too old to be an orphan."

"You're an orphan."

"What?"

"Is that why you had a boy and girl, to make up for the matching set you never had at home?"

"That's nuts, and you know it."

She paused, tight with holding back. Then the words burst out. "Your mother put you in Geggo's potato bin. And *split*!" she said.

Louise looked at her, stunned. Forget lies and vice. More often then not, it was your deepest wounds that indicted you. "Who told you that?" she said.

"Geggo."

"My goodness, must've been one of your favorite bedtime stories."

Mighty nodded minutely. "She said *sweet* potato bin, actually."

"She told me plain potato."

"Maybe she thought sweet potato make you sound more adorable or something."

"Or something."

"The stories always get better. It can't be helped."

"Really."

Mighty twisted her fingers this way and that. She bit her lip, plucked a lash. Her Sunday punch had knocked the wind out of both of them. "Let me alone," she said in a low voice. And Louise left quietly.

She found Trover and Frank watching Great Railway Journeys of the World on PBS. Nicked primitive railcars were climbing high into the Andes. Ruddy-cheeked Indians embracing crates of hens and geese squawked and larked as mountain lakes and snowy peaks and clouds sucked by their windows. Trover pointed out tourist spots, proprietarily; you'd think it was his own homeland they were passing through.

They sat on the sofa against the wall, Frank nodding in abject fascination. Their bodies rocked and swayed with the ponderous rhythm of the rolling stock. A bowl of popcorn was wedged in the fissure between them, but nobody offered Louise a crumb. Her lot to be lost, motherless. Motherless, motherless, motherless. "I always thought the Orient Express would make a lovely trip," she said without great feeling. She imagined herself beige and featureless as a potato.

"Shhhhhh," said the tandem travelers.

Trover leaned forward. "It's way up there but you can't see it," he said reverentially. "Machu Picchu!"

And that silly nun squinting, pretending to be impressed.

Louise looked up to see Mighty between the rooms, beckoning. Louise rose, scooped back for a clawful of popcorn and followed her daughter out to the kitchen. She emptied her hands into Mighty's. "What now?" she said.

The crimp around Mighty's mouth had softened, and though the flash was out of her eyes, she glowed with opportunity. "Know what I was thinking?" she said.

"What?"

"It's Christmas." She examined a kernel of popcorn, then tucked it neatly between her teeth.

"No kidding, Dick Tracy."

"Well, would a person who was really serious about throwing someone out, do it two days before Christmas? Maybe you should reconsider. I mean, for your own good. Remember Hofecker?"

"Oh, yes, Kenny Hofecker."

A carpenter of sorts, Hofecker was one in a sorry series of hirelings in the long harrowing home-improvement era. An excon, he was penniless, inept, lazy. Trover, who culled these tradesmen from the lowest rungs of his clientele, bought him hand tools and gave him Louise's car to get back and forth in, although, as it turned out, the man generally preferred to stay over. In the evenings with his own hands, he fashioned little scrapwood boxes for Louise; in return, he asked only that Louise's hands make his bed, iron his shirt, fix his dinner. He singled out two chairs for himself, one at the table, another in front of the TV; he menaced anyone who touched them. He also slept and watched soaps on the job, and once she returned from town to find him entertaining a local waitress in the guestroom. She let them finish before dismissing him. Stupidly. For only later did it occur to her that she'd sent him away forever, in *her* car.

"That was my last carpenter," Trover fumed when she told him what happened. "And what a shabby thing to do to a guy right before Christmas."

Certainly it was. How low-down and heartless of her. Quickly, she set to phoning every flea-pit hotel in Neisstown until she reached him. She made extravagant promises to lure him back. Better lunches, higher pay. Oh, people branded you, stamped you with their bad habits, their handiwork. Once they found a niche in your house, your house had a new owner. You were theirs and they were yours. Louise saw her mother, upswept do, wartime shoulders, depositing her babe, then out the door, off scot-free. "Why can't *I* get rid of anyone?" she wanted to know.

The girl gave her an expectant look and a nub of buttery corn.

"You know where that damn kid is?" Louise said, chewing. She swallowed hard.

Well, of course she did. Mighty nodded but cautiously.

And Louise nodded, too, ruefully: *Go ahead, get him.*

Louise went back to Trover and Frank and sat down. She followed the almost comically raucous course of the train across the ridge below the lost city, through dusty Indian villages and back down the mountain where it came to a smoking, choking halt. Passengers swarmed out and started to walk. Louise felt silly just sitting there. She rose and for several moments stood staring gravely down at her husband and friend. "You two might be stuck here for days," she said. "Not me."

She started upstairs to bed, then stopped. In the dim stairwell she sat, head against the wall, waiting. It was no time at all until she heard them come in the kitchenway. The two of them speaking in the subdued tones of the newly rescued, *tump* of the freezer door, clink inside the fridge. Ice cream, beer, Gideon pulling out his chair. And she noticed too that the barbells and the thermometer-barometer-skiwax register she'd tossed out not two hours before were back in the house, leaning against the piano. From the sound of it the train was back in action too. How had her life drawn these people, these things? How had her life arrived here?

CHAPTER

24

"Another theme Christmas," Mighty said as she filled an ice pack for Maddy, who had arrived damaged from the long bus ride.

Michael was locked in combat with a fifty-pound sack of Alpo and a stiff sheet of gift wrap. "I don't get it," he said. "You mean, like Christmas in other lands or something?"

"I mean like Christmas right here. The theme is us. Nutso. Did you catch Gram checking out our little manger scene? I doubt she deems St. Beethoven an acceptable substitute."

In a fit of impatience Michael tore off the foil and crumpled it. He tied a big red bow around the bag instead. "Wait'll she sees the tree," he said.

The tree was a lamp. The lamp was analogous to bootleggers in the family, some plucky crime you faked penitence for in public but took secret pride in. It was Christmas personalized and Christmas remade in their own image. In this he could see how each family, happy or not, created its own character, and even those who resisted that character unwittingly contributed to it. Early Kleeves might have boasted a coat of arms. This branch had a Christmas lamp.

The tradition had its roots, of course, in chaos. It had begun seven, eight years ago, when just after supper Christmas Eve they discovered that with all the last-minute frenzy, nobody had thought to buy a tree. Louise refused to let them cut a live one from the hillside. Irritable, disgusted, they proceeded to comb, cursing, the closets and cupboards in search of a passable substitute for a Scotch pine. That was one thing they had, still did have, a streak of crotchety optimism that got things done more often than not.

Then Louise had summoned them all to the guest room. "Wasn't it perfect?" she cried, indicating the flea market lamp on the dresser. It boasted a greenish base and a leaded glass shade that swirled shades of paler green with if not exactly red, then a kind of sunrise puce. She resituated it downstairs on the drum table, and with hardly a mutter of protest, they set about adorning the fixture. They hung gold and silver balls from the lower trim of delicate filigree, tinsel from the flared, lacy crown. Then she all but declared it heaven-sent when somebody spotted on its base the embossed words "Tannenbaum Lamp Company." They laughed at her, but when the chain was pulled, it lit up in a way it never had before, as if the Victorian lampmaker had only them in mind when creating it, its sole purpose on earth to redeem their deficiencies, to illuminate that very moment of their lives.

Fortunately his grandmother napped through the brief time it took them to trim the lamp this year. But now Frank came downstairs, and Louise said, "Oh, great." When Maddy arrived, the woman had been romping around in jeans and a Panther Power sweatshirt. Louise glanced into the next room, where Maddy, crowned with ice, was sleeping off the green of motion sickness. Louise drew the nun aside. "Great!" she repeated. "What do you expect my mother-in-law to make of you?"

"It's Christmas," the nun said. "Some things cannot be gotten around. I wouldn't dream of going to mass out of habit." She squinted at the lamp. "No tree, Louise? No tree?"

Then Maddy was up on wobbly legs, swaying, disoriented. Michael wanted more than anything to shield his grandmother, for he had a sudden picture of himself—all of them—through her eyes, and they looked not unique and proud and inventive at all, but lazy, lawless, a slipshod lot with a silly lamp. She stood pink-eyed and dazed, like the rabbit he'd shot, supporting herself between the walls of the archway. He watched her absorb, adjust, overcome. Then she was on the march, tapping at Trover. "You takin' me to midnight mass, Bud, or do I have to thumb it?"

"Gram," Michael said, "I just called. Midnight mass is at seven."

"Well, if the fourth can be the fifth and Columbus Day on the tenth, they can hold midnight at noon for all I mind—and what do you call that contraption?"

"Oh, Tannenbaum," Mighty belted out, never missing a chance to bait this frail but bitier prototype of herself.

Maddy twisted her lips clockwise. She gave the sudden nun the once-over. "As you say, Bud, shut yer eyes a lickety instant, and boys, oh, boys, they switch the bejeesus out of things."

Sprecher had refused their dinner invitation. So Mighty and Michael drove over with his presents. For him, a set of polypropylene ski underwear and a check. The Alpo for Joe. Mighty spotted Sprecher's eyes beaming them in from his back window as they climbed the steep lower part of his driveway, and by the time they reached the house, he was out on the stoop, legs planted wide, waiting.

"Thanks," he said, taking the gift box and check from Mighty. He kept close tabs on Michael, who was busy lifting the massive sack over the tailgate onto his shoulder. Head cocked, Sprecher nosed closer. "That dog food?" he asked.

"Yep," Michael said. "Merry Christmas to Joe from Bagel and Caroline."

Sprecher arched his thumb. "In the shedt," he said, with dour exasperation, as though he'd been directing dog food deliveries for days.

The shed smelled of mold and bologna and burlap and grease. Michael propped the sack against a bag of lime and felt the fuzzy meat brush the back of his neck, even if it didn't. Turning to go, he happened to glance out the single, very filthy window. He was amazed to see that parked beneath a makeshift lean-to outside was a bright red, shiny new Massey-Ferguson, far too large for the garden or yard.

Stepping through the doorway, Michael said, "See you got yourself a Christmas present, Mr. Sprecher?"

"Yep."

"Cool."

A grunt.

"Merry Christmas and all that," Mighty said, itchy to go.

The old man nodded. Then he hitched his chin ever so slightly. In a man of few and economical gestures, each nick and notch were fraught with meaning. He meant for them to wait. After jerking open the slant door to the cellar, he disappeared into the earth. He emerged with something big and tinny, which he shoved at Michael.

"Mr. Sprecher, we don't want anything," Michael protested.

"It's a bean dryer," he said. "From Cho," he added with hard-bitten, almost bitter finality. "Cho don't take nothing for nothing."

They took two cars into the Catholic church, the only one in north Bauscher county. A small, white Christmas card church, its atypical, almost abject simplicity gave it a look of desperate longing to fit in among the Reformed and Lutherans, the Amish, Moravians, and Mennonites and other plain sects that abounded in and about Lorraine. The Kleeves' worshiping was, in the main, timed to coincide with Maddy's visits, a fact hardly lost on her since no one seemed to know the pastor's name or the mass schedule or the words to any of the hymns. They didn't know when to stand or sit or kneel either, and so they always contrived to sit in the back behind rows of competent models.

Sometimes, having stumbled into bed after his Saturday night match, Michael, waking early and grateful, would quite unaccountably rise and get dressed and go in to rouse his mother. And if, after the lick and promise of his christening, she had never gone out of her way to catechize him, neither did she quite have it in her to refuse to take him to mass when asked. She'd drop him off at St. Joseph the Worker's and then go, uncombed and cranky, for the Sunday paper.

He'd fall in with the knots of softly conversing parishioners outside, ladies smelling of hair spray and cold, their infants sniffing suspiciously the fragrant hush of another Sunday, husbands with their noses in handkerchiefs or hands in their pockets.

He loved the easy slide from one end of the body-polished pew to the other. He loved the little creaks and throat clearings, the gathering buzz of expectancy before the priest appeared. He did not try to follow the service or make the proper responses, and often his thoughts strayed to wrestling or Erica Lavender, most often, though, to food (the pew had a meaty grain that tempted him). There were no stained glass windows to make the light noble and holy, and the music was singularly unbeautiful, one woman always bawling above the rest. So, in his ignorance and outsiderness, in a church that also did not fit in, he observed the stretchings of a people toward a God and a promise so absurdly distanced from the fuss and fluke of their daily lives that not belonging became a kind of condition of membership, and all that was alien and unimaginable drew close, the unknown opened a crack, and he felt gladdened in a way he would have been hard put to account for.

And even after he got home, the essences of St. Joseph the Worker would cling, the perfume and tallow and furniture oil, and he'd feel dipped, as a candle is dipped, and lit, and the light would last for hours.

From Luke now, the priest was reading the common details of an uncommon birth. And the Holy Name men were sponsoring a mackerel breakfast in May. The pert little priest wished them the joys and abundance of the season and, rejoining his servers, swept back to the altar. Maddy's rosary had huge crystal beads that struck the pew in front with the clunk of hailstones; her lips twitched with prayer.

She was the only one of their group to go up to communion. Later, in the shuffling lull before the ceremony's close, she elbowed her grandson. "You happen to take notice—did that there nun receive? Did your daddy?" Michael knew enough to understand what she was really asking, but he shrugged, reluctant to divulge the color of anybody's soul.

They exited to a full-bodied chorus of something joyous and jazzy, the loudmouthed woman caroling harder than ever. Outside, it was raining, coming warm and fast. Were it snow, his dad would rev up the Jeep when they got home, and whoever was in the mood could go along. Michael remembered starry nights after a southern snowstorm. Not a soul about, the houses smoking and tight. The undiminished thrill of being first to incise, to sign the fields and yards and highways. They'd ride high off the ground, safe and powerful. They knew where to find the highest drifts, and he'd let them take turns busting the snowbanks, and each time they broke through, everybody cheered, reconfirmed in their faith that as a team they were unbeatable. Then on through somebody's windswept pasture, Trover pounding time on the gas pedal, happy as an urchin slapping through puddles. His dad was never so at ease with them, his children, as when they could all be children together.

The next day he'd come home with books about snow crystals and glacial formations and tons of seed and suet for the wintering birds. He'd be busy then with snow until it melted and some other sudden but equally fleeting passion would spirit him away to the stores and books and the various playgrounds of his mind and desire.

But for now his snow phase would have to wait. It was a savage, slanting rain, and bits of broken twig littered the back roads. When they turned into their lane, the headlights seemed to snag on the sorry slump of rot and ruin off to the side, plucking at one section in particular. Under the hammering rain, the chicken shed was beaten almost to earth now, a long collapse of jagged shambles tugging on the part still attached to the barn, the part still holding on.

At home they immediately fell to arguing in the measured, dispassionate mode of regulation debate. Whether to open now or wait until morning, and since the holdouts for morning were at least as greedy as the midnight people, the former always capitulated early, and only Maddy, who had conceded too much already, hung in past the point of ritual surrender. "Bud," she said, looking to him, her own kind. "Bud, we always opened at first light."

"Leave me out of it," he said good-naturedly.

"Oh, go 'head, you'uns always do what yiz want anyways." Opening her purse, she knifed sharp white bank envelopes around. "Frozen assets," she said in a voice as crisp as the bills. And they laughed, knowing she'd kept cash in her freezer for years. She produced as well two makeshift packets for Gideon and the nun, five ones in each.

Mob gratitude enveloped her. "Thanks, Gram." "Yeah, thanks," "Wow, thanks, Mrs. Kleeve." "How sweet."

"Bud," she said, "you remember them old Applegood sisters back home?"

"Vaguely."

"They's both croaked now, kicked off a month apart."

"I didn't know that, Mum."

"Way-el, betcha they's a lot you didn't know about them two. Betcha didn't know they was practicin' cannibals."

Everybody left off scavenging and looked up. "Yep," she said, "they always had them caretakers and handymen around—you remember that, Bud. Drifters mostly. Homeless folk. Well, after them two gals went, the county come in, and what do you s'pose they found?"

"A million bucks," Gideon said, all ears.

"Noop. One of them upright freezers, full of parts. Not chicken parts, by garsh, but hunks of them fellas—rump roast, loin chops, plate boil—"

"Gram!" Mighty cried.

"No lie, chickie."

"We believe you, Gram," Michael said. "It's just that, well, maybe some people'd rather not hear cannibal stuff on Christmas. He patted her shoulder. "Thanks a lot for the moola."

She punched him. "Don't blow the wad in one place."

"I won't, Gram." He play-poked her nose.

Louise slipped a package onto her husband's lap. Michael made his fist into a microphone and started circling the recipient. "He's giving it a good shake, folks. He's guessing its weight, taking his time." It was his Dutch Howard Cosell number. "Ladies and chentlemen, he's ready, I believe it. Ay, he's goink for it. He's got the rippen between his teeth. Such a pahrful bite. Here it comes, folks—*ach du liever,* it's chogging shorts, not two, but count 'em, folks, six, eight, ten pairs of cute little runnin' pants. It's a new, let me confirm that, ay-yi-yi, it's official, a new werlt record."

Trover set the bright-colored nylon aside. Michael plunked down in his lap, holding his fist under his father's chin. "Any comment, kid?"

"Mr. Cosell," Trover said, "puh-leese."

Michael got his sport across the board: new warm-ups; a takedown manual; a subscription to *Wrestling News.*

"Now you got no excuse to choke at states," Maddy said, cuffing him.

It was Mighty who came up with the pièce de résistance. "They're hand-blown," she told him, rotating the glass wrestlers under the Christmas lamp. One man on his stomach, an opponent at right angles trying to turn him with frangible arms, the two men connected by a mere speck of matter, a glass scar. Smooth and cool to the touch, they shivered with gelatinous peach-tinctured light. "Guy made them in five seconds," Mighty said, minimizing. "Squiggle, squiggle."

And Michael took her up into a fireman's carry and pinwheeled her around the room, prompting Maddy to ask, "Say, I's just wonderin', what kind of year them Pack boys havin'? Kickin' butt, I hope."

Gideon's gifts went directly from box to body. If he turned them into secondhand quick, maybe no one would want them back. In his fisherman sweater and cap, his gloves and T-shirt and socks, he sifted through litter, prospecting for more, happiness messing his mouth like jelly.

Frank opened two slim similar shapes from Louise. One contained three pairs of black lisle stockings; in the other, an assortment of panty hose in sheerest nude, navy, magenta, and pearl. "For all the women you are," Louise said in that breezy, tossaway diction she used to mask meanness.

And Maddy, frowning, unfurled one of the nude ones, exhibiting it by an appalled pinch of gossamer. "This kind don't wear for beans," she said.

"Well, dig in," Mighty said. "If you must." And Louise did, jabbing holes in the wrap, ripping handfuls away from the rectangular flat thing in her lap. It would never occur to her to loosen the seams and proceed. Intermediate steps played no part in her logic. Michael was reminded how she clawed cigarette packs open and gouged out onion bags instead of untwisting their ties. The physical world was an endless obstacle course for her, but now she had her prize. The frame lay facedown in her lap. Turning it over, she regarded the image at first with uncertainty. Michael leaned close, too. Was it? Well, yes, no, yes, it was his sister. Or her ghost. Something that had escaped her unawares.

The portrait person was poorly lit, flickering almost, oddly set back so that you wanted to look behind the frame for the rest of her. A lovely young woman, doelike, vulnerable, eyes darkly patient, waiting. Her full, beautiful mouth softly pursed, a wistful chagrin, a sweetness he'd never seen before. Louise was speechless. She stared from her daughter to the girl in the photograph.

"Hey, look," Mighty said, shrugging. "It's a mystery to me, too. When I went to develop my last roll of film, that thing turned up on the contact sheet. I don't remember taking it, but it's me, isn't it? *Isn't it?* It scared me, Ma." She shrugged again. "I thought you should have it."

"Why, it's exquisite, it's—"

"Mercy!" cried Maddy, whipping something voluminous out of a suit box. It was a quilted circle skirt and vest to match. "It's giant potholders!" Then she elbowed Louise to show she was kidding.

"I just hope you won't be too hot in it," Louise said, scratching lackadaisically at the taped edges of the small box Trover had given her. No overeager package savaging here. She picked it up and held it to her ear, fearing not a bomb, Michael knew, but another watch. Wearing a stiff, precarious smile, she proceeded daintily, advancing on it a layer at a time until at last the hinged lid opened upon a bed of indigo velvet. She looked in without condescending to it, holding her head unnaturally high.

"Looks to me like a key, Louise. Mebbe a key to your hubby's heart." Maddy winked, and Trover rocked happily back on his haunches.

"The key to your *heart*, is it?" Louise said.

Trover stroked both corners of a wily smile. "Anybody else hear Santa touch down about an hour ago? Could be he left something nice outside."

"In the rain?" Louise said.

"Grab an umbrella," he said, still insinuating, mysterious, acting as if he had something heartwarming planned.

"We don't own an umbrella," Mighty said.

"Come on," Trover insisted. "Little rain won't hurt the collard greens."

And how easily he had his way with them, his eyes requiring their attendance, his whistling obliviousness, "Oh, Tannenbaum, oh, Tannenbaum. . . ." But it was his bearing, his badness—the rhythmic himness of him—*that* was the tune that drew them; they'd follow the man anywhere. Even Maddy, otherwise impossible to nudge into nonsense, even she rose and, with adoring eyes fixed on her only son, went out with the small band to see what waited in the weather.

The rain had let up some over the past hour. In the chill drizzle Trover strode, now strutted onto the gazebo floor and threw the switch. He led them around and down to the flagstone walkway girdling the lower circumference of the building. "Surely not!" said Louise, still shockable after all these years.

In the ocherous light the vehicle gleamed wet and unwanted yet somehow as snugly dug in as Gideon McThee. Lovingly, Trover swept clinging pine needles from the roof and dried his hands on his pants. Michael felt sorry for the vehicle, as though it were some mutt that had followed his father home and had to wait in the rain for clearance.

"It's a Vanagon," Mighty said wryly.

"Merry Christmas, Bibs." Without batting an eyelash.

But Louise had stopped coming as soon as she saw it. Hanging back behind the bushes, she seemed somehow guarded by them and the shadow ladders cast by the red oaks towering off to her left. Her face was cross-hatched and unreadable, but Michael could imagine her struggle, not for control (she would be beyond that) but for organization—what damages to brandish first, what code to invoke, how many purgatories to promise, how to say what she had said so often, so unprofitably before.

"It's not bad," Michael said helplessly.

Trover consoled the Vanagon with a pat. Then he trimmed his mouth to prim and disgusted. "That's what I mean about your mother," he said, as if the whole purpose of this junket had been to bring to light Louise's secret defects. "There's no pleasing a woman like that."

"How do you know, Dad?" Michael argued. "You don't *try* to please her. You never get her what *she* wants."

"She doesn't *want anything.*"

"You say that the same way someone else might say she wants everything."

"Same damn thing, Son, same thing."

Mighty sidled up to her mother. "Don't ruin things," she whispered ferociously.

Louise had been preparing to say something imperious. He could tell by the way she tried to make her body stretch further. But Mighty's injunction had reduced her to trembling. Injustice on top of outrage. "I said—I told you—you were warned, m-mister," she said, turning too fast, slipping, scrambling up over the vinca and away.

Michael could almost feel the steam come off his father's body. Maybe the rain would put him out. He was snorting hard, old dragon breath, and his eyes darted around for the quickest way out. Throwing open the door to the driver's side, he let the smell of new baste them. Then he clambered in and slammed the door. The Vanagon leaped into gear, loped onto the lawn, brushed by the vinca bank, caught the retreating wife in its lights, and rocked onto the driveway. Now *they* were the betrayed, a trusting clutch of abandoned disciples. In a camaraderie of wounded silence they moved closer and watched him disappear into the holiest of nights.

"Well, there you are," said Gideon. "He *did* keep a set of keys for himself."

"And what if he did," Maddy said, "what's it to you, fella?"

Michael awoke cold, his chest inanimate again. Afraid to strain himself, he rolled his eyes toward the illuminated dial on his clock-radio. Three-thirty, and all was calm. Gingerly he laid his hand across his chest. A blip. Pip, p-pip, pippip. Tum, tump, tump. Whewwwwwww, it was working again.

He sat up in bed. The dark, tapered shape on the floor was Gideon in Trover's mummy-style sleeping bag. Maddy was in his sister's bed across the hall. He listened into the dark as he had, just moments before, monitored his murky heart. And he heard his grandmother's crying, not loud and anguished, but soft silky wasp-wing beats of weeping.

He swung his legs around; he groped for his robe and stopped. For it had come back to him, how deftly she had brandished that cannibal story. She had literally battled them back with it. If he entered that room now, she would take her hurt and hide it under the pillow, as if he'd caught her reading *Playgirl* with a flashlight. To show up now would be the same as stealing her grief. Her husband was dead, and her daughter-in-law was not the one she'd prayed for. Her son, who helped smut merchants survive, was loose in the night in a world boarded up for the holidays. Close your eyes for a moment, and everything changed. You woke in a strange room in the treetops, and nothing around you was yours. It was raining cats and dogs for Christmas, and blankets didn't help because the chill was inside, the cold, steep quiet of the grave inside you.

A lick of light grazed the lower branches of the sycamore outside his dormer, and then the double roar of a gunned engine, the aggressive way he said, "I'm home." Then stillness and dark again and the steady rain. The father was home, the husband home, the son, the sobbing next door subsided and died, and Michael slipped back into his sleeping body, hoping his heart would last the night.

CHAPTER

25

Light pried him open. The rain was done, but his soggy bones would be a week drying out. Today Sprecher weighed a ton and did not try right away to rise.

Morning: still, white, tight, a shell you had to crack before the day yielded its tasks to you. So it was when time was another kind of skin, taut as his own, and when daylight licked him awake, a fair-haired woman kissed him.

But today nothing tugged; nothing demanded his time or attention. What month was it? What day under heaven? The days hung low now, low and slack, big baggy things he got lost in. Days that held the shape of his life, the way Perma's underdrawers (he kept a pair under the mattress with other important documents) carried the fleshly press of her, though both, days and drawers, were empty long now.

One day, when they had been married nearly half a century, Sprecher had to fetch her all the way to Neisstown to the female doctor. Backing out the lane, he noticed a tomato stake leaning. He climbed down from the truck and went to the garden and pounded it back in with a rock. Returning to the Ford then, he headed for town. They didn't talk much, he and

Perma, never did, but he had joked her about the size of the holding tank on the brewery roof. And she had chuckled, hadn't she? When he got to the big lot in front of the medical center, he parked and started walking. He stopped at the lobby door and turned around: *now where did that woman get to?* He clumped back to the truck. He looked inside, checked the floor, even the truck bed. No Perma nowheres. At last, completely ferhuddled, he made for home. He found her setting out slug bait between the bean rows. "Ach!" she said when she saw him. She flapped her hand in disgust. As it turned out, when he had gone to fix the stake, she had run back in to make sure the gas was off. *"Dummkupp,"* she said, "you run off withott me."

But that was the point. He had not gone off without her. He knew for a fact she'd been with him all along. The place next to him was occupied. After all that time, the very air had grown around her, taken Perma's shape, felt and smelled and laughed like her. After fifty years the flesh was nice but not so necessary. He touched the depression on her side of the bed. The sheet was still warm, he swore it, the space beside and inside him as lumpy with her bulk as always.

Sprecher woke every day now to the expanding world of what wasn't there.

His mind scouted. He thought of the Knoll, good now till March. He had no logs lined up outside the planing mill; Tumbling Run with its sullen promise of vandalizing brats come spring, so peaceful now it depressed him. Nothing to do but housekeeping. He hadn't scrubbed or redd up since Perma died. That was her job. He was handy with working the dirt in the fields, but there was something bewildering, beyond him, in the way inside dirt collected from nowhere. It unsettled him. He thought of time itself sifting down, the dry bodies of dead farmers. A baby sister buried behind the old farmhouse. On her tiny stone the words "So soon I was done for, what was I begun for?" He didn't disturb such evidence. It was right now that he should live between the dirt he loved more than life and the dust his life would surely come to.

Maybe the men in white would show today, men with soothing voices and straitjackets. Lately he'd found himself listening for them, his nerve ends hot with the mixed tingle of dread and expectation. His blood, like a dog, wanted to run. "Quick, sic 'em," he'd tell Joe. He'd go for his varmint gun, poke its nose through the window screen. Ay, he'd raise heck with those hospital men. He'd truss them up as they had him. He'd lash them together and keep them in the root cellar till potato eyes sprouted on their bums.

Ill will warmed him, whumped him out of bed. He rose in his grimy layers and triple socks and shuffled over cracked tiles to the toilet. He pissed quick and snugged himself back in. He went to the refrigerator. No damn oatmeal. Today he needed meat. And body heat. He hacked off a chunk of the greenish beef he'd begun the day before. He unscrewed the horseradish lid. He turned it upside down; he looked inside. He upturned it again and shook. A single dollop splat onto his beef. Ach. The horseradish was all. His last jar. *Scheiss!*

"Haa gott heilich schtann gewitter!" And when he left off his curses, he saw that it was half past six. Wetzel's Superette would open at seven. Simple enough to drive into Kemp for more. With a little thrill he recognized the opportunity in this. It was the toehold he wanted. This small need gave him access to his day. He was back in business.

In grateful tenderness he fondled the jar. He held it off from him, still farther away until the label clarified. Why, sure! He knew that he knew that girl's grammy from somewhere. Ada Clauss. RD 2, New Jerusalem. Pure, fresh horseradish. Why, sure—she was his horseradish woman. When she wasn't picking through for spotted apples.

He sat back. She'd have some give to her, the Clauss woman, low, soft songbird bosom, always chuckling to herself. She'd overflow a chair like Perma, same mouthful of raunchy jokes. Sleeves rolled up to the dimpled elbows, hands red from paring roots, knuckles raw from the grater. He hoped she didn't have a puckered mug from licking all those labels. Once she would have been the same sassy shade as the granddaughter. Ay, such a red one! And respectful, too. He went down the cellar for the jars. He fed Joe cold oatmeal from yesterday, a few rinds of beef. He climbed into the Ford and went off with the empty jars chattering beside him.

"Well, now, what's all this?" Effie Wetzel stood, hands on hips, her eyes like two startled mice under her movable hairline.

Ay, so dense. Didn't she know horseradish jars when she saw them? He set his basket on the counter with a twisting emphasis generally reserved for setting something in cement. "And I'll have four"—he held up fingers— *"four* new chars."

The woman looked in the basket, looked at him. Fixing her lips as if to whistle, she went to the dairy case to fill his order. "You cleaned me ott," she said. "It'll come you three-ten. Bag, Earl?"

"Don't waste no paper," he said, tucking the goods in his deepest pocket. She lay her palms across his jars. "Now how 'bout these?"

"Chust see to it they go back where they come from."

"Your only returnables anymore are the birch beer quarts from Neisstown Beverage and the glass cider chugs."

"Schwetz nott so dumm. Why they're good yet," he said.

"Believe me, Earl, the company could care less about its empties."

"What for company?" he said. "Look it." He flashed the label at her. "Lady named Ada Clauss puts it up. Comes from right out New Jerusalem ways."

"Now I should know my own suppliers, not? And I'm telling you, Ada Clauss is a good-size outfit with a full product line. Bacon dressing, apple butter, chowchow. Why, Ada Clauss is nationally advertised. Don't you watch TV no more?"

"Not since they took off *Let's Make a Deal.*"

"Ach," she said with ill-concealed distaste, "such a carryin'-on."

He raised the bushel an inch or two and let it drop, jaw set.

"Now, Earl," she said, "you best watch your step. Get that blood pressure up, you'll soon be in bed with the doctor."

"Never mindt my blood pressure. Now how 'bout them chars?"

"Earl, I told you—we got no pickup procedure. It chust wouldn't pay them people to chase around creation for empty chars."

"You *ferrickt* or what? Chars cost goodt money. Old chars hold the same as new chars—"

"Ah, the light dawns." She tapped her skull. "You want a refund, Earl?"

He stomped so hard his toebones sang. He shook a black finger in her face. "I don't want nothing from no chiselin Wetzel. Chust give over them chars to that poor Clauss woman before she hass to run out for more."

"Now, Earl, you're getting me mad. I'm tellin' you for the last time—"

"She can't make no living that way. All the time buying!" He swung a steel toe into the tongue-and-groove boards around the counter. *"De Gluck!"* he said under his breath.

When Effie Wetzel flinched, her hairline strayed. Sprecher'd love to know what she kept under that rug. She grasped the counter edge with two hands and leaned forward, fixing him with eyes like aggies. "There plain ain't no Ada Clauss," she said.

He wanted to kill her. Her crime was murder, *murder.* He couldn't speak. Effie Wetzel drew her lips into a thin wiggly line like fish bait. His only comfort was that his enemy uglified as he watched.

The thought placated him somewhat. He felt the rage drop off from the dangerous space near the top of his head. He puffed out his chest. "Them bug eyes run in your relation," he told her matter-of-factly.

Effie Wetzel's jaw dropped.

"They wass none too schmart neither. Why, your mum Verna was so dumb she roasted once some hens for Harvest Home, guts still in the belly." He held his nose.

"For *Gott's* sake."

"And your grammy, the ragk lady—"

"And chust because they give your Sprechers fancy names like Earl and Rex don't make you no royal family."

"One nice thing I can say abott your grammy, why, she never wore no wig the cat drug in." He hoisted the basket and let it drop hard. He was not taking no for an answer.

And with that, the storekeeper took a giant step forward, and setting her goodly bulk against the basket, grabbed both handles. Sprecher kept pressing, keeping one hand free to menace her. It amazed him how she was able to dodge and arch and glower at him without once letting up the pressure. Between them they managed to crack the splines and then crush the basket; jars flew, glass broke. Curses flew both ways.

"*Heilich avich!*" the woman muttered, whipping her flyswatter off the hook. Glancing furtively around the store, she then lowered her pitch to an ancient malicious whisper. "*Heeva havva!*" she said, hoarse with satisfaction.

He drove home halved, the first part steaming mad, the other part, deeper down, so swollen with glee he thought his gut would split and the cold splash out of him for good. That *gretz, wunnernaus,* old busy body with her swatter, all worked up and plain as a woman could be without getting shot for it.

"*Heeva havva,*" she'd said. How long since he'd heard that one? Years ago the *heeva havva,* with his black teeth and muddy boots, used to go from farm to farm in the breeding season. He was the husky one you hired to guide the bull into the heifer. And that's what fancy-pants shopkeepers and other uppity folks used to call the hardworking farm populace. *Heeva havva:* hayseed, clodhopper. The hubbub inside him was half laugh now and half the heat of sweet remembrance. Warm barn, restive animal flesh, Perma turning in her sleep.

Calves came easily enough, heave and cry and blood slide. Perma's belly swelled but not with child. No broad-backed son, no daughter to say, "Mum, you work too hard. Let the dishes set awhile." But they'd kept track of those five little girls from up north. Perma snipped their pictures from magazines and sent birthday cards and cried for a week when Emilie died. But then the world lost interest; the Sprechers lost track. He wondered if they lived yet behind a big window with husbands and youngsters and a nosy public still looking on.

He made a hard left that put him on the road skirting the base of the Kleeves' place. He glanced up as he came around. Above him, like a ship's prow, loomed the lower wedge-shaped tip of the Knoll. Come summer that high shale ledge would be studded with a strange snaky plant that punished the picker with invisible itchy prickles.

He chugged around the next curve, by the stone dam. Water from that reservoir was pumped uphill into the pool. All winter it collected mud. First nice day he'd have to shovel it out. He saw also that several stones had heaved up at the lower end. Good. The prospect of work formed in his head as future. Mud, a slap of wet cement, patch of grass around the dam, the pleasure of raising the sluice gate to let the water in.

Across the street Minnie Grimm pinched a pin to the line, the other hand waving to Sprecher. *Heila heila, hinkeldreck*—the chickenshit woman, they called her. Spells, incantations. It was said she knew things she shouldn't. People died in her mind before they died in their beds. They said she had the power, but it was Sprecher's guess she got the bulk of her education from her six-party line. Well, she had her signals crossed this time, hanging clothes outside. The temperature was dropping fast; in no time she'd have a family of stiffs doing the cha-cha-cha across her yard. And that red union suit—wasn't that the cock of the washline? Despite the range and strength of the lively world inside him, his face held, impassive as the rock cropping on which nothing grew but that itchy Pennsylvania cactus.

He hadn't noticed on the way to town because the red barn would have blocked his view from that angle. And he might have missed it now had his eyes not first been drawn along the linear flight line of a pheasant family shooting out of the roadside scrub into the waxy barnyard grasses. He was seized at first with strangeness, that dizzying sense of something as yet unnamed amiss. To the right of the barn, a bafflement, a wallop of white air, something misbegotten here. He turned into the lane and came warily up past the barn to where his perspective took in the whole of the wreckage wrought by the Christmas rains. This was not absence so much as failure, of nails, of matter, of men against heaven. Instead of his endangered but abiding chicken shed lay an abomination of parts. A dump of boards and rot and debris. Clods of rich manury floor dribbled onto the roadway.

And the rubble above was nothing as against the ruin within. Even the gleeful demon lay crushed under collapsed ribs and the useless heap of heart and lungs and liver. Sprecher tossed his memory down with the rest. He wanted nothing of it now. No sassy reds, no bantam named Esau in peacock colors, turquoise and russet and cream. No huddle of hens, air silky with billing. No carpet of soft underfeathers. He had never felt that river of hot wind streaming down from the meadow above, never heard the rattle of cornstalks in autumn, remembered nothing of husk ribbons lifting in the air currents, rising like tiny birds, crows scolding from all the trees. No seed dust, no rub of sun on his back, no pretty red hens. No, if it must go, let it be all, let it leave him alone forever.

And even now not a muscle of his face twitched. He stared at the ruin until tears came, and the bones of his broad cheek took them as the stolid polished rocks of the Maiden Creek took the shallow waters that ran now in winter.

He sat motionless for a long time, dying, he hoped, though he did remember to turn off the ignition so as not to waste gas. He sat until his eyes ran dry, and drained now, he watched a fat *grundsow*, roused from hibernation, slither out from under the pile. The creature looked at him with stars of burning in its eyes, then waddled off into the brush. And gradually, as the afternoon wore on and cold settled around him, he heard, like distant thunder, the rumble of his stubborn heart, and there was that rise again of mind and will and powerful awful rage.

The fool, he was filling again.

CHAPTER
26

As would any right-thinking woman, Louise waited until after the holidays to call the lawyer. One thing was clear: She could not go on forever minting ultimatums and printing up I-must-remember-to-hate signs. To buckram her resolve over New Year, she did repost the premises, but he-who-would-be abhorred accorded the signs no more than snorts of contemptuous skepticism. Trover remained unconvinced.

Though unwilling herself to leave (shouldn't the guilty party be the one to go?), she packed the "hers" piece of their matching Airway and let it stand in the hall as a memento mori, a reminder of their dying. She reshuffled the household to free the guest room for herself. She hoped he was satisfied.

Her guest room stay began with the same pain she'd experienced those first months in the country. Her life spiraled deeper, exile inside exile. And who would have guessed the tug of his flesh from two walls away, his scent stealing in? She grieved and slept little. Lovelessness could be medicated with dogs or cats or card games, but how did you go on turning in this black socket of self-restraint, not loving, with the one you loved just yards away in his sweaty bed, his lawless heart both drawing and stopping you. Keep it up, you would die, die like wiper blades frozen fast and pulling to go.

And then one day, after a week or so, the connection attenuated some; her nerve ends stopped burning. She began to sleep, albeit contortedly, twisted into weird aches around her perfectly good reasons. One night the air seemed to give up something with an audible sigh, and the hurtful distances shrank like skin around lost pounds. And this easing grieved her most of all. What if she could get used to life without him? Then she would have lost him for good.

She found her lawyer in the Yellow Pages. The name Nimson Ickus, she thought, carried a certain hybrid strength, a blend of tact and ferocity, whimsy and intimidation. She imagined him to be wily and nimble and eloquent, a rumpled churl, just the man to challenge the likes of this artful mate, bait him, beat him—this last a wish she could not mean yet, not when it had been the habit of her entire life to anguish over the courtroom fate of Trover Kleeve and his low-life clients.

When she called he told her to come right in. It was a gray, ugly day, snow forecast, but the long sad drive to Neisstown was relieved somewhat by the difficulties posed by a broken index finger on her right hand, which resided now in a huge padded splint shaped like a snub-nosed gun case. It jammed against the dash when she tried to turn the ignition, and she shifted gears only against the doctor's orders to keep it raised. Its throbbing distracted from the pounding of her heart.

Opening a door marked with only a taped-on calling card, she found herself in a small room before a desk from which presided neither receptionist nor secretary but a flinty-eyed ancient. His liverish face wobbled at the top of a column of colored rags, a canny conical nose aimed at the very heart of her sorry affairs.

"Is this a bad time?" she asked. She seemed to have arrived in the midst of a seating crisis. But the fact that she had nowhere to put herself seemed to faze this person not at all. "Well, should I just get started?" she asked, sniffing: The smell was eucalyptus oil and bacon.

He cleard *his* throat, which she took to be a sign of a sympathetic bent.

"Just to give you some background . . ." she said. "Uh, don't you need a legal pad? Shouldn't you be taking down my name and address and well, you know, the *evidence?*"

He waved her on.

"All right," she said. "Maybe you've had a few dealings with my husband. Maybe you already know what an insufferable know-it-all browbeater he can be. On the other hand, you might have some acquaintance with the other side of him, Mr. Nice Guy, defender of the poor and downtrodden. Wit, raconteur. Maybe he lent you money or bought you drinks all night. But well, all I can say to that is you don't have to live with the man."

"I wouldn't mind," he said. "Would he take the wife, too?"

"Beg pardon?"

"Just tweaking you," he said. "Been a bachelor all my life."

She gave a grudging chuckle. "Well, getting back, what I'm trying to say is you have no idea how selfish he can be. And perverse. And violent."

Crepy lids flickered.

"Well, maybe not—yes, 'violent' is exactly the word for it."

Ickus sat up, staring at her damaged hand, obediently elevated now. "The monster."

She took the part back, clutching it to her breast, lest it be used unjustly. "Oh, no! Trover'd never break my *bones*. This was an accident; happened Christmas Day, in fact. My daughter was about to mash the potatoes, and I saw her struggling with the mixer—it's the old-fashioned, freestanding kind you can still pick up in flea markets. I offered to help. I was trying to get the beaters in when somehow she turned it on and—"

Ickus winced. "Sure you're divorcing the right person?"

"It was an *accident*, sir, a minor one as such things go. I think a body has to allow for breakage—"

"Wait and see, that finger's going to be crooked. You'll get arthritis in it."

"Look, we were discussing my husband. It's more like *things* he beats on. Good things. Living things sometimes."

"Good God! Kids? Puppies?"

"More like plants," she said. "Houseplants. I can't keep greenery like normal women; it wouldn't be fair to them. Nothing's safe from that Hun, except maybe the ball cactus. He bought it for me on our honeymoon. It was only a couple inches in diameter then. I tell you, it's unholy the way he keeps tabs on that plant. 'Louise, doesn't that thing need water? Louise, the needles are bent.' It's enormous now and very, very hazardous, and hardly a week goes by that he doesn't start in about repotting. Well, Mr. Ickus, believe me, I have looked. There is no bigger pot to be had. Unless, of course, I'd fill the garage with topsoil and . . . is this more than you need to hear?"

"I'd call your local farm agent."

"Who?"

"He knows his plants. He'll tell you what to do with that cactus."

Panic clogged her esophagus. What would she do with this, her best story, if even her own lawyer ignored it? "Lum Motors." She pressed on in desperation. "What do you suggest I do about such people? He lets them run right over us."

Ickus leaned forward, flushed, ireful. "Lum, that son of a sea captain!

Few years back I bought this Jetta—top-of-the-line item. Cash sale. Hey, I didn't have the thing a month when—" Ickus sat back, giving up with a sigh. "Ha," he said, "can't blame your hubby for that. Every life has a Lum or two. Men with the repugnant charm of a carbuncle. Something you can't keep your hands off of. The gumboils, abscesses, scabs that obsess because they're ours. When the spirit needs to touch its open sores, it visits Lum. Lum never disappoints."

"I see you worked that one out pretty thoroughly."

"What else?" he said.

"Let me see. Well, he's a man of ridiculous, dangerous extremes. You just don't know the half of it."

"Hey, remember me—I don't know any of it. What kind of extremes?"

Her mind blanked. The only thing that came to her was—"Jarlsberg cheese," she said.

"Cheese is extreme?"

"When it's the only kind you've touched in six years."

"Grates on you, does it?"

"It's not funny," she said. "Besides, that wasn't a good example." She racked her brain. "OK, he's 'into' things. He's a one-man hobby conglomerate. There's woodcrafting, reloading, body building, clockmaking, running, climbing, rafting. Now it looks like mountaineering is next. And that's just scratching the surface. No sooner does something catch his eye than he runs out and equips himself to the teeth, and then just about the time he's got it all, off he hops to something else. Honestly, it's more than any reasonable woman can bear."

"Do you want for anything?"

"Yes, some cleanness of line, a touch of austerity."

But Ickus's head had begun to droop. Austerity, it seemed, wasn't especially rich in entertainment value.

She began to dig deep for significant particulars, showstopping facts she might hurl at the phlegmatic old face. He'd need a helmet she'd get so rough. "Helmets," she said. "He has a helmet for every occasion—motorcycle, bicycle, hockey, horse racing—and, I kid you not, a ski helmet. Just imagine your basic little bookish type, weekend intermediate, cruising along on a pair of boards as long as a bus and wearing a crash helmet. His daughter refuses to be seen on the slope with him. And speaking of skis, the man owns six pairs, imagine! Conditions change, he says. Why, you'd think he could just strap all six pairs to his back and use them like golf clubs." She forced the words out with the last of her wind and then drew in deeply.

Ickus came to with a jerk, hitched his lids to half-awake. "Hell, a man needs seven, eight pairs of socks. At least that."

"Skis," Louise squeaked. "I said skis."

"Well, the man's a piece of work all right."

"Hold on here," she said. "I want to be strictly fair. The only time we went skiing together somebody stole my ski poles. In their place I found a pair of tall, skinny, bent ones. I was afraid to go back out without my own poles, and so Trover took me back into the lodge for cocoa and yogurt. Sometime later I happened to spot a young man at the snack bar. The reason I noticed was that his shape reminded me of the poles left behind: He was very tall and lean and bow-legged. You know the type. What's more, he was clutching a pair of sturdy yellow poles just like mine, hugging them close as though afraid they'd get swiped. Without thinking, I pointed him out to Trover. The boy went off with his teeth in an apple, and Trover took off in the hottest pursuit you'll ever see over a pair of ski poles. I followed in shock. Well, he grabbed that tall, cocky kid, the small, cocky man. He spun the kid around and confronted him. 'Yours?' he said. 'Yes or no?' He demanded to examine the poles. The boy made for the men's room, Trover hanging on his coattail. They scuffled inside, and out came Trover with broken glasses and both ski poles."

"Most touching," said Ickus, "but can we get back to villainy? Tell me," he said, "this hotshot shopper, does he also stock up on"—he blew his nose— "let's just say, software?"

"He's been talking about getting a home computer, which I'm fighting tooth and nail, of course."

"Of course."

"And once he bought an electronic chess set named Boris. Oh, you mean other women? Look, Mr. Ickus, what do you want? He can't commit everything."

The old man dipped into an open jar of Vicks, then lined the inside of his nostrils. "Women get you a lot further in the courts than cheese and helmets."

"I thought we had no-fault in Pennsylvania."

Ickus perked and turned puzzled. "No-fault? Oh, no-fault." He paused, still sputtering with uncertainty. "Then how come you keep bringing up the poor bastard's faults?" he blurted.

Her turn to be stumped. "Because," she said. "Because I didn't want you to think I'm proceeding frivolously."

"Counseling," said Ickus, like a line come back to him. "You two twerps tried counseling?"

"Trover bare his soul to some beard behind a desk? Never. Anyway, it's his contention I just want to humiliate him in front of strangers."

"Any truth to that?"

"Some," she said. A lot, she thought. Anytime she'd ever suggested counseling, it was perfidiously, with an eye toward the ambush. She wanted nothing of analyst, healer, teacher, or impartial anything. What she wanted was a judge in her pocket. She'd rattle off the rap sheet, and the counselor would attend, tight-lipped, appalled, worst case he'd ever heard. What did she know from no-fault? No-fault was insult. What other contract had a clause whereby one party could escape just because he or she didn't feel like living up to the terms? Somebody had to renege, somebody had to be wrong, and that somebody was Trover.

"Besides, it's gone quite beyond that. I—I . . . how can any self-respecting woman keep taking it this way?"

"I know, I know." Ickus shook his head sadly. "Way it is these days, a husband has to be defended like a Ph.D. thesis. Especially the frisky ones."

"He's a big baby," she said.

"Hey, me, too!" Ickus said, stabbing his breast hard, pupils wide with the light he was casting on the matter. "This old fart is just a lot of husk over a tot about yea high." He raised a speckled hand above his desk. He shook his head. His eyes took on a desperate intensity. This was a point he had to make while there was still time. "Hey, I still look both ways. I hate it when there's nuts in the pudding. Every once in a while I experience this wild forward surge, as if my life, by George, were still out there somewhere, waiting. Damnedest thing . . ." he said.

"Mr. Ickus, I didn't even get one mother. Why should Trover have two?"

"Woman," he said, "I don't have a wife. What I got essentially is a sister—and I tell you, it wasn't always easy. Forty years ago she started going funny in the head. I took her in to keep her out of the bughouse. I hired people to look after her while I ran my practice. Many's the time I got calls at the office. Nettie fell down. Nettie wandered off. Whhhhew!" His gaze drifted, and he dragged it back. "Then here about ten years ago, she got up one morning and sneezed. Blood gushed out her nose and ears, and well, what do you think?"

Louise smelled a miracle. She drew closer.

"Honey, from that moment on her head was clear as winter. That sneeze blew the craziness to bits. She recovered just in time to be the companion of my old age. Hey, what's a wife, a sister? What's a mother? You make your relatives out of what's available. People can be anything, you know. People are good that way."

Louise was seized with the conflicting edification and resentment of somebody told something she already knew. Or should have. Didn't she open cans with screwdrivers and make electrical connections with bottle caps? Didn't she have a Christmas lamp? The light in her house, sudden light in the sister's mind. It was all quite remarkable. She was glad she came. "I smell bacon," she said.

He tugged at the rags around his throat. "Fried bacon and mustard," he said. "Best thing there is for sore throat. Nettie takes good care of me. Some women look after their menfolk."

"My husband would never wear bacon," she said, provoked now, defensive.

"Simmer down," he said. "Anymore you can't say anything you libbers don't get your Irish up."

"Aren't you supposed to be on my side?"

"Foursquare," he said rakishly. "And I would be if I was still serious about practicing law. Been retired now since 19—well, since Nettie got her marbles back. And even back then I wasn't idiot enough to screw around with domestic stuff. Junk cases, no winners."

"Then why do you still come into the office?"

"You're not very observant," he said. He tapped a horny fingernail on the top edge of a brass nameplate. "Late-life career change. Something closer to my circumstances, you might say."

"Shadyside Memorial Association," she read in a halting, incredulous voice.

"I'd lay odds you two half asses haven't taken care of this little matter yet."

Louise stared at him.

"Sure, you can always get accommodations when the time comes." He erected a finger. "But you'll pay more." He leaned close, puffed with inside information. Rummaging in a drawer, he produced a pamphlet. "Take this home and talk it over with hubby. Doubles start at four-eighty-nine-ninety-five."

"Doubles?"

"Your choice of side by side or vertical. I'll tell you right off—our vertical vaults are cheaper. But side by side has a cheerier ring to it, I always think."

She sat up straight. She was trying to get out from under, and this galoot wanted to seal her up with Trover for good.

"Ten percent cash discount. It's something to think about anyhow."

Clutching her brochure, she turned vaguely toward the door.

"Hey, look," he said, motioning her back. "Things really get rough . . ." Wetting his thumb, he flipped the pages of an old bar association directory. He quibbled down the lists. "Fat cat. Pompous ass. Shyster. Playboy. Idiot. Deceased. Ah, here we go. This chap's a hell-raiser; he'll give that rascal of yours a run for his money." Underlining a name, he tore out the page and handed it to her.

Banfer C. Kleeve, she read. Ickus looked so tickled with himself she didn't have the heart to say anything beyond "Thank you, my best to Nettie."

The phone was ringing when she got in. His voice carried the same taut bravado as the day he called to say he was in love with Cathy Koolbaugh, his ex-secretary. "I'm going for a walk," he said belligerently. "What, if anything, do you want from the bakery?"

"I have bread," she said. He knew, he knew! Uncanny how he always found the end of her rope and hung on.

"Sourdough, yes or no?"

"I can't tell you what to do anymore," she said.

"Good-bye," he said, but the click was not forthcoming.

"All right," she said, "I went to see a lawyer this morning, if that's what you're fishing for."

Pause. Then: "Hope you had a good time running around making a nuisance of yourself."

Louise held her tongue. In the context her silence was eloquent, precise, decisive.

"Hope he told you you're making a big mistake. If he didn't, he was remiss."

"On the contrary, he thinks my decision shows character."

"Who said that? Don Briggs? Chip McLaird?"

She held her peace.

"It *was* McLaird, wasn't it? Yes or no? Hope he told you right off what I did to him in *Bruce* versus *Pudliner*. The man's a lightweight, Louise. I think you should know that."

"Thank you," she said.

"So it is McLaird?"

"I didn't say that."

"Dammit, Louise. You always do this. I cannot have you calling my office day and night, getting my juices flowing, disrupting my schedule."

She held the receiver away as if it were crazy. "You called *me,*" she told him.

"And you always have to have the last word," he said.

Louise set the receiver back, staring into the silence he was hiding in. Instead of closing him off, it opened for her into his world, opened with the sudden rich intimacy of a View-Master scene. For several moments she couldn't find him there. Then, *voilà*, he enters fretful, face pinched and red. He's thinking fast, scrambling for rebuttal. Now he braces his arms against the edges of Drummond's fine old desk. He wheels out of her vision and comes spinning back. He reaches for the phone. Louise hopes he isn't planning to call Chip McLaird, whoever he is. Her phone rings once and stops. He rocks the receiver back in its cradle; the fingers of his left hand run the rim of his fedora like a flute. Now he slaps a stack of papers, crumples the top sheet, flips it into the gorilla's lap, shakes the sleigh bells, and bounds off beyond her power to invent him.

CHAPTER

"Debbie," he called, "can I see you a minute?"

No answer.

He called again.

"Hold your horses," she said.

He stood and spun his chair. He paced. He made mutterings and thumps and farty mouth sounds to project his condition, acute distress on top of broad dismay! "Hey," he heard her say, "he's bumming out in there. Call you back, Darlene." Moments later she sauntered in and took a seat, buffing lilac nails on her shirtsleeve.

Trover steadied his chair and sat. Removing his glasses, he regarded the girl closely. "Question number one," he said.

"Fire away," she replied.

"What do you think of a woman who'd dump a guy just because he bought her a new car?"

She shrugged. "He playing around?"

"No way. He's a nice person and a darn good provider."

"What case is this? *Wertz* versus *Wertz?* That new guy, geek type, wears his pants around his ears?"

Trover popped his glasses back on, as if to expand *her* vision. He stared at a smudge of ink on her lower lip while his thoughts wandered off.

"And question number two?" She prompted.

He whisked at the air. He wanted her to stop bothering him.

She was not a hard person to dismiss. He watched her go, a tiny girl in heels just high enough to give her a pretty, reedy sway. He knew that she thought *him* little and *pestiferous*. Later, after he'd taken off for the day, she'd phone that Darlene person back and use pithy terms to disparage him: geek, peabrain, dipstick, drip. It used to be he didn't care what anybody said. Now he found himself thinking how could he stop her.

He juggled several phone calls and two appointments. Apparently nobody's life was the one the teachers had promised. They came to him bankrupt, brokenhearted, bored. They demanded an explanation. They wanted him to make things stop. Or go. Mrs. Reeser was plain beside herself, and how could he blame her? Yesterday not even the Chicago-bound Boeing she'd been expecting but a small craft, a single-engine Cessna, had flattened the house across the yard. She'd been standing at her kitchen window, watching a neighbor set the table for one. The woman, her best friend, had vanished as she watched. "They're picking us off one at a time," she told him. And of all days to call, when Trover's own foundations were trembling beneath him.

"Let me sleep on this one," he said. "Call me tomorrow."

Mildred Gaugler stopped in then to pick up her peacock teapot. There'd been no need to file suit. Her sister, Doris, had surrendered it with philosophical goodwill the first time he asked. Inspecting it all but microscopically, Mildred discovered a lid chip that hadn't been there before. Her eyes lit up. *"Now* can we sue?" she asked.

In the wake of high-minded holiday raids, bookstore owners came to him more deflated than irate, long-suffering souls who did not hesitate to show how deeply their faith was shaken. Thoughtless clods had wrecked their Christmas. Was nothing sacred? What could be done? When Trover's own woes were all he could juggle right now. He poked his head outside the door. "Deb," he said, "go the hell home." Let her libel him on her own time.

He plugged the phones, took his pulse, his blood pressure. He filled his pockets with office chocolates and considered his options: Should he converse himself or go berserk? Ribbet, ribbet. He locked the door and left.

He headed out to Life Cycles. "What do you have assembled and ready to go?" he inquired of the fresh-faced clerk.

"Everything you see in the racks." Behind the boy, beyond the plate-glass window, the snow was just beginning.

Trover took the fancy foreign job the clerk offered and stepped over the bar. He bounced from the knees. "Throw on a pannier," he said. To those purchases he added an electronic odometer and a tiny rearview mirror on a long stem that attached to the rim of his glasses. When everything was bagged and paid for, he said, "Put the small items in the pouch and throw the bike in the back of the van."

Over three blocks and up two. He parked in a loading zone and walked to the bakery. "Noo, noo, noo!" cried the cheeky matron in response to his polite request for sourdough. Then, when he asked for doughnuts, her scowl deepened. "Wednesday is *cruller* day!" she snarled, crossing her arms high: The woman would defend this declaration to the death.

He settled for six French crullers. "Make that twelve," he amended. Once, when he was a kid visiting a friend, the boy's father came home with a dozen potato buns. His friend took one out of the box and sank his huge front teeth into the tender dough. With his sugary mouth stuffed, he said, "I'd offer you one, but there's only enough for the family." Three people, four apiece. Trover had never gotten over that. "Make that a dozen and a half," he said with a ferocity equal to the cruller lady's own.

Then on to a downtown pub buzzing with blue collar camaraderie and Superbowl talk. A grizzled lush in a stained overcoat was making the rounds with a chewed-up newspaper. When he came to Trover, he spread the local section across the bar. Trover looked down at a full-page feature story: CITY KICKS OFF CLEANUP CAMPAIGN. A photo showed an empty Tiger Rose bottle in the foreground. "See that jug?" the bum said. He grinned and thumped his breast affectionately. "Mine!" he boasted. Trover bought him a drink and left.

He stopped at a seedy lounge on the outskirts of town. He nursed his lambrusco. The wine was powerless now to reverse his sense of urgency. A secure domestic life inspired in him the same confidence as his prepaid slot in the parking garage. Now if he didn't hurry, his place would be taken. He pictured Chip McLaird trying his chair, paring his cheese, sugaring his Mini-Wheats, shaping to Louise's spine as he slept.

Often anymore, when he tried to summon her, the image shimmied, and superimposed upon Louise's sweet curvilinear vagueness would be the flatter, more forbidding planes of Maddy's face. As if his mind simply forgot where to draw the lines. Or had she, living with him, been rubbed, pumiced to this keener definition? Was she wearing through to some steely other underneath? Lately she moved into her day more deliberately, her instincts quicker, her arms not quite so likely to wander off the job onto somebody's person; skin whiter, smile tighter. Women took middle age the way middle-aged men took mountains. The day was at hand when she would take one look at that nineteen-year layering of chaos, and order would form like a decision against him. The day she had enough, it would be like that: She would reach deep into her own funds, her useful skills knowing no bounds. She would leave him with a clean house and a goodly supply of soap on a rope, toilet paper on all the spindles. She would leave in glee, the person she thought he always wanted her to be—neat and crisp and reliable. She would think that, and she would be wrong. Because that was only the initial phase of it. True, he wanted Louise to be more like his mother, but that was only so that she could then evolve into everything he'd always wanted his mother to be, which was something more senseless and capacious and tender, something very like Louise Pegeen Kleeve.

Well, there you have it, he told himself. Jewel-colored light filtered through the stained glass transom over the tavern door. Truth in booze, the first whiff of wisdom. Pitiless insight where before, he'd had only the steady blaze of whatever beast he was persisting in itself.

The van still smelled of vinyl rolls and part bins. Wide and high, it didn't have the tight interior division of a family car so he had to wear the whole hollow thing himself, and he felt lost in it. The snow was starting to stick; he hunched forward, squinting into the distance. He imagined himself lugging uphill in this chunky bus, those known curves of the Knoll bearing him effortlessly on, the fantail of soft pines ushering his vision onto familiar ground. But, wait! For the first time ever his house is locked. When he knocks, the nun opens the door but a crack. She's done up now in full dress black, choir harmonies wisping behind her. "Families may visit Sundays one to three," she tells him. The Church has converted his home, within which his wife and kids are cloistered off from his misdemeanors.

One night he stayed up late, hoping to take on Boris, the chess great, in privacy. Suddenly Frank was kneeling on the floor beside him, one hand on the chessboard, the other on his knee. Her face was tipped toward his with an expression of such fearful expectancy he saw no human choice but to kiss her. But the knowledge of who she was punished his tongue later; it was a strange aftertaste, a dry acridity, like ashes or catacombs, and he had to wash it off with a drink. Still, he'd not been entirely unstirred by the press of a lifetime abstinence on his person. And Louise was jealous.

If it disturbed Louise, he felt compelled to dish it out. If she slept, he wanted to wake her. If she slipped from him, he had to evoke her. Let lightning split a tree, he had to blame her. Louise indignant, appalled, pissed. Louise come gunning for him. Fireworks were required of her. They flashed back the spark of his own personality, blips on the blank screen. They marked his place in time, were evidence of crime, mine, mine. Ah, like the shine of the drunk's wine bottle in a back alley.

Omitting most of his accustomed way stations, he drove straight out the narrow pike that bisected all the tiny towns and threaded the isolated stretches connecting them. At Womelsdorf he pulled off the road and went into the hotel. He ordered a quick one on the rocks for the heat he expected to need. Guffy Derr, the plumpish keep, sat on his stool, watching the six o'clock news. A prison riot, major earthquake, world hunger, national shame, but once again, Neisstown's big story, the newscaster insisted, was a center city house fire.

At the commercial break Trover said, "Hey, Guff, you don't mind if I leave my van in your lot overnight?"

"Bat-tree troubles?" Derr wanted to know. "You need a jump?"

Trover shook his head.

Mrs. Derr appeared in the kitchen doorway, scraping dough from her elbows. "Ay, Kleeve," she said, "you missed the last bus. It left at five thirty-five—in 1959." The couple exchanged glances that set them off voluminously.

Watching them laugh, Trover imagined the snap of transit lines, his house cut off, lost in the glaucous dark of God's country. He hadn't meant to take them so far out. Had he? But he kept the cupboards stocked and lavished transportation on them. Why couldn't Louise admit the wisdom of those few spare vehicles, just barely enough to keep four lives in continuous circulation?

"Bertie," said Derr, "fix him some crumb cake."

Trover held up his hand. "Thanks," he said. "Save me some." And he went out.

He rolled the new bike out of the van. He put the crullers in the pannier. In his coat pocket he discovered gloves and a wool scarf that had probably been balled up there for years. He turned his collar up, and not thirty yards out the wind swiped his fedora away. He managed to grab it back, holding it tight against the handlebars. He could barely see for the tumultuous air; he felt faintly dizzy. Only five miles to home.

Off to his right sprawled acres of fruit trees; prunings lay between the rows like the tangled gleanings from Louise's hairbrush. Somewhere in the blur beyond were the mountains, lumbering north as he pumped west. Someday he would follow them to Maine. Tonight his house seemed as distant and steep and difficult as Katahden, and that's how he wanted it, wanted her to know he'd gone some, in hardship, to get there.

Later tonight the fields would fill with the ribboning moans of snowmobiles. A sleigh would suit her better. He'd start checking the classifieds for an old-time sleigh, with the fancy scroll sides. Snowy nights he'd take his wife out the old road to Persia, over the double-covered bridge, across the lower tier of gamelands while snowmobiles ran pretty rings around them and led them down hidden roads and secret trails through the woods.

It was a rare occasion that Trover flirted with a romantic plot. Once when they lived in Neisstown, he let Louise talk him into going to the park after dusk to sit by the lake. It was a mystery to her why others weren't about, why children or fornicators weren't flocking there like geese.

They sat first-date stiff on a cement bench at the crest of a gradual rise from the water's edge. It was a stifling night, sluggish lapping, splash of sunfish and frogs; distant traffic skipped broken tones across the water. On the other side, fireflies bright as minor stars. The darkness, he thought at first, was playing tricks, clotting, subdividing, dark clumping like tumbleweed. It was a moonless night, and when their eyes adjusted, it was clear that they were looking out over a small but lively college of water rats.

Even then she would not give it up. "So," she said. "They're not bothering anybody." They jiggled a pinch closer and didn't speak or, but for an occasional prolonged shudder, move after that. They kept their eyes hard in front of them. At last Louise let out a stagy sigh and allowed how the night air was making her drowsy. Then and only then would she permit them to abandon the hard seat, the water, and that malefic consistory of creatures.

She could never be wrong, never suspend a course of action just because it proved unworkable or exhausting or erroneously undertaken. She couldn't discard a foul-tasting cheese until it lay in the refrigerator long enough to produce a repugnance quite apart from its own bad character. It had to beg to be thrown away. The thought gave him heart.

His toes numbed; pedaling grew onerous. A barnyard dog took chase but unhungrily, as if he were just doing his job and it bored him. He followed a wide turn that wrapped like a protective arm around a gray clutch of farm buildings. The dog dropped back now, and when Trover hit the straightaway, the northern flank of the Pinnacle slammed into view, a smattering of night skiers dancing down the eerily lit trail for beginners. One of his favorite terror fantasies involved sneaking up there after the lifts shut down for the night. He'd carry his skis to the top and come down Sky Dive in the dark, feeling his way, nothing but the wind and the scrape of his risking skis.

Now settled dark hemmed him in again. All along the countryside dairy cows shivered in their stanchions, their lowing the lullaby of country nights. Wind swept across the open land beyond Job's Station, swaying him leeward. Wind against him. He hoped that was not a bad sign. He had never loved any woman but her—a statement that was truest in times of trouble. How many times had he said it the day he found out about Julio? Louise didn't know it, but he'd bought a gun around that time, and once he'd actually skulked in the bushes near Julio's house, fondling the cold weight in his jacket pocket and crying hard, too heartsick to be homicidal.

He passed through tiny villages where families named Dutt and Schmeck and Hoffmaster were unbelting from ponderous dinners, snapping off lights as they moved through rooms. The smell of woodsmoke tugged him gently on. No longer did his tires carve through to contrast. When he glanced back, his track was like a white rope tying him to where he'd been.

He had to concentrate now to keep from skidding; in the quiet his breath raked harsh and disembodied, a quiet roar. By now his pulse rate was chasing the upper ranges. He should have worn his wrist monitor. Why did it offend her the way he checked his functions? Did she want him to miss the skip, the hiss, the creeping diastolic? Did she want him to be taken by surprise (his father humming to himself, his arm in a sleeve of morning light, reaching for a clean shirt)?

The day he bought his blood pressure equipment, he came home hoping to practice on the family. "Hey!" Mighty protested. "Get away. That's private." Michael wasn't home. He decided to try it on Louise. He never did again. That row of militating beats threatened to confuse his own heart, trick it into arhythmia, the way one drummer can be thrown off by some unsynchronized other banging nearby. Worse, he heard the life thump into her veins, he heard it cut off. He'd ripped the stethoscope from his ears, the light of day suddenly too bright for his eyes.

The air seemed colder, drier now. His tires made an aggressive tacky sound as he pedaled into Kemp. In the window of his filling station George Groff was turning his sign CLOSED side out. Trover waved stiffly, turned at the hotel, and headed out the home stretch.

It was very dark as far as the cloverleaf, where overpass lights swept a bright path before him. As he rounded the first curve beyond that, the Knoll loomed into view, the three-tiered house burning like a birthday cake somewhere in the heart of the storm. Left now around the base of the hill. He wobbled up the short rise past the dam, past the Hinkeldrek woman's house; he checked his mailbox and troubled on.

Under normal conditions he could make it all the way, no sweat. He'd pump, pump, pump, taking the entire tilt of the hill without stopping once. But the lower roadway was slick and rutted now and he was able to make it only as far as the wreck of the henhouse. His legs gave up; the tires shimmied to a halt. Climbing down, he began to walk the bike.

On the upper side of the cement bridge he stopped to rest. Sounds drifted in from far away. He inclined his head, puzzled. He listened this way, that, trying to wipe the blindness from his eyes. What *was* that? How odd to hear anything on a snowy night but the sound of snow deepening. The churning firmament confused him now, and he couldn't quite pinpoint the source of the sounds. Snowmobiles? Not hardly. This was a plodding, stolid, hardworking hum. A farm machine. But who would be working land this time of year?

He pressed on to higher ground. At the half apogee of the first curve he stopped and surveyed the bleary landscape. His own fields stretched like the apathetic dead, white and silent. But behind him and off to his left, the area jutting above the tree line was streaked with wands of red and yellow light. He measured the angle with his arm. That knob would be Tumbling Run. What the devil were they doing up there? He shrugged. What the hell business was it of his?

He made his steps high and lively now to encourage himself. The hum followed him the rest of the way around the turn. Up and up he went, the questions forgotten as the going got harder. And still higher, breathless, bone-tired, and now back on the bike, coasting cautiously downhill through the gate and between the larches and under the mulberry boughs, past the white-tipped shrubs around the ghostly gazebo.

He came to a halt just yards from his front porch. He stood straddling the bike a long time as snow continued to powder his crown and spackle the creases of his sleeve, cake under his collar, hat in his hand still tipped as if for alms. He listened and listened, but the sound of snow muffled everything now except the sound of his heart.

CHAPTER

28

The trouble was Louise did not see the trouble at first: not see the rippled rug, not notice the broccoli wogs in the sink, not perceive at all how non-alignment rankled the common man (magazine corners jabbing this way and that). But the messes always caught up with her. How they'd gather in the unconscious, hunkering away until the wee hours, and then pock-a-bam! They'd go off like cluster bombs. She would wake with the full calamity of it flashing at her, every neglected nook and corner exposed, her flaws almost fatal at this hour as the husband slept innocently beside her, the house he paid for hardly possible anymore. Nearly crushed under the wide load of this secret shame, she would writhe and whimper and then finally struggle out of bed, start sorting through the quiet rooms, desperately, as if her soul were in danger.

Now today, having returned from the lawyer's office, she stood in the doorway similarly stricken, stunned by disarray. Surely it was the same house she'd left earlier. Surely nothing had changed but her perspective; the glance she'd honed on Trover's flaws, still deadly, zeroed in on her own, even more visible delinquencies. The range hood gray with gunk and dust, cobwebs knitting her corners closed, a half-eaten pretzel on the blender lid. Shoving the pretzel in her mouth, she went after the worst of it.

She straightened and scraped and unclogged her corners. She scoured the bathroom tiles with a toothbrush. She released the soap-sensible pungencies of substances long dormant under the sink. The snap of pine and citron and lemon-oil cream. Then the multi-layered fragrance of scrubbed wood. At fifteen she had helped houseclean the chapel for the feast of Christ the King. While her friends lathered kneelers and aisles, she'd rubbed tung oil into the rosewood pews. The mingled scent of soap and resin cut through her longing for home, uplifted her.

She moved quickly now, sniffing suspiciously into cupboard and crisper drawer, jabbing her monstrous padded finger behind bookcases, radiators, and other places she'd never dream of touching with the living flesh. Even mutilation had its uses.

She made a pot roast and then, softened by sadness, with Gideon's help, baked a pie for dessert. Afterward, she put everything away, including the butter, and Mighty said, not without fondness, "Well, well, little Suzy Homemaker." Then brother and sister went upstairs to do schoolwork.

Louise had already apprised Frank of the day's developments. In recent days the nun had begun more and more to retreat into herself or, worse, into Trover's library, his college of self-help from his art-of-living phase. How to say yes. How to say no. What to say next. How to say it devastatingly. Frank, Louise saw, was plumbing these secular sources with the same ardor she'd once sought out the wisdom of saints and prophets. Living between systems was awkward at best, and she often seemed confused as to whose beatitudes were applicable. Now, in an effort to console Louise, she set to pointing out her "Penalty Zones," those obsolete, self-defeating attitudes wittily listed in the best-selling book of the same name. "So," she said, her hand between the pages, "it shouldn't take you more than a day or two to get over your Trover. Just retool"—she tapped Louise's brow—"your thinking. You chose to love him. You can choose not to."

"I don't know," said Louise. She looked at the author's photo on the book jacket. Dr. Bob Hoxie was a balding man with a brittle grin and a liberated V of chest hair. "I were you, I'd trust Christ over this guy."

Looking perplexed, put-down, Frank went upstairs with a gothic novel.

And that left Gideon. Gideon, who seemed to know everything without being told, who made in-house business his minute-by-minute concern, Gideon kept patting her head. "Hang in there, kid," he said. "It's a bummer."

"Thanks," she said, slipping into the Room. She sifted through odd lots, separating screws and nails, gaskets and washers, cotter pins and wing nuts. In time she ran out of shoeboxes. Well, fine, she'd codify the screwdrivers. Toes tensed, stomach in knots, she couldn't decide: Should she divide them by function, Phillips first, or according to the handle, reds through blacks through blues? Should she hang them in descending order, large to small, or work the reverse? And the stubby? What of it?

Better take a break to think this over. She collapsed on the sofa. She smoked two cigarettes without encountering a clue to the definitive way with screwdrivers. She lit another and lay back, covering her legs with the afghan. "Gideon, did somebody turn off the furnace?" she called.

"You bats? It's like an oven in here."

What was wrong with him? Couldn't he feel the warmth leaving the house, slow degree by slow degree? It was snowing out and blowing, and even the *idea* of wind was stealing heat from her home. Wind and fatigue were making her afraid. But she had pushed, and something had given, and once she started a project, wasn't it both her strength and stupidity to see it through?

Frank had graciously marked key sections in Trover's guidebooks. Divorce set forth as attractively as some California travel club's best getaway vacation. Zestful, aggressive advice about "hurdles" and "stumbling blocks" and "new horizons." About "finding oneself." As if the self that loved and suffered its fools and served were somehow lost, pinned in the wreck of misguided alliance.

What did the books know that she didn't? And why didn't they know how her hipbone wept, how her nine good fingers grieved, hurting worse than the broken one? That Trover was about to be a ghost, the amputated part that kept prickling and niggling her. Bet on it, Doctor.

And why couldn't they see how age had reshaped their faces, years of unconscious mimicry making them each other? It wasn't sex that made them one but the rubbing, the tumbler of days, the sly seizing of limbs as they slept. No, she had to be prepared to go off lopsided. Listen, Doctor, I leave him now, I leave myself, as he made me, as I made myself to oblige and defy him. Don't make light of it, Dr. Bob. This is serious as I get without dying.

She sat up, smoking hard. Where was he anyhow? How could she leave him if he never came home again? Well, wouldn't that be just like him. Shyster, he'd outslick her to the end. He'd disappear as he always did when she was closing in. He'd leave town forever, and she'd end up divorcing a chimera, cursing air. The slippery creep. She kicked off the afghan. She was warm, warmer, burning up.

Now Gideon bopped past. He spun around on the balls of his feet, remembering something. "Mind if I borrow the blowtorch?"

Louise shook her head absently.

"Thanks," he said. "Hey, why don't you go in and watch the rest of *Bloopers*? Get your mind off things."

She gave him a slow, unfocused look. "*Bloopers?*"

"Yeah, you get to see all their flub-ups. TV and movie outtakes. Much better and funnier than when they get it right."

"I see," she said. "A celebration of blunders."

"Great mistakes." Gideon plunked down his Coke can, and Louise automatically tapped her ash into it. Then something thumped on the wooden porch. They exchanged baffled glances, and at that moment the door flew open and *he* was standing there.

"Lord!" she said, for at first she did not recognize him. He could have been something summoned from the icy sleep of a hundred years. He stood pigeon-toed with his arms bowed out. He lurched forward, lifting each leg as if it were triple-plated. His face, cascading crystal, was dazzling and lavish under the chandelier.

Gideon dropped next to Louise, and they stared in wonderment as Trover, beginning to thaw, turned translucent, the melt beading off his lashes masquerading as tears.

Gideon squinted close. "You ride out in a convertible? Roof of the Vanagon fall off?"

"B-b-biked home," Trover said between working teeth.

"What bike? Your ten speed is on the porch."

"Don't grill," Louise said. "I'm in no mood for non sequiturs."

"You want tea?" Gideon asked. "I'll put the water on."

A stiff arm came up to stay the boy. "Cocoa?" said Trover. "With a dab of marshmallow cream?"

"All we got on hand is Ovaltine," Gideon said.

Trover nodded but creakily, as if his neck, like him, had determined to flex only so far. Taking several sidewise skips, Gideon shot off toward the kitchen.

It was monkey business all right, bike out of the night and icicles. And Trover waiting for her to buy it. She eyed him charily at first and then not at all.

He said, "Could I trouble you for a spoonful of your peanut butter?"

Her peanut butter indeed. She squirmed and muttered something that refused to be human speech. In the dead calm that followed she stole a peek through her fingers. His eyes on her were red, raw, bovine. He looked wretched and marginally thriving. *Remember to hate this man.* She jerked away; death to witness this.

"Any broken saltines you don't want?"

The man was shameless. Why didn't he ask for bread and water, permission to scavenge the trash? Why didn't he sit down instead of standing there, emitting the subversive rays of cold and hunger and melancholy?

She stared down at his soaked cordovans, deeming the view safer than most. Right toe angling left, those inevitable double furrows. Once, when Trover was lost in the mountains with his father, two of his toes took frostbite. He told her that story shortly after they were married. She slept the night backward, his toes in her hand, and all night long she who was yet childless was sorrowful mother to the child he had been. "Wouldn't hurt to take off your shoes," she said, from the helpless depths of better times.

"If that's what you want, will do," he said. *Say but the word, and I'll toss each toe in the fireplace.* Slowly, painstakingly, he departed each shoe. He sank into the cushion next to her and proceeded to remove his socks. Louise watched the way Mighty must have watched Michael dismantle her crib, watched in fascinated horror, caught now in the implacable machine that was nothing more or less than her plus him.

Though patches of painful pink marbled his feet, he made no move to rub or cover them, his face still damp—indecent man!

Knowing he was in no position to rant against smokers, Louise lit up. Facing away, she stared through the next room at the black windows beyond which snow unseen was falling, falling, filling in. She imagined the tumultuous funnel under the arc lights, the serene reaches beyond, the arms of the giant spruce dipping lower and lower. Her own arms ached. Bagel, sensing her burden of emptiness, sprang into her lap to replace it. She hugged the dog as the unregenerate woman in her longed to embrace the man, melting felon, adored poseur at her side. She hugged the dog and thought of snow.

Lackawanna snow, more earnest and lasting than these eastern teasers. Snow dolloping the little pink house. Snow ice cream with sugar and fake vanilla. The heavier Geggo's drapes, the louder the snow always sounded. By now her mother was old and cold, and snow where Geggo lay, and snow deeper yet on her dad, and a down quilt Geggo spread over her, at thirteen, in the chill of her first period. Ready or not, peace was stealing in with Bagel's heat, peace and sleepiness.

Bagel, oversqueezed, squealed and lumped out of her lap, turning then to look up with that cocked doggy consternation. Louise clung to the sofa arm for support. The TV audience was in stitches over those great American mistakes. Was Trover still coming on? It was hard to tell; he was skilled at bearing down on you without seeming to budge.

"Bibs," he said, "Bibs, Bibs, Bibs . . ." He snapped up the matchbook and, with an expert one-handed flick and a flourish, chivalrously lit her.

She smoked and spoke not a word, her splinted finger beginning to droop. Trover gave her elbow a shove upward.

"Louise," he said firmly, "I feel you should hear me out." That reminded her of other times, she deep in her dawdle, and suddenly he'd be calling her, urgently, burningly, and down she'd come, from upstairs, or down from her art, only to find some tap-dancing ant on TV. Or that lapping cat. Or worse, whatever once-in-a-lifetime wonder gone. It's going to be something dumb, she thought now, but not unhopefully.

In accents most artfully wrought, he detailed his recent findings: insights he'd gleaned from the chilly night, the big hollow van, the bakery. She listened aghast to the newspaper parable. Trover was the drunk, it seemed, she his wine jug shining in the alley.

"What are you talking about?" she said. Certainly he meant well, trying to talk Louisespeak, third-person ironic, allegorical mode, but really, she had no choice but point out that he had likened her to litter. "Litter!" she repeated gravely.

He patted her thigh. "It's nothing to be ashamed of, Bibs."

How serious he looked. How proud to be a romantic type with a baroque approach to things. She had seen that look before, half swain, half desperado. He was trying to lure her into his logic; then there'd be a sudden twist, a serpentine turn, and the man would slip out through a loophole. She eyed him narrowly. "And?" she said.

His hand had remained on her knee, transferring heat to her femur. She stared at his hand, her body tense with the effort of holding out, with the certainty of lost ground if she succumbed. "And?" she asked again.

He squeezed her knee.

In shock she watched her own bandaged hand light down on his for one split second before flapping off to the less treacherous ledge of her own shoulder. "AND?" she demanded.

"What do you mean, 'and'?" he said pleasantly.

"Well, what's to be done then?"

"About what?"

Delicately speculative, she turned to survey him. "If it's true you've had this great revelation and you admit to mixing me up with wine bottles, well, then, how might you be correcting that in the future?"

His face erased. He stared back, stumped. Fear of rehabilitation had set in. His eyes sped away, but now, after the long day, Louise hadn't the strength to chase him.

He had cracked her nonetheless, and knew it. So stuffed full was the Coke can that when she dropped in her stub, the hiss of extinction didn't come and the rancid smoke made Trover grab his throat. And now that their thighs were practically flush, was it her imagination, or had he actually bumped his body an inch or two away?

"Hey." It was Gideon with Ovaltine for two. "Hey, I checked out the new two-wheeler. Pretty awesome."

"It's just an inexpensive little touring job."

"Like heck. Fifteen-speed. Campy derailleur, alloy spokes—"

"Where's the Vanagon?" Louise said.

"Typical diesel engine. Unreliable as hell in cold."

"*Where?*" Gideon prompted. "She asked where."

Louise waved the boy back. "Drop it, Gideon." She was not interested in any complicated odysseys involving cars and bicycles and vans.

But Gideon had swung a leg around the coffee table, establishing himself square where Trover was trying to situate his cup. "You gotta start making sense, Mr. Kleeve. Straight answers to straight questions." Trover raised a brow. "And all that merchandise you keep trucking in, like hey, you're crowding Mrs. Kleeve out. You should do the manly thing and cut down on the shopping."

"I'll *buy* that," Trover sassed. He seemed to relish the rebuke as Michael used to enjoy the displeasure of his teachers.

But Gideon continued to glower like some lower-court magistrate. "And look, Louise," he said, paddling down the table. "Hey, you gotta get your act together, too. Try to keep your mind on what you're doing. Shut the dishwasher door for starters." He shook his head, eyeing her injury. "That finger's a disgrace. Looks like you used it to clean the oven." Then he reached out to tug at a plastic stem depending from her sweater sleeve. "When you tear off the price tags, why can't you just get a scissor and finish the job? Easiest thing in the world."

Louise forced a miserly smile. Nobody wanted to get mad anymore. In this tiny fiefdom of peace they all were model citizens, battle-shy, wry at worst, compliant. In strained amiability they sat stretching fishy grins. "Hey, wait a minute," Louise said at last, for it had just sunk in. "What's the blowtorch for?"

"Oh, that," said Gideon. "I wanted to P-Tex my skis."

"I didn't know you had skis," Trover said.

"Those old Dynastars of yours. You haven't worn them for years, say not?"

Trover rolled his eyes to heaven. "Take them," he said.

"Hold it, Gideon," Louise said cleanly. Here's where ambivalence ended. "You are not using the blowtorch in *my* house!"

"Then can I borrow your iron?"

"Go, go, go," she said, rowing him away.

Gideon eyed the deescalating couple. "Oh," he said, "you two want a little private time?"

Up popped Trover. "No!" he said. "We're all talked out."

"We are?"

"Where do you keep the peanut butter?" Trover asked.

"Three guesses," she said.

"In the kitchen, right?"

He left the room more nimbly than he'd entered it. Bagel, sniffing the word "kitchen," followed him out. (That damn dog loved Trover best anyhow.) Louise heard him now in the dining room. The table was always spread with the hurried deposits of cluttered days: schoolbooks; junk mail; a month of hats and rubber bands. Trover's purchases waited there for room assignment. Bag rattle, the crackle of stiff paper. A pause. Oh, damn. Why couldn't she learn to hide things? She knew what he'd happened upon.

"Shadyside Memorials!" he boomed. "This is your scourge of the courts? Nimson Ickus?" Then he was back in front of her, waving the flyer high above his ears. "You went to see *Digger* Ickus?"

What could she say?

He snickered and snorted and roared in disbelief. Then he sobered up abruptly. "It's my earnest hope that you didn't give the guy a down payment."

"On a divorce?"

"Louise, Ickus doesn't *do* divorce. On any, uh, *properties.*"

Spite lived too close to her tongue. "Don't worry," she said, "they'll both get used."

"You want one, Louise, fine. I've never denied you beans. Just don't bother shopping for me." But for a split second, instead of livid, he looked waylaid, somebody taken at noon by a black apparition. "Admit it, Louise," he said then, thinly, "sometimes you act like a nitwit." Bagel, bored, started upstairs to bed.

"Prove it," she said, with a confidence born of that slight jog in his aplomb. The shadow of death had taken the gloss off his act. "You're always calling me things. You never have supporting evidence. Prove it!" she repeated.

"OK," he said. "OK." As if life itself had driven him to measures he'd otherwise consider sadistic, unthinkable. "How about the time you rigged the deck in your favor and gave *me* a double run in hearts?"

"So, I learned something about the reciprocity of cheating."

"The time you left your purse in the Acme parking lot all night?"

"I got it back. I always do."

"Hear that, Gideon? My wife lives in the safekeeping of angels."

And Gideon was champing at the bit. "Louise, don't forget when you were vacuuming with your shoes untied and that power thing gobbled up your laces and the motor burned out."

"Gideon, go home."

"But you said, 'prove it' " Gideon reminded her. "Nobody but a nitwit would say that to a lawyer."

"And where may I ask is the Vanagon? Did it die on the highway, poor thing? Is Lum in charge of funeral arrangements?"

"You're a nag, Louise."

"No way am I a nag."

"Well, then you're plain nasty."

"That's right," she said. "At least call it what it is."

"See, Gideon, see why I never discuss things with her. I mean, you come home, walk in and say, 'Hello, Louise,' and right away she starts yelling and screaming."

"She's not screaming," said Gideon. "You are."

"I knew I shouldn't have come home tonight."

"Who the hell invited you, fool?"

"Simple solution," he said, snapping a hideous grin at her. "I'll leave."

"Good thinking!"

He took the stairs with a hammering hauteur that rivaled Michael's years ago when they sent him up to bathe. The ceiling shook as slamming, stomping, he plundered closets and drawers. "He's a very noisy man," she confided to Gideon.

And then Trover was downstairs, crackling past them in a nylon parka, dragging a bedroll. Head high, he strode into the Room, where he ravened bangingly through the entanglements for a while before slipping out the rear door.

Gideon and Louise hadn't moved from the spot. They exchanged glances; they shook their heads. Then ka-lunk! he was coming in the front, marching magisterially by. With an air of grateful riddance, he dumped the bag of crullers on the rug. Then the exclamatory slam of doorboards again, and Gideon looked at Louise and threw up his hands. "I tried," he said.

"Yes, you did," she agreed, shivering in the wake of the wintry blast Trover's several leavings had let in. The slap of cold had an immediate tonic effect. She felt refreshed at first and then stupidly hopeful and then laced through with that lunatic exuberance she'd experienced the first few moments after she'd broken the hold of the car wash. A moment's rush, the racketing madness and then—then only the chill of sanity, the icy circle she stood in. Panicked, she ran for the sweeper.

For some time then she raked back and forth across the carpet, her stroke too maniacal to have much to do with cleaning. But her blood was warming again, and now, more slowly, in a steadier rhythm, she went through the kitchen, the bathrooms, the long, long room that Trover's very last carpenter built. The hour turned late; she began to drag, how silent the house; the mantel clock amazingly still beating.

Long after Gideon fell asleep on the sofa, she kept it up. What she had been unable to achieve in the name of compliance, defiance was driving her to nicely. As fast as her life deranged, she was setting it back, sorting its parts, dusting its sundry adornments. How could she ever leave a clean, serene house? Now every stroke took on the eager solemnity of a nuptial vow. But weren't they a devious pair, whacking these pathways, finding each other over the worse, the most convoluted routes around? When the clock struck three, she snapped off the sweeper.

Put your ear to the heart, any heart, and listen to its awful logic, unreal as the ticking clock in the sleeping house. And sometimes only the heart knew what it meant, and the left side of the brain frowned upon the right. And vice versa. Even the parts of the self were mistakenly paired, a contentious and unfortunate but irrevocable marriage.

Returning the Kirby to the closet, she hung its hoses from the hooks Gideon had installed reproachfully some weeks before. Then she went to the front of the house and switched on the floodlights to see what the storm had created. The snow was still coming but less generously now. The tire tracks were nearly filled in, and pretty knife-edged drifts reshaped the lower curve of the rose garden. And then she saw it: a great round thing, the metallic gleam in lights made silver by the slanting snow.

There it sat like a fallen moon, or the simple truth, bottom flattened out where it came to rest against the earth. But of course, it was no moon, no more a wonderment than he was. It was only one of those pretty space-age tents she'd seen in Trover's Early Winters catalog, something he'd trundled in God knows when.

She switched off the lights and stood with her back to the snow-lit night. Her muscles came undone like ribbons, the smell of snow was sweet. No wonder she hadn't heard the usual ferocious kabooms of some engine racing before takeoff. He had gone, yes, but not so far. As usual he was camping just outside the thumping, ridiculous mystery of her wifely heart.

CHAPTER

29

And Michael woke early to dread. Sometimes that stalled-heart dream of his left him heavy like this, dejected. Yet he was quite certain the night had passed without fatality, dreamlessly indeed. The dormer window framed a brothy square of mixed light and night. Wrapping a quilt around his shoulders, he hauled out of bed. He went to the window and cranked it open. He waded an arm out to check the temperature and drew back, shivering.

Through the open window, along with the waves of damp, drifted a thin strand of tractor rattle. Could it be old Sprecher was already up and clearing the lane? Sprecher abominated cold and often made them wait for a warming trend before plowing them out. Conversely, if a dink of a spring system left a lick of slush on the roadway, he'd be up first thing to scrape it off. Michael studied the road; it looked a little rough but not impassable.

He was about to close the window when he noticed the alien shape at the far left corner of his perspective. He hung out, clutching the jamb. What the hey? A big gray bubble under the naked arms of the Japanese maple. Would the morning keep yielding up these domes of strangeness? The one out there, the one enclosing him?

He cranked the window shut and slunk back to bed. Switching on the radio, he waited hopefully for the school closings. If they weren't forthcoming, Spot would pick him up as agreed at seven-thirty. Mighty had finally lowered the boom. Make her late one more time, she'd said, and he could find another chump to lug him to school. He had, and she'd held firm, and thank God Spot had been good enough to save him from the bus the past mornings.

The announcer seemed afloat out there in the half-light; his voice projected a sort of disembodied, halfhearted bravado. He threw out school names like bait. Some were closed all day. Only city schools would start on time. Upper Lehigh, Lower Longswamp, Effort Secondary, and Lorraine, all starting one hour late.

Good, go back to sleep, boy. But the best he could do was snuggle deeper into his white nest of apprehension. Closing his eyes, he saw snow again, and it scared him. He flung the covers off. He stared straight ahead to the big window where his trophies stood black against the coming sun, coming weakly, the trees like tall ships across the morning. He returned to the dormer window. What were campers doing in his yard? Gideon? Gypsies? Drawing his knees up, he wedged into the alcove sideways and closed his eyes. Maybe he dozed, and maybe he only bided time, but when he peeked out again, a scallop of frailest blue was showing just above Pulpit Rock. The edge advanced, rose swiftly, thinning across the ridge. He watched it stretch, ominous, soft-pawed. A bear come over the mountain, the first woolly blue drift of nothern air; he was watching a cold front come in.

Now, when he craned down toward the tent, someone was emerging from the igloo-type foyer. The man was clad in heavy outerwear, fruit juice colors vibrant in the slicing light. Crawling to the side of the tent, he appeared to survey the main lawn. He was looking toward the orchard or the hills beyond. Then he scrambled to his feet and, facing the house, shaded his eyes against the white-skinned sun. The man was his dad. But what was his dad doing in a tent? Trover turned again now and set off across the snow in that awkward toddling gait even grown men employ to negotiate depths. Seconds later he came high-stepping back through his tracks. Then his voice was careering through the quiet house. "Louise! Louise!" Then: "Louise, get up!" Impatient hiking boots shucking on the stairs.

From the top of the attic steps Michael heard his mother bump out of bed. "God, why is that person yelling?" Michael came down to the second-floor hall.

His father was blocking the bedroom doorway. "Louise, you tell Sprecher to remove the fruit trees?"

She regarded him blankly.

"Well, if you didn't, who did? Because that's what he's doing. This very minute, trust me, Louise."

Michael squeezed past. "Sprecher's pulling out the fruit trees," his mother told him, and she sounded almost drunk.

Trover presented his wife, as if she'd just caught on.

"Oh, wait . . ." Louise smiled. "Isn't this the time, the most favorable time of the year to prune?"

"He always prune trees at the roots?"

She stared at him.

"Hey, last night on my way home I heard a tractor running up at Tumbling Run. What d'ya bet he rototilled the campground and moved on down to us."

"Oh, God," she said. "Do something."

Like someone about to sneeze, needing Kleenex, Trover scanned the room. He found his son. "Michael, get out there and tell that nut to knock it off."

"Me?" he squeaked. "Me? I'm only fifteen."

"The pears!" Louise cried, flapping irascibly after the sleeve of her robe, babbling like a goose. "Those lovely old plums, did he get the damsons? Oh, why would he—what gets into that man?"

"Fine, let's all sit down and discuss the psychological underpinnings."

Louise took a deep breath. Then she cast off her robe and addressed her son directly. "You," she said, "wake Gideon and your sister. We'll all have to pitch in."

"Way to go," said Trover. "Deputize the whole damn town."

"What town?" Michael said. "Sometimes I wish we had a town."

At first view of the damages Michael stopped dead in his tracks. The entire upper orchard lay in a twist, a vision all the more savage for the acres of solid white quietude enclosing it. He thought of herds of slain deer, their fine racks branching from the ground, bits of broken antler scattered, their sweet stiff flanks cradled in snow. But they were not deer, only insentient trees, and still his knees went weak. Roots thrust out of clumps, menacing as live wires; the snow was rubbled with yellow clay and scree the same shade as his shadow.

Down in the center section Sprecher stayed his course, unfazed. Apparently done now with cherries and apples, he drove between the rows of alternating yellow peach and early apricots. The mild winter had been, as ever, his ally; since the ground could not have frozen much deeper than an inch or so, his task was that much easier. He rode his own tractor, spanking red as Mighty's nails, and if he noticed the small stricken party looking on, he paid it no mind at all.

At the upper edge of the wreckage they crowded close, Louise hunched up in her coat, the cold front creeping silently, deepening furtively overhead. The sky was now tenuously divided between clean cerulean and the shifting liquor left from the storm, the blue traveling rapidly, its eastern flank now lapping, now slitting the sun free of its haze so that the tips of Mighty's scant lashes caught sudden fire and her face went white and underexposed. And Gideon, shielding his own profile from the glare, said, "Wait a minute! He can't do that! I'd sue I were you."

As to a more immediate cure, Michael hadn't a clue. "Where's Dad?" he asked. And everybody started swiveling and dipping, looking behind each other's knees and back across their tracks, as if he were something mislaid in the confusion. The sun on the snow drove their eyes back, but it was soon clear that Trover was not forthcoming.

"I don't believe it," said Louise, letting her finger drop for a second.

Mighty propped it aloft. "High time you did," she said.

In stymied silence they watched the caretaker back up to within several feet of one of the older Elbertas. Lumbering down off the tractor, he took a chain attached to the rear bar and dragged it over to the tree. Wrapping the free end several times around the slender trunk, securing it, he climbed back behind the wheel.

"Hurry up," Gideon cried. "Call the staties. Stop him."

It was a thought. Involve the cops. Let them handle it. A couple of beefy types yelling, "Stop or we'll shoot." And one thing for sure, that mulehead would never listen, and what if they got carried away and blasted him out of the saddle? Michael shuddered to think it. Scrap that one.

Tears stood in his mother's eyes. "It's like getting murdered in your bed," she said.

Mighty screwed up her face. "What is?"

"The trees, dormant, trusting, Sprecher coming at the crack of dawn."

Gideon's eyes flew open. "Hey, My, what'd I just get done saying? Didn't I say 'Grim Reaper'?"

Michael let out a hefty sigh. His father had abstained, and he, Michael— His eyes darted with failing hope from one face to another. Well, who else? Years from now he'd tell his grandchildren about the day he became a man. "OK," he said miserably. "But don't you guys dare split."

Affecting a casual stance, hands in pockets, Michael approached the old German, who was inching forward, watching behind him, the chain tautening between tractor and tree. He nodded as he might on any morning, curtly, two quick jerks of the heavy jaw, preserving intact the crags and concavities of that gray, impregnable face.

"Whoaaa!" Michael hollered, to no discernible response. He circled around to the downside, wagging his arms in some indefinite semaphore he prayed translated "stop." But Sprecher kept hard ahead. So he returned his hands to his pockets and reviewed his options.

A low, slow-moving vehicle, slow old man manning it. One hop and he'd be up there, headlock, bear hug, and down would come one Dutchman, duck soup. But in Michael's imagination, the brittle old bones shattered as they hit, and he could almost hear Sprecher break with the indescribably icy tinkle of Mighty's glass wrestlers the day he inadvertently brushed them off his trophy ledge. No way to get that extra bit of leverage that let you throw in the upward hitch that broke your opponent's fall.

Wait, wasn't there a way to slice through metal? Surely, in all his frenzy of possession, Trover had acquired such a cutter. He could sever a chain link as Sprecher tugged. But that meant slogging back to the house to rummage through tons of junk for something he'd never seen before. By that time the Knoll would be an official disaster zone.

Precious seconds passed as he deliberated. He continued his fruitless rounds, and so indifferent was Sprecher, so resolutely impervious that Michael felt like a turkey buzzard circling Pulpit Rock. When he slipped and fell on his can, Sprecher ignored him. He got down and pounded the ground, and Sprecher peered at him impassively before shifting back to his operation. It hurt something in Michael's mouth, the creak of the peach tree, the roots holding on, clinging to bone.

It was not a young tree, and in past years the fruit had been puny and sparse. But Michael remembered well the almost obscenely fecund state of the orchard the August day they moved in. He and his mother and sister out walking, surveying their domain, everywhere wild with surprise. In the orchard they acted like drunks, the sheer abundance, the windfalls turning to wine under their feet. They hardly knew what to sample first. His mother's teeth were in the peach when Sprecher came up from behind. He'd come from exactly nowhere, and there he stood in his awful grizzled dignity, his coveralls clean and creased, thumbs hooked under his straps, much older then because they were so young. So overwhelming was his presence, so proprietary his stance that Louise let drop the piece of fruit, and the three of them stood bowed like intruders as wasps thronged to the peach to sip from her toothmarks.

The Hummers had never mentioned Sprecher; nobody had warned them that he came with the place. After many minutes had passed, he plucked another peach and placed it in Louise's hand. "Help yourself, missus," he said. He nodded and started back up the hill and they watched him go in shamefaced silence. He'd gone home to Perma but a black after-image lingered, and they no longer felt free to taste the fruit or continue their explorations. They went back to the house that was not yet a home. They took turns keeping watch.

Michael looked up to see Sprecher come off the tractor again. Now was his chance. Easy tackle, no one gets hurt. But when he really looked, he was stopped by something so solid and indestructible that the task seemed suddenly too much for him. He might just as well try to uproot one of those trees by hand. Instead of striking, he found himself trailing along to the base of the tree. He peered close as Sprecher lowered the chain and looped it tighter. He watched in diffident, apprenticelike attention, and somewhere up there Mighty was shouting, "Mike-kool! Michael Kleeve, stop pissing around!"

"Sir," he ventured, drawing Sprecher partway about, "uh, looks like we're in for a cold snap."

"Ay," Sprecher said, "it's nippy."

"Oh, one more thing," Michael said, "I was just wondering, well, how come you're ripping out the trees?"

Rising stiffly, then turning, the old man got a bead on the boy. But Sprecher's words suggested nothing of hostility or condescension. Just a simple pledge, chiseled in stone: "I do the same as all the time. First I clear the fields; then I plow; then I put in seed."

By any reckoning it was time to shout, "Not on the Knoll you don't. This look like a dirt farm, Bub?" But Sprecher had stooped to the slipping links again, his broad back taking the snow as it clumped off the branches. Rust bloodied the snow where the chain lay. In some world, even if only Sprecher's own, his claims had to be valid. Now it was given to Michael to challenge that claim. And if Michael couldn't say "ours, mine," what could he ever say with any conviction? He was good in trig but didn't have the head for this sort of figuring. The logic was there; all he had to do was take it one step at a time, up the courthouse steps, through the revolving door, and down the hall, rifle a file, and there it was, a deed with the name Kleeve on it. What was wrong with that? The terrible swift spear of linear thinking. So why did he have to see instead the big bat-wing shadow of Sprecher's soul purpling the snow? Why was nothing clearer to him than that?

He turned and looked uphill for help. He watched Mighty climb aboard a root-ball, the better to oversee him. His mother burrowed deeper into her coat, and Michael could almost see the bat-wing beating over her, too. She would be useless when it came to counsel.

Mighty climbed higher. She stood with her arms folded across her chest. Even without glasses she managed to project the tapering disdain of one peering *over* them. God, she looked just like his grandmother. She would not say more, he knew. She would just nudge him into trouble with her little chisel of a chin. Well, he had to do something, didn't he?

Feeling unbearably dumb and unsupple, he crept around and behind

Sprecher. He spread his arms and opened and shut his fingers, practicing handling for a while before risking an actual grasp on the man's coat. Then he laid the other hand opposite. Sprecher tipped back, then stood, his torso sliding easily up through Michael's indecisive grip. The old man turned quietly into him. From the upper banks they would look like a young man and his grandfather locked in an awkward hug of hello or good-bye. Sprecher was smiling, blue lips slicing to one side, sour heat wheezing out. Sprecher took a step uphill, thereby adding to his moral advantage over the boy the boon of extra height. And Michael, steeped in the dreamy wonder of the surely unreal, didn't see it coming; as Michael gawked, Sprecher hauled off. A chop to the shoulder that sent him reeling, reaching for the tree. He missed, slipped on the snow, and went down.

Instinctively he rolled to his belly, Sprecher hurling himself on top. Michael's mouth, still agape, quickly filled with snow. With Sprecher's not inconsiderable weight on his chest, it was hard to breathe. He was splayed flat, spitting snow, all desire to escape pressed out of him. A rope of curse words and grunts lashed the back of his neck. *"Haa gott Heilich schtann gewitter dunnerwetter fadommt!"*

Sprecher's gutterals were cut with yelps of panic coming from Louise. In trying to drag the old man off, she succeeded only in adding to her son's cargo. "Gideon!" she cried, shaking that graying finger around. "Mighty! Mr. Sprecher, we'll work something out. Please let Michael up. You'll crush him." And Bagel came running, ripping around the pileup, yipping for the pure joy of sport. Mighty, he suspected, was off somewhere smirking her face off because they were all fools, everybody but her.

Gideon crouched near Michael's nose. "On your knees," he said. "Up! Up!" And that set Michael to laughing. That and the snow tickling under his collar and the funny helpless syllables his mother was spooning into the confusion. The pressure eased off his upper body and settled lower. "What's he doing?" Michael asked his friend.

"Holding down your bum, peabrain."

"Yeah, but what's he *doing*?" he whispered.

"His Rushmore act. No ants in them pants."

The image undid him. With both hands he made a dry nest for his face, a pit for his giggles. His mother was saying, "Earl, would you like some Ovaltine?"

"Good thinking," said Gideon. "We got crullers, too."

"Crullers?" said Louise. "Really?"

With great difficulty Michael lifted his chin. He tried to say "oatmeal" before another wave of hysterics crashed him back into his hands.

"Oh!" Louise said with phony cheer. "Who could go for oatmeal?"

The offer drove Michael even deeper, his silly mouth melting the snow between his fingers. He was laughing so hard he didn't notice right away when the burden lifted. Lightened, he was free now to float off into his life. The little hollow balls of laughter stopped, dropped back into his chest; the dread tamped in again. He was slow getting to his feet.

In the nest their bodies had made in the snow, he sat with his head resting on his knees. His mother whisked caked snow from his coat and someone shook out his toboggan and recapped him. The Massey-Ferguson was riderless, too, now, and there was Sprecher tacking uphill, cracking through the thicket of defeated trees. Not one person spoke as he passed under the pines and started up the steps by the pool, then vanished over the upper rim of their perspective. When he was gone, Michael staggered to his feet. "I feel like a SWAT team," he said.

"We stopped him," said Gideon, with a limp, abstracted sagacity. "Isn't that what counts?"

The nun was up when they got back. Giving the returning party a cursory glance, she said, "I do hope I missed something exciting." She was sipping coffee, flaking a cruller with her thumbnail.

And Trover strode onstage dressed as a chap, a country squire. Trover, in his scratchy tweeds and shiny shoes and woolly socks. Rosy and fragrant, he dandied in and out of rooms. A privileged man exempt from the heat of his own boundary squabbles. Let the peasants brawl in the fields. Oh, he'd been trimming his grin in the mirror as a crazy clawed up his earthly garden, and he was stuffing warm toes into fluffy socks as Michael assaulted an old farmer. He did not ask the outcome. He shook Mini-Wheats into a brandy snifter, and he sang "My Boy Bill" without a trace of irony. Bagel looked at him adoringly.

Louise stood by the counter, working the bread drawer in and out, pumping away the urge to cry. She bit her lip, thoroughly curdled. She had wept for almost every living thing they'd ever lost, the trees broken by wind and eaten by disease, the plants deflowered by groundhogs, the groundhogs the dogs got, the dogs, the cats, the fledgling wrens. Michael had never seen her cry for Geggo, but all that summer little deaths had leveled her, the zoo flamingo broken by vandals, a wingless bee. One day he found her sobbing out by the laundry basket. It turned out she'd found a gypsy moth egg cluster on one of the pin oaks holding up the clothesline. Nearby the female was beating its feeble wings, weakly, weakly; then the wings breathed their last. He finished hanging the clothes and led his mother home by the hand. If she ever found the real loss, he worried, would it kill her?

"They were good trees," she was saying now, "happy trees. And him, well he's gone, that's all." She meant Sprecher, and she spoke as if they'd slain him.

Mighty tried to save herself with severity, but her arm seemed to rise of its own volition. It came to rest across Louise's back. "He shall return, Ma. He always does."

"Sure. He'll come back and rip out more trees or he'll go someplace and die of bitter old age." She framed the next question around one face at a time. "When do we get to choose between good and better?"

"Have some OJ, Sister," said Trover. "Another cruller?"

"Thanks," said Frank archly. "I will." They exchanged glances. Clearly they were the only sensible heads in the room.

"Gotta run," said Trover. "Mighty, drop me off at my car."

When they had gone, Michael watched his mother come around. She dried her tears, eyes shining as she took her first nervous slurps of tea. Michael had witnessed this transformation before, and it still amazed him. He could swear her spine lengthened, and the cords of her neck stood out. She looked suddenly taut and scrawny, a body electric, one step ahead of itself. She would try again today, with her untalented left hand. Whatever happened she always seemed to recharge in time for work, the way he revived for wrestling practice, even if his heart had stopped the night before. No ordinary job would dare resurrect you like that, grab you back from the past, from grief, deep or immediate. Watching her now, he felt a low, sad longing. He wanted to tag after her today, make something of clay himself, a kid imitating his mother, his mother a kid imitating God. He wanted to stay until the magic waned and she was common again, a klutz with a hopeful heart and no particular grip on things. He wanted to stay home today with his mother.

So distressed and unsteady did he feel that his mother's leaving seemed cruel, an abandonment. She had left him behind with Frank. Their eyes met skittishly across the table. He felt too heavy to rise. The nun continued to watch him with studious, amused interest. She smelled his fear, he thought. She saw how dopey he looked with all the courage drained from his face. Setting down her cup, she smiled. "You have a certain light, Michael. Oh, my, yes. Any fool can see it."

"Yes, ma'am," he said. "I mean, Sister."

The weighty subjects covered, they were stuck with what was left between so disparate a couple. She liked speckled bananas. He preferred black. They talked toilsomely about leaky pens and a particularly obstreperous kind of hard chalk that wouldn't erase cleanly. And when Spot called from Mrs. Grimm's house to say he couldn't get up the hill, Michael was still in torn sweats over flannel pajamas. He was sorry to have to leave the nun just when he was getting to know her.

He dressed quickly enough, but then his all-star coat disappeared. "It couldn't have walked away!" he said. In desperation he grabbed a fat yellow goose-down parka that he'd never seen before. It had a fur-lined hood that made him look like the cowardly lion. It took him another five minutes to make his way down the slippery hillside to where Spot waited by the dam. He glanced up once before climbing in. The mountains, with their white cliffs, limned a clean nautical line against the scintillant sky, and it was perceptibly colder.

Showing not a snip of impatience, Spot punched Michael's padded arm in friendship. The Leper, with its bald tires, balked a bit on the first rise, and then they were off. They clattered through Kemp. Already sidewalks were shoveled; driveways, cleared. It was in local bones to look after things immediately. Not even the birds had to wait, lawns pocked with crumbs and etched with the delicate glyphs of tits, finches, and chickadees. A housewife left off shaking her mop to watch the birds bob and dance in her yard, and the creatures seemed to come from nowhere, as if that sky had spun them earthward just to preserve its curve of perfect blue.

The old-timers had wasted no time collecting in front of Groff's Garage. They'd be talking weather, of course, marveling on and on, as though snow were a once-in-a-lifetime phenomenon. Then someone would mention the storm of '32 when nineteen inches had collapsed the roof of Umlauf's Danceland. And the men would nod, still awed, still needing to be awed, after all these years. Around here only birth and death and dirt were givens. Every single one of these men had immaculate wives, headstones bought with hard cash. Some had buried babies, and Michael had heard them speak of such in the same proud breath they mentioned the living children's "gradiations" and weddings.

"Slow down," Michael said. Spot had hit the seam hard, and the jolt lifted them roughly onto the covered bridge. Beneath them the dry boards replied with a comforting thrumming rumble.

"Gotta watch?" asked Spot.

"Heck, no," he said. "Don't you?"

"It's busted," said Spot. "I don't see nobody at the bus stop. Guess we're late."

"Maybe a little."

Spot was not speeding exactly. Maybe nervousness over the time was butting him from behind, causing him to run a bit fast for conditions. It was almost impossible to take these stretches tentatively. Every dip and figure were too well known; the tires turned and turned, and the sky tumbled by, whisking you with it. So with hardly a break in rhythm Spot went bounding down off the main road and headed south over the mountain shortcut to Lorraine.

They passed an Amish church with its surrounding wicket of covered carriage stalls. They swept the generous S called Kauffman's Hill. They drove through open country, through the struble of twisted grasses, through two-toned fields, the silver and gold now echoing the checker of the cob itself in late July. Down in a crease between hills, a car on some nameless road shone in the sun like a shovel load of embers, flared brightly and blinked out. They crested just as the woodland began; they descended into shade. Hemlock branches hung low overhead, and how silent and dim it was through the long hall under the white archway. For a second Michael was riding in a train, wind rushing by outside, a train flashing across a rickety trestle, thundering into the dell. A night train with dim yellow windows. The nun had looked; she saw his light, she said. His light so deep and small, yet most of the time that's all he had, all there was to go by. Riding, he rocked and watched his lap. He looked over at Spot. He'd wanted to say "stop" but stayed dumb as one in a dream. His friend seemed far away, damp with shadow.

Into the fog hollows and then up again and flat out across the plateau. The feed mill, the Ironmaster's House, and then they came to the lip of the long grade that pitched to the left and switched sharply back before straightening out to follow the river through the narrow valley at the other end of which was the town. This was Michael's favorite runout, the exquisite precipitousness of the dip; you could almost feel the lurch of the earth beneath you. "By the way," Spot said, "you never did tell me what was left on your plate that time."

"What time?"

"That smorgasbord pig-out your Dad took you to. Remember, you were so stuffed you had to leave something on your plate. You said you couldn't stop thinking about it. Well, what was it? You promised to tell me, remember?"

Michael tried to smile. "It was no big deal," he said. Spot was rolling, the landscape contagious. What could be done? "It was . . ." he said, then caught his breath as they entered the turn, a wide curve but blind as a boot. And Michael saw the trouble in the same breaking vista that held the long welt of straightaway, the sweet resume of farm country, barns suddenly as wonderful as ships drifting out. "A raisin," he managed to say, in amazement.

There were two compact cars stopped dead in their path, one facing south, the other north, the drivers' windows contiguous, the drivers hanging out, holding hands. He had spotted them oddly, without alarm, and in that longest instant of his life Michael recognized Yoder and, without ever having laid eyes on her before, Erica Lavender. It surprised him mildly that Erica Lavender was not fair. The sheen of her black hair was unbearable in the blue-white light. It hung between him and her face. He could smell, taste her breath—like apples or milk. His own word reverberated. *Raisin. Raisin.* How strange.

Wasn't his aplomb remarkable, his thoughts still unreeling at their customary leisurely pace? He felt only a vague regret that now he would never see her pretty face, never contend again. He thought of the powdery mystery his mother moved in, her poor finger; he left her his messy room, his sister's soft sorrowing deep in the Christmas picture, his father asleep in the cold last night.

Even after Spot jammed on the brakes and the Leper whipped twice around, he was not afraid. Time continued to expand and contract. No rush, he had not time but forever to think. His mind lay quietly down, stretched out smooth as time, as a clean bed, white, unwrinkled, ready. He thought nothing at all now as the Leper decided, aiming straight at the two small nuzzling cars blocking the road. Then he was air, or airborne, and he knew death to be something white and sun-starred through which you rose or fell—a whole note, held long.

CHAPTER

30

"Easy," said Louise. "Right here." The Landers rocked to rest between a batter jug and a stack of bills where they sat pat, set in their ways. "Thanks," she said, holding her bad hand out from her. "That's that." In a slow, speculative arc, her eyes moved from the plaster family to Frank. She touched the jagged stub where the crook of Trover's elbow was missing. "The earth has no particular liking for us creative types, doesn't do diddly to make our little projects stick."

"Likes nuns even less," Frank said.

"Neither of us produces a thing worth beans in the scheme of things. If you're not hoeing turnip rows or having kids, the planet dismisses you as irrelevant."

"Irreverent?"

"That, too." She continued to pick at the chalky wound.

"But, Louise, you whacked that elbow off yourself. I saw you."

She had. Attacked it with a flashlight the night Trover ruined Christmas. Louise scrunched her mouth. "The planet made me do it."

"I thought Trover did."

"Same thing. He's in on the mission. We all are. Create and destroy. Do and undo. If it's flawed, revise. If it threatens to become perfect, for God's sake, stop it!"

"I thought it was our inalienable nature to self-perfect."

"But it's equally true, don't you think, that we go out of our way to miscalculate, overstep, misbehave. Sometimes the clearest signature we have is our simple fallibility. It's a kind of chauvinism, I'd say, these demonstrations, yelling and stomping and goofing off, this hopping, awkward dance with one foot in the grave. It's like that Irish pride in their stumblebum drunks. *Look at me, Lord, I'm Louise Pegeen, planet Earth, human as you made me. You can't catch me!*" Louise crisscrossed her chest. "But, oh, God, *catch* me."

To which Frank dryly replied, " 'And the last shall be first, and the poor inherit,' and only the losers of life shall keep it. Abominate your own faults, but abide other morons fondly. Love the defective. Human flaws—didn't somebody once say they were the wounds in the hands and feet of man?"

"Those somebodies paradoxed us half to death, didn't they?" Louise grinned. "Now we think life is dull without fifteen rounds a day of weighty contradictions."

"No wonder we don't get along with anybody."

Louise quickened; this was her kind of dynamic, the pull of puzzle, the hidden twists. She'd once read of a man whose ruling passion was knots. He wrote the book, in fact. He'd spent his life trying to isolate and codify the endless ramifications of a single scrap of yarn. Each loop and hitch locked in another pattern, another plot. In trying to exhaust the possibility of knots, he succeeded only in inventing new ones: slippery hitch, Turk's heads, true lover's. In unraveling the great secrets, Louise had fared about as well as the old knot master. She, too, stumbled with a weird, thwarted joy on new variants. "Here's one!" she said now. She drew a deep breath and recited: "Love the green earth and the great pyramids and the funny inventions of dusty little men. Watch the sun come up if you will, but keep your middle eye on the unseen."

"Who said that? You?"

Louise grimaced. "Could you tell?"

"Well, it's not as pithy as Proverbs, but with a little practice, Weeze, you could get a job on the Bible."

"There's a local legend," Louise said, "about an old man who had to be buried sitting up. He needed a special casket. They couldn't untwist him."

"Poor soul. Arthritis?"

"Or maybe he just tried too hard to reconcile his views."

"Louise, you always take things one step too far."

"OK, OK, help me look for that broken piece, will you? I'm sick of messing around with that monstrosity. Especially now that I'm disabled."

In the room variously called Purgatory, workshop, mud room, front room, back room, Room, they got down on their knees and searched. Louise frisked the bottom shelves and sifted through little dunes of sawdust. Then she lurched up and sprang to her feet, and as she did, her vision went white and fluttery. Frank reached out to steady her. She helped her friend to the couch.

"I went all fuzzy," Louise said. "It was snowing inside me."

"You got up too fast. All the blood rushed out of your head."

Sighing, Louise leaned back and shut her eyes.

"Find it?" Frank asked.

"No."

"You all right? You look a mite peaked."

But Gideon had appeared at the foot of the steps, combed and shaved somehow too slick.

"Gideon," said Frank, "you didn't see a little gizmo, so long, with a crook in it?"

"You mean Mr. Kleeve's elbow?" Holding up a finger, he skipped off. He returned moments later with the part. "It was in the dish with the beer nuts," he said.

"How 'bout that?" said Louise. "Thanks."

"Anytime," he said.

"Where you off to? Surely you're not going to *pick* in weather like this?"

"Why not? I come as a happy surprise on a snowy day. Catch the widder ladies off guard. Mind if I take the Jeep?"

Louise nodded halfheartedly. She hoped this would not be recorded anywhere as abetting against the elderly. "Oh, Gideon, while you're out, could you pick up some epoxy?"

"Anything else?"

"Just glue, thank you."

Her house had heavy doors. When they slammed, the rooms shuddered and stillness struck like a stopped guitar. How the clock on the mantel pounded. Louise felt like an only child left home on a snow day with a small friend. She was thin, impotent, commended to the whimsy of things. Drawing her legs up, she hugged herself close.

She glanced up quickly and found herself staring at the opposite wall, where her daughter's eyes burned through to her from all that time and life behind the frame. The Christmas gift face suspended from an eightpenny nail. "You act *so* smart," she once chided Mighty. "You make us all feel stupid."

Mighty had shrugged. "So? That's how I am."

"Wait a minute," Louise had protested. "You don't accept *us* so damn philosophically. You make it clear that *we* have to change."

"So?" the child replied. "That's also how I am."

Louise slid deeper yet into the clog of bothered thought. She could not decide what she'd done well in her life, what meanly; she took furtive comfort in the blur of bad feelings in general, guilt indistinguishable from hurt, all of it ancient and unresolved as a row of ghost ships. Cold white thoughts drifted in, the air thick with terrible waiting. What was she waiting for?

"You're shivering," Frank said.

"I'm still a little dizzy, from before."

The steady, ticking calm clamped down again. It was Frank who eventually broke the silence. "I have to do something soon," she said in a small voice.

Louise let her own life go and turned to her friend. "You can stay as long as you like," she said.

"No, don't be nice. I've been here nearly a month." She lowered her eyes. She squirmed. Her hands, upturned, started to work as if she were weighing or shaping something, then dropped like rocks into her lap. "I told you about that minicourse system we have at school, a little of this, a little of that, for kids who can't take much of anything in one gulp."

Louise nodded.

"Well, they had me teaching one called Astrophysics for Poets. Just another way of saying gravy course actually. One day I got in much deeper than the curriculum permitted. Black holes. Dark matter. A world breaking away at the speed of light. The kids weren't scared, but I was. That's when I wrote to you. I expected to write again shortly, joke about momentary madness, cancel out. Instead, when the day came, there I was, stuffing a nightgown and stockings into a paper bag. When my homeroom went to first period, I slipped out the alleyway and walked to the depot. I called myself plucky. I considered myself a humanist."

"That's hardly like you—to run off like that."

"The planet made me do it."

"Touché."

"I'm serious, Louise. There I was, staring into endless, measureless everything, and all around me the simple finitudes were piling up. And I don't just mean people *dying*. Nuns enjoy an enviable longevity. Isn't that odd? You'd think that we'd just rush to meet Him. No, I mean the little deaths mostly. Sister Edith waking up blind. And one day little Sister Leann forgot what came after 'My soul doth magnify.' The next day she forgot not to sing 'High Diddle Diddle' at benediction. And we always have at least one menopausal paranoid in the infirmary, rocking pillows in her arms, berating Him like some she-devil. And I began to imagine the eggs in my belly, one by one blinking out like those prehistoric stars."

"I see, just the ordinary pressures. Oh, Frank, do you want a child?"

"I want an extra life. Two extra, three." She sat up tall. "I want *options*, Louise."

It was a lame, little-girl demand, and it made Louise smile. Deep in shadow they sat, surrounded on three sides by other rooms. They sat, Louise saw, in the thick distillate of lives from which much of the stock had boiled off. Lives they'd somehow chosen and remained, for the most part, faithful to. Lives with body and consistency and savor, yes—deepened in that way but still unquestionably reduced. Lives thick on the skin as middle-aged flesh on the bones. Louise rubbed at herself.

"I have these dreams," Frank said. "Oh, Louise, I couldn't begin to describe them. You'd be scandalized forever."

"I probably would, so exercise good judgment if you're going to pursue this line."

"Well, just let me say there are mornings I wake and the only thing alive on earth are the birds and my chirping flesh. And not enough spirit in me to spark a *Te Deum*."

"It gives one pause. How did Augustine do it?"

"Sometimes I don't care how he did it. I think he was a fruitcake."

"And sometimes you do care."

"Most of the time" she said. "That's the part that can't be gotten around, quite." Steepling her fingers, she tapped her lips gently. "If I could just have a little time to give the unused parts of me a run. . . ." She popped up a finger. "One word and I'd take all my doubts and double dares and this third world of a body, I'd go downtown and carry on like a fool. I'd make the most of my sabbatical. Take up skating and exotic dance, court dangerous men and philosophers and other threats to the dedicated mind. Let them test me."

She was running double time, ticking her head as she talked. She had caught something of Louise's fever, that superheated rush when she was chasing some crazy train of thought, eyes burning hard ahead. She lighted a cigarette. "Doubts make muscles, don't you agree? Oh, I'd say anything. I'm a desperate woman, Louise."

But Louise was leaning, ignited herself. She wanted in on this requisition, this cantical of demands. "I want things, too," she said. "And I'm talking a lot more than my health. Remember that snapshot that made me look like Piper Laurie. Well, I want it back. I want to be a Tamburitzan. No, a Rockette. I cried the first time I saw those girls, working like clockwork. I want to be God's best girl and humble as mustard at the same time. I want my husband to be more of a husband, you know, the supportive, mannerly model Dr. Bob recommends. But just let Trover try it, let him become something other. Why, I'd be disconsolate. I'd feel like a widow."

"Whew! And Trover doesn't think you want *anything*!"

"What I don't want is easier for him to find in the stores. If he ever set to pleasing me, he'd turn into . . . a knot, no doubt. And he's clever enough to play dumb."

"Maybe the stupidity of men is survival. Pure instinct."

"There's certainly something in us that cannot be appeased."

"So, what'll I do, kiddo? I have pretty dimpled knees. Nobody will ever know that."

"If it's any comfort to you, I can say that a married woman has something of the same fear. A body given to a twenty-year spouse is a body common as the backyard, a body passed through at times as if it were the only path to the soul still open. Women my age get drunk at piano bars and strip for strangers."

Frank looked contrite. "I've been out of line, Louise. And who am I to question your choices? Anyhow, I'm beginning to see why you stay with Trover."

"You do?" Louise said. "Then you're smarter than me. If I have my reasons, I rather think they begin, not end, with him. I have a particular man and have to go around inventing the general idea to support him. All my ideas die in time of stupidity or boredom. Every last theory eventually fizzles out, and lo, there *he* is, bigger and brattier than ever."

"I think you get that man mixed up with God."

"Frank, I have always given my heart to missing men. The first was my father, poor soul. Then I had that teenage crush on Christ. In a way, Trover's the easiest case of all." She paused. "Seems to me there's a lot of reciprocity between heaven and earth. What's *your* idea of Christ, Frank? Whose eyes have you given Him? Whose dear familiar cheek?"

Frank nodded and smiled and leaned closer. "Last summer I went to Chicago for a seminar on illiteracy. It was late afternoon when we left O'Hare. Several minutes after takeoff, I looked out. We were passing over a brace of very high, shiny buildings at the lip of Lake Michigan. Then we were over water, the wing dragging a kind of purple darkness. The light was indescribable, timeless. Then the buildings began to fan out weirdly and fade. I watched the quiet curve of the lake sweep wider and wider. Then it was wholly in sight, a bowl of lustrous blue, and the city sat shimmering on its distant edge. Chicago was the color of memory now, and the light was the color of God."

Frank's hand spread open across her breast. "Louise, I thought I would burst. There was a fearsome surge of, well, sweetness. And longing. And sorrow. Oh, it was love all right, as pure as I've ever felt it. A love that was a kind of exquisite suffering. Love, I thought. *Love! Lord, what a thing!* And seconds later I was in utter despair, crying my eyes out. Why? Because I couldn't decide what it was I was loving so. The City of God or the city of men. Either way seemed like a betrayal."

"And why not both at once? Isn't it all *one* city?"

"That was too huge an idea for that little plane to bear."

"We shouldn't talk like this. We'll scare ourselves, like you did."

Frank's faint fillip of a smile faded. "I have to go back, don't I?"

"Even if it's only to leave again, politely. Like I had to go back to the car wash."

"What a wild analogy. But I accept it. I've made quite a spectacle of myself bumping around in your life. I feel like some pimply adolescent, smoking too much, loafing, stuffing myself with junk comforts. And I miss my girls. How often over the years I'd catch myself thinking, 'I'll leave when the kids grow up,' only to remember with a jolt that they're always the same age to me, a steady procession of sixteen-year-olds, one big corporate kid who never goes off to college."

Now Frank laid tapered hands emphatically on her knees. "Know what we are, Louise? I'll tell you what we are. We're *committed women.* They'd call us the same thing if we were locked up in some asylum."

Louise giggled. Then she pursed her lips and frowned. "Maybe the only alternative is to enlist in the exclusive service of self. Sometimes I think there's no way out of that insanity. I don't know, we get so tired and miserable and bitter. We curse what we love best. Then the next day we wake plump and rested and ready to empty again. On the other hand, the in-turned tend to eat themselves and starve to death. Either way we wear down. The difference is, in the former case, ordinary sleep will restore us."

Her friend looked distant now, wistful. Louise reached for her hand. She had boneless, indecisive, Jergens-softened hands that never seemed to match the steely rest of her. Just moments ago Louise had watched those hands nuzzle like chubby children in Frank's lap. Louise imagined them waking restless and hungry, squirming off her knees, Frank crying, "I have no milk, no place for you to sleep." Louise hung her head.

It shamed her now to think how intolerant she'd been of Frank's clumsy attempts at flirtation. A good friend was generous and giving. Should she have offered a taste of Trover as she'd offered nuts and crullers? As if Trover were donatable! Indeed, as if she were all that philanthropic. And Louise could no more help corrupt a nun than she could seduce a priest.

Yet once many years ago, not long after having Michael baptized, she was visited by a young monsignor with a gaze as dark and sharp as winter-green. She was washing storm windows in the yard, and he offered to help her. She gave him rags, and the two of them knelt with the glass between them, rubbing, watching each other clarify through the polished glass. That was all. Still, she had been smitten. For nights she'd lain awake, wanting this man of God, turgid, verging on that full-bodied, succulent faith of her formative years. She had nearly forgotten how the sap of both body and soul had risen in her adolescent self at the same time. Raging into so many awakenings at once, she had thought her skin might split and the fullness of life leave her a drop at a time. Now she was nearly twenty-three. Her breasts leaked mother's milk at an embarrassing rate, and all the wild and sublime desires had come to sourness and fatigue and disappointment. Thinking of the beautiful priest, she pitied herself. She wept and wept and, when Trover tried to touch her, sobbed, "I married beneath myself!"

Had she said that? She hoped not. Yet the possibility of it shocked her now, knocked a small, sharp cry from her chest. Frank was looking on with a faintly quizzical look. Then she said, "Can I come again, Louise, if I get a little crazy?"

"Of course."

Frank's frown lines deepened. "What if times moves too fast for us?"

"Bet on it."

"But what if we stay put too long and suddenly it's too late to retract? We'll be . . . we'll be . . ."

"What? Tell me."

Like some bearer of terrible news, Frank squeezed Louise's fingers tight. "More and more," she said, "we'll miss everything we ever renounced or allowed to lapse or stupidly neglected. We'll look deep in the eyes of passing strangers. We'll yearn in our beds and yearn in our pews, and the second we get what we've most ardently yearned for, we'll miss that lovely gloss of possibility. And every single thing we love will come to grief."

And Louise arched back, harking away from that much high heat and heartache, far more than she'd bargained for. "What about happiness?" she asked sharply.

"Good heavens, Louise, happiness isn't our sort of thing. Too bland and available. We grew up on the numinous. They filled our heads with incense and visions, taught us to pray in an ancient language. We were enjoying transports when other girls our age were getting a buzz from cherry Cokes. Joy's a drug, I think, of the sort that keeps coming back on you, flaring up for no reason at all except that we live and love what we can, at hideous risk, as fierce as we're able, all of it so tenuous and absurd and because, because . . ."

"Because God is with us?" Louise said, as if expecting an argument.

Frank flashed the pretty smile the sisters had given her. She bopped her one. "Amen, Louise. Praise be."

Reflective, expectant, they eased back against the sofa. They were two friends pinned for a moment in the sea wrack of time, plain pagan time they loved more then they were taught to. But they could be any two women, sea wives staring out, bag ladies with little tilting smiles; what worlds tinkered into being behind their eyes? Who knew what worlds blinked out? They could be Louise and Frances Jane riding downtown on the D Street trolley. Or stuck in a bus. Two women waiting in the thick for traffic to move.

And then the telephone rang.

CHAPTER

31

"Go two hills past three hills. Chust up a ways from the House of the Seven Sours."

Louise did not remember to thank Mrs. Grimm or say good-bye but set the receiver back with the respectful delicacy of an explosives handler.

In the archway between rooms she paused. The message passed from her eyes to Frank's. The message cemented them, and for a long time neither woman moved. Then Louise came and sat rigidly next to her friend. After several minutes she bent close. "Come with," she whispered. "Please."

"I'll do anything you want," Frank said. Louise nodded slowly, loath to rise, unable even to breathe. She could not go back to the time when her boy had not been. She had raced to the hospital; his birth she always knew had been too easy. She would not rush to deliver him up again. She would not be the one to do it.

Frank rose. "I'll get your coat," she said gently. Louise looked up, hating her face. It was the blanched, bankrupt face of the friend who, knowing you were broke, did not offer, could not offer. Not a dime. Not a single lie to finance this journey. She brought Louise's ski jacket instead. She drew her arms through the sleeves. She tied a woolen scarf under her chin and tucked a clutch bag in the crook of her arm. "Sweetheart," she said, "call your husband. You must."

Obediently Louise tiptoed back to the telephone. A sudden move or sound would snap every bone in Michael's body, the thin web connecting her to him. His life was suddenly ancient lace in her clumsy hands. She was unfit to handle fragile things. How had she managed to hang on to him this long? Her own voice startled her with its absurd formality. "There's trouble," she told Trover. "It's your boy, Michael." She had repeated the *hinkel-drek* woman's words exactly.

And Trover was offended. "Why do you believe everything anybody tells you?" he said. "Lay you odds it was a fender bender. You hear me, a fender bender. They're a dime a dozen in slippy weather!"

Unlike him, she dared not educate fate by stating her preference. Yet hope fought in her throat alongside the freight of the unspeakable. Words could not break this logjam. She made not a squeak, not a whimper. So why was he shouting at her, "Stop crying, PLEASE. You're hysterical. Get hold of yourself!"

When he finished yelling, she said, "I'm going over there now."

He replied with injured silence. Then: "So be it, Louise. You go, go ahead, just go," as though sending her to a place he'd hitherto forbidden her to visit. "You go see for yourself. Calm down. Take the Jeep, it's safer."

"Gideon has the Jeep."

"Well, take the white Rabbit. Get the oil checked."

"Oil? What?"

"What?"

"Oh, Trover, I can't go."

"God."

"Oh, God."

Neither Rabbit would start, so they removed to Gideon's little Triumph with Frank, presumably the calmer of the two, at the wheel. Having had limited experience with snow and ice, she spun them immediately onto the ropes on the Maiden Creek side of the highway, and twice local men had to free them from snowbanks. Louise closed her eyes, suffering danger and delay as patiently as a passenger in a dream that always ended the same way. Finally, on the flat stretch leading out of Kemp, Frank began to get the hang of it, and for the first time the speedometer needle shivered past fifteen.

"Slow down," said Louise. As long as they were en route, they wouldn't be there. *There?* Never before had the word carried such exact meaning. Every road she'd ever traveled all these years had been heading nowhere else but there. There! And traveling time was all there ever was to her life, all that was left of it, and however long it took, that's how long her son had to live.

But he could be bleeding, in shock. What if he needed blankets, compassion, the sight of his mother's face? She had to choose between saving herself and him. It was no choice at all. "Please hurry," she urged Frank, who responded the same to "Hurry" as to "Slow down." She squeezed Louise's hand and proceeded at the same careful pace.

The morning circled, its curve as hard and clean as a band of sapphires and diamonds. They seemed to be not moving at all but standing still, as the landscape sped by in strips swift as freight trains. Could it have been just moments ago that she'd so cheerfully ticked off that silly wish list? She wanted not one of those things, not peace, not love, not even God Himself. It was, in fact, as if all those wrongful wishes had converged now to form the one rushing real one, so forceful through her veins it threatened to tear her body apart. All she wanted now was the plain sight of her living son. She dared not even pray on the off chance God was another Trover and, hearing what she wanted most, would offer a substitute. At five, when Michael was deep in his divinity-seeking stage, she tried to explain that nobody knew if God was male or female. "But God's a *man's* name!" he boomed, and fuming, she sent him to his room.

So Louise was abandoned to the care of chance and a narrow country road that intended no better than carry her to truth. Either he was or he wasn't. "Stop!" she cried, and Frank gave her a look of blinking uncertainty before steering off to the berm.

Louise disembarked in tottering confusion. Frank followed her, and together they stood on the spine of roadside snow. Louise was pointing into the glade, a small scrap of bottomland spiked with battered plumes of pampas grass on scrubbed white stalks. Louise took her friend's arm, and together they stepped over the highway cables; their shadows, blue as the hills, ushered them into the dell like a single silent bear.

Louise immediately set to gathering the spikes. Working with driven efficiency, she handed them to Frank, stacking her high, running all the plumes the same way. Frank's eyes shimmered with tears flecked with the same blue as the winter sky. Frank wept, and her breath hung white in the shameless air. Louise stopped to watch, blue-white wafers of miraculous breath, ghost after ghost smoking out, like the blank souls of all the children she'd never conceived. "Oh, Frank," she said. "He's all right. I know it now. If he were gone, he'd be hanging around me, dawdling. I'd feel it. Look!" she said, slicing her hand back and forth like a magician demonstrating space around a levitating form. "It's clear space."

And Frank, stacked to the chin, dropped her gaze and knocked her tears loose. Gemlike, they shone among the seed stars of the decimated fronds. Louise unburdened her friend; she laid the weeds gently in the snow, keeping but one stalk. "Let's go," she said now with quiet resolve. Frank walked ahead, her shoes sinking deep. How solid, how absolute she looked, her black against the fragile matter of snow and sky.

The car was gone. Frank had forgotten to apply the emergency brake. They found it downwind, nose in a snowbank. They dug out with their bare hands, Louise shoveling with her splinted finger, and when they were moving forward again, Louise was seized with a fear so large it squeezed from her every assurance her heart had only moments ago so magnanimously bestowed. She huddled against the door, and Frank said, "Dear, can you tell me, are we almost there?"

"Yes, yes, I guess. Almost."

Again the Triumph slowed. Louise opened her eyes.

"Weeze," Frank said. She wet her lips and did not seem to know whether or not to risk the conjecture. "I saw . . ." she began. Then: "Louise, someone's sitting on the porch back there."

Louise shaded her eyes from the sun, from false hope.

"Well, I mean it looked like an abandoned building . . . a ramshackle place set a good way back from the road . . ."

"The Ironmaster's House," Louise said. Her entire being began to shake, for now she did feel him near. But in what form? Why would a live boy be lounging on an open porch in the dead of winter. A vivid particular would help. "A hat?" she asked. "Was he wearing a hat?"

"I saw a blur of yellow, that's all—"

"Did he look hurt or anything? Did he look lost? Was he—"

"I had but a glimpse. I just thought it odd, you know. . . . Louise, we're going back." She looked for a place to turn around. Spotting a shoveled driveway, she slammed on the brakes, and the little car fishtailed, and almost miraculously, they ended in the lane opposite, pointed back the way they'd come.

The Ironmaster's House. Sally Ann Furnace. Louise had heard the earnest accounts: fire still glowing in the smeltery rubble, faces afloat in the windows, children's hymns rising from the chimney in clear high German. Why would her son come to such a place? Was it a way station for the misdirected dead? Would they make him wait on the porch before admitting him?

Now they were rounding the bend, but Louise was afraid to peek for fear he'd be gone, that his appearance was, in the mode of such sightings, a once-and-done affair, and blinded by timidity and distrust, she'd missed it.

"There he is!" Frank shrieked. "It *is* him. It's *our* Michael." She lay on the horn, as if the jolt might bolt him to the spot where he sat slumped on a three-legged iron settee. It was winter's spareness that opened this vision to them. Come summer the house would be engulfed by the greater mansion made of its weeds and creepers. Vague depressions remained to indicate where the wagon trail had once cut back to the glen in which backyard pig iron was cooked for Union cannons. And just beyond the house the woods began, second-growth hemlock that slathered everything below in a thick melt of iron gray shadow.

The boy on the porch did not glance up but sat hatless, neck bent, arms hanging between his legs. He wore a puffy jacket that reminded Louise of the boat Sprecher had vandalized. Never before had she seen such a stop-light yellow coat. Was he wearing the rubber raft, dredged from the landfill or wherever spirits went to scavenge their outerwear? A buoyant coat made for floating. If she rushed him now, would he float away, and if she touched his arm, would her hands fill with nothing but the down from a phantom jacket?

This time Frank remembered to lock the brake in. She got out and came around. Opening the door for Louise, she held out a hand, which Louise refused. She sat pat, craning around Frank's bulk, her eyes now pinning, now rocking the boy on the porch. "OK, then," Frank said. "Wait here, I'll be right back."

A broad swale lay between the road and the house. Weeds bleached bone-white snapped as Frank racked past. Yellowed Queen Anne's lace and stained yarrow, pennywort, the silk torn from their delicate frames. She battered into banks where clusters of scarlet sumac berries still clung and ash saplings thrust through the snow like spears. She picked around the fragile ribs of tiny trees. Then she was moving directly along the plane between Louise and her son, stopping what might be her last sweet drink of him. Louise cried out, spreading desperate fingers against the glass.

Now Frank was beside him. She turned toward Louise, and moving to the boy's right, she touched his shoulder. Whatever he was was substantial enough to support the minor weight of a nun's hand. Louise almost fainted with the rush of grace into her head. Throwing herself against the door, she rattled and kicked it open. She went stumbling across the path her friend had blazed for her. She ran to him like a wild thing. She beat on his shoulders and chest and hammered his padded parts with her cold bare knuckles.

She checked his pockets for gloves and, finding none, rubbed his hands between her palms. When she pulled his torn coat close to his body, he started coming apart like a seedpod. Silently he sat in this tiny private squall of fuzz and feathers while his mother tried desperately to slap him back together.

"My God," she said, "where's your shoe?"

"Don't worry," he said dully.

"Louise," Frank said, "don't you think we should have him checked out?"

Standing back, Louise scrutinized him. His eyes had given up half their color. They were the watery blue of Frank's tears as they stood dazed among the pampas reeds. "Your dad was right," she said. "He told me it was nothing, a fender bender; he said not to worry"—and she laughed too heartily—"for once your father was right."

She went on in manic haste, talking loud enough to disturb ghosts, and Michael touched her cheek in a gesture that was half slap, half tenderness. "Mom," he said, "I flew a long way in the air. I landed in a shrub bank, one of those, you know, snowball bushes."

"Hydrangea?"

"I guess. It was full of real snow, too. It was a much softer landing than I deserved—" And he looked out and down toward town.

She closed her eyes. And hadn't she known from the first moment she saw his face that there had to be more?

"They're all"—and he sucked back a sound that was like a terrible braking—"oh, Mom, I think they're all—dead."

Frank stiffened, and Louise dropped to her knees before her mind caught on and reminded her that this matter of faith was by no means agreed, that only moments ago she'd withheld her truest wish from heaven, treating God like a trick question. "They're all dead." Her tendons prayed and her toes curled up in their pews and her knees refused to relinquish the cold Catholic comfort of earth and ancient stones. She bowed down in gratitude—and in shame for giving thanks when others were dead on the road. Her mind pronounced her a ridiculous sight, and still, her bones hummed and the sudden abundance of life nearly crushed her.

But the nun was tugging her upward. "Come on, Louise, your son could be injured. He should be looked at."

"I can't go home yet," he said. "I can't go anyplace where it's warm. . . ." His voice trailed off, his eyes looking far away.

Something about the way he said it made the statement binding. So the women waited awhile longer. Frank sat next to him on the slanting bench, and Louise stood near in the open doorway as cold drifted in and out. She listened to tall trees shiver away the snow, the crack of shifting timbers; everywhere the smell of dry rot and age was cut by the clean, sharp blade of the solemn cold front. Chips of blue buttermilk paint remained on the wooden shutters; traces of blue sky flashed through the latticed roof.

How foolish Louise felt, remembering the scope of her immense outrageous relief. It occurred to her how it could have been otherwise, sorrow unloosed, devastation hurling her to the ground with the same vehemence. Then they were always there, she thought calmly, grief and cataclysmic gladness, waiting in the cells, waiting to liquefy, like the dried blood of the early saints. If it was in the swag of sanity and balance that we lived, was it the swing of extremes that knocked us into God? Louise felt immensely bruised, abraded beyond the bone.

Then Frank came and took her arm. Together the two friends helped the boy from the bench and led him to the car. They started to get in and stopped. They looked at one another with small, foolish smiles. The Triumph was a two-seater. So Louise took Michael on her lap, and "Louise," said Frank, "keep that finger elevated. Or you're going to lose it."

Louise, amazed that this small matter should loom important again, looked at her. Then she raised her hand as high as the roof allowed.

CHAPTER

32

They held him for observation. All night interns and nurses came and went, hardly observing him at all. Serenely indifferent, they interrogated him on the hour: "What's six times two? Your street address? Who discovered America?" "Sasquatch," he said. "Good, good, go back to sleep."

His head hurt. His thoughts were rocks knocking around in his braincase. When he tried to doze, the load shifted. He awoke, surprised all over again.

He was hammocked in branches, a boy born in a bush, his eyes risking sight one at a time. Maybe he had never been unconscious at all but merely passed rapidly through the little ages of himself, all the stages of dying, and in his eagerness to destruct politely and well, he had huffed the air out of his lungs, let his flesh go numb as punk. Giving himself up to darkness, he had waited for the milk of light, the sight of God. And he had awakened instead to the milky light of a Pennsylvania winter.

He swam down through a web of slender limbs and crawled out from under the wide skirt of a bank of hydrangeas. He stood then and looked and beheld the simple divide of blue sky and graphite line of mountain, walls and roof of his plain everyday life, and they seemed not so much common as disturbingly familiar, the framework of a place he'd passed through long ago, expecting never to return.

The hospital wrote him up and set him adrift on mended sheets. His mother and the nun went home, returning several hours later with Gideon and his sister in tow. His mother was dazed, insatiable. Mouth-sprung, she touched him so often, so probingly that his heart felt hunted and his skin hurt. His bones were buried treasure; his body lay like a gem in bed. He would never again be so prized. One by one they reached out as they filed by, as if he were the saintly relic of himself.

His family, his friends. Why was it that the closer he looked, the more unlikely they seemed to him, like common words when you tried to analyze them? Bed. Butter. Mother. The world shaken separated strangely. Who were these talkers and walkers? The girl with skimpy lashes, the boy somehow jumping out of his skin. The nun's good smile a shim off-center. He turned so that his angle of vision was more askant. Better not to observe the world in aftermath directly.

He had landed in somebody's yard. Not two feet away was a woodpile as long as a bus that he'd mercifully missed. A Christmas tree lay on its side on the porch, shiny bits still clinging. A white house with yellow curtains. Immense quiet but for the birds strung out on the overhead wires. A clash of sun glints hit him from the road, from the roofs of the two small cars. A slow-moving man and his wife, both in hunting jackets, she sobbing softly, poked in the wreckage. Michael approached them as would any neighbor roused by a jarring sound from his morning chores.

"Anna Mae fetched the ambulance," the man told him, shaking his head. The cars were inextricably combined. Yoder had been tossed like a toy into one of the back seats. Erica's face pressed against the windshield in the attitude of one trying to get a better look at some fleeting wonder.

"Down the road a ways there's more yet," the man said without glancing up. Michael turned, and his world filled up again with its precious accessories. The swift immediate detail of boy, truck, tire, tree. The two-century oak by the door of the old schoolhouse had received the Leper like an old friend. Stillness strummed, a notation of crows on the telephone lines. The crunch of the man's work boots in the snow was deafening.

They came with gifts. Mighty brought him an electronic game for geniuses and the cleansing grace of her citric scent. That big phony, frozen grin of hers. She was like some rich eccentric aunt, saying, "My, my, what have we here?" And watching from their steep perspective, those eyes his mother said came all the way from China, at once hostile and hurt and frightened and wise.

Gideon brought him flea market books, *Our Friend the Atom. What We Can*

326 / Sharon Sheehe Stark

Learn from the Wombat. Both first-person plural. Breezy, congenial titles. Gideon was his friend. Most of his friends had come by way of Mighty. Michael was his pretty sister's brother, his mother the sculptress's son. Spot was gone, but wasn't Michael fortunate to live in the shining radii of bright women? Women were wonderful. They sweetened your troubles, broke in your buddies. He leaned into the stream of Mighty's lemon fragrance. Emma Jean had already come and gone. She, too, had smelled good. "Nice dress," he'd said.

"It's old," she replied. He knew she was glad to slip out when his family came in.

He was beset with a sense of trembly expectation. For what? For the pain maybe. The same way it takes awhile after you've struck your thumb. Spot? Yoder? Her? But his body was as far away as Mighty's eyes, and his heart didn't care. He remembered now how he'd started to walk, how he'd stood in the middle of the road, turning in circles. Should he go home? Continue to school? Looking down, he noticed that one shoe was missing. Half-shod, he hobbled uphill. He wanted that lopsided struggle, tug of events at his back; at the time all his choices seemed closely considered and devoutly sound.

Now that the gifts and sympathies were tendered, all honors coming to him paid, Michael saw that he would not reap survival benefits much longer. Already his popularity had begun to wane and boredom took hold like a pocketful of August. His mother and the nun were gray with fatigue. Michael wanted to say it was all right, he understood; they had rejoiced as much as the occasion called for. Relief was bliss, but it didn't stretch very far. "Go home," he wanted to tell them. Gideon peeked at his watch, picked at his teeth. Then Mighty said, "Don't look now, but aren't we missing something? Where the hell's His Nibs?"

Louise showed her empty palms.

Mighty's pupils turned to pellets. "Michael came this close"—she pinched the air between two fingers—"and the donkey-breath creep can't even . . . Ma," she said, "you tell him he's low."

"I called him right away from emergency. I told him—"

Mighty huffed. "What'd he say, 'fuck off, I'm busy'?"

"Don't be ridiculous." Louise brushed back her bangs. "He just didn't come to the phone. Debbie buzzed and buzzed and buzzed. I had her all but kick down his door. We couldn't get a rise out of the man. God, I began to think the worse. Heart attack. Stroke. Finally I told Debbie just to yell at the top of her lungs, 'Michael's fine!' What can I say? He picked up immediately. It's my guess he'd spent the day under his desk."

Mighty crossed her arms high. "The man's always been a rock for us in times of trouble. A pillar of pudding."

"Mighty," said Louise, "don't start."

"You die first, Ma, he'll embarrass you. Guaranteed. Shit, he'll probably just walk out and leave you in your deathbed. He'll leave the country. Oh, Ma, get out and find someone nice while there's still time."

When they left, he slept. He dreamed. He woke briefly and dozed. He slept again. He and Spot are trudging up the switchback streets of some hill town in the coal regions to the north. Higher and higher, the way worsening until finally they are inching across a craggy mountain trail, rock croppings riddled with icy spikes and deep crevasses. When they stop, they are looking down the dazzling white face of a frozen waterfall. Spot laughs sadly, shaking his head. "We were wrong," he says. "This is no road."

He awoke frozen. He slept again, in a rocky bed, brain flashing faces and places and textures that made his skin crawl. He awoke to find a huge hat in his room. Because of the downtilted crown, the silhouette was flattened into a hawklike shape against the light coming from the hall. Then the brim lifted, unfurling a cocky panache and the full forward effect of a great Stetson. Sickly lit, the face beneath seemed to be weeping. With the beard and the disconsolate eyes, the man might be some lost apostle. "Hi, Dad," he said.

His father belched or caught back a breath—it was hard to tell.

"Dad, I knew you'd come. But how did you get in?"

Trover seemed disinclined to reply. With eyes already somehow too full, he drank the boy in. Then he shook his head the way he did when Michael pulled a stupid move on the mat.

"Mighty and Mum are gunning for you. This time they're really pissed."

Trover reflected on this. "I'm not a very nice person, Son," he said.

"Sure you're nice, Dad. *Extremely* nice."

"I let good people down. Or didn't you know that?"

"You have a lot of excellent qualities. Remember the time—"

"Wanna know what old high class Harry was up to tonight?"

"Dad, it's cool. Honest. I'm just glad you're here."

Ignoring him, Trover went on. "Your old pop just spent about nine and a half hours holed up with the philosophy department down at Banana Dan's."

"Tavern?"

"Hold it, I take that back. Philosophers, hell, they were biologists, more or less, *marine* biologists. We got into a big kefoofal over who was smarter, poodles or porpoises. (You listening to this?) Shoot, I don't know poodles from pineapples. But hey, God bless you, boy, you have to hand it to the dolphins. What those suckers couldn't tell you if you'd just take the trouble to sit down and learn sonar."

"That's an awesome hat, Dad."

"Want you to know, Mikey, me boyo, this is my one commendable deed of the evening. Bought myself this hey, hey, hallelujah hat. Bought it right off the gentleman's head."

"One of those marine biologists?"

Trover thought a minute. "No, this guy was more"—he grinned—"a demand-side *economist*." He hunkered close, confidingly. "A burglar," he whispered. "Hat's probably hot off the premises. Ain't it a peach, though? Comes fully equipped. Hey, you want one like this, I'll get you one. Hell, what am I saying? You can have mine." Taking the hat in both hands, he solemnly presented it.

"No, thanks, Dad. I wouldn't feel right accepting your hat."

"It's yours, m'fair-haired boy, prince of my kingdom."

"Dad, you keep it, please."

"You need anything else? Use a little cash?"

"Not at the moment."

He wiped his glasses and jiggled them back on. "Couple clients came in to see me today."

"Yeah?"

"Old couple—about ninety-six years old apiece. Come in for a divorce. 'Whooooooa,' I say. 'How many years you two nice people been hitched?' 'Seventy-five,' they say. 'And every year more miserable than the last.' So I look at these two pips. 'Hey,' I say, 'if it was so bad, why didn't you get out before now?' "

"So what'd they say?" Michael asked on cue.

" 'We were waiting for the children to die.' "

"Come on, Dad. That's a joke, right?"

Trover produced a grimace of fake contrition. "You caught me red-handed, kid."

"Dad, under the circumstances, don't you think it's sort of in bad taste? I mean, about kids dying."

"Boy, is your old man ever a yahoo."

"I love you, Dad," he said, closing his eyes. He felt the air stir, felt the heat from his father's hand just inches above his brow. He pretended to fall asleep to let his father drift away as unceremoniously as he'd drifted in. Sometime later, when he opened his eyes, the cowboy hat was on the chair and his dad had vanished.

He had some frostbite on his foot. No big deal. But his head still ached. Who knew but that he didn't harbor yet some deep undetected wound, a frayed vein, a thinning blister about to drown his thoughts in blood?

If he died now, would any of them have the strength to mourn again?

* * *

They would be buried from their own towns, Yoder from Alsace, Erica from Lorraine. The paper, which recounted the scene insinuatingly, pointedly added that arrangements for both were private. No flowers, no donations, meaning the bereaved were too mortified to come out of the house. People should be careful not to die compromised. The tears, Michael thought, would taste funny; they wouldn't think twice about cremation.

Michael skittered in and back from the edge of sorrow. He circled the deaths, not knowing quite what to make of them yet. He had known not Erica but his golden version of her. Now both were beyond him, and her leaving was the slight loss of light when the door is closed another inch.

Spot was laid out at Itterly's in Lorraine. Michael had once spent a night in that house. He was staying over with Kib Itterly the night before a summer tournament. They put him in a finished basement bedroom just under the viewing parlor, which lay between him and the Itterly family quarters on the second floor. He stayed awake a long time, trying to catch the drift of absolute silence above him, but the hum of blood in his ear interposed, and the sporadic rumble of truck traffic through the empty streets of Lorraine soon bullied him to sleep.

It was understood and accepted now that Trover abstained from all viewings and funerals. It was not even his wont to bring home unpleasant news, so that Louise often ran into the widow a year later and, not having heard, happily asked, "How's John?" And when Trover read that the Air Force band was already rehearsing Richard Nixon's funeral, he rattled the newspaper angrily. "Government ghouls," he said. "Sick, sick!"

Clothe the naked, bury the dead; nobody dared even hint as much to Trover. Prudently they refrained even from inviting him along. The four of them got ready to go, moving circumspectly, casting him smiles like scraps of meat, careful lest they rouse in him some jiggle of guilt, a stitch of shame. Shame would split him into a team of leaping devils, each one more than they could, even collectively, handle. They didn't argue. Hell-bent nonetheless, he argued back. He accused them of disapproval, pursued them with excuses. He felt the grippe coming on. Tons on his mind, lives and fortunes resting on his head. He made lively debate from the doorway to the Room, where he hung upside down in the heretofore unused gravity boots. "Hey, I'm wrecked at the end of the day," he said, his face cherry-red. "Or didn't you know that?"

They tried to ignore him, tried to be nice. They brought him everything he asked for: the newspaper; Chapstick; a cup of Ovaltine. He chased them up and down three flights until finally, inevitably, somebody balked.

"Damn!" Mighty said. "How can he read the paper like that? How can anybody drink cocoa upside down?"

"Peristaltic action, dodo," he said, trying to lift his chin.

"Oooof!" Mighty said. "Why does he want so much?"

Louise jammed her feet into knee-high boots. "Mighty," she said, "if you were hanging by the heels, wouldn't you want everything, too? Everything!"

He came down from torment with the air of one harassed out of his favorite chair. He couldn't find his watch and accused Louise of stealing it. He wanted Gideon's junk out of the garage. "Not tonight. Not tomorrow. Now!" And Mighty, Miss Wiseacre, just wait, she'd get educated someday! "Michael," he yelled, "get in here. Toot sweet!" When his son slunk in, he said, "See what you did."

"What?"

"Shit for brains!"

"Just tell me straight, Dad. What'd I do?"

"Pick it up, will you?"

"Huh?"

Michael peered down and found himself staring at the cloth arm protector from the green chair. A minute inspection failed to uncover anything remarkable about the thing. He cast a puzzled glance at his father.

"I knew it! You *are* planning to leave it. Good old Michael can't be bothered with the mundanities."

"I didn't put it there."

"What you're saying is you refuse to pick it up."

"That's not what I meant."

"Fine, I don't wear singlets, I won't pay for them. I don't eat all the food, so why should I work my ass off to feed ingrates? And who's gonna pay for your education, huh? Don't look at *me*, I already got mine!"

Mighty flew in, her upper lip half-painted. She pointed her lipstick at him. "Can it, Dad. Don't you know what this kid's been *through*?"

"Fine," said Trover. "Simple solution. Every time there's a tragedy in town, we'll all run around throwing things on the floor." Swooping up his saucer, he let it drop to the rug. A double-barreled stomp, and it cracked in half. Then he wiped his feet on the fallen arm protector.

"Who's thumping around?" Louise called from somewhere far away.

"It's him," Mighty yelled back. "Didn't I tell you he'd go ape-shit today?"

"You said ignore him." Michael chided his sister quietly. He was so small now they probably couldn't see or hear him. He was a speck in the center of perplexity.

"Get out of here," Mighty said, watching her mother approach. "You'll just make him worse. He can't resist showing off for his girl. That's you, Louise!"

Louise lowered Mighty's outstretched arms and battered through to her husband. "Now you stop agitating. This is no time for one of your numbers." Her big erect finger made her seem more formidable than she was.

"Right," Trover said. "Times are tough. Let's all live like Okies. Here, I'll get the ball rolling." He emptied a jar of pencils and pens into a deer's-foot fern. Rocketing around, he swept all the magazines off the end table. He pirouetted and slid on their slippery covers.

A running jump, and he was aboard the sofa in the adjoining room. "Wheeeee!" he cried. "Come on, gang. Let's go for broke. Jump on the home decor, that's what it's here for. Right, Mighty, old friend?" He flashed a mean, seedy grin and hopped over the sofa arm and, gesturing behind him, like some kind of music man gone mad, beckoned them to follow wherever the spleen would lead him.

In the kitchen they watched him fill the sink with water. A squirt of air from the empty Joy container. "We don't need this," he explained to the nun, and, snagging up the blender, plunked it in the drink. He added the carving knife. "This is a highly sophisticated tool," he said. "Not for these hillbillies." The toaster, the yogurt maker, the waffle iron. "We're above life's little facilities," he said. "Hey, the Mixmaster's a killer!"

"Gideon, take an end." He was back in the living room now, bending over the long cocktail table. When Gideon demurred, he grabbed the scalloped table edge himself and, heaving up, easily flipped it.

The boys set it immediately upright. Frank scrambled to grab up the burning butt she'd left in the ashtray. Bagel was hiding under the end table. Dropping to her knees, Mighty fell upon the two halves of the clay old lady she'd made in third grade. The statue had a speckled liver-spotted breast that had run into the neckline of her bodice. It was a squat, stupid piece she'd never treasured. Until now. Madonnalike, golden hair veiling her downcast face, she clutched her creation close and wept.

"Oh, woe is me!" Trover taunted from his post on the bottom step. "Thespians, bunch of Meryl Streeps!" But his voice was threadbare now, and as he stood clutching the banister, panting hard, the women came together like a trinity of keeners, all three groveling in the rubble, broken things in their hands.

Glancing up, Michael caught a pinch of inquiry around his father's eyes, then a split second of such profound remorse that his irises seemed to glow around the brown rim, a meltdown fierce enough to destroy an ordinary man. Not Trover. With a visible effort he hauled himself back from the brink. "Just doing my bit, good buddies," he said then. "Like to give you guys a head start turning our life into—landfill." He started upstairs. He backed down two steps, raising a hand. "No need to thank me."

When he was safely upstairs, Frank turned to Louise, her face splotchy with disgust. "What do you want with that, that—"

And conjured immediately all the treasures of Michael's someone had questioned at one time or another. What do you want with that rock, that root, those rusty beer cans? What do you want with those IBM brochures, that dirty turtle shell . . . ?

"That, that *maniac*! You put up with that stuff, you're wackier than he is."

Mighty spoke more matter-of-factly. "I'm killing him," she said. With the same demonic ardor her father had shown she scampered from otto-man to sofa arm to piano bench. She landed on a step edge and hurled herself over the banister. Stumbling with rage, she fell up the steps.

"Should I go after her?" Gideon asked.

Louise considered, then shook her head. "Let her be," she said. "As long as she doesn't have a gun."

Thunk. Crack. Clunk. From the sound of it she was beating on the door with her shoe and kicking with a stocking foot. If she couldn't get at him, it was because Trover was bracing the door. "Come out of there, rat! Cow-ard! Why did you bust my great-grandmother? You come out right now. Answer me, you twerp." More furious pounding, then slow token thumps, and then it seemed the ire started to die of its own frustration as once more his ramparts held. Michael imagined his father on the other side, terrified, biting his wristbone.

Mighty came down in slinking defeat. Flushed, mussed, she was exquis-ite. Louise brushed a strand of wet yellow hair from her cheek. "Oh, Mighty Mack," she said, "I didn't know that old woman was Geggo."

"How could you?" Mighty said. "I just now figured it out myself."

When Louise reached for her, Mighty let herself be taken. Hunched stiffly under her mother's wing, she drew deep breaths until the trembling stopped. "Let's go if we're going," she said then, tonelessly.

Louise let her go. "Give me a second to get myself together." Gideon sat down with Michael's BB maze; Bagel came out. To the rhythm of Trover's thumping overhead, Louise started pacing the house. She returned from the dining room with a hat in her hand. Smoothing the orange and emer-ald pinfeather, she said, "Remember the night he came home with this hat?"

Mighty sighed. "Not that ladybug sob story again."

But it was as though a door had opened to a whiff of something oddly, imprecisely inviting. That state of not quite sober, not quite drunk when

Trover was as lovable as they come, when wobbly of will and mentally slack, he was theirs for the asking. "Yeah," said Michael, "I remember that."

"Well, after you kids went to bed that night, your dad and I watched a movie about an amazing nuclear-powered bus. He's fun to watch junk with, you have to give him that. He'd left his hat out on the kitchen table. Every commercial he'd run out and check on that insect's condition. Sometimes I went with him. We'd hold hands and gaze down. It was a way to be close, you know, loving something simultaneously. 'But what do they eat?' I finally asked. 'She'll starve. Ladybugs don't eat hats, do they?'

"Well, he looked at me, his face so deep and serious. 'If she wants my hat, she can have it,' he said." Louise's smile was small, a seed needing the full light of her children's complicity. She expected them to know just how much she had loved him at that moment.

Mighty girded herself anew. "Maybe bugs are more his speed. Maybe he loves bugs and tears the legs off people."

Gideon grinned. "I got it. You guys dress up like bugs so he'll be nice to you."

"Shut up with the bugs," Michael said. He felt oddly crowded; something bad was gathering at the soft edge of his consciousness.

But Mighty was looking her mother over. "Bottom line, Ma. Truth. You'll never leave him, will you? No matter what he pulls. Hell, he's home free."

"Oh, won't I?" Louise sucked her cheeks, carving out a stark angularity she had no natural claim to. "I've been thinking, these things aren't optional; no, it's the least he can do. Your father doesn't show up at that boy's viewing tonight, that's it. I've decided."

"*She's* decided!" Mighty sneered. As if addressing incredulous multitudes. And Michael had a sudden picture of a family's life, a photo made of a million tiny dots, the countless soft decisions some sucker woman made *not* to send the guy packing. One *hard* decision could erase all that. Oh, yes, he'd seen the glint of alarm in his sister's eyes.

And now Gideon was poking her. "Shhh, he's coming down."

Lest he somehow escape their notice, Trover descended with increasing emphasis on each step. At the base of the staircase he threw open the closet and started to shove the coats around. Incredibly for a man so recently under siege by a girl with murder in her shoe, he was whistling, well, not whistling but piping jets of tuneful air.

"Where's my new yellow parka?" he grumbled.

"It's all in shreds, Dad. It was in the accident with me. I think it helped save my life."

"From now on nobody take my stuff," Trover said.

"Ass!" from Mighty.

He settled on a plaid mackinaw and an Irish tweed cap. These, in concert with the red beard and ferocious eyes, created a crazy vision of maniacal cockiness—some freshly sprung jack-in-the-box leprechaun, a larking sort who added spice to insipid lives (and got no thanks for it). Such verve, forced or not, offended the hurtful strictness in Michael's heart. Mighty looked but said nothing.

Popping in two sticks of gum, Trover made a case of masticating it, chomping like a wise guy. He was obnoxious, too, with his keys, rattling them, deliberating at great length: *Zip-uh-de-do-duh, let me see, think I'll leave to a lively beat.*

"Oh, no!" cried Louise, for at that moment—and Michael felt only a blessed wrench into rightness—he heaved off his seat, hurling himself at the spiffy figure stopped in the open doorway, storm door partially ajar. Taking Trover around the thighs, he gave not a thought for leniency; it was only by dumb luck he missed whipping him into the newel-post or against any number of deadly edges and angles as, spinning with him, running, he dumped him savagely onto his back.

Michael's heart sputtered and thundered. The storm door clicked shut. Father and son looked at each other with the mildly miffed surprise of friends crossing paths in a strange place each had been keeping secret from the other. Then Trover's eyes slammed shut, and Michael plowed him hard against the baseboard.

Part of the shock was how easily his dad had been felled. Michael hadn't wrestled him since junior high, when for the eighty-seven-pounder, it was boy against side of beef. Now the older man seemed small and dry, the meat of aged pine. Michael could hold him at bay with one smallish hand.

Trover was landlocked on one side, a regional champ strapping him in on the other. Shackled, totally exposed, he managed to take a lusty swipe at Michael's face. Michael ducked, then turned to the gawking onlookers. "He's still trying to hit me!" he said in amazement.

Michael looked down at his father's battened face. Now what? What was Michael to do with this man? What mischief would he commit if Michael let him go? What about food, water? What about school? Spot's viewing? For a gentle boy his next thought was shocking: Either finish him off or move on.

Now, as he stared, Trover's eyes flew open with an aggressive suddenness that made Michael flinch. Just inches beneath his nose lay those bottomless brown depths of irreversible injury. Almost immediately Michael suffered a giddy collapse of bicep and resolve. What's more, Bagel's teeth were in his belt and she was trying to pull Michael off the man she loved.

He felt himself reel as the moment merged with his struggle against Sprecher. He could still taste that snow. Poor old man, he'd done similar damage up at Tumbling Run, and they'd filed charges. As a result, he was back in Neisstown General's wacko ward. He'd never get out now. Michael winced, weakened. Turning away, he tried to hide his misgivings behind a moronic smile.

But wait! This was *his* game. He was boss on the carpet. His body, knowing as much, brought him back from silliness. He shook the dog off roughly and gave his dad a quick, unforgiving glance. The mouth was drawn so tight you'd think it was a purse Michael might pry open and pilfer. And that mouth was what inspired Michael's next move. "Say it, Dad," he said sternly. He was taut, tough, running with expertise and inspiration. "Now *you* say it," he said.

Trover tightened and twisted sideways.

From somewhere out there came Mighty's voice, nervous, uncertain. "Michael, maybe you shouldn't push . . . maybe . . ."

Michael drove in hard enough to hurt. "Say it, Dad," he said. Say what? Like a soldier of fortune summoning plunder, Michael's mind chased the possibilities. What gems could be wrested here? *I'm sorry? I love you? I praise the day you were born?* No, he could not hear his dad speak any of these things. Moments passed. Then he shackled tighter still and smiled icily. "Say it, Dad," he said again. "Say, 'Son, you can eat my hat if you want to.'"

Trover said, "You'd better have a good job lined up, boy."

Behind them somebody laughed. But Michael was suddenly drained, devoid of comeback. He had caught that ether whiff of sorrow. He wanted to lie down and cry; he wanted to sleep. "Oh, crap," he said, dropping his full weight across Trover's chest, their two hearts thin walls apart. Michael laid his cheek against the carotid pulse. He breathed his father in. With his last pennyweight of strength he wedged his head under Trover's chin and pushed. He hadn't the heart for more.

"Kids, get your coats," he heard his mother say.

Then Michael rolled off, and Trover was unloosed. Like some stuffed thing that got sat on, he plumped up slowly, moaning. He shook his head; he sat; he stood. He wiggled each foot and swung his arms in arcs of diminishing amplitude. He shook his head again. He would never get over this!

"Where's my hat?" he demanded, obviously too broken in body and spirit to search for it.

And Mighty seemed to come from nowhere, bearing not the Irish cap but the famous ladybug fedora. As she pressed close, dropping it with lofty unconcern on her father's head, Michael heard her whisper, "Get your ass to Itterly's. Or *she's* leaving you."

Trover removed the hat and, taking it urbanely by the pinch, made a case of jiggling it to just the right raffish tilt. He walked out like a man of the world.

Spot's father received them dressed in faded jeans, a pretty friend at his side. Around his neck an eminence of chunky turquoise and silver, proof of pedigree, totems of his lost tribe and their proud but peaceable ways. He had the pallor, too, and the stoop, of one who'd been at chemical peace with himself since the stunned sixties. He kissed each burning cheek as the wrestlers slouched past into the candlelit parlor. Incense pots smoked among the flowers. Michael thought of Yoder, father of sons, fixer of toasters and tricycles. Once he'd watched him chip ice from his wife's windshield. The small misery of jock itch. The solid common Yoder he knew. But what about the floating Yoder, the man dancing all day in class, in secret raptures because Erica adored him? She looked on him with love in her smoky purple eyes. Was he, Michael wondered, was Yoder smoke by now?

Michael had forgot. Spot's real name was John. The brass plate said "John Jacob Grayrain." It shamed Michael to look. To stare at a friend's death was knowing something bad about somebody nice. The knowledge itself seemed aggressive. Still, he could not look away. He lingered too long. Spot in his warm-up suit. Just two days ago he'd been gaunt, gangly, four shadows sunk deep in his face. Death had somehow rounded him out. Nobody would say he looked hungry now.

People kept brushing up to him to say, "Kid, it doesn't come any closer." They looked deep in Michael's eyes. Did they expect him to look older or holier? But he could marshal no sense of what it was he'd escaped. He understood nothing. Wrong as it was to stare, he persisted, shamelessly surveying this incomparable stillness. Squinting, he imagined himself in Spot's place, he Michael, laid down in dark, flesh embedded in cold. He looked for death inside his own heart as one might search for mercy or truth. Was death a dull ache, the white ache at the heart of a stone? Was it dense as stone, weightless as an ache? He looked and looked and learned nothing. It was like trying to see into the dark outside without turning off the lights. The division between the living and dead was not like the line between Pennsylvania and Ohio but a wall as thin and yet high as the sky. The wall was his life. He stood in sublime stupidity behind it, and not even grief came to ferry him closer.

Two sniffling cheerleaders flanked him, then dropped back with a strange, graceful synchronism. He looked again. Why had he not noticed before how the white patch had expanded? Spot's head was now as solidly white as Mr. Grayrain's. He thought of high school actors playing old men with powdered heads, their pink mouths and bright carmine cheeks, their youth shining through no matter what they did to mask it. Spot forever young; he would wait like that, an adolescent granddad, while Michael and the Packs plodded past him. And some of the wrestlers would die in middle age, others blend into real old men, and then just like that none of those increments would mean a thing, and they would be a team outside time, old or young or however forever arranged things. Spot in his wrestling magentas forever.

He felt himself sway as if he were fighting heavy winds high above the boy in the box. A succession of friends joined him, made attempts to console with the same awkward gestures they used to buck up the kid who'd been whipped on the mat. Then Spot's dad drew Michael aside. "Not a mark on him," he confided. He said that almost proudly. "Brain stem," he added, touching the back of his own neck. It came out in the local cadence, rising at the end like a question. And Michael thought he could hear the delicate snap of the stalk, the flower head perfectly whole, so improbably dead.

Michael had scratches, a puffy eye. These wounds, he knew, only added to the man's confusion. His life, the size of it! His very presence was an assault to the sedated eyes of the man and girl. She wore a lacy blouse and smelled of musk oil and ironing. Your kid was trucking, he should confess. Because I wasn't ready when he came for me. I own no watch. I gave no warning.

But guilt came no more easily than grief. He withdrew into deeper distance; the room looked suddenly vast and hazy and recessive. He smelled its secrets; he suspected the falseness of its walls. This was too much, beyond his power to have caused. Who was he but a fair to middling middleweight? He had no weight at all in this dimension.

In his great unbearably arid remove from things, he took the particulars in, the little pinwheels of benign gossip. Two out of three Panthers were tying their shoelaces, faces hidden between their knees. His mother sat with Mrs. Kern on a velvet settee, Louise listening with a strange lacquered intensity.

He still hadn't come up with a single consoling word for Steve Grayrain. He took his hands out of his pockets. His fingertips were cold as roller bearings. He tucked them back in. Mr. Grayrain turned and tried to hug him. "Chin up, young Kleeve. Our seed is sown on the wind. Honor the flux."

Michael nodded minutely. He looked at the man's pupils. Pinpricks. Eyes defending against light, and loss. They had been buddies, he and his son. They called each other Chief. Lived in squalor, ate out of cans, their life together one long bivouac. No woman to nudge them into prickly intimacy. Honor the flux. No woman to worry and shop and do their public mourning for them. The word "flux" hovered like some clumsy shorebird. Michael had the sudden lunatic urge to punch the man and seize his girl. Ashamed, he wrenched his gaze away.

Two women teachers came with their arms out to Mr. Grayrain. Michael gratefully stepped out of their way. He stood breathing in the fumes from the incense and flowers; the summery air and whispery talk made him light-headed. At first he thought he was seeing things. Just inside the double doorway, where Mr. Itterly was directing entries into a big black register, a latecomer was signing in. Small, balding, he had a decided lean to him and a funny hunch. And incredibly, like some kind of suitor, he carried flowers. Didn't he know any better? Of course, he didn't. He had so little experience in this area. And he was probably half-plastered.

Trover came timorously across the forest green carpet; it seemed to take him days and days, so great was the distance, the effort even greater. Michael knew what the gesture had cost him.

He watched his mother rise, finger shushing her lips, face lit with a kind of radiant pain, as if she'd been bitten by a miracle. She stepped forward, then stopped, smiling at herself. It was, after all, no big thing. Just one man among many come to confront the dead.

Mouth crimped in benevolent interest, Trover dawdled now like a tourist. He clasped the flowers behind his back. Every several feet he stopped to gaze wonderingly up at the terraced baskets of carnations, daisies, and glads. From there he proceeded falteringly forward; he stopped several feet from the candlelit grotto. He bowed his head before remembering himself. Removing his hat, he bowed down again. Several seconds later Michael watched him lift, more from the waist than from the toes, peering in for just an instant. Then, in the same barely perceptible stretch, he reached out with his gift. Balancing the bouquet on the rim of the casket, clutching his hat close, he strode briskly out of the room.

Just before the accident Michael had experienced a rumble deep beneath him, like a tectonic shift. He remembered it now as while he watched his dad, it happened again: the dizzying lurch of something huge and immutable budging the tiniest bit.

CHAPTER

33

DEAR RITA,
Every time I get to feeling righteous or wise, along comes another longhand
bill of particulars whistling with exclamation points to instruct me otherwise. I'd thought it was settled: God is my judge, and I His. But since you
insist, I suppose we can always make room for one more in the vast
bureaucracy of opinion mediating between us.

Unopened in my hand, your letters already weigh on my conscience. It
came as a great relief this time to find the heft much taken up with redun-
dancies and summaries, lengthy elaborations of old matters, rather than
the twelve or so pages of brand-new damnings I shudder to imagine. Still,
Rita, you should understand that with every disapproving word, you
power us deeper into our idiosyncrasies, our houses shunt farther apart;
soon you'll spin us off entirely. We will be like the Falasha Jews, left to our
tents and quirky texts. Generations hence some curious scion of your line
will trace back and find us, the lost tribe, the dark and forgotten ones, and
then somebody wise will have to rule on whether or not we qualify for rec-
lamation.

But, Rita, don't mistake my tone. In matters of taste and diet and de-
cency, we concede nothing. If we slump in our chairs at your house, it is not

only to stay low against raised eyebrows but to hide the heights of a reciprocal "attitude." We don't approve of you either. Privately, you know, Mighty snorts at your "wall treatments" (she has small appreciation for mine either). Trover thinks you eat too high on the food chain. We watch appalled as your youngest gobbles butter by the chunk. We own cars without troubling to understand them; you know their parts too intimately for our taste. We buy the best and wreck it. You keep ugly things shining. Rita, not so many generations back, we were hucksters, miners, mulekeepers, seamstresses. Huns before that. What a marvelous sight it is, all of us so bright-eyed and bossy now, bopping around in the middle class. We can only pray that we accustom ourselves no deeper than is necessary to cover our debts and stay out of jail.

I am sorry that Maddy left here nursing a "bigger headache than she arrived with." But it was Christmas, and the casualties here are pretty general. (You heard about my finger.) I must say, however, from the face of it, most of what she reported back to you, though rooted in fact, carries the distinct ring of the Lackawanna rewrite, that arcane procedure whereby the two of you, over coffee, make deathless family legends out of tidbits and quibbles. The Dutch have their quilts; the Irish, their stories.

Take the mouse affair, for instance. It began not in "squalor and irresponsibility," as you claim, but with a simple need to deal effectively with a mounting pest problem. There were the usual complications, technological snags, inclement weather, the muddying drug of compassion, all of which factors somehow managed to accrue, as is often the case, to the good of the hunted one. With a little duct tape the humane trap Michael had used to catch the mouse easily converted to a capacious cage, its webbing so tight as to allow in precious little more than light and his daily ration of peanut butter. Escapeproof, Michael assured us. Who could have imagined that the little dickens could make himself intangible? (The Masai of East Africa have a similar skill. Rarely can they be incarcerated for more than several weeks before they slip out through the bars. Only their bodies remain behind. Thus for them every imprisonment is a virtual death sentence.) The mouse, as you know, did not die but found a new life next to the giant *M* in Maddy's handbag. We don't doubt for a second that she is unaccustomed to "cuddling up with rodents," and we deeply regret her subsequent distress. Still, I hope you can see that the crisis arose not from malice but from the playing out of conflicting decencies. We felt terrible, I assure you. And the mouse? I suspect that he's more at home in the middle class than we are. In any case, he remains at large to this day, living more traditionally, by his own wits and the grace of plates left out and unswept cutting boards.

As for "driving out" her son on Christmas Eve (her words or yours?)—but yes, I guess I did, though it was a passive-aggressive driving out if ever there was one. And there was Maddy, husbandless, suddenly sonless as well, commended to the disgruntled company of people who were, without

Trover as go-between, practically strangers. And yes, she read me right. I did resent her that night, and bitterly! For giving him life, for not suffocating him in his bassinet, for loving him too much or not enough, for whatever excuse she gave him to live out his married life as a gangster. But it was just a thought, Rita. Mean, but fleeting. After all, it *was* Christmas.

You're right. My son is too thin, and it's unquestionably "criminal" to deny food to growing bodies. But wrestlers and their coaches have perfected affectionate techniques for quelling maternal protest. Hugs and head pats, go home and fuss no more. At the moment Michael is thinner than ever. (He's dropped a weight-class for states.) What starvation hasn't taken from him, the accident has. He goes about hollowed out, lit with a kind of set perplexity, as if he were listening to something that won't come closer. He never cries. It seems almost miraculous that he's come through the postseason rounds undefeated. Tell Maddy it's looking good for states. If he can just stay healthy another week or so.

To that end we've been holding him in what might be called protective intensive custody. He's kept warm and out of drafts. Lord knows the boy is accident-prone, so he's monitored constantly. Let him as much as attempt to unstick a cupboard, Trover yells, "Break a finger, dodo, and it's all over!" If the stores sold germ-free environments, Michael would be a boy in a bubble.

Gideon McThee moved quickly to fill in, eagerly taking on jobs outside Michael's current limits. What a blessing it was—a strong back not being saved for something better. He helped transport my families. He provided a fresh outlook by rearranging the furniture. He repaired leaks and helped us locate those elusive notions, cuticle scissors, Scotch tape, the terms of Christian existence. He checked out a pile of water-damaged small appliances and declared them pretty much defunct. He organized the Room for me, but now that he's gone, the old comminglings are beginning again as the family personality creeps inexorably back, so if Maddy wants to see neat, she'd better look fast.

And speaking of Gideon, I find no connection whatsoever between that boy and the "breaking down of the fiber of American life." True, he and Mighty lived under the same roof; we all did. There is only one roof, truly. It's been an odd, many-way relationship. I believe he wanted the corporate, symphonic us as much as any single one, especially as Mighty began weening herself away. She had introduced a functionally homeless kid into her household, and once it appeared the graft had taken, she cut herself loose. She's since fallen in with a colorful bunch of country-style punkers at school, where she polishes this new facet of herself with the fastidious abandon of some housewife liberated after twenty years of rocking babies and rolling socks. And Gideon, who apparently was not about to begin his life until he had some place real to shove off from, finally left with our blessing. Last week we traded him the Jeep truck for his little Triumph.

The very next day he headed west with a load of golden oak for the insatiable California market.

So please let Mighty be. Insinuate against her again, I'll have to punch you. That may be the only way I know to defend my daughter, whom I love in the dark, in the nervous reprieve of all that remains unsettled between us. With her, I am always at such a loss, as inept and debt-ridden as I used to be with the most draconian nuns, especially the ones who seemed to look askance at the authenticity of my "calling." She, too, makes me feel like a prisoner of higher, prior knowledge. Her eyes weld me to my impostorhoods. As mother/other woman I am known as only the enemy must be known, even as its ways remain inscrutable.

It goes without saying that she's more of your side than mine. I stir her thus to frights of xenophobia. But her father perturbs her even more, for he will not take up the burden of their broad similarities. Will not or cannot. In any case, as a natural ally he has failed her. And she makes him pay. And I try to translate them both into easier terms. And Michael looks at us these days as if we were *all* dying. We carry one another like hot potatoes of the heart. What *will* become of us? Someday I suppose we'll know the full scope of our vandalisms. (I know she didn't mean to grind up my finger, but . . .) Some of the damages will wax silly, some negligible, but up against the profound and irreversible injury we'd better know what forgiveness is for or gear up for group therapy (another prickly bunch, bet on it).

I must say, your new tack caught me off guard. I was used to letters that went to every length to spare Trover the dose meant for me. This time you dump it down his throat. It turns out you don't even like his pretty beard. What happened to the Eagle Scout? you ask. Where is the boy who worshiped the ground his mother walked on? Rita, you should know better. He's far too smart to answer such questions.

But I'm not. The Scout, from what I can determine, is coming crankily awake after a thirty-year snooze. Trover looks more and more to the hills that prowl like galleons out behind our house. More likely than not of late he takes the back roads home, even the ones that miss us, as they say, by a country mile. For several months now he's been breaking in a very relentless-looking pair of hiking boots. He's looking into boats and quotes frequently from Michael's *Wonderful World of Knots*. Whether or not these developments have any material effect on the personality disorders implied by the Scout question should make for an interesting follow-up study in years to come.

As to the thing between a man and his mother. Oh, Rita, don't we both know how it goes? For better or worse, under sly disguise or brashly, with stumbling wonder or tender awkwardness, they will have their dance, long after he leaves home. Rita, we're lovers for such a short spell before the new stage is set. Begin the bad dreams and the scratchy throats, those grown men start calling with small voices, calling your kids by their siblings' names. And those eerie times when they're looking right at you, no, through you—beseeching some other.

True, there's supposed to be a new breed hybridizing out there. Men in aprons who aren't afraid to say "sauté," who know where the fever thermometer's kept. Let me say I approve without much enthusiasm, for I trust little in the stability of the line. Certainly the social transactions of the past two decades have put some fear into them, but behind the complaisance and the pieties, I detect the glint of the same sort of guile developed by overscolded, extra-gentrified peoples everywhere. These men aren't so much new as retooled for new uses. Granted, they show some humility, tact, manners. Good. An A in deportment is no mean achievement. And serves the general tranquility well until the gentlemen get tired or fired or influenza, in which case I understand that with rare exception they revert to the more primitive form. And when they die, they'll cry not "wife" but "mother," meaning no doubt both of us, as did their fathers and grandfathers before them.

Adulthood comes to us all, I think, not as a systemic condition but as a hat we're old enough to wear. On a windy day, on a high mountain, when the hat flies off like a hawk, all pretense rises like the heat from the top of our heads: we stand as children before Big Government and God. So we ascend and descend through forms that nestle like Russian peasant dolls. We take great pride in the large days. Some of us are heroes but never all the time or in every way. Think of the old ones, aching, enfeebled. It takes more strength than they can sometimes summon to sustain the face of dignified age. They regress, we say. They stop taking losses like a man. Or, more aptly, like a woman. For women are better at this, don't you think? We have learned early whence the comfort comes. We are mothers to others and mothers to ourselves. So we stomp and whine, then rock ourselves to sleep.

Does that answer it? By now you must have forgotten the question. It would be simpler for all of us if you just did the natural thing and defended your brother as before—blindly, blindly. If you don't, we will. In terms of the nest of peasants, Trover's a bad one over a good one over a bad one, and what can I say but that we want all of them and especially the something good that pulls us toward the core with the ticking promise of a cache of pure uranium? This he cannot hide. Nor the fact that he's funny and generous and incorruptible. He will not be bullied except perhaps by lesser men, for which phenomenon I offer no rationale beyond behold! Another discrepancy heard from.

I must tell you that my first impulse upon reading your letter was to hide it. I wanted to *protect* my husband; he's had more than his share lately. Death, domestic strife, night court, day court, no wonder he drinks. In addition, he's thrown himself into a major legal offensive against a local car dealer named Lum, who, having recently acquired a fleet of distributorships and several Heap Big Cleans, has apparently conglomerized himself into a target large enough for Trover to take on. I hid that letter for love, I swear it. But you know how these kindnesses can turn. First serious spat we had, I released it with a force only enlarged by the righteous strength with which I'd held it back. I let him know exactly who and what he was and used your letter to prove it. So, Rita, unless you don't mind being brandished, I suggest you take care what you commend to the weaponry of print.

Tell Maddy to simmer down. Sister Innocent bussed back to Pittsburgh some weeks ago, so we're no longer "running a shelter for runaway nuns." I miss her. When she came here, a circle closed for me. My life became of a piece somehow; both parts, the then and now of it, began to flow together. We were mirrors, too, to each other, to the flicker of unlived histories. We eyed each other slyly, and we talked even more than we used to, though I noticed that neither of us could discuss goodness and truth or sex at first without some blushing. One day somebody mentioned the nuclear age, which still seems new after forty years of prowling out there. She confessed to me that every time the subject comes up, her first thought is, God, what if a bomb goes off, she'd get separated from her tweezers and her eyebrows would grow together in the middle. I laughed that day and felt happy without knowing why. Maybe it was just that brave little fear in the face of the big one, the human eyebrow asserting itself over the unimaginable. It made me feel free to love my life: However menacing, it's mine. I want it!

She writes that she's finding the tighter rhythms of convent life rather restful after the bucking exacerbations of ours. The nuns can be just as touchy and coy and stubborn and glum, she says, but we family types are fully combustible, as it seems blood laces relationships as nothing else can. I understand that she was well received at Mercy, that for the first few days after returning she shamelessly raked in the proverbial joy over one proverbial recovered lamb. But by now, I suspect, it's out of Proverbs and into the unclassed middle of things, which is where most of us plod on, with the vigor and bewilderment and occasional transcendence of the not-yet-saved.

So Maddy considers my sculptures a bunch of fish faces and a waste of time. No fair. Mothers-in-law may criticize the slumgullion but not the art. I caught her inspecting them when she was here. "Why, they's white as ghosts," she said, frowning down upon my people. But I was thinking how very pale *she* looked. It was the blanching wash of winter light she stood in; it was that terrible unuttered grief bleeding her in secret. She whitened even as I watched. She and Michael share this translucence now; it's almost as though they can't help shining through themselves in spots. As I sit here, I am looking at a little Swamproot Cure bottle that Gideon dug for me in a local dump. In it is a bone of frailest February light. If we may think of the soul as a bone of light, then I say we are nothing until we are whittled down to that bone of bones, raw to every onlooker. Michael heard his grandmother cry one night. Although reluctant to expose her so, he reasoned that if we knew, we'd be more careful, handle her with the delicacy due a little pink widow, with a mouth on her.

Which we devoutly promise to do if Maddy should decide to come down next week for states. The team, as you can imagine, has suffered great convulsions of adjustment in the time since the accident. The assistant tennis coach was pressed into service, but so apparent was his distaste for the sport that the boys took it upon themselves to choose Yoder's successor. When Shirley Kern, president of Wrestling Mothers, was approached, she reluctantly agreed to take over for the championship rounds. Up to this point "Kernie's" been rather splendid, suffering only a minor drop of nerve and ferocity after her own son lost in the last seconds of district semis. I regret to inform Maddy that her main men, the Pack boys, went down in order consolation finals. Unfortunately, only Michael is left now to shoulder the burden of school expectation as well as single-handedly carry posthumous honor to his fallen colleagues: Everywhere fly the beseeching banners, "Go, Kleeve, for Yoder and Grayrain." Though we cannot promise a champion any more than the priest-producing aunts can guarantee a bishop, we do vow to act our age while Maddy is here, which should prove easier in the somber damp of early March than under the spell of all the glitter and ghosts of Christmas.

I've purposefully left several of your minor contentions stand. To quarrel with every point would smack too much of litigancy, the filing of an Answer to a Complaint in Replevin or Trespass. Or Divorce. A last-ditch defense before the blame is laid for the final break. Heaven forbid. However true it is that we can't go back to Lackawanna, it is truer yet that we cannot safely disengage. Despite that our interests and visions diverge perhaps indefinitely and the generations grow more distinct, this branch from that, we all are nonetheless attached at ground level, fed from the same roots. I've seen local writers leave the farm for high church and gentility, where they learn to construct without mud, prettily indeed. I know an aging painter who comes home weekends to find that certain shade of late light without which his work goes soulless to market. Oh, here I go again, evoking art, dissipating myself in vagueness. Enough, I say. Call us gypsies, pigs. I tell you, woman, we will not be cut off. I will not permit it. I will say "pig" back and dig in; it's an act of love I learned from your brother.

Best from your sister-in-law,
LOUISE

CHAPTER

34

The tournament opened just at the cusp of the equinox, the day like a bated breath, a blur between seasons, the backcountry palette melting behind a clicking mesh of gentle rain. A perfect day for preliminaries. By now Trover knew the weather patterns in this part of the world. Behind the veil you could already see the gathering brightness, feel the close warmth building. Later on there would be luster on the hills, milky light lacquering the black pines. A pearl of fine weather, of false spring. False in relation to what? thought Louise. Was April everlasting? Was May? "Magic light!" Mighty cried, grabbing her camera.

At the big arena Trover bought a program and immediately set to filling in the rosters. Louise tagged along, watching him copy information as the chart from each weight class was posted. "What are you, official statistician?" she asked happily.

"Commissioner of make-work," he said, agreeably brisk, carrying his data back to the bleachers, where he proceeded to burn further anxiety by mulling over the brackets, starring his favorites with such triumphal emphasis that one might think his professional reputation hinged on the accuracy of his sports forecasts.

From time to time he looked up. "Hello there!" he said to almost anyone happening by. "Hello there!" he called jauntily to Sterl LaWall, coming up the aisle with Fuzzy, who'd hocked out of school for the day. LaWall caught Louise's eye behind Trover's back. He winked at her and made a collusive O with his fingers. "Hi there!" said Trover to all the vaguely familiar faces he half remembered from summer tournaments. "Hello," he said, in the same impersonal tone, to Maddy and Mighty returning from the snack bar with sodas and soft pretzels.

He saluted Len DeTurk down in the lower aisle. Levi was still alive but up against a three-time champ in the opener. Doom imposed on Len a dopey look, his eyelids lowered as if his head were the home of some family of fat, sad thoughts.

"Yo," he said, blinking up at Trover. "See who's in at thirty-two?"

"Chart's not posted yet, is it?"

"Just went up. Judge Bogpother's kid, Wesley. Top-seeded no less."

Trover considered this development carefully. He scrubbed the salt off his pretzel. "Ribbet," he said.

"Looks like your boy drew a bye first round," DeTurk added.

Now Maddy, face all knotted, shot forward from the row behind. "He'll get stale as samwich crumbs settin' all day."

"Nonsense," Trover said.

Not until late afternoon, then, did Michael see action. It was a maddeningly hamstrung match between two boys goony with diffidence, stiff with fear. Michael won by a fluky reversal early the third round. Afterward Trover conferred with Kernie. "He was a little stale," he said. "Nothing to worry about. . . . Let's go," he said to the rest after flushing them out of their scattered perches. When they stepped outside, it was into that promised light, the polished opal of a fine day that seemed to foretoken a coronation or at least a trophy as tall as an adolescent king.

It was the start of the third day. Dulled by sleepless nights in a noisy motel, by the drone of events they had no stake in, they were stale themselves. The DeTurk boy was long ago eliminated. Bogpother's kid, a gristly, grim-faced loner, was still seething with heat and authority. Nonetheless, Trover managed to enter the stands chipper, hugging his clipboard, tasting the eggy morning light in his beard.

Louise settled into the limp interim, hours like interstates loping along as though it were possible to be this long between things. As if the road itself were nowhere and time passed in transit without outlet to the hard little mill towns of the mind and heart, the secret scenes blinking through the trees. But waiting time turned out to be a town unto itself, all the citizens about. Trover's head bent over his busywork. When Louise leaned over him, her own face swam in the shiny spot where nothing grew, and her heart hovered. Touching her own cheekbone, she summoned her mother's face, the knobby contours, in the only photograph she owned of her. Where was she now? Dead? Or alive in the poverty of bottomless regret, too queer by now to see straight?

And two seats over, Maddy's fingers flew as Mighty dozed prettily beside her. Once, when Louise had nodded off in her chair, Mighty shook her awake. "Oh, Ma," she said, "please don't. You look so *old* sleeping."

Maddy's needles purled a burgundy river, the first row of a new afghan. The color purpled Louise's thinking, stained it like wine. The Landers' pallor still offended her. She'd thought to leave them blank, call them bisquelike, and be done with it. The undone, it turned out, was irresistible, the porous surface always sucking at her, taunting her with possibility. Soon she'd be getting up demented in the middle of the night, grabbing her paints, making the piece hideous maybe. Did God, too, suffer these restless, furtive nighttime tinkerings? Did He fret and did He pace, poking in the stubborn imperfectibility of the perfectly created?

Maddy scowling over her stitches; God sick with omniscience when His work was done and the mud held, the pods filled with peas, and all the tiny joints and jaws functioned as planned. He added parsley; he added salt. And still, still ... He had everything and nothing, for nothing gave Him trouble. Was man the Maker's gift to Himself, the one He wanted to woo? Each life a knife to His perfect heart, a plot to boggle His boundless mind?

Was He, too, hopelessly in love?

Chittering needles, the purple row, the blue and white and scarlet bleachers, moan of the crowd, the hours running now like colors. Too warm in her winter clothes, Louise drooped and started to doze before remembering Mighty's rule about older women and public sleeping. Jerking awake, she cast about for her boy.

There he was, down with Shirley Kern, in front of the empty yellow section. He was standing very still, Kernie circling him nervously. Four feet ten, she looked even smaller in Yoder's warm-up suit, two fat blue doughnuts of rolled cloth rubbing her ankles, gray bun tucked under a duckbill cap.

She was clever, enterprising, Michael was finding out. It seemed he was always waiting for her to return from some minor spy mission with valuable data on his opponents' weaknesses, strengths, their secret weapons. "Leg man coming up," she might say. Or, "Look out for the guillotine, friend." Now she was saying, "Shame on you."

Spotting his mother, he crossed the varnished floor and mounted the steps. "Kernie's ticked," he told his parents. "I was four ounces over at weigh-ins."

Trover sat at full alert. "Go outside and spit," he said.

"I did."

"Well, go pee."

"Did."

"Shit," said Trover.

"Can't."

"Damn."

Michael winced. "What if I lose?"

"No problem," said Mighty. "With your brains and looks, I'm sure you'll find a good home somewhere."

"Thanks."

"He won't lose," said Trover with a weird, shivery cheer.

"His color's bad," Louise said when the boy was gone. "He's cold and hungry and exhausted."

Trover sized her up. "He's fine," he said challengingly.

"Something tells me he's in deep trouble."

And Trover swerved at her, shooting a look at once accusatory and shocked and affronted, as if she'd just placed a hefty bet against their beloved son. Quietly she watched his eyes burn to worry raw as her own. He blinked, then gave her injured paw a gingerly pat.

They'd been there so long they belonged, stuck like seeds in the cotton of off-white noise. The dense general hum, the shriller pitch of critical instants, the loudspeaker voice had a soothing rockaby lilt as it swayed the contestants' names together and named the winners and sent losers off to consolations and coaches off to the office and called for doctors and fathers for the bleeding or weeping. When Michael was summoned on deck, the family dispersed, each fleeing to some prescouted spot in the stands.

"Pack 'em," Kernie yelled as the match got under way. "Put him where he can read GE on the lights." Michael pinned his man in a minute six.

They came together again gelatinous with grace. Good luck made goodwill; goodwill made them one. Maddy poked arms, ribs for good measure. She waved her burgundy stripe like a banner. "It's official," she said. "We'll finish in the chips."

But Trover was motioning toward the floor, where the other thirty-two-pound semi was just wrapping up. He glanced up at the scoreboard and back down in time to see the winner's hand go up. "Bogpother," he said. "Wouldn't you know? Couldn't happen any other way."

Mighty said, "Who? Huh?"

"His old man's on the bench out in western PA. Guy'd pay twice to see me on my back."

"Whose match is this, yours or Michael's?"

"Forget I said anything," Trover said. He was watching the judge wrap his gavel arm around the dripping kid's shoulder. He ushered him off the floor like a dance partner. Trover turned to Louise. "Guy's a lot less likable in person," he said.

Louise laughed out loud.

"No, really. He's one of those dry, punctilious types, much given to o-rotund pronouncements. What do you bet he'll consider finals a classic match between good and evil?"

"Which is our side?" Louise asked him right between the eyes.

"That's your department," he said. "You call it."

Michael and Kernie looked far away and small waiting so late into the night in that eerie emptiness of yellow seats. The educational channel people had mounted their cameras at strategic points, and the final rounds were presented now on a tray of gray illumination, the yellow-gray of insomnia or melancholy.

Immediately after the award ceremony for the nineteen-pounders the family diaspora began. Casting a lingering look back to her son, Maddy went off to find a seat in the blue section because blue had a tendency to pull her. Mighty headed for the side aisle. "Bye now," Trover said to his wife, and watched her disappear into the starry glare of the lights above the very top bleachers, where cushioned by space and braced by strangers, she would soon turn stiff as her splinted finger. But what was she afraid of? Trover suspected her of nothing more corrupt than mother love, that dying a thousand times each match because her boy might be bumped too hard or bloodied. "Say ten 'oh, my husbands.' " Trover used to tease her when she came to him contrite in the tender give of their early years. Oh, my husband, she thought now, it's loss, not scars, at the bottom of it. Like you, I want the kid to *win*, my blood to prevail. Winning, didn't you feel smart and shiny and absolute? Louise understood the folly of it all, and even so the cold rose and coated her heart, and she sat in fear of what a single loss would tell her.

Now, in the caul of heat hanging under the press box, Louise sat straight and pious. Below, the contenders moved with the sleepy diffidence of a priest and his servers. Then, *ite, missa est*, the mat was erased and waiting. Out strode Trover, toting his camera. The loudspeaker voice called Bogpother and Kleeve. Michael entered, Kernie behind him lugging Gatorade, a bucket, and those scratchy Panther towels.

In a dimness not conducive to knitting, Maddy's fingers drummed and scrubbed at herself, and the feeling inside was fierce and Irish, hungry for hell to pay. Something wanted indemnity. For what? Old man, she thought. Then young man, as Michael, head hanging, gave his arm to Kernie for last-minute massage. Old man, young man, what did that mean? Her fingers twisted with the tangle of too many thoughts as for a moment, in his stoop, the sweetness of the boy, she felt her husband near.

Incensed, unhinged, she stood and shook the ghosts out of her lap. She settled a lacerated gaze on Mighty. Mighty on the aisle step shuffling with energy and impatience. The feisty tilt of the chin seemed to bespeak Maddy's own attitude exactly. Young woman, old woman, she thought, nodding. And she saw herself, saw even the lavender Life Strides she wore the day she stole her granny out of her grandpappy's house. He was too feeble to care for a massive stroke victim, too feeble even to know it. He wept as Maddy lifted the wasted old woman onto small, strong shoulders. Shook his fist as she pulled away in a borrowed Packard, the grandmother lashed with velvet ribbon to the passenger seat. Maddy took her home and, every morning after that, pinned a ribbon in her hair, tied her upright in a bentwood rocker. She kept her vacantly alive, chin wiped, jasmine-scented for eleven years. Now she watched Mighty's sharp little profile. She rocked in place, her fingers fluttering like ribbons.

And feeling the press of attention, Mighty whirled around and winked. She knew the old woman saw but preferred to pretend otherwise. But *Mighty* preferred to make her look, and with the full force of youthfull will she drilled back until Maddy returned the glance, albeit crossly. Mighty's eyes held a wily triumph they both understood. Now where was Louise? Feeling a small stab of panic, Mighty scanned the stands. There she was! Up top. Her upraised hand made it look as if she was waving hi or holding a candle. Louise was very strict with that finger these days.

Mighty still winced to think of it. Louise grabbing back her hand, her look of mild surprise, left fist dripping blood. It would be fine, she'd said, trying to bind the wound with a paper napkin. If they hadn't dragged her off to the hospital, she'd still be running around with a body part hanging off.

The break should have mended weeks ago. But Louise was Louise was Louise. Nobody could tell her anything. Because she hadn't kept her hand up, infection set in, the bone had to be rebroken, and so the whole bungled up, extravagantly packaged affair lived on and on as a reminder. Deep down had Louise planned it that way? How had Mighty managed to hit the mixer switch in the first place? Who could know these motives? She imagined some great collective unconscious just below the flow of things, an endless sea of unsolved crimes. *I didn't mean it, Ma.* She plucked a lash. *Oh, God, I'm sorry.*

Then Mighty wrenched her gaze away. She turned back to the mat just in time to see Kernie take the boy by both shoulders. With the fire of her own eye she meant to cauterize all doubt, ignite the fighter in him. Then, slapping each cheek gently, she sent Michael off.

He halted just at the edge of the mat, a bit taken aback by who was waiting there with Bogpother. It was his favorite ref, the black dancer. Where had he come from? No matter. How glad Michael was to see him. Perhaps he would pick up something of his deftness and delicacy, his cool good humor.

The boys shook hands and locked horns. Never had Michael felt so free to proceed. He felt the skill in his limbs almost as a kind of iron-rich blood, and his heart was charged with courage. Head to head, the boys bullied back and forth. They gave each other up and came together again with the brutal urgency of feuding lovers. Pleasantly tense, weightless, Michael prowled high above his terror. The state was dreamlike, impenetrable. He slipped a notch in time, the time he went skiing up east. The thermometer atop Mount Snow registered twenty below, and once everyone had passed him, a beginner, he stood alone and wobbly in fragile air, the sky so silent and blue he imagined that anything less than a gem-cutter's skill on skis would shatter the day like fine glass.

Michael broke away at last. Then he came back in and picked an ankle. Cracking the leg like a whip, he brought Bogpother resoundingly to his rump. The move drew gasps from the crowd. When his man was secured, he threw in a leg. He rode him perhaps a moment too long, incurring a frown from the black man and a warning. Grinning, Michael cranked the boy halfway onto his back. "Drive it!" cried Kernie. "Follow through, Mikey. Go!" Her voice seemed to keep ringing in the icy air of his heightened state.

His opponent had a following. A safety net of a thousand voices swung under him at all times. "Up, Wes!" someone urged. "Wes, stand up, get out of there. Now!" So insistent was the crowd that when Bogpother squirmed free, it seemed entirely by popular demand, as if the voices themselves had jostled him out of Michael's keeping.

"Shoot, Wes!" And Wes shot. Michael threw in a whizzer and went down nonetheless. When the kid attempted a chicken wing, Michael nimbly pivoted on the winged elbow and rolled Bogpother around a split second after the buzzer ended the period.

Michael glanced over at his coach. One pant leg had unfurled; wet strands strayed out of her cap. She made praying hands at Michael while he squinted the sweat out of his eyes.

Bogpother drew bottom position. Clamping down on him, Michael went to work like somebody's monkey wrench: tightening, loosening, levering this way and that. He tried a ball-and-socket into a half nelson. He went to a cross-body ride, giving it up first for a scissors, then a figure four. Nothing was working because the kid underneath was unworkable, inert. He'd need a crowbar to pry this guy off the mat. Michael paused to make incredulous eyes at the ref. *Hey, make him wrestle!* But the man seemed happily taken up with his own contortions. Michael saw him crab sidewise around their bodies. Then he leaped to his feet and pointed his toes, scissor-kicking across the boys' torso. He crouched and bounced on his haunches.

Locking legs, Michael rested dead weight on Bogpother's butt and waited. The crowd, too, drew a breath, and in that brief lull, he thought he heard the purr of his father's camera, felt its tolerant eye, the heat of its eagerness for him. Was he dreaming now, or did the ref spin on his toes and bow both to Trover's camera and to Channel 29? And did he lay his finger on his lips as if to say, *shhhhhh,* just before calling the bottom guy for stalling?

Michael held his man for the rest of the second period, and then seventeen seconds into the third reversed with a granby. The ref celebrated by humming. "Amazing Grace." Michael tied Bogpother in knots and checked the time. "Never mind the clock," Miller scolded. "Forty seconds, and you're up four-three."

Out of discomfort or pique, Bogpother jiggled his hips, just enough to let Michael under him. Moving quickly now, Michael posted his hand, cross-faced, scooped Bogpother up, and set his heart on death by cradle. "Amazing Grace" dissolved in the pounding pulse of the crowd, the noise like a balloon buoying them high, so they seemed now to float just under the rafters. The boy in Michael's arms was struggling. He was craning, straining up as one with something urgent to say. And Michael, always the gentleman, tipped his ear, attending. "Huh?" he said.

The voice was low and opprobrious. "Stuhhhhd!" it said.

The ref's fine small head bobbed near theirs, as though making a myopic search for backpoints. Michael pondered the message, then looked down at Bogpother and laughed. Who was this kid in his arms, the bull-like neck lifting a burning, hungry, hard-breathing face to his? His breath was warm but odorless, smelling only of life itself. The life leaving Yoder, Spot's last breath left on Kauffman's Hill. *Stud!* he thought. *Me?*

Stud? It was the funniest thing he'd ever heard. Funnier even than his mother's wrestling moves. Funnier than Sprecher sitting on him. Michael was giggling and ashamed of giggling, and he couldn't even use his hands to quell himself. Pursing his lips, the ref tilted back on his heels. "Myyyyyyh goodness," he said.

And Michael clung to his kid and giggled still, his hands on that strong neck, thick stem, brain stem, fragile flower. The gusting seared his throat now, and it wasn't until the moment passed and the Bogpother kid had reversed the cradle that Michael understood that he was sobbing wildly, that the world was slippery with tears.

"Oh, crud!" Kernie groaned, and then she was down, pounding the floor, shouting, "Get out, Guy, you're one down."

"Twenty seconds," his dad said tightly.

"Mike-Kool." Mighty's voice like something unsprung from the crowd. He could even hear his mother's stillness and Maddy's silent grind of fingers.

He looked for comfort to the ref, but he only shook his head and lowered his golden gaze. Then, in one smooth slice of motion, the man was belly flat against the mat, and Michael rocked onto his other shoulder to clear a space between him and humiliation.

"You promised!" his father called. "You promised!"

Like some small efficient furnace, Bogpother took in great drafts, firing himself with oxygen. The ref was busying back and forth now, pivoting, swiveling, springing from knee to knee. Now he stopped, prostrate. "Th-three seconds." Kernie fibrillated.

For a moment or two Michael thought he could hold out forever. His heart rallied, ambition flared, but sadness and gravity drew him inexorably downward. Light blossoms filled his eyes as the ref's hand slammed the mat and the buzzer sounded now, too late to save him. Bogpother, hard pressed to hide his surprise, rose and helped Michael to his feet.

The first face Michael dared confront was the black man's. His smile was wide, blinding. He shrugged and let his glance gambol among the crowd. He turned again to Michael, showing the innocent pink of his palms. "See," he said, "it's not so bad, is it?" He took Michael's hand, and he took the other boy's hand and raised it high. Then he flung both children from him.

In the morning they rose and had breakfast in the motel dining room, packed their bags, and left. In sullen passivity they sat as Trover drove aimlessly around and around the outskirts when all they wanted was to get home with their dirty clothes and disappointment. At the entrance to every shopping mall he scanned the list of stores; he slowed through commercial strips. And, finally, when the wanting grew ungovernable, he bolted off the road by a roadside kiosk. In short order he bought two sheepskins for the Vanagon. At an adjoining sports shop he found a poster of some young shot hotdogging over a frozen waterfall at Jackson Hole, Wyoming. And a regulation soccer ball.

"A soccer ball?" said Michael.

"Don't worry," Trover said amiably. "It'll get used."

"Not in this life," piped Mighty, regarding him coolly, this burning furnace of a man.

What did a consumer consume if not the sums of loss and dread he couldn't take with him?

He found a small mountaineering shop, dashed in while they waited glumly in the car. When he came out with rag socks all around, Louise spoke in an odd atonality, as if interpreting reality for the rest. We have scads of socks," she said.

"Kids," he insisted, catching their eyes in the rearview mirror, "if I didn't tell you before I'm saying it now: Never hesitate to invest in good wool socks."

"Words for the ages," Mighty muttered.

Louise took the socks with a sigh and handed them back to Maddy, who chucked them farther back into the cargo hold. Then she clapped her grandson hard between the shoulder blades. "They's still next season, kiddo." It was the first reference to the disaster since it happened.

"Ain't that the truth, Bud?" she added.

"I'd rather not discuss it," Trover said, braking past another access ramp. He backed up and shot into a small shopping center containing a Polestar Bowling and a Jetco discount. This time he took Mighty in with him. In twenty minutes they came back, staggering with packages. They unloaded a complete line of small appliances: blender, toaster, yogurt maker, waffle iron, hand mixer. "Good job we have this vehicle." Trover said that for Louise's benefit, pausing to give her a chance to concur. "Admit it, Bibs," he said. "The Vanagon's been a godsend."

"By garsh, you'uns can't say it's not roomy."

Hand on the ignition key, Trover waited Louise out, holding home as the prize for compliance.

Louise looked at him with that pale, embattled face of hers. "I'll agree about the car," she said. "But not about the socks."

"That should hold him," Maddy said.

"You kidding?" said Mighty. "He won't stop until he gets it all."

Trover twisted the key, booming into business.

"Well, Ma," Mighty said, "you can always get another Digger Ickus divorce."

"Ribbet."

"Now can we go home?" Michael was exhausted.

"I'ze a-going, gang," Trover assured him. "I'ze a-going."

That's what he said, but what he did was come off the highway again an hour later, just one exit before their coveted own. He straightaway made for the hinterlands. The change of pace and direction jiggled Mighty out of a sound sleep. "What? What? Where the hell are we?"

"There's something you have to see," Trover said. "I'll take only a second of your valuable time." As he spoke, a red-shouldered hawk splurged at the windshield, its wingspan immense, threatening. The bird glared in, funneled upward, and was gone. A weather-silvered bridge slid by like time. "Why is a covered bridge covered?" Trover asked.

"I want to know where we're headed." Mighty fumed.

"To protect the cars?" said Michael.

"To protect itself, dummy," Trover said. "It's made of wood. Rain would rot the floor out, of course."

"Oh," said Michael, and Trover geared down and down again as the van labored up the switchbacks scoring the mountainside.

"Holy hell," said Mighty. "He's going to drive us off a cliff."

But her father's face held his hidden purposes with a sweet, inviolable intensity, his eyes pecking ahead. So intent, so oddly momentous was he that Louise widened her eyes to take in the whole of him. *Him.* Why him? The din of the past days seemed to die around her now. The world was so busy with itself, the bumping and tumbling of hungry bodies, the trembling leaves, the traffic. The world did not stop to explain itself. But now in the silence of the van, in the sudden sadness stretching like a glassy sea between heartbeats, there was also a flicker of clear sight. Not just the "knowing," that recurrent surge of faith that kept saving her. But a fact that stabbed her through. I could not, she thought. *I could not bear for this man to die!*

Around and around, then two more loops. The van rasped onto gravel. Trover pulled off into a narrow kerf between thickets. "This is as far as we go," he said. He hopped down and, sliding open the door, extended a hand to his mother. "Raus," he said to the reluctant others.

Mighty cased the place warily, then shrugging, grabbed her camera and followed. Still flabby with failure, Michael lumbered out and gawked around until his mother steered him onto the footpath behind the others. Everything smelled ripe and rich and deep. The sunlight had clear sailing through the naked trees. Single file they sludged along, captives of him, slaves to the driver. Not a word was spoken until Trover stopped and turned to them. "Now do you know where you are?" They looked doubtfully around as he tempted them farther out on a wide flat ledge. Large mica-flecked boulders jutted out on either side. Scrambling onto one of the big rocks, Trover struck a Balboa-like pose, his face lit with incipient vindication. "*Now* do you know?"

Michael peered out. "Whoaaa."

Then Maddy, scanning with hawklike eyes, said, "Way-el, guess we died and went to blessed heaven."

"Speak for yourself, Gram," snapped Mighty.

Below lay the first day of spring as lavished over the lands of the countyfolk.

"Not bad," Mighty said. "That bronzy thread, that the Maiden Creek? There, that's got to be the river of rocks."

"We got purtier cricks and hills back home." Maddy made a peppery face. "Mercy, what's that snappy shade of green?"

"Winter wheat," Louise said with pride. She loved, trusted this country in a way you never could the place you came from.

Trover rotated Michael a half turn, so that he faced the wide coliseum wall of mountain range as it curved northward. Michael counted down along the scarps and lookout points. "This must be Pulpit Rock, right?"

"Excellent," Trover said earnestly. "Now over there, that little grouping is New Jerusalem. Windsor Castle below that. The Virginville Dam. The little burg squeezed in the wrinkle is Long Swamp, home of the *boom-bas* and the world's largest scrapple plant." From up there the misty light showed not so much pervasive as patchy, hats and scarves of it floating far below.

Now Trover spoke louder, addressing them generally. "Look here, *now* what do you see?"

"Where?"

"There, where I'm pointing."

"Another superb example of the earth's curvature," Louise said. With her upraised hand she seemed to be blessing the universe.

"*Look,* goddammit."

"Why, that's yins own place," Maddy blurted, peeking closer. As a light wind stirred along the ridge, Trover pinched his mother back from the edge, at the same time gripping the rim of his fedora. Bits of white fluff fluttered along Maddy's hairline. "There's that there gabizmo," she said.

"Gazebo, Gram."

"And there, your swim pool. Shiny as glass."

Only a jut of white porch and part of the dormers showed through the ring of pine trees, but Mighty pointed out the shape of the rose garden, the black scrimshaw of orchard rows, the gap that marked the uprooted ones.

Michael said, "Take a picture, My, why don't you?"

She gave him a sidelong look. "I don't do kitty cats, or landscapes."

"There's the old VW bug," Louise said, intrigued. "Looks like a polished apple in the sun."

"And what's that other red thing?" said Michael. "See, over there, to the left of the pool."

It was like a game in which they scored by finding hidden figures in some intricate, trick-ridden picture. Under Trover's edified gaze they puzzled down upon the world. They squinted; they stretched. Michael was indicating the wide oval sloping away from poolside where the green, in contrast with the great billowing sails of winter wheat, remained scab-colored from winter kill. Something impudently crimson stitched along its small circumference.

"Shit," Mighty said. "I don't believe it."

"That's gotta be the Massey-Ferguson!" Michael said.

"It's him. Who else?" Louise said. "Sprecher's back."

"Chust like robin rettbreast," Mighty quacked. "Ay, don't that beat everything."

"Well, bless his heart," said Maddy, clapping.

They watched in silence as his circles tightened and the hard light from the sun knocking at noon cast a family of midget fidgety shadows. "OK," Maddy said, "let's shove off. How 'bout we find a Hardee's? My treat."

But just at that moment the wide firmament behind them began filling with birds. Red shoulders, silver-pink in the sun, scores of them riding the thermals soundlessly as arrows. They watched openmouthed, enthralled. Then, as the great migration thinned to a few stragglers, Trover shook his head. "Whewww. Wasn't that something? Now aren't you glad we came?" As if the hawks were some traveling spectacular, something he'd booked for them in advance.

"Right," they said. Sure.

And as they made ready to leave, Mighty stopped them. "Wait," she said, fast-stepping backward with her camera. She got them in her sights. "Hold it right there."

"What about you, chickie?" Maddy said.

The question seemed to catch Mighty unawares. She stopped, head tilted prettily to one side. Eyebrows arched, she scanned each face appraisingly. Michael still watery with loss, his eyes unearthly pale in the frail mountain light. She watched Louise stretch to full formal height. Louise straight-faced, resigned to her one gesture by now, unabashedly pointing up. Trover rested one hand on his wife's shoulder and peered sternly out from under the arm holding his hat down.

She looked at Maddy flapping in the wind. "You're on, Gram," she said.

Mighty steadied her camera between two rocks. She set the timer for seven seconds. She hurried to get in.